Jill Dawson's novels include *Fred and Edie*, which was shortlisted for the Orange Prize and the Whitbread Novel of the Year Award, *Watch Me Disappear*, which was longlisted for the Orange Prize, and most recently *The Crime Writer*, which won the East Anglian Book of the Year. An award-winning poet, she has also edited several poetry and short story anthologies. She has held many Fellowships, including the Creative Writing Fellowship at the University of East Anglia, and in 2008 founded Gold Dust, a mentoring scheme for new writers. She lives in the Cambridgeshire Fens.

~

'Jill Dawson has always had a knack for spotting sensational true-life stories and making from them intelligent, thought-provoking and terrifically absorbing page-turners. Her latest is no exception . . . The sights and sounds of vibrant Seventies London pop off the page, and the whole thing crackles with life, ideas and – hurrah – unapologised-for female desire.'
Daily Mail

'The nanny's-eye view of these posh, emotionally stunted people is entirely effective . . . this beautifully written novel achieves its aim: it gives the victim back her voice.'
Andrew Taylor, *Spectator*

'The complex intersections of the mother-baby-nanny triangle and the loneliness of childcare are beautifully depicted . . . The narrative's progress towards the terrifying evening in the dark basement kitchen has the ineluctable pull of tragic myth. We know what must come, but this knowledge never detracts from the memorable beauty and intelligence of the novel. By focusing on the victim, Dawson allows us to completely rethink the original story in a way that honours Sandra Rivett's short life.'
Sofka Zinovieff, *Guardian*

'Gripping . . . This dazzling novel combines the pace of a thriller with moving, poetic writing.'
Joanne Finney, *Good Housekeeping*

The Language of Birds

Jill Dawson

SCEPTRE

First published in Great Britain in 2019 by Sceptre
An imprint of Hodder & Stoughton
An Hachette UK company

This paperback edition published in 2020

1

A CIP catalogue record for this title is available from the British Library

Paperback ISBN 9781473654556
eBook ISBN 9781473654549

Typeset in Sabon MT by Hewer Text UK Ltd, Edinburgh
Printed and bound in Great Britain by Clays Ltd, Elcograf S.p.A.

Hodder & Stoughton policy is to use papers that are natural, renewable
and recyclable products and made from wood grown in sustainable
forests. The logging and manufacturing processes are expected to
conform to the environmental regulations of the country of origin.

Hodder & Stoughton Ltd
Carmelite House
50 Victoria Embankment
London EC4Y 0DZ

www.sceptrebooks.co.uk

For Sandra

'The joys I have possessed, in spite of fate, are mine.'

John Dryden

ONE

The first time I heard the voice, I was six. It was a swan. I was walking home across the fen and this bird was in the beet field, and it stretched up its neck – it looked like a great big white coat-hanger nestling in all that green – and it spoke to me. I got the shock of my life. I was on my way back from church but I started running, tripping. I almost fell in a ditch. I was crying, and when I got into the kitchen, when I got out from under all that fen light beaming down on me – *Jesus loves me this I know* – I tried to tell my mum.

I had been thinking about the horrid minister. *Jesus Christ. The same yesterday, today and for ever*, the sign at our church said. I'd been reading it and trying not to think of anything else. Afterwards, I'd been walking home as quickly as I could on my short legs. There was a sound in the sedge beds, like snapping, like a fire. Then, in a big bluster, the swan was up and flying past, its neck like an arrow and shouting: 'You're not normal! You never will be!'

I fell down on the edge of the ditch and started crying. Then I shot up again, in case the swan came back and knocked me into the dead water. The sky above me was white. It looked like smoke and nothingness, with just this one tiny thread of geese in it, a long way off, like the tail of a kite. I thought – maybe the swan wants to sweep me up there with it. I ran until I got to the sprouting tractors and bits of old machinery – our back yard – and I was sniffing and snuffling, and trying to get the words out. 'Mum, Mum. A swan shouted at me!' I said.

My mum, she was always pale. That day she was so flimsy, like the little flame from a candle, and I was afraid she'd go right out.

I was always scared about that. She turned around from the oven, tucking a strand of hair behind her ear. She came into focus a bit, and she took off her yellow pinny and folded it and put it in a drawer. I could smell roast potatoes: Sunday dinner. She didn't look worried or scared. I was waiting and waiting to see what she'd say about the swan and how weird and white it was, and what was it doing talking to me and in a beet field?

She just smiled. She didn't even ask me what it said, either, and I never got to tell her about the minister. 'Oh, you're just like your granny,' Mum said. 'You've got the gift.'

Granny Otterspoor. She was a funny woman, with a fat tummy and thin legs. I thought she looked like a bird herself but she was kind, and because Mum was nearly always ill or in bed, she looked after me. Granny was born in another century and she used to tell me she was a witch. Granny might have been bonkers, but no one ever called her that. It was only me they ever said that about.

My brothers all worked for my dad on the farm and I was the only girl, the last, the baby. I sometimes thought it was me who wore Mum out, the worst, being the last, and her being older by then, maybe too old to have another. I was the one with opinions, too, and Mum said I was a Daddy's Girl. They said I should be a teacher or a preacher.

I did well at school. I flabbergasted them all: the first child to pass exams and even want to go and do a course at Chelmsford College. My brothers were all, 'What's wrong with the farm? Why do you want to go off there, then?' And Mum just smiled and said she was proud of me, but she coughed for a long time after she said it and sounded wheezy. I thought she was flickering, more than ever. I was scared to leave her.

Chelmsford. To do a course in child development and psychology. There was a brand new nursery on site, with brand new babies in it for us to observe. I don't know why I picked Chelmsford, really. Picked it out of a hat. It seemed close but not too close. As for the course, well, Granny had fourteen children and Mum had had four, with me the only girl, and I suppose children and thinking about them, it was something I thought I could do.

All of them piled my stuff into a van and drove me there, singing, 'Three Wheels On My Wagon' all the way. All except Mum. She was coughing again, and fading out. She tried to wish me luck. She gave me a tea-towel and some cups for my little room, and a hug that felt limp and final. Why did I want to go? I was thinking. Go to my vast future, without her? And then angrily: Why *shouldn't* I want to go? I was clever. I was the only one who was.

And I was lonely and I fell in love. His name was Dr Mills and he took me to the theatre a few times, and then I realised he did that to everyone, even the kissing and the cuddling. I'd been what my brother Danny would have called clout-headed. Daft. And then suddenly one morning they were at it again: the birds. This time it was wood pigeons outside my window. At first I thought somebody, maybe another student, was tooting one of those annoying paper party whistles. On and on it went.

Then I heard them clearly: they were saying, 'Hey, Rosy! Go back to Ely and throw yourself under a train.'

I remember the station master and the porter in his uniform walking along the track, softly talking to me. A kestrel, trying to listen in, hovering overhead. I remember them, and the waiting room, and the police. Through the window of the police waiting room I saw a dead crow. Velvet, its wings spread, face down: a supplicant. Like me.

That led to a spot in The Poplars, which was good, yes, that was a good thing in the end, because that was where I met Mandy. And Mandy changed everything. Mandy introduced me to something, an idea that Mum had never managed: there was such a thing as happiness. Despite all that had already happened to her, Mandy was often laughing. Smoking, laughing, making naughty faces, she was . . . oh, I don't know . . . she was *lively*.

She was the opposite of Mum. Not feeble like a candle flame but burning steadily.

Joy. You could expect it. You might not get it, but at least, well, you knew it existed: it was a thing. It was worth dreaming of. Mandy was my first proper friend, and she was in there for a kind of breakdown. They sometimes said mine was psychosis, but we helped one another: we laughed at them, we took the pills, and when we met Dr Ryan, we were so amazed by him, so under his spell, we stopped the pills. We hid them. That was what he told us to do if we ever wanted to get out of there. Mandy didn't think I was bonkers, she never called me that, but also, not being religious, she didn't think I was gifted either. I told her about Granny and how she had imps, familiars – that was what witches had – and hers were crows and surely mine were birds too.

Mandy said, 'Blimey, Rosemary, do you really believe all that? And, God, you're fascinating.' That's the exact word she used. She was the first person who did. I liked being fascinating and normal for a while, under Mandy's gaze. From the window in The Poplars there was a line of trees, like bristles on a chin, but the birds were at a distance, out of earshot.

I could see pheasants strutting in the fields, lapwings flipping – they always reminded me of fluttering handkerchiefs in the wind. There was a buzzard, fierce and suspicious, stuck on a post, but birds never spoke to me when Mandy was around. It helped me to get out of The Poplars quickly. That was when Mandy came to live with me at the farm. Those were the best times. I saved her, and she was grateful.

So there was the swan that day when I was six and then the pigeons at Chelmsford telling me to go home when I was eighteen. In the years between those times I listened. I was nervous whenever the first whooper swans started to arrive, congregating in the fens (were they all talking about me? What were they saying?), but there was nothing. I couldn't hear them any more. My voices were silent after The Poplars too, just like Dr Ryan promised. He said it was only a 'rare visitation' and that I might be prone in times of stress, but could otherwise expect a quiet life. He was right, too. He made me feel confident that my life could be normal. They were silent through Norland College, all through my new job with Lady Jane in Belgravia, thank God. I thought they had left me for good – I even missed them a bit. But that night, an autumn night, a Thursday in November 1974, a conker-coloured sort of evening – the same colour as Mandy's hair – it started up again. Not birds this time. That night a new voice came: Mandy's.

Mandy's voice was lovely, young for her age, sweet. It had a sort of husky, cigarette-thickened sound. What did she say? Dr Ryan had insisted that four per cent of the Western population hear voices: 'Don't worry, Rosy, it's not as rare as you think. And two-thirds of these voice-hearers don't think of it as a sickness, as schizophrenia or anything like that, either, but actually *experience the voices as helpful.*' That was what he told me. Mandy used to say that everything is chance – the way a leaf falls from a tree: *which one, when?* The throw of dice on a game of Monopoly. Ending up in Park Lane not Mayfair – she didn't believe in Fate, or God, or destiny so how could you foretell the future? 'The future doesn't exist yet. It's going to be made up tomorrow. It's just *random*, Rosemary,' she'd say.

The night it happened, the Thursday when Mandy went down to that basement kitchen, I was in Belgravia. I was washing up and a bubble of liquid popped on a long wooden spoon and I looked at it, and I can remember standing by the window staring out at a great drooping cherry tree that Lady Jane had in her London garden, and it was dark so I couldn't really see the tree, just shapes. Quarter past nine. Instead I saw, I was seeing, Mandy's little navy court shoes for no reason at all, as if they were in front of me, seeing them right there in the black pane of glass. I mean, truly vivid: shiny, navy patent, small, scattered. Footless. That was the word that popped into my head because she wasn't wearing them. Then: *footloose* and fancy-free.

It came at me with a slicing pain in the head and a scream and a shock like the swan and then a chilling, icy trickle. A lovely sweet voice, young-sounding. Saying my name, over and over. 'Rosemary – Rosy!' she called. *Help me*.

TWO

Long before she was twenty-six, the age she was when she came to London, Mandy River had learned to trust her intuition about people. Starting with her mother, she knew that people were mostly cowards and self-deluders. She might be small but she was brave, *brave*. Cowardice was the trait she despised most in others.

Gulls wheeled as Mandy leaned over the solid brown river, taking deep, smoke-scented breaths and wondering at the marvel of it all. She let her hair stream out, whipping round her face and behind her – what a mess she was making of it and how her mother would have something to say about that. Beattie River was a mother who always had an opinion and didn't let her own ignorance, lack of education or experience get in the way of a firm view, energetically expressed. More often than not, these opinions were about her daughter. Mandy's hair, her eating, her tidiness or lack of it, her clothes and whether her skirt stuck out at the back or her collar looked 'ridiculous', her dolls and their tidiness, their clothes, their hair, whether they should be dressed or naked: all came under Beattie's scrutiny and most were found wanting. Beattie thought of herself as an excellent mother, despite the straitened circumstances in which she found herself. A static caravan, for goodness' sake. Brian losing his job – well, no doubt all that cheap labour coming in after the Fanfare for Europe meant he'd never find another farm to take him at his age. Another baby to care for at *her* age. It was fresh lemon and honey for sore throats, hot-water bottles for stomach-ache, but it's true she was lost, completely lost, when it came to *feelings*.

Mandy's father was silent when his wife went on the attack, though if it was about the IRA or joining the Common Market and those 'bloody people' on the telly, he could sit up from his prone position on the sofa and be as wide awake as the next man.

In 1963, when Peter John River had come along, both parents had decided that the less said about him, the better. Peter was poppered into a white, brushed-cotton romper suit, kissed and cuddled, welcomed into the family. Beattie was secretly pleased that, despite the inconvenience of his arrival, so late in her marriage, right when she thought she was done with mothering, he did at least have the good sense to be born a boy. Mandy remembered seeing her father standing looking tired – so *tired* – by the bed in the blue light of the early hospital morning. One extraordinarily beseeching glance was directed towards her. She couldn't read it. She had never thought of it until now, standing on a bridge, her hair flying out behind her, staring into the river Thames. Perhaps she had been wrong about him. What had her father meant?

So much that was puzzling. How come she hadn't known there would be seagulls in London? Surely they only existed in seaside places, like Hunstanton or Holkham, their cries a lamenting backdrop that echoed her own (once as a girl she had thought it sounded a bit like calling *Help! Help!* And when she met Rosemary she discovered that for some it was more than a thought: it was a conviction); but here they were and maybe they'd come from home, too. She was here, she'd made it, joining the damp-speckled late-blooming flowers, the pigeons and magpies and glittering tourists that littered the pavements. Shiny benches with winged, gilt-tipped arms, foreign voices, people endlessly stopping to take photographs, the sounds of wet tyres sloshing, an abandoned champagne bottle floating in the river: nothing was as she'd imagined it would be. She could even shake her head and erase, almost successfully, the picture of Peter on his birthday a few weeks ago, intent on his train-set, kneeling on the strip of maroon carpet at the bottom of his bed that passed for floor space, placing the little wheels more solidly and securely on the track, his blue eyes not on her but the train, and think: My God, I'm here, at last. I've arrived in my own life. They'll all be fine. It's done.

She had in her coat pocket the folded envelope, scrawled with the address of the agency. It reminded her of long ago, another address on an envelope, a place near Newmarket that stank of the farmyard, a place that had terrified her, The Poplars, a place that, somehow, she had always known she'd visit, at least once in a lifetime.

People: Mandy liked the ones best who knew their own badness or weakness. The ones who wanted to open things up, kick a molehill apart, see the soft blackness spill and know a living creature was down there, that just because you couldn't see him didn't mean he didn't exist. That was the main thing. Things that didn't exist. Things that Rosemary was certain of and Mandy only caught a glimpse of once or twice, could only guess at. She liked Rosemary's 'wackiness'. She couldn't share it, she had a deep constitutional scepticism that only occasionally splintered, but what she liked best was that Rosemary's soaring thoughts so contradicted Mandy's mother, planted as she was so firmly in the Fens soil. Beattie.

Beattie was certain that so many things did not exist. Like money. 'That's not for the likes of us,' she'd say. Or desire. 'It's all very well for a man – they're just animals, really. Women have to be *responsible*.' Or happiness. 'No one has it easy. We all have our crosses to bear.' Ease, or a life without crosses to bear, did not exist.

Then Beattie's other favourite saying: 'Some folks don't know they're born.' This was an attack on the privileged, on some television personality who had just divorced and ended up with a palace and a stash of jewels, but as a child Mandy had always felt it angrily directed at herself and countered with 'I do! I know I'm *born*!'

Born *again*, perhaps, like a Christian? She almost did a twirl, right there on the bridge. She would walk to the agency, she decided. She took the envelope out of her pocket and studied again the address Rosemary had written for her, circling the word 'Knightsbridge'. Rosemary had said, 'It's like *Upstairs Downstairs*. You'll love it.' She had as a safety net a second suggestion, West London Nannies, and Mandy had decided to register with both. She paused to study her *Geographer's A to Z* to calculate the distance . . . Maybe a twenty-minute walk from here.

London was abuzz, a streak of red from a squealing bus as it passed her, a dark man with thick hair in the style of Uri Geller calling out something only loosely translatable as '*STANDARD, Evenin' STANDARD.*' The newspaper had a cover photo of two pandas. The new arrivals seemed ridiculously happy, too, draping the bars in their cage at London Zoo. She would go there one day, she thought. She walked quickly, her mood lifting with every step. *I did it. I did it.* Who could imagine what it had taken, the length of the leap? She would visit the zoo with her new charges, whoever they might be. She pictured herself with a pram, with twins, perhaps, or toddlers, wheeling them round the zoo: gurgling, happy babies, knitted hats. What child could resist a live cuddly panda bear?

When she reached the address, the agency building surprised her: it seemed more like a house, not a shop front, as she'd imagined. Spotless white steps, fancy black door, a bell with several names next to it. She rang the bell beside 'Knightsbridge Domestic Services' and a woman who seemed too young to be wearing her hair in that stiff blonde bun answered and led her wordlessly to a reception room. It was just as Mandy had suspected: everything in London was unreal and unspoken.

Mandy wondered whether she dared smoke a cigarette, and decided against it. She sat with legs crossed at the knee at first, then remembered that crossing at the ankles was more lady-like. Talking about herself, why she wanted this kind of work, deciding which details to give. She began biting the skin around her nails and her voice was suddenly called. Miss Amanda River.

'Mandy,' she said. 'I'm mostly called Mandy.'

The stiff blonde led to her to another room where an older, friendlier-looking silver-haired man stood up from his leather chair to welcome her. He was Mr Reed, she'd been told. He sat back down, indicating the chair for her in front of his desk.

'Do come in, Miss River, and tell us all about yourself. Marvellous reference here from Miss Rosemary Seaton, a Norland nanny with a lovely family. Did you both train at Norland?'

'No – I— We're friends from Ely. Rosemary's been working in London for a while and – she loves it. I'm experienced, though. With children, I mean.'

Now was the moment to mention so many things. But, really, why should she? And wouldn't it just – get in the way?

'I wanted to come to London. You know. Leave Ely and . . .' (Could she say, 'I'm looking for something better?' or did that give away too much, suggest she'd come from a poor background, or was leaving trouble behind? She hadn't expected to be inter-viewed by a man: she'd definitely pictured a woman, a fierce, matronly type, but this was all to the good. The old gent was fiddling with his tie and straightening his cuffs; that usually meant something. His gaze on her was keen, lit-up and prickly. She was used to this. It had started when she was fourteen and then it had surprised her; it didn't any longer. She crossed her legs again, this time at the knee. His gaze followed.)

'And it's *Miss* River, is it?'

'Yes.' She closed her mouth so hard she could feel her teeth clamping together.

'Let's see what we can find, shall we? You didn't train at Norland. I see. That was the referee who recommended you. Well, not to worry, plenty of our girls don't . . .'

He stared at her for a second and then began flicking through a leather ledger. 'There are new families on our books includ-ing . . . Where is it? . . . One from a lady I know well, a countess in fact. Where is it? Lucinda! Lucinda!'

The door had been left ajar and the blonde appeared, black-lined eyes flicking over Mandy.

'Her ladyship – this morning? Lady Morven? Do you have the piece of paper where I jotted it down?' he asked, drumming fingers on the blotter in front of him.

The note was produced and he began copying details onto a piece of headed paper. 'When I read your form I thought, This girl is perfect. She's worked with boys of exactly this age – the boy is ten – and a nice recommendation . . . warm and unflappable. That's what this poor Countess of Morven needs. She's had a rather difficult time of it lately. There's a baby too, a year old. You have experience in a hospital, and with new-borns . . .'

Yes, she had experience with babies. Her mother had had a late child, her brother Peter, and she'd helped to bring him up. Oh, and she'd worked with an elderly couple as a help, and in a hairdresser's (not relevant, she guessed, but showed she was versatile) and briefly in a hospital, where she'd considered training as a midwife.

'And decided against it?' the gent enquired, when she paused for breath.

She nodded. No need to tell him more. She should bite her lip now, and wait.

'So what I'll do is telephone her ladyship and ask her if she might be willing to interview you this afternoon. How would that be? Or tomorrow, if you prefer. She sounded rather desperate. Her other girl left suddenly and, of course, she can't manage a baby and a ten-year-old boy. Though why he's not away at school at the moment I don't know. Summer holidays, I suppose. He'll be gone in September and then it's just the baby.'

Mandy nodded and allowed him to make the appointment, sitting silently while he chatted on the telephone. She was thinking: Why *can't* this countess manage a baby and a ten-year-old boy? Women did it all the time. But she and Rosemary had talked and she knew that such thoughts had to be suppressed. Posh women couldn't manage their own children and that was that.

They never had and they never would and thank God for it, in Rosemary's view, or where would girls like them find work?

As Mandy listened to the telephone conversation she realised with a bolt of joy that it was a live-in post. She'd have a room, a home. That problem might be solved too, in one swoop.

Mr Reed held the phone to one side for a moment and whispered to Mandy, 'Do you drive, my dear?'

'Yes, yes, m'lady, she does, of course,' he boomed, into the phone. 'Friendly and experienced, she's trained as a nursery nurse and midwife, so babies are no mystery to her, yes, yes indeed . . .'

Mandy kept still as the lie was told, though she'd had an impulse to lean forward and protest. Still, in essence he was right: babies were not a mystery to her. It was all set. An interview that afternoon, two p.m. at the house, close by, in Knightsbridge. He gave her the address.

Mandy stood up, straightening her cord pinafore dress, and offered her hand to thank Mr Reed. He held it a little too long and his palms were sweaty.

'Let us know how you get on. Lucinda will follow up with a call to her ladyship.'

'How will I . . . What should I call her?'

'Oh, she's very informal. But start properly, of course. It's "m'lady" until she gives you the nod. Or Lady Morven at a pinch. She's young. She's not old-fashioned. She's perfectly charming when not in a crisis. Where can we reach you to find out how you got on?'

She gave him Rosemary's number. She couldn't let him know she'd arrived in London by coach only that morning, with no address but his in her pocket, and the sum of twenty pounds.

On the way to the interview Mandy bought a pair of red boots. Sloane Square dazzled her. She was salivating: the colours, the swirls, the patchwork leather and suede and flower patterns. In one window: shiny boots, cherry-coloured patent leather. Her hands were shaking as she took the ten-pound note out of her purse. Eight pounds. That would leave her just twelve pounds; the thought made her giddy and she stumbled with the change, shoving notes into the wrong part of her purse, dropping coins, flustered. The girl in the cheesecloth smock didn't need to know that. She tried to straighten herself out. She could just imagine what Beattie would say. But whatever was said would be followed seconds later with 'Oh, but after all . . . I was more reckless than you at your age. The *things* I did!' Beattie's only real interest in the end was herself – her only hobby – and the ways in which her daughter extended her or not. All roads led back to that. Mandy promised herself she'd try not to mention the spending or the boots to Beattie, no matter how tempted she was to blab.

Outside the shop she took off her old grey pumps and bundled them into a bin. Put the box and the tissue paper in with them and zipped her stockinged feet into the leather boots right there on the dirty pavement. Then she stood up, shook back her red hair and smiled at whoever was looking. Lucky boots. She hoped this countess, whoever she was, liked them.

The interview with Lady Morven was at her house at two o'clock, so there was time for some lunch. She had to walk far to find the kind of place she was looking for. Away from Knightsbridge, in the direction she'd come from: towards Victoria station. She ordered a fried-egg sandwich with ketchup from an Italian café with a board outside and the promise of Full English for twelve and a half pence. A man was staring at her, she felt, and she wondered for a moment if it was the shiny boots, or if perhaps even in London women didn't eat in workers' cafés on their own (she looked around and that seemed to be true). She tried to return his gaze in what she hoped was a friendly manner, but he pursed his mouth around his pipe, then slowly and rudely turned his head away. Was he the man she'd seen somewhere earlier that day? On her arrival at the coach station, perhaps. Was he the man who had asked about her case and acted strange and disbelieving when she'd said she hadn't one, just her navy hand-bag? Why should she explain to a stranger that she'd planned this for months? That she'd sent boxes on ahead, to arrive at Rosemary's, so that Mum wouldn't get wind of her plans to leave.

Outside the light rain had stopped but a cloud passed over the sun and the sloshy late-summer day had darkened. Perhaps it was nothing, just that this fellow looked a little like Mr Barr. An older version, but the same prominent brow, overshadowing dark eyes, like a cliff threatening to crumble. She lit a cigarette – something to do with her hands, they were shaking again – and tried to remember if the job had been non-smoking. Had the old gent Mr Reed mentioned smoking at all? What if she didn't get it, what then?

Rosemary had said she might be able to stay with her but only for a night or two: it would be 'inconvenient', Rosemary had said, to bunk up because her employer, Lady Jane (three children: Clemmie, Rupert and Snaggy), was strict and rules would need to be broken. Rosemary wasn't above breaking them: that was why they were friends. Rosemary would do anything for her.

Suddenly, as she stood at the till counting out the coins to pay, she knew. It wasn't at Victoria coach station, no. She'd seen this chap outside Knightsbridge Domestic Services. He'd been across the road and nodded to Lucinda as she opened the door. He'd given her a fleeting stare as she'd stepped out after the interview. She was sure it was him. She left now, glancing around without wanting to acknowledge to herself that she was doing so, for the Mr Barr lookalike, the pipe-smoker, but he had left. Seeing her new boots, adeptly avoiding a small puddle, she realised the inspiration for them. Not exactly Chelsea Girl, more Paddington Bear. An impression swam towards her then, herself reading in bed to Peter, squashed into the cupboard-sized room in the caravan, the rain sheeting down on the tin roof, he in his Paddington pyjamas, smelling of hot chocolate and Matey bubble-bath, his blond head warm against her shoulder. Peter would be fine. No need to worry. Mum would read to him now; she would do a good job. That was the strange part. Beattie was a good mother to Peter. Reading to children: that fitted with Beattie's version of herself; there was no conflict there.

Mandy arrived early, paused opposite the house in Knightsbridge trying to assess it. But her experience of London streets was limited. These were town houses, were they, these beautiful white buildings with the little arches over black-painted doors, the white steps (could they be marble?). The terrace seemed more like a row of flats to her. She couldn't imagine the interiors, how they must miraculously open up inside, like a Tardis. And did they even have back gardens? She stared up at the windows, trying to understand which room they conveyed, which windows belonged to which house. That must be the basement, the window to the left, low down behind railings. She imagined herself describing it to Beattie – *And they just leave these huge fancy pots of flowers outside and they don't seem to worry if anyone will nick them* – then felt a pang: Beattie would have got her note by now. She would be – what? Angry or resigned? *Mum, I'm sorry I didn't tell you sooner and had to leave like this. I thought it would be better this way.*

You would have tried to stop me. You'd have made me feel sorry for Peter, and guilty. She didn't write that, but that was what she meant. Or this: *For God's sake. I know I've made mistakes but I'm twenty-six years old and if I keep bouncing back like this my own life will never begin. At this rate I'll never leave home.*

She rang the bell at two o'clock and, as she stood there checking her watch, admiring the gleaming round toes of the red boots, she heard a wailing baby. There was a long wait before the door was opened and the petite woman standing there, with a howling baby in her arms, hardly seemed to acknowledge her.

'She's been like this all night. I haven't had a wink of sleep. I'm at my wits' end.'

The woman – jiggling the baby rather roughly against her orange and green striped T-shirt – didn't invite Mandy in, but instead glanced out at the street and nodded, with a grim expression, to someone behind Mandy. Mandy turned her head, but didn't see anyone.

'Bloody private detective,' Lady Morven said. 'I'll make us a cup of tea.'

The friendly handshake Mandy had prepared, the 'so pleased to meet you, m'lady' she had practised (feeling ridiculous) were not required. She stepped over the threshold – a much bigger space than she'd anticipated, a high ceiling of powder blue, a soft rug, silvered mirrors and the scent of freesias – and the baby was placed in her arms.

The promised cup of tea never materialised. Instead Mandy found herself following the small form of her potential employer down the stairs to the basement kitchen, where Lady Morven burst into tears. 'Oh I'm exhausted, exhausted,' the countess said, sinking into a chair and burying her head in her arms. 'Could you take the baby out for a walk or something? The rain's eased off – if I don't sleep my head will explode.'

'Of course,' Mandy said, between the shrieks of the hot baby, who hadn't settled at all, and was trying to squirt out from her arms, like toothpaste from a tube. 'But I thought – Mr Reed suggested this was an interview?'

'Oh, it's perfectly fine – you're nursery-trained, aren't you? The last girl left three days ago! Three days and I've had no help at all!'

Was this the moment to say that she wasn't a trained nursery nurse? She didn't think so. Lady Morven clearly didn't care. There was a smell of Milton disinfectant and several buckets of soaking terry nappies around the kitchen floor. Stockings and bras dripped from a radiator. Dirty dishes, baby bowls and spoons, and opened jars of baby food were piled next to the sink. From another room, perhaps upstairs, came the canned laughter of a television set. Mandy's impression was that most of the living in this home happened here, that the powder-blue graciousness of the hallway was just a front.

'I'll have a lie-down. Have your stuff sent on, won't you? James is upstairs, glued to the goggle box. I'll ask him to come and show you where everything is.'

The baby's screaming drowned her out, and when Mandy called to her departing back, watching her slipping wearily in her stockinged-feet up the stairs, 'What's the baby's name, m'lady?' she didn't quite catch the answer.

The boy appeared. He was fair, sweet-faced, and the soft, silent way he slipped into the basement kitchen made Mandy feel he was used to being invisible. Or perhaps hoped to be. He was almost the same age as Peter, but nothing about them was similar. Peter seemed so robust – huge – in comparison.

'I'm Mandy,' she said brightly.

He held out a hand, stiff and old for his years, and almost stood to attention. 'James. Mummy said I'm to help you with the pram. It's in the hall.'

She followed him upstairs – he had bare feet and his heels were chapped and tender-looking – and he showed her the Silver Cross pram. It was brand new and smelt of rubber sheeting. Mandy jiggled the baby in one arm and moved the dummies, cotton scratch mittens, soft Snoopy dog and muslin square that lay in a heap, smoothing out the bottom sheet ready to lay the baby on it. James was putting on socks and smart shoes, carefully tying the laces.

'What's his name? Or is it a girl? I've forgotten.' The heavy baby – a year old, Mandy remembered Mr Reed telling her – was wearing a neutral yellow romper suit, and the screwed-up, rather dish-like red face and tufts of ginger hair didn't give much away.

'Pamela. But Mummy calls her Diddums.'

Mandy knew that once this child was lying in the pram her screams would only increase in intensity – until she could get her off to sleep – so she was trying to do as much as she could with the child held awkwardly in her arms. Yowling babies were hot and tiring. The child was batting at her, and hard to contain; Mandy's heart was beating hard and she was already sweating.

The spattering of rain had stopped so no bonnet or woollens were required, but what about a door-key? James showed her where a bunch of keys was kept, on a little shelf above a coat rack. The keys were attached to a brown-leather fob decorated with a crest of some kind. Two wolves with a gate between them. He was watching her looking at the crest and seemed to be biting back the desire to say something.

'Is there a park to go to?' Mandy paused to stare back at him. He had thin arms. He was wearing a blue T-shirt that said, *Remember you're a Womble.* 'I might get lost on the way back,' she added. Some instinct told her this boy liked to be needed. 'I'll buy us some ice cream.'

'Is that man there?' James asked suddenly, stepping close to the door to peep through the spy-hole.

He stared for a moment, then drew back. Pamela screamed with renewed fury as Mandy laid her in the pram and tugged a crisp white sheet with embroidered bunnies up to her chin. It was immediately flung off and the dummy Mandy offered spat out. Mandy could see the little tongue vibrating in the wide-open mouth. She shuddered with a primal terror of this child, of the ferocity of her despair.

'Who is he?' Mandy asked, jostling the pram up and down – movement, movement, that's what babies like – but hesitating before she opened the door.

'Daddy sends him to spy on us. Sometimes Daddy's there instead. I wave to him. But he never waves back,' James said, and flung the front door wide.

It felt to Mandy as if the baby's cries filled the whole street and announced her arrival with aching simplicity: Fraud, fraud, fraud. The baby can't stand her. Here she is, folks. The *nanny*.

* * *

23

Outside Mandy felt weightless and random. A white ping-pong ball bounced noiselessly past her feet; it must have come from an open window, though she didn't see who had hit it. She walked for a while with James beside her, rocking the pram with one hand whenever she had to wait to cross the road. It was big and springy, and manoeuvrings were required to get it down and up each kerb, but James helped, pressing down on the pram handle with experienced precision. There was no sign of the chap with the pipe, or the man James was anxious about. For about ten minutes Pamela lit up Knightsbridge with her squalls, then finally released herself and slept.

Mandy spied a phone box and went in to ring Rosemary. James stood patiently beside the pram, sentinel stiff, staring straight ahead.

'Yes, I got it . . .' Mandy said, pushing ten-pence pieces in when Rosemary picked up. 'I don't know her first name. She's . . . I just tried calling her "m'lady". He's not there, but he's the Earl of Morven or something. Yes, not that far from you.'

'Wow, that's fab. And when's your night off?'

'Oh, she didn't say. It wasn't much of an interview. She disappeared.'

'Well, try and make it Thursdays, like mine. Then we can go to the pub together. I could bring your stuff over this evening, if you like?'

'Yes, yes, do. And, Rosemary, I told her – she seemed to think . . . What if she asks to see my certificates or something?'

'Oh, don't worry. I'll bring you the Meering handbook and you can crib from that. Is your room nice? Mine's tiny, and I accidentally killed off all the plants.'

'I didn't get to see it. But I think there's a car—'

'Fab! Give me the address, then. I'll see you after I've put them to bed. Got to go – I've left Snaggy in the playpen.'

Mandy gave the address and shoved hard at the door to the phone box, glad to be rid of the dank smell of cigarettes and cats. She smiled at James but his big eyes only widened, faint eyebrows disappearing into his hairline.

'Why does Daddy send a man to watch the house?' she asked him. And then, thinking of the man with the pipe she'd seen outside the café after her visit to the agency: 'How did he know I had an interview at your house?'

James shrugged. 'His friend Lucinda works at the agency. The last nanny drank a beer. Daddy said that was deplorable.'

'Daddy doesn't live at home, then?'

'Daddy called Mummy a Neurotic Bitch from Hell. Mummy said he should take his stinking cigars with him and she was sick of lamb chops for dinner.'

Mandy tried to hide her smile, taking hold of the pram and turning around, heading for a little park in a neat square close to the house. It had a gate and a rather enormous padlock, but she had a hunch that one of the keys on the handful attached to the fob that James had given her might work. It did, and she let them both inside. A grey squirrel was sitting primly in a corner, as if waiting for a bus. On seeing them it swirled up a tree. James chased after it. She was glad to see him run, glad that he had it in him to do spontaneous child-like things. She had begun to wonder.

After pushing the pram on a tour of the gated garden – very pretty, very small – Mandy sat down on a bench and reached for the cigarettes in her handbag.

'Excuse me, Nanny.'

A woman was approaching her in the unmistakable brown uniform of a Norland nanny, huge pram sailing in front of her, a little coronet decorating its raised navy hood. A doll-like girl in a gingham dress followed her.

Mandy put away the cigarettes and looked up, smiling and ready.

The woman parked the pram and ostentatiously put the brake on with a black-shod foot. 'Is your mummy a titled mummy?'

Mandy's smile sank. 'Yes. She's Lady Morven.'

'Oh, that's all right, then. You will excuse my mentioning it, but this is the bench reserved for titled mummies' nannies.'

Mandy leaped up as if the bench was on fire. 'Oh, yes, of course. Well, I'm new. I'm Mandy.'

The black-haired child was staring at her, dangling a toy troll in one hand, twisting its lurid turquoise hair around her finger.

'I'm Nanny Richmond,' the woman said, taking her place on the bench with a creak. She was a well-turned-out woman of around sixty, grey hair closely cropped, not a scrap of makeup. Her mouth reminded Mandy of the chewed end of a tied balloon. Or an anus. 'I'm astonished your mummy approves of those.'

She nodded towards the pram where Pamela was sucking noisily on her dummy. Mandy vaguely remembered that Rosemary had told her how the Norland training had frowned on such things but, really, if they wanted their babies quiet the whole time, and the mother wasn't breast-feeding, what option did she have? The baby would be as fat as a pig if she gave it a bottle all day long.

'She's young, Lady Morven. I suppose she has new ideas. Well, lovely to meet you – actually, I was just going . . .' Mandy tailed off, looking around for James, calling him once, rather feebly, then rattling a row of plastic ducks on elastic strung along the inside of Pamela's pram, pretending to be entertaining her.

'So much trouble in *that* family,' the nanny said, settling in for a satisfying gossip, shooing away her black-haired charge with a wave of her hand.

James materialised in his characteristic way: silently, from nowhere.

'Must be off,' Mandy said again, grateful. James took hold of the pram handle and walked carefully beside her. The word *loyal* sprang into her thoughts. She felt a little surge of affection for him.

After the spell in The Poplars and the magical bit when we lived together, Mandy and me, in the cottage on the farm, I came up with this plan, after Mandy left, and my dad said it was a good one. Norland College. To train as a nanny. Maybe there was some life insurance from Mum or something – I never did know how Dad paid for it – but he was happy, so happy, he said. He was embarrassed, feelings always shamed him, but he stood in his faded yellow shapeless sweater and the smell of the dogs clinging to him and said he was proud, so *proud* of me, and he loved the uniform and the idea of his daughter looking after the children of toffs, lords and ladies. Maybe even royalty. He said Mum would be looking down at me from her place up there with Jesus and she'd be proud too. I thought I'd go first, then Mandy could do it. Join me. That was the big adventure.

Oh, I was pleased that Mandy got herself to London. I'd been scared she wouldn't. I missed her, the months I spent here on my own. Much more than when I'd been training at Norland because I'd had other friends there. I always felt sane when Mandy was around. I couldn't wait for her to join me. Every little thing – Clemmie calling me Nanny Seaton, the time I accidentally said to a guest at a wedding, 'Oh, how beautiful this castle is, never knew people could hire places like this,' and she said snottily, 'I grew up here . . .' All of it would have been all right, been a laugh, with Mandy here. We had been scheming for her to join me. She'd been forwarding her stuff to me in parcels so she didn't have to tell Beattie, and I'd been hiding them for her. I got that together now in a suitcase and a bottle of Chamade that Lady Jane had given me (bit of a pong – I'm not sure Mandy would like it) and a little cashmere jumper in a gorgeous kingfisher blue. That would suit Mandy's colouring more than mine.

Clemmie and Snaggy were asleep. Rupert was still up since it was the summer holidays but that was OK: it was my night off, I was allowed out.

I got a black cab right up to her door and the driver knew exactly who lived there. He wanted to talk about John Aspinall and his private zoo in Kent, big cats that lived in the bedroom with him, walked around the place, slept with his wife – had I heard about that? Weren't they friends of 'this lot', the lady of the house? I waited at the back of his cab while he got the case out of the boot, pretending to know nothing, and I didn't tip him either – nosy bloody parker – when I got out. The telephone was clanging as I rang the doorbell. It was late, after nine thirty, so naturally Mandy rushed to answer the phone as soon as she'd let me in – we just stood there grinning at each other for a second before she dashed to pick it up. I waited, admiring the circular table in the middle of the hall and the lovely soft blue Chinese rug. I worried that the bottom of the case I'd brought would mark it.

'Hello, hello, it's Mandy, the nanny,' she was saying. Most people said their telephone number but she obviously didn't know hers yet. I had it written on a piece of paper and looked for it in my coat pocket, but Mandy waved away my help and put the phone down sharpish.

'Crikey,' Mandy said. 'Third time that bugger's rung.'

'Who?'

'I don't know. Clicks off when I speak.'

'Weird.'

There was a strong smell of cigarette smoke, and these beautiful white flowers, and when I hugged her, the lovely familiar smell that Mandy always has – what is it? – makes me think of the mint we used to pick in the back yard, to put on the new potatoes.

'Which is your room?' I asked her.

'She still hasn't shown me!'

There was a creak, and a door opened, and a small voice: 'Who's there?'

'It's me, Mandy. This is my friend, Rosemary.'

She was a beauty, this Lady Morven. Thick brown hair in the same style as Mandy's, big brown eyes, little turned-up nose, pouty full mouth. She looked like a film star, like Natalie Wood or something. She was so slim too. And kind of liquid, not quite solid in the doorway, as if only her holding onto it was keeping her from melting.

'I should have watered the lawn. But it's dark now,' Lady Morven was saying. She wore a navy quilted dressing-gown and fluffy slippers, also a pearl necklace, a green velvet hairband and black eye-liner that was smudged and half rubbed off.

'What time is it?' she asked, seeming to get a bit more solid, firming up. 'Is there supper? I'm ravenous.'

'The children are in bed,' Mandy said, with a sideways glance at me. 'I asked my friend Rosemary to bring my stuff over.' I stood beside the suitcase, fiddling with the leather handle, not quite knowing if I should pick it up and take it somewhere. I didn't quite dare look at Mandy, and I didn't know why.

'Well, if you let us know which is my bedroom, we'll shove this in there and I could make – I could make an omelette?' Mandy suggested.

Lady Morven gestured towards a door. 'Oh, I feel marvellous! Refreshed. Extraordinary what a nap can do. Where's my Diddums? I'll give her a cuddle.' As she said this, she put on a babyish voice, raised her shoulders up to her ears and clutched her hands together, like a squirrel.

'She's asleep!' Mandy said, alarmed. But Lady Morven had already scampered up the stairs. I supposed that was where the nursery was. I heaved the case towards the door she'd shown us, and we collapsed on the bed – a four-poster bed! – in Mandy's new room, trying not to laugh.

'What's your place like?' Mandy asked, when I'd checked to see that the door was properly shut.

'Strict. It's all right.'

'Do you have to call her "m'lady" or something?'

'Yes. You should too. M'lady.'

'It's so odd,' Mandy said. 'I've been here until now with the kids, just sort of on my own. I felt really funny using her stuff, you know, and poking about in the kitchen. I mean, she's only just shown up. There was a moment when I thought she'd topped herself. Crikey. Would you let someone in like that and then disappear?'

'Oh, yeah. I'm getting a bit sick of it. Nobs. *Nanny Seaton, could you "desist" from giving Clemmie ice cream?* And then the minute my back's turned, she buys her one.'

I kicked off my summer sandals and opened the suitcase to show Mandy what I'd brought. 'Your stuff came in boxes. I had to use Lady Jane's case but I have to take it back. Here's the Bowlby book and the Meering. I doubt she's bothered about your qualifications, though.'

From the nursery above we could hear mewing, like a kitten. Unmistakably the sound of a baby, who had been deeply asleep, wakened.

I opened a window, found my Silk Cut and matches and lit two cigarettes, handing one to Mandy. I wandered around the bedroom, touching things, approving. It was so much bigger and better than my room. The furniture was posher, too. The heavy blanket box. The dresser with a silver mirror, silver hairbrush. I opened the wardrobe and the wooden hangers knocked together noisily. The phone was ringing. We heard Lady Morven scuffle down the stairs to our floor, then across the carpet to the hall in her fluffy slippers and then her voice, high-pitched: 'This is getting ridiculous. I know it's you. Would you kindly leave me alone?'

Her voice was sharp, rattled. I looked at Mandy.

'I don't know,' Mandy whispered. 'Her ex-husband? Maybe the same person who rang just now. He's having the house watched. She hasn't said anything about it, but the boy told me. They're divorcing. I did worry earlier . . . Do you think she's on something?'

I nodded. 'Yeah. Sleeping pills? Or something else?'

There was a little knock at the door, and Lady Morven was standing there with a mewling Pamela in her arms. 'Poor little mite seemed terribly overheated. Did you leave the blanket on? No need for it in the summer . . . just a sheet is fine . . . She's awfully *sweaty*, aren't you, darling? Her little tummy is absolutely *slithering* in sweat . . . Did you mention an omelette? I'm awfully ravenous.'

I took her cigarette from Mandy as she reached out for the baby. We went downstairs, carrying a now-howling Pamela.

'Flipping heck,' I said, in the basement kitchen and out of earshot of Lady Morven, but Mandy said nothing. She's always been mild like that, not irritable, not like me. The kitchen wasn't so fancy. I mean, the china and everything was nice but it was poky, a bit dark down there, not like upstairs. Upstairs was all velvet and lovely pale blue wallpaper with little red birds on it, the heavy walnut furniture and the smell of freesias and peonies.

Mandy showed me her new cherry boots. They were beside the kitchen door. She hopped with Pamela round the kitchen, flicking one off her toe, trying to get it on without putting the baby down. In the end I took Pamela from her, laughing. We laughed so much that Pamela looked at us as if she was scared. We didn't know why. It was as if a switch had been flicked. 'I can't believe I'm here!' Mandy said.

Just then the door opened and Lady Morven appeared. We immediately straightened up.

'I'll make that omelette for you, m'lady,' Mandy said, glancing round the messy kitchen. There was a second when I could see she was considering passing the baby to Lady Morven, but instead passed her to me. 'Hey, Rosy. Pop her back to bed, will you?'

'Oh, call me Katharine, for goodness' sake. And might I have one of those?'

Lady Morven held out her hand for a cigarette. We gave her the last from my packet of Silk Cut and I took Pammie up to the nursery.

Other people's children. It's a bit too *intimate* sometimes to hold somebody else's baby. To smell it. Peel off its little things, to swab at the most private and tender places with Vaseline and shower on baby talc, like shaking pepper over a steak. It's a funny old job. Do you think we ever really love them? I suppose some nannies do.

Mandy and I talked about it a lot. Taking care of children. *Should* it be a job, paid for? We both had mothers who'd been . . . I don't know, *eaten up* by motherhood, in different ways. Mandy's came on too strong and mine faded out too much. When we lived together at the farm we spent a lot of time talking about it. Was motherhood a job, exactly? Wasn't it something else, more of a *feeling*? Mandy thought that wasn't quite it. She thought some people really didn't have it and back then, well, the trouble was, I didn't know *what* I thought, which was why I so loved talking to Mandy about it.

This one, Pamela, was big for her age, weighty and warm. She had some fine tufts of gingery auburn hair, which was strange because her mother was a brunette. I guessed she was over a year old – I can't remember ever being told. She had big eyes – though right now they were screwed up. The sounds she made weren't a full cry, but as if she couldn't quite get rid of something from her throat.

I paced the room, propping Pamela upright against my shoulder, patting her back now and then between pausing to stroke the walls, the soft lemon-velvet curtains, the dangling mobile of little ducks and sailboats. I loved noticing all the pretty things. After a while I could feel her settling and she began looking at them too.

'Duck,' I said, showing her.

'Quack,' I said, holding it up to her face.

'Birds,' I said, and Pamela grabbed at the duck and pulled it towards her mouth.

It's weird how, in the end, Mandy was more the maternal type than me. I mean, she's glamorous and sexy, yes, but I could always tell that she was more genuine about kids. That she didn't mind their messiness, that she was good at thinking about them, about how they saw the world. I was more in doubt. I was the one who'd done the training, who'd spent all those years at Norland, but it was a career, a theory. After seeing what happened to Granny Otterspoor, to Mum . . . and all sorts of ideas were changing and being a mother was . . . well, it was being *denigrated*, I suppose. Who would want to be a drudge? Who would want to be like Mandy's mum, Beattie?

It felt good to be pacifying Pamela but that would never be enough satisfaction to make up for the hard graft of it all. I tried to imagine myself with my own child. Did I want one? There was a giant baby doll, plastic-scented, that we used at Norland College to practise on. Tracey we called her, for some reason. If I'd had a daughter I would have called her Clodagh after Clodagh Rodgers. Or probably Mandy. In my picture of myself as a mother it was always a girl, and she was sitting by a window in a beautiful house, with smooth red hair, and quietly reading. To get this girl, the mess and filth and chaos, breastfeeding, any of that stuff, crying, sleeplessness, being like the sow snuffling in our back yard with all the little piglets tugging at her, that was the part I couldn't imagine.

At Norland I remember the hours of classes about the baby's 'routine'. There was a picture in one of the books of a baby in a pink pram with a flowered sunshade. Our uniform had to be pristine at all times. The little hat could not be taken off. The watch (actually, I loved mine: it reminded me of a toy one on a nurse's uniform I'd had when I was five) was the most essential element for the help it offered with baby's feeds, and nap times, and half-hour of free play before tea time. The routine was soothing. I was particularly good at it. But I knew that was only possible at the college or at work, with other people's babies. My own would have been . . . Oh, I don't know. Always when I got this far imagining it my mum popped into my head. The last time I saw her. Weak. Crushed, I always thought. Like I'd sucked all the life out of her.

Pamela was clutching at her little duck, stubbing the tail end straight into her mouth, making the mobile tip and threaten to topple. Her eyes were closed. Teething, probably. There was a hot red spot on one cheek. She was calm now, mesmerised by all the sucking she was doing, so I untangled her, prising each finger off, and laid her in the whopping great cot. A family heirloom, no doubt. She fell asleep straight away. It was like I'd swept my hand over her and cast her under a spell. I kissed her little face, all lit up in the gold and blue glow of a baby lantern that rotated over her.

What do babies remember? *There can be no contentment and real happiness for the person who is not emotionally stable; nor can he be a useful member of society.* It was an essay I wrote as part of my diploma. About the emotional development of babies. Highest marks of my year, but that was just theory. Actually handling real-life messing wailing things and being on your own with them was different.

I kissed Pamela again, breathed in the milky vanilla and Johnson's baby talc smell of her, and felt something shifting – some molecules in me rearranging themselves, my future opening up and closing again all in one moment. There were ducks everywhere in that room. I stared at them – the pictures, the yellow felt ones dangling from the mobile, plastic ones. Ducks and ducklings. Birds. I felt a little shudder. Even Bowlby had famously used the example of greylag geese when discussing how mothers teach their children.

Dr Ryan had once said to me, 'Come on, Rosemary, is it *so* controversial to admit you don't want any of your own? Seems reasonable enough to me when, these days, for the first time in history, women have some control over their own bodies.'

He meant the pill. He was always on about the pill and it made me blush, him mentioning it again like that. We didn't talk about the pill in the Fens, and I didn't know anyone who could have got hold of it anyway without being married.

I shook my head then and didn't answer him. I wished I could shake him out of my head now, stop remembering him. Pamela was quietly snuffling and I crept out of the room, feeling like I'd escaped something. I listened hard outside her door once I'd closed it, but all the dangling birds were silent.

The girls escaped to the pub a few yards from the house, Mandy throwing a light tan jacket over her pinafore dress and putting the cherry boots on again, wanting to show them off. There were gold-framed pictures above the bar of yellowing city scenes. Walls the colour of nicotine and an unlit fire in one corner. Their arrival was noted by the men at the bar and in the snug. The place shuffled and adjusted itself, a prickle of something in the smoky air. The girls noted this and took it as their due. Mandy ordered a Snowball. 'God, a Snowball!' Rosemary said. Her drink was Dubonnet and lemonade.

'What would you do instead?' Mandy asked, as they squeezed into a brown leather banquette that was slippery and snatched at her bare thighs. They sipped their drinks, then placed them carefully on beer mats. They were self-conscious – they had hesitated outside, goading each other to go in. They had actually never been in a pub by themselves and would never have gone into The Lamb without a man, without Rosemary's brother Danny, or a boyfriend. But here, London, you had to do things differently. It gave you a little thrill; it made even the smallest things an adventure.

Rosemary looked blank.

'I mean, if you didn't work as a nanny,' Mandy said.

'Oh . . . retrain. Social worker or something.'

Mandy picked the cherry out of her Snowball and bit into its stickiness. She could tell that a man was looking at her from his position standing at the bar, the glasses hanging behind him, framing him. Before turning her head to check, she wondered if he was the one who'd been watching her earlier, but when she turned she saw him. A big beard, sideburns, masses of hair. He was handsome too. He struck her – something in his stance – as self-conscious. Like he was daring himself to be there.

This man was tall already, but a huge black felt hat floating on top of his springy hair made him taller. It reminded her of a prince or a circus master, someone in charge. He was magnificent. She'd never seen anyone like him. He was smoking a big cigarette, watching her. A full mouth above the beard. A yellow T-shirt with a black slogan on it. He had a handful of keys and was jingling them impatiently.

'If the kids get attached to you they move you on,' Rosemary was saying. 'Lady Jane's outraged if Snaggy puts out her arms for me and not her. Says I'm spoiling her and then goes shopping in Sloane Square for the best part of the day and wonders why her baby hardly recognises her. Read one of the books I brought you – John Bowlby. With the blue cover. *Child Care and the Growth of Love*. I'd rather deal with – you know – deprivation. Lack of money. Not those who've got all that and make such a mess of things. I'm bloody sick of them.'

The man was coming over. The keys were jingling, something frantic in the noise. His eyes were brown, soft. A gold chain at his throat. 'Buy you a drink, girls?'

He was confident. Cocky even. Mandy always liked that as a trait and found herself smiling over her glass and asking for another Snowball at the same moment as Rosemary said, 'We're just leaving.' Rosemary was standing up. Mandy glanced up at her friend, unsure what to make of this sudden movement.

'I really must go, Mandy. Snaggy wakes me at six. I can meet you next week, too, if you ask for Thursday as your regular night.'

The man stood there as if he had all the time in the world for the girls to sort out this little spat. Mandy glanced sideways at him, his profile – he was like something glittering dropped in a pale dull pool – to see if he was offended. Others in the pub were watching them. Rosemary held her handbag close to her body and nodded her goodbyes.

The man slipped into the seat Rosemary had vacated. Mandy slid over a little. He seemed amused rather than offended.

Mandy's legs were sticking to the leather; she tried to pull down her pinafore dress. Above all she must demonstrate (to whom? To him? To the pub at large?) that she wasn't like Rosemary. That she didn't care what other people thought. She tried to disguise the drumming that had started up in her chest by smiling and looking straight into his eyes, as boldly as she could manage.

Rosemary had once said, 'Anyone would be confident if they looked like you.' Mandy disputed this. What Rosemary called 'confidence', Mandy thought of as courage. Her courage always outweighed her caution. Mandy secretly thought that Rosemary was cowardly where men were concerned. She feared rejection so much that she stepped out of the way of them.

'Of course, men are more important to you than they are to me,' was Rosemary's next jab.

Mandy hadn't agreed with that either, but she'd let it pass. 'You're the first proper friend I've ever had,' she had told Rosemary. This was true. Because of Beattie she'd always imagined everyone was talking about her in the same searing terms Beattie used. Their time at The Poplars, the confidences they'd shared and then their months living together on Rosemary's farm, brief though they were, had changed how Mandy thought of herself. Other people liked her, she discovered. Even admired her. For a time she basked in this. Then Rosemary left to train at Norland, and later to work in London. Years where the long arm of her mother caught Mandy in its reach again. The gap between them opened up, like a grave, then was piled instantly with deep, deep earth.

His name was Neville. He bought her another Snowball and some salt and vinegar crisps, without asking which flavour she liked. His voice was deep, his accent unlike anything she'd ever heard. She had to concentrate to understand him. When he came back he pulled out a wooden chair opposite her banquette, scraping it with a horrible noise across the pub floor, and bashed his long legs against the table as he sat down. 'Ouch,' he said, smiling at her. 'Clumsy. Mum would say, "What that phone ever do to you, man?"'

When Mandy didn't laugh, or respond, he said, 'You know. Thump the receiver down – smack! Once broke a towel rail just giving it a teeny tiny lickle touch – a tickle like a baby's . . .'

She giggled then and sipped at the sweet Snowball, nudging it away from a sticky spot on the wooden table. She was out of practice. And ridiculously, giddily excited. Her first night out! And this man, Neville, was chatting her up. His eyes were so brown, the colour of a peaty fen, so beautiful. She'd never seen a man with eyes so lovely. And the jingling, agitating keys, what was that about? Like he wanted to whisk her off, lock her up? Even the sideburns – she could grow to like sideburns! Maybe they'd chafe your skin at first, maybe that beard and moustache meant kissing him would make her mouth raw. But his arms were nice! Shapely, like Popeye's. Oh, they were good. His wrists, his hands. His fingers were long, the nails were clean and he was . . . She searched for the word. Deliberate. *Definite*. He was the most *vivid* man she'd ever looked at. He crackled with it. He jangled. Nothing about him was casual. There was an angularity – a certainty – even in the lines of his nose, his profile. And yet a soft fur of hair, very light, on his wrists.

Oh, and a wedding ring. Now that she was looking, watching him light himself another cigarette, she saw a gold band. A wedding ring. She shook her head to his offer of a smoke. She glanced around at the wooden-panelled bar, trying to take it in. A wedding ring.

And he smelt of . . . What was it? Something familiar, something sharp. Was it lime? Was it that men's aftershave, an old-fashioned one? He smelt good, that was all she knew.

But that ring. So that was it. On the make. Had she looked like an easy target? A country girl. She was, of course.

Neville was talking about bombs and the IRA. The IRA had been threatening some big cheese (perhaps he'd said 'big chief' but she'd heard it as big cheese) at Scotland Yard because of his probe into a betting coup on the bank-holiday race at Cartmel. Neville was interested in racing. She couldn't really get excited about it but she knew she was on her own there. Everyone else wanted to discuss terrorism all the time. The IRA had threatened to burn down the chief of police's house.

There was a red jukebox and someone had put 'Waterloo' on too loud, and she could hardly hear Neville over the cheery sounds of Abba. Kidnapping, threats to their homes, intelligence . . . Beattie was always on about it too, a soldier shot dead in Ulster, threats of bombs. Mandy grew tired of hearing about them because to Beattie and Brian they loomed so large, made London so terrifying. When should she ask him? When should she say to this Neville, 'So, you're married, then, are you?'

He was also telling her about a club nearby they could go to: Annabel's. A bloke he knew was some big race-horse owner and a club member. This man could get them in as his guests, he said. It was full of toffs and West End actors: did she fancy it? The keys. They were now on the table: a great bunch of them. He did something in security. He was tense, she thought suddenly, like a powerful person locked inside a slim, elongated body: I'm determined to belong. I've every right to be here.

He's like me, she thought. *I've got the key of the door, never been twenty-one before*. A music-hall song that Brian used to sing floated into her head. When to mention the ring, when to mention it, when to ask him? She'd been there: she couldn't go there again. The disappointment was making her tongue-tied and he was looking at her enquiringly. He must have asked her a question.

'What, this evening?' Mandy said, realising that an answer was required. Now the jukebox was playing 'Stoned Love', the

Supremes. She started wiggling in her seat, her heart pumping a little. She wanted to clap her hands. Would it be strange to do that? Would it be OK to jump up, to grab him? Did they ever dance in pubs in London? Anything was possible, once you'd escaped Little Thetford, surely. Oh, but I'm old, old, she thought. I'm twenty-six, not a girl, for God's sake. I have two children who need me – and then: Oh, my God, I'm still here, I'm here, I'm here in the world, and how beautiful he is, the loveliest thing I've ever seen, he's like a big old tree that's just burst into blossom, he's like a head of corn that's glittering in the sun; and she went right back, back to her bedroom, fourteen years old, before it all, before everything, and there she was, there she always was – a girl with auburn hair in bunches, freckles across her nose. Blood pumping, heart leaping, dancing alone in her bedroom, once her parents had left the house. Moving the furniture back and really shaking herself, throwing up her arms, wriggling: everything she had seen Pan's People do. And the excitement and the tendrils and the feeling, the whole world I love you you're all mine I love you all, and her desire, such desire: it began so early to connect with everyone and everything and to reach them and to think of them, all the people she'd ever loved . . . Oh, how sexual this feeling was: it came from deep within her, in a place so expansive she knew it as her only true place, a place where she wanted to change the world, to do something. What it was she could never say, just a phrase from school that had got in early, lodged in her, never left her: *I shall do such things*. This was who she was, she existed, she was unique, she was what? Rapture, her English teacher once called it, and the moment the word was uttered, it had clicked. It was the truest part of her and had been there since the first. And this stranger, this extravagant stranger, had just kicked it into life.

She clapped her hands once, shyly, as Barry White took over from the Supremes and Neville was still talking, still smiling, and someone else in the pub suddenly shouted, 'Yeah, exactly, yeah!' The music – it was probably only the music that had done it, or maybe the drink . . . Did other people feel this, ever? Is that what drugs, LSD, were all about? She found herself standing, reaching for her tan jacket, beginning awkwardly to slip her arms into the sleeves. He stood up to help her.

She tipped her face a little towards him, over her shoulder. 'It's my first night here. I'm really, *really* tired, suddenly. I have a new job.'

They were close enough to kiss. She saw, gratifyingly, that he was about to do exactly that, and had to recalibrate. He had moved forward, just for a second, just a fraction, and then had to move back because she was fiddling with the collar on the jacket and he had misjudged. well, hadn't he admitted he was clumsy? That had been his opening remark and it was a nice quality, a vulnerable one: it only made her like him more. Not as smooth as he thought he was. And as he looked at her she felt certain they would end up in bed together, and she didn't know how she knew this, but only that she wanted it.

He asked for her phone number. The noise in the pub was so strange, like being in a hen-house. Two barmaids were pushing each other, play-fighting, catching her attention momentarily. He had to ask twice.

Mandy said she didn't know it, but he could walk her home. They pushed through the door, leaving the smell of furniture polish, cigars and beer, and the cold fresh night greeted them. They fell into step. Lady Morven's house came up too quickly – she pointed out the door – so they walked around the block, towards the park where she'd taken James and Pamela on her first day. He was talking to her about his jobs. He had a lot of jobs. Sometimes art students drew him and he took up uncomfortable poses at the Royal Academy for people who wanted him to stand tall, pose with a spear. It was good money. She should come along, he said, she'd like it. He'd only been in London six months. He'd come here to find his father. 'Did you?' she asked. He said he'd never found him and his father was a bastard, had never sent money home. His father had come here and wiped his mind clean, like washing grime from a window, of them all: his wife, his four kids. Came on the SS *Winston Churchill*. Twenty years later Neville had followed him to London. All he had was an address in Kensington. He'd come to tell him what he thought of him, but the address he'd been given was out of date.

'But you're married,' she wanted to say. 'What about that?'

Every step strengthened the decision, made it more and more impossible to go back. She had a job. She had people who needed her – James certainly did, Pamela did, and now Lady Morven. Katharine. Well, despite her dreamy, drifty quality there was something else about her that Mandy liked. Maybe it was just the hairband, but she kept thinking of Alice in Wonderland. She remembered Katharine eating the omelette she'd made for her, forking each mouthful delicately in, so neat, then suddenly solidifying, coming into focus, as if a full beam was switched on, and saying, 'This is delicious. Thank you. This is the first time I've eaten properly in weeks. Did we agree a wage? How does twenty-five pounds a week sound?'

How big her eyes were, behind the little round glasses she'd put on her nose to read the letter from the agency. And then the sudden smile and that wide, surprising mouth. Her slender, white arms in the T-shirt with skin that Mandy had never seen before – almost blue, it was so luminous and pure. Everything about her seemed to Mandy to be just that bit more special and glittering and magical than anything or anyone she'd ever met back home in Little Thetford.

Mandy and Neville stopped outside the house. She had the sense of someone there: was a car behind them? Had it stopped at the same time they had? She glanced around. Neville watched her but seemed unbothered.

He asked if he could come in, and stood nuzzling her ear. His masculine smell of sweat, warmth, she didn't know what, it was dizzying.

'No. It's too soon. You know where I live now. What about you?'

He said he lived over the pub. That was strange. She'd thought he said security, or something. Or perhaps it was only that the keys had suggested it. Still, she didn't remember him saying anything about working at the pub.

'How come you were fraternising with the customers then?'

'Everybody entitle to a night off. Having a swift one on my way up to bed, then saw this pretty girl with red boots, she look new in town . . .'

He kissed her then and it started up again: the escalating feeling. Something looming in so close and real that had been, so far, so unbelievable. The city, London, the chaos, the danger and the wildness of so many people: the unknown. Beattie had said she would never do it, never get here, and here she was, kissing a stranger on the street, but not really a stranger. This man, Neville, had already made her laugh, told her about his father who had written in a letter that he worked as a clippie on the buses, so Neville had ridden all over London, hoping to bump into him. And something, she thought he'd said something about owls hooting on his way to school, and how he missed the green. He tasted of beer, of the cigarettes he'd been smoking; his beard tickled her mouth, but it was a good kiss. She felt like steam in a kettle, rising. Something was happening in her.

He had long eyelashes. Girl's eyelashes in a deeply masculine face: the beard, the chin, the nose, his profile, the shock of hair.

'I have to go in,' Mandy said. She was pushing at his chest slightly to move him away. 'My first night! What if she's watching us, up there at the window?'

No curtain twitched, but Neville let her go. He smiled, he doffed his big black hat, giving a theatrical sweeping bow, spot-lit by a streetlamp. He looked tousled and young suddenly, and happy.

'You're married,' she said to him.

43

She picked up his hand, showed him the wedding ring. She was surprised at herself. How warm his hand was. And he didn't pull away from her. He made a sound, sucking the air in through his teeth, said, 'This my mum's ring. It her wedding ring. She don't have no use for it after that bastard leave her so she give it to me when I leave. For good luck.'

Mandy wanted to believe him. He kissed her again and pushed his hands inside the jacket, ran them up and down her until she had to push him away and tell him to get back to the pub.

Again he made a funny little clicking sound with his tongue – he seemed boisterously cheerful, teasing. He backed away from her, giving her a little bow, putting the hat back on his head.

She turned away and fumbled for her key, the one with the crest, but the moment she stood on the step, all the bubbles inside her popped. She could hear that Pamela was crying. Loud, heart-felt, abandoned wails. She flung her jacket on to the hat-stand, rushed to the nursery, still wearing her boots, and found the room in darkness, with only the feral heated-baby sounds – impossible not to think of it as desperation, impossible to slow her heartbeat soaring in terror to meet it – rising from the cot.

How on earth could Katharine not hear this? She picked up the hot, squalling baby and began pacing the room, holding her against her shoulder. The smell of milky sourness rose from her. Mandy changed her nappy – provoking a peak of high-pitched protestation – then began the walking again, and the cries slowed to little shudders and occasional sniffs and sighs. There was a funny blue and gold lamp that rotated and threw patterned horses on the walls; she could feel Pamela's interest fix on them. The baby's eyes were open, watching over her shoulder. And then Mandy became aware that someone else was in the room.

The nursery door was open but she could swear he hadn't come in that way. Had he been there in the darkness all along?

'James! It's late. Go back to bed!'

He was wearing blue and red checked pyjamas of the sort grown men wear. They were too big for him and too formal: they sat stiff around him as if he wasn't wearing them but was pack-aged in them. The sight of those pyjamas plucked at her heart. He must have been sitting in the dark like that, arms around his knees, all along. He stood up now, cowering a little at her voice, and she softened. Pamela's cries were quieting and intermittent, so she patted and jogged her and said, over her shoulder, 'See? Baby's doing fine. Don't worry. Did you come to help her? That's very sweet, James, but I'm here now.'

'Where were you?' he said.

It was unmistakable, the accusation. *You weren't here. We were left alone.*

'Yes, it was very naughty of me to go out. But Mummy was here, and I did ask her. Thursdays are going to be my night off, and tonight is a Thursday, see. You were all tucked up in bed, but Mummy was looking after you.'

'Daddy came. They were shouting.'

'Oh? Well, see, I didn't know that.'

'Pamela needed her nappy changing. I could smell her.'

'Yes, that's all done now. There, there, all fine now. See? Baby's nice and clean and everyone needs to go back to bed, and then I'll come and tuck them up . . .'

James didn't move. He had picked up a toy, a strange knitted thing that could have been anything: bunny, fox, bear. It was long and stuffed, a caramel colour, with two brown felt ears and no definable head shape. He was batting it lightly against one hand. Mandy wanted to ask more about the father but knew that wouldn't be conducive to the sleepy calm she was trying to create. She found a clean-looking dummy on a shelf and popped the rubber teat into Pamela's mouth. The baby began to suck in a determined way. *I'm so good at this and yet it's not true, is it?* But she was tired – the day had been so long with an extraordi-nary number of parts to it. Was it still going on? She closed her eyes.

James's clear voice piped in the semi-dark, 'Mummy fell down. He gave her some pills and now she won't wake up.'

45

Oh, Lord.

Mandy's eyes flew open. He was standing very close to her. She could smell him: a sort of warm brushed-cotton-pyjamas smell that reminded her of Peter. 'Is Daddy still here?' she asked. Blue and gold shadows circled her. Prancing ponies. Fairground shapes.

He shook his head.

'Maybe she's just – tired. Did you go in her room?'

He nodded.

Pamela had grown heavy, her body rising and falling in synchrony with Mandy's breathing. She could risk laying her back in her cot now. There was a complicated mechanism to let the wooden side down; James helped her with this and she placed Pamela on her side, pulling the cover over her, removing the pillow (surely she was too young to have a pillow), switching off the lamp.

Ushering him out of the room with a finger to her lips, she paused, once the door to the nursery was closed and they were outside it, and said she'd check on Mummy. She said everything would be fine and he was to go back to bed. Her arms felt light without the baby. The Snowballs, the earlier surge of emotion, all the newness: it was exhausting.

She padded downstairs to the middle floor; James was following her. She was thinking, How to enter the bedroom of my new employer and check if she's still alive (and what do I do if she isn't?), when she heard the sound of the lavatory flushing and Katharine appeared, sleepy and guileless in her navy dressing-gown. She seemed unsurprised to see them there, outside in the corridor at that hour, and simply smiled as she slipped back into her bedroom.

Mandy patted James on the back, and pushed him gently towards the stairs up to his bedroom. Katharine hadn't said a word to James for being up so late. Mandy stared after her departing figure. A mother with no interest. Was it just an act? Perhaps it was temporary, due to whatever she'd been through, the pills she was on . . .

It was a relief to observe it, though. After Beattie and her admonishments. Up until then Mandy had thought such liberation impossible, had believed herself unnatural and alone.

———◆———

'What do you talk about with Dr Ryan?' I asked Mandy once. I didn't like that Mandy got to talk to him too. I thought sometimes he was mine – I fantasised that he was going to marry me. Once, I'd asked him, 'Surely I can't apply now to train at Norland? There's a reference required. Fitness to practise. They'd say I was bonkers.'

And he'd said, 'Oh, Rosy. I cannot think of anyone more fit to practise than you. You've hardly spent any time here and you were never a danger to anyone. Of course you must apply.' I loved that he called me Rosy. I loved his faith in me.

So when Mandy told me he'd said the same sorts of thing to her I was . . . disappointed. I thought it was just for me, his kindness. I was shocked that others got it too. Mandy told me he talked to her about her feelings, about her fear that she was a terrible mother, a failed mother. 'And he would say, "Maybe you're just too young. You might make a better mother later."'

That was his trick, his magic. Dr Ryan: he got you to venture your most dangerous feelings and you thought he'd take them from you, make them safe. That didn't happen. But something else did. You felt you had dared to feel things. You felt so much braver.

I arrived two nights after Mandy did, with a police accompaniment, because I'd refused treatment. Mandy was a voluntary patient, which was different. My arrival came with shouting, with police, with me waving my arms and flapping, shooing a doctor away from me. I had a file too that said things like 'vague and woolly thoughts'; 'Auditory hallucinations especially those including comments by birds. Religious admonishments. Says she feels tormented and torn to pieces.'

My father had told them those details. He gave them the wording: he told them the pigeons had been instructing me to kill myself. He told them all of it. He was embarrassed, and because my mother was ill, was in hospital at the time, he couldn't visit. He was glad to get a break from me, he told Dr Ryan.

Dr Ryan asked me quietly if I'd read an important new book called *Sanity, Madness and the Family*.

I hadn't. I was lying on the floor because there wasn't a bed in his consulting room. I lay face down in the position I'd seen the crow in beside the railway line. I was practising, I told him. Practising what it would be like to do whatever I wanted, when I wanted, no matter who was in the room.

'What would it mean to do exactly as you please?' he asked, in his soft, walnut-wrinkled kind of way.

It was a trap, but I lifted my head from where I'd been lying and picked a piece of fluff from my mouth. 'Well, I might stay a virgin for ever, for example,' I said.

'Anything else you might like to do?' he asked.

He seemed interested, which was surprising. I looked at the walls for a moment. They were painted lavender. Lavender. I'm sure some idiot must have told them it was a soothing colour. It was a particularly disgusting shade of lavender. 'I might like to leave Ely. Little Thetford. And go somewhere else.'

'Weren't you studying at Chelmsford? Would you like to go back there?'

'No. Because there are too many – it's too . . . I don't know. I want to go somewhere else.'

'Did something bad happen in Chelmsford?'

'No. Yes. Yes, I just found it – too noisy.'

I was sitting up now. His questions were quite gentle and there was something nice in his voice. He wasn't – for once – telling me things about myself. He actually seemed to want to find things out.

He asked me if I'd read a book he liked very much. A book called *The Divided Self*. I had been studying psychology at the college, hadn't I?

Yes, but it was only child development, and I hadn't read it. And if I had, I wouldn't tell him I had, I said.

He smiled at this.

'I'm hungry,' I said. He asked me about food, about what I liked to eat.

I talked for a while about the pink sponges and yellow custard from school, and the meals my mother cooked, the fish, the smoked eel, the faggots in gravy and the Bird's Instant Whip – my favourite! For the name, I said, and Birds Eye fish fingers too. He nodded, and his foot, crossed over one leg, waggled.

'Mother's dying,' I said. 'I've worn her out.'

'Is that why you came home, really? Not the failed love affair but the feeling that you needed to be with your mother?'

'God, no. I wouldn't want to – get in the way. I would just be in the way. She has Dad. And my brothers. That's plenty for her.'

He had very dark eyebrows that lay over his eyes like caterpillars. They made me want to laugh – what if a bird flew in and picked them off? I did laugh, and he smiled back at me.

'So. Noisy in Chelmsford. Is the noisiness your voices? Is that what you mean?'

He had a Scottish accent. Glaswegian, I thought, surprised that I'd only just noticed. Usually voices are the first thing I pay attention to. Then, just as I was about to answer, I got a lovely whiff of something foody and my stomach rumbled. A smell like school dinners. Shepherd's pie, chocolate pudding with chocolate custard. I stood up now, went over to the window.

'Mine was a virgin birth,' I told him. 'And that's just the way I like it.'

'Do you mean you've given birth to a child?'

'Me? No, of course not! I mean my parents. They found me, like Moses, in an eel basket in the Fens. And Father would prefer it if I stayed that way. A virgin, I mean.'

49

'I see.' When he frowned, the caterpillars inched closer to one another, their little heads touching.

'And have you talked to the new girl, the girl in the bed next to yours – Mandy? Did she tell you anything about why she's here?'

'No – why should she?'

Mostly they would stop there, the doctors. You ask them a question and they clam up. But he was different, Dr Ryan. His trousers were crinkled at the knee. At his ankle I could see a green sock and a defined ankle bone. He had a tiny pot belly, but a long, skinny frame. There was something unthreatening, perhaps tired, about him. He struck me as truthful, which was odd.

'I've seen you talking to her. I think you know why she's here. And you were kind. You were sympathetic. You didn't judge her, which I imagine was helpful. And a little unusual here,' he said.

Yes, I knew all about Mandy. A little bird had told me.

He asked me then about my course again. Child development. Psychology. Did I think feelings had to be managed? How would it be simply to *feel* them? He tried to ask me about my mother, but I said that the first time I heard a voice it was the swan's voice long ago, after church. It wasn't related to my mother's illness. And then he asked about my granny, my mother's mum. How she'd practically raised me because Mum was ill so often. Was I close to her?

I didn't want to talk about Granny. She was born in another century.

'But birds have come back recently to talk to you after a long silence. Do you think this is significant?'

'Of course it's *significant*. They want to tell me something. The trouble is, I can't understand it any more. When I was little I could hear it, you know, work it out. But now it's another language.'

'They come to say unpalatable things and you refuse to understand them?'

This was a startling question. This struck too hard. 'Not refuse. I don't refuse! I want to understand. I try . . .' Maybe I was shouting. A little flicker in his eyes told me that I was.

'Your father already said that your mother was very ill when you were a little girl, she was often ill, and her death was constantly expected. Her approaching death is an experience you've had many times and must be very painful for you.'

'It's not painful. It's just what is. Mother has always been ill, and this time, she's very ill. She doesn't want me beside her. She wants my dad.'

'That must be very hurtful,' he said quietly.

He looked upset, which was uncalled-for. I shook my head. It wasn't hurtful. 'My granny at Grunty Fen was a witch. She used to cure the fen ague. I know some things, I sometimes see things, that I can't explain. If you put the placenta on a fire after a birth, the number of times it crackles is the number of babies you're going to have.'

He said he hadn't known that, but it was very interesting. 'Is it how many *more* babies you're going to have, after the birth? Or the total?'

'The total number. Fourteen crackles. For Granny. But for Mum it was only three crackles. So I was extra. I was – a surprise. I wasn't really meant to be.' Damn. I wasn't going to talk to him about her. About that.

He smiled then, and only nodded as if he agreed. It was probably just a technique to, you know, put me off. But, in a way, it worked. My guard came down because I wasn't used to people believing me.

'If you see a chimney sweep when you're pregnant you'll have a baby with black skin.'

I watched his face, then continued, 'But Granny said that one was rubbish. She said, "When did you ever see a chimney sweep in the Fens? You'd be more likely to have a baby with black skin if you looked at one of the coloured Americans on the airbase."'

He laughed then.

He said he was from Glasgow, Dr Ryan. He didn't tell me much, but he listened to me, and listening, not talking, seemed to be the cure.

'I was born at midnight, and in a thunderstorm. You know what that means?'

But he didn't and I refused to tell him.

Mandy was in the next bed to mine. I returned after my session with Dr Ryan and said to her, 'He's nice, isn't he?' She said nothing, and didn't stir. 'Do *you* know what it means to be born as the clock strikes midnight and in a storm? So that the milk is tainted with brimstone and sulphur?' She did, I knew she did: she was from Little Thetford after all, but still.

'It means you're special,' I said. 'You have special talents.' I thought she was listening but there was no sign. The cover on her bed was smooth and neat.

'If a hare runs past this window, there'll be a fire,' I said. Mandy's hair – vivid red, like the hair of a fox – was all that I could see of her above the bedspread. She'd been sleeping and sleeping, like she was in a big sleepy sludge. She probably knew that one too. I mean, there was a big fire at Fordham in 1956 and a hare had recently been killed in the exact spot it broke out, but still she didn't say anything, so I tried one last time: 'You don't want to have a baby on May the first, do you? Granny used to say if it was due then, you had to jump up and down on April the thirtieth to bring it on because the first of May is a terrible date for a baby.' At last I saw the red hair stir. And then her face appeared. She looked at me over the blanket. She seemed – I don't know. Amused, or curious. She was very lovely to look at. And friendly. I was pleased that I'd got her to see me at last.

Then one day a man came in to see her. I tried not to listen. He brought her flowers and a big bar of Galaxy chocolate. A copy of *Honey* magazine. At first, I thought he was her father: he was older than her with this big bald dome of a head and glasses. He pulled the chair up close, put his face close to hers and whispered; he stroked her cheek as she lay on the bed. I think his name was Thomas; I caught it once. Nurse Bingham was soon standing there, looming. Visitor's Hour was over. One hour, once a week. The smell of the farmyard came in through a door; the place had once been a farm and a small barn next door was used for occupational therapy. Visitors were discouraged, because they were 'unsettling'. It was true that afterwards Mandy sobbed, quietly but unmistakably.

I tried again to talk to her. 'Don't ask for the tuna. It's like sawdust,' I said, and she shook her head at the next dark dead baked potato on the tray on her bed, a foil-wrapped oblong of butter that could have been soap beside it. She glanced up at me, a look I got to know well. So swift, so clever, she took in everything in one sweep.

'The tuna is the deadest of the dead,' I told her, and she nodded, and we began to talk.

———◆———

Mandy spent Friday finding things in the house and discovering that Pamela, in the daytime, and with attention, did not cry piteously but pulled herself up against the bars of her cot, grabbed your nose and hair, smiled, chatted, pulled an earring out of your ear and tried to eat it. If you set her down on the floor she was off on all fours round an invisible track, like a toy train. If Mandy gave her a wind-up turtle she would sit for a long time, putting her finger over the tail, delighted to feel the mechanism flickering and reviving when she moved her finger.

She could cruise her way around furniture and the wooden bars of her play-pen and burbled happily – meaningless sounds – when she was strapped into her high-chair and given a plastic spoon and a bowl of baby rice. The bowl always ended up capping her head, and when James laughed, she did. James loved her. He seemed to want to spend all his time in the nursery with her, wave toys in her face and hand Mandy nappies or find the Matey or the rusks or the nappy-rash cream.

Katharine emerged at one o'clock, asking if anyone knew where the keys were and saying she would show Mandy the car. It was parked on the street close to the house: they left James minding the baby (Mandy strapped her into the high-chair) for the five minutes it would take.

Mandy tried to hide her disappointment that it wasn't a Mini or a convertible or a Roller or whatever else she'd imagined titled people drove. It was a big car, boxy and ugly, and, well, she hadn't properly taken note, but she thought it was a Corsair. As they were sitting inside it, Mandy turning the key in the ignition, Lady Morven – Katharine – showing her the little ashtray that flicked out, and where the lighter was, how to adjust the rear-view mirror, though their heights were very similar, Mandy thought, so probably not necessary, Katharine suddenly said, 'That damned man,' and they both looked across the road and saw a balding man in a suit, bulky and sinister, standing on the pavement opposite the house, arms folded, making no effort to hide the fact that he was staring at them. It wasn't the same one from the day before but his stance was the same. Defiant.

'Is it the private detective?' Mandy asked. Katharine was opening a cigarette case to offer her one. Her hand was shaking a little but both women strove to seem unbothered, unobserved.

Katharine nodded. 'I suppose it must be another of them. The way he stares at us – it's so rude, don't you find? I've a good mind to—'

They lit their cigarettes and drew on them. Katharine wore pink lipstick and nail varnish and was crisper, better turned-out than she had been. She had small pearls at each ear and a pussy-bow tie on the collar of her blouse. She seemed to Mandy less molten, more firmly defined.

'I hope you don't mind me asking—' Mandy began.

'My husband? You'll meet him tomorrow. It's his turn to have the children. Saturday to Sunday, every other weekend. That's what the court decided in its wisdom. I spent a little time in – well, I suppose you'd better know – some institution. And so, of course, one knows they'll say one's mad and not fit and all of that.'

The mention of an institution prompted a tremor in Mandy, as if a cold zip had been pulled up and down her spine. Katharine noticed and added smoothly, 'Oh, don't worry, he's only ever beastly to me. And then not when there are witnesses.'

That hadn't been Mandy's question. But it felt rude to ask, and impossible. Although Katharine was friendly (there was something sweet about her, something girlish, surprisingly open and willing to confide), Mandy held back. She was her employer, after all, a very new employer. She spoke with a plummy voice that Mandy had only ever heard before on the radio. No one Mandy knew said things like 'one knows'. She was frightened by it. Such a person could only despise a girl whose parents lived in a caravan. Mandy felt sure of that.

And so, Saturday morning, he turned up. The Earl of Morven. Richard. He let himself in with his own key and there he was suddenly, on the landing, wafting the smell of cigars, his hair oiled and his moustache reminding her – she didn't know why – of a neatly stacked hay bale. Mandy was coming up the stairs from the basement kitchen, carrying a tray of home-made ice lollies in Tupperware containers.

'Dickie,' he said, extending his hand to her. His voice was loud, his hand thrust out at her.

She struggled to balance the tray with one hand and take hold of his with the other. She wondered if she was supposed to call him 'm'lord' but, then, he'd said Dickie. The smell of cigars for her meant Christmas: the only time her father had ever smoked them. His palm was warm, but dry, completely dry. She thought of an advert then, on the telly, for hand-cream, which showed a 'before' shot of a hand that looked like a dried-up leaf. Dad would say Earl Dickie, Lord of All He Surveys, had clearly never done a day's work in his life. And that baby blue roll-neck he was wearing was a bit cissy for a man.

'I'm Mandy. They're – I'll get the baby ready. I didn't know what time you were coming.'

'Oh, no rush. I've something for them. James! Get down here.'

James appeared, dressed to go out: brown cords too wintry for a summer day and an over-sized green T-shirt. Everything was oversized on him; his arms hung like pieces of spaghetti. He glanced at the lollies, then obediently back to his father. Next to the bustle and confidence of Dickie he seemed paler, more ghost-like than ever.

Dickie was showing James a basket, an ordinary shopping basket, with blankets inside. And in the blanket, the face of a tiny black kitten. 'Pick her up. She won't bite you,' Dickie urged. When James hung back, Dickie picked up the kitten himself and waved her in front of his son's face, as if she was a glove puppet. The boy broke into a grin.

'What shall we call her, eh? Sootie? Blackie? Sambo?' the father boomed.

'Can we call her Bengo, like the cartoon dog in the *Blue Peter* annuals?'

Dickie thrust the kitten back into the basket. Mandy had left the lollies on a little side table and was coming downstairs from the nursery with Pamela in her arms and a bag of things she'd put together: nappies, a change of clothes, her bottle, her favourite sock-toy. She felt embarrassed handing this to the earl – surely a man wasn't capable of looking after a baby. What should she tell him about Pamela's routines, about the rusks she'd included and the baby rice? There was no sign of Katharine but it was obvious she had heard Dickie arrive and was hiding in her room. Mandy's next problem was: should she let on by asking the children to say goodbye to their mother?

Dickie was staring at her as if she was a new car he was buying. He stopped when she noticed and smiled, ducking his head politely at her. Mandy felt as if a silent compliment had been paid. It was unmistakable: she'd passed some test. He approved.

'Will you be needing the pram?' she asked, stumbling a little. Pamela was holding out her arms for her father and squirming towards him, like a genie trying to escape from a lamp.

'Lord, no. I imagine the nanny has such contraptions if she needs to take them out.'

Ah, so another nanny would be there. Yes, how silly of her to assume that earls took care of their own children any more than countesses did. She offered James one of the lollies, popping it out of the Tupperware holder, and the boy began sucking. But he never took his eyes from his father.

'Who's Daddy's baby doll, then? Who's his little Babykins?' The earl had taken Pamela from Mandy. For an instant she thought he was going to plunge her into the basket with the kitten. But he was opening the front door and there, coming up the steps, was a slender blonde in Dr Scholl's and a Laura Ashley dress. A girlfriend? The nanny? Whichever, the baby was handed to her and she started down the steps towards the car.

James needed a small push – the kitten in the basket placed in his other hand – to be persuaded out of the front door to follow his father and the young woman.

'And what time will you be back tomorrow night?' Mandy asked, in loyalty to Katharine. Dickie was bluff: she didn't feel sure he'd deign to give her an answer, but she didn't want to say she hadn't dared to ask.

'We'll be back seven p.m. on the dot,' Dickie said. He clicked his heels together and saluted. Then he gave her a wink and a glorious, sweeping glance from her feet to her head. Mandy felt herself blushing. It was as if a big dog had licked her up and down.

That night Mandy dreamed of Neville. She couldn't remember the dream except that she woke up a little sweaty, disturbed.

Wanting Neville disturbed her. After all she'd been through, couldn't this part of her just give up the ghost? She thought of his hair, the texture and smell of it, and when he'd kissed her, the way his beard had tickled all around her mouth. And in the strong lamplight she felt she had seen everything about him, right down to the pores. She thought of his nose, and his hands, and his mouth, which was very full. She lay in bed, luxuriating, going through every detail as if she was drawing him. The eyebrows.

He might claim he had no wife but he had admitted to a son. Mark. He hadn't said how old he was. Mark was back home, being cared for by his mother. When had he told her that? She had been giddy, she could barely remember, but perhaps it was during their walk around the block, before they'd gone back to the house. So why hadn't she asked him then? Oh, OK, a son. What about your wife? That had been the moment to ask. The discovery of the son had made her gasp, but she didn't reply properly, didn't tell him a story of her own. It was too early to tell but it just made her feel closer to him – he spoke of his son with gentleness, tenderness, but he was open about it. He said his mum was doing a good job but when he had money and a proper place – not just a room above a pub – he wanted to bring his son to England. He sent money home: that was the point. Not like his own bastard father. He worked hard. He was a baby-father, an expression she'd never heard. She tried to imagine someone – a man – caring for Peter in the same way, sending him money, but couldn't.

Would she dare mention the wife, the wedding ring, again? Who was the mother of his son and why wouldn't he tell her? If she was going to see him. Was she going to see him again? He had never asked – he hadn't called her but she knew where he was. Mandy knew with certainty that she would see him again.

So that first weekend when Mandy's kids went off with Dickie, we went to Annabel's. Mandy had met someone, the bloke from the pub that first night, and he'd rung her, she said. 'A friend of mine is a member. We can go as his guests. Pretend you're debs,' he told her. 'It's very posh.' Mandy asked him what a deb was, but I don't think he knew: he'd just heard the word on *Upstairs Downstairs*. 'Aren't we a bit old for that? They're young, aren't they?' Mandy said, to me. 'But Neville says we have to dress up,' she told me.

He probably couldn't get us in anyway. I thought he was bluffing to impress Mandy.

On the Saturday evening we got ready at Mandy's new place. Lady Morven came into Mandy's room with her arms full of clothes in black dry-cleaning bags and heaped them onto the bed. Then she disappeared and came back with three martinis on a tray, clinking with ice, and a little dish of olives, and cigarettes in a silver case.

The bed bounced a little when she joined us. 'Most of these are barely worn. When would one wear them?' she said, unzipping some of the bags and laying things out. The room had the buzz of the changing room at Miss Selfridge but the labels were ones we'd only ever seen in magazines: Gina Fratini, Zandra Rhodes and Celia Birtwell, Ossie Clark and Mary Quant – Mandy's eyes in her frosted blue eye-shadow widened with every new peeling of a zip. She was sitting smoking in a nylon slip, but I was too self-conscious to undress.

'Annabel's. I always loathed the woman,' Lady Morven murmured, pulling a black velvet dress from one of the bags with a great waft of scent and showing it to Mandy.

'Oh, m'lady, it's not a person's *house* . . .' I started, but Mandy shushed me. Apparently we should call the countess *Katharine*. I suppose 'm'lady' made her feel old, and now she was sitting here between us, the most wide-awake and giggly I'd seen her, she did seem younger. Probably not much older than us, maybe twenty-nine at the most. It's easy enough for Mandy to call her 'Katharine':

she hasn't had my years of training. I mean, the proper forms of address for nobs were drummed into us at Norland.

'You're about my size except for the old bazookas. I wish I had a bust like yours,' Katharine said, as Mandy tried the dress on. We fell about laughing and shrieking and she topped up our glasses from the bottle she'd brought.

'Doesn't she have any friends of her own?' I whispered to Mandy, when Katharine went to fetch more things, wraps and boleros and fur capes, but Mandy had only been there a couple of days and said she didn't know.

When the black velvet dress was produced, Mandy had said, 'That's so generous of you, Katharine. Surely not that one – that's *too* kind!' but really she was thrilled, I could see that. Now she wriggled into a sort of floaty chiffon number, a maxi-dress, with bell sleeves and a low neck, all patterned in orange and green swirls, and turned back to me from the mirror, her cream bosoms sort of bursting out of the top of it.

I said, 'Wow, you look like a model,' and Katharine came back in the room and agreed: 'Zandra Rhodes. Perfect.' She was suddenly serious, all giggles gone.

Then Katharine turned her attention to me. I was embarrassed, of course, but she made me stand up and try on a Gina Fratini red silk dress. That was a bit formal, she said, she suggested a Bill Gibb, with red swirls on white chiffon.

When I pulled a face she said, 'Nonsense, darling, it looks stunning on you. No need to hide your light under a bushel, eh? You have a stupendous figure and men love all that creamy skin and that fresh-faced-just-finished-milking-a-cow look. Like something out of an Edna O'Brien novel. They'll be wanting to bend you over a milking stool at the first opportunity. Now, what size feet are you?'

I glanced at Mandy. We burst out laughing again and Katharine joined in. It was shocking to me to hear someone so posh talk like that. If I'd told Dad – well, I never would tell him, but if I had – he'd have been dumbstruck.

We slugged back more of our drinks and Katharine went to get shoes – I had the same size feet as her but Mandy was one size smaller. We hobbled about in gold platforms and tried on her Oliver Goldsmith sunglasses, and then we looked at the time and Mandy shrieked and Katharine said we should just go onto the street and hail a taxi to Berkeley Square. We left her sitting on Mandy's bed, suddenly small again and deflated, like a child playing dress-up, surrounded by all the abandoned clothes and shoes, and as I glanced back, Mandy whispered, 'Should we have asked her to join us?'

But I said, 'God, no, of course not. That would be weird,' and we called out, 'Bye, thank you so much,' over our shoulders.

The evening had a dry and yellow feel to it, the sky a bit of a washed-out blue handkerchief. An end-of-summer feeling, with all the plane trees in Berkeley Square drooping and heavy. There were lots of people outside Annabel's. We stepped into a cloud of eau de Cologne, cigar smoke and petrol fumes. Motorbikes revved – they were practically on the pavement so that the blokes on them could chat to the girls gathered there. I don't know how they could hear themselves think, over the car horns, the hissing of brakes from a bus somewhere and even a police car shrieking past. A Bentley circled us like a shark. Over the street I watched a man in a velvet suit taking photographs of a girl in thigh-high boots and a cape.

I had a funny thought for a second about how Dad would be impressed but Granny would have said it was the Devil's Playground, and then I squashed it. I sort of shook the thought out of my head.

We smoked our cigarettes, leaning against the railings. I was finding it hard to balance in the platforms – I kept feeling like I'd fall off them. Mandy squealed: 'There he is!' and this Neville appeared, in his top hat, like a magician. Blimey, that man fancied himself. I couldn't understand what she saw in him. He had a beard and the most crazy bush of hair – his hat wouldn't really sit on it properly – and he was in a black velvet suit, all flares and wide lapels and, yes, well, yes, OK, I did notice the way the other girls sort of bristled like electricity as he passed them. It made me laugh, really, because they were so obvious about it, but, well, that kind of flamboyance, cockiness, that's not my type. He looked perfect with Mandy, though, in her Zandra Rhodes dress, I could see that, and I saw how she glowed when he came up to us. I watched him carefully. How he looked at her and how she looked back. It was interesting. I'd never seen anything like it. Do faces sometimes change? Does falling in love do that? It really did seem a bit spooky to me. I knew it was something I didn't understand.

Anyway, once Neville had arrived we clattered down some stairs, with me nearly breaking my ankle in a Dick Emery-style walk.

It was nothing like I was expecting. I suppose I'd pictured silver disco balls, the Beet Club, that kind of thing. Instead the walls were painted this plummy red and it was all boring paintings of things like horses and dogs, country castles, portraits of dull couples. It was like some posh person's front room or a golf club. And lots of old men in suits. Mandy drew me to one side to go to the cloakroom. She gave her 'wrap' to this woman, who one of the other girls in there called Mabel. Mabel had a face like a crumpled tissue, seriously scary. Next to her at the sink she had a saucer and the other girls were putting ten-pence coins in it. Even one fifty-pence piece ('That's a lot for a pee!' I whispered to Mandy, and we giggled). There was this enormous bottle of Calèche on a dressing-table and I saw one of the posh girls squirt herself with it, but I didn't quite dare. A blonde girl was redoing her lip gloss with a little brush. Another was doing up a velvet choker around the throat of her friend.

I glanced at myself quickly in the mirror and thought about what Lady Morven had said. Me bent face-down over a milking pail, my bum in the air, my skirt all rucked up. The thought of it made me feel funny. I remember that I'd said to Dr Ryan once, shyly, 'I've no idea if men ever fancy me.'

And he'd just laughed and said, 'Who cares? Who do *you* fancy? Isn't that the point?'

The first room we came to was like a perfume-scented, satin-lined jewellery box. We picked out glittering lights in a dark, smoky place. The walls were covered with gold-framed paintings. Each of the tables had a glowing gold lamp, and once my eyes adjusted to the dark, I could see it was all emerald-green-velvet-curtained areas and marble and oak panels and glossy red-painted doors, leading off into other mysterious spaces. Everyone was in evening dresses, I was glad we'd made the effort, and the men in suits. Neville went to the bar, waving his pound note above his head, like a flag. We found a table in an alcove and plonked ourselves at it.

'I haven't spotted anyone famous,' I said grumpily.

We stared at the tiny dance floor, sort of wooden and sunken with this scattering of lights on it, like stars. The bar area was a scrum. All that strange artwork above it: what a horrible mix of paintings.

Mandy said: 'There, look! Molly Parkin! She's famous, isn't she?'

When I said nothing, Mandy asked, 'What's wrong?' and I pretended not to hear. I felt sulky and stubborn. I'd thought when she got to London, after all our planning and manoeuvring, our real fun would start. I'd been helping her, I'd been saving her stuff, I'd been waiting for her to get to London and join me. And instead, five minutes after arriving, here she was, with *him*. But I couldn't say that. She'd have teased me because, really, didn't girls always give you that feeling, that friendship was nothing, girls were just temporary? Surely everyone understood the rules, until blokes came along. Only an idiot didn't get this, but somehow I hadn't. I felt silly and humiliated. Mandy was right and I was wrong, of course: men were the real thing and only a girl would expect things to be different. A weird girl like me.

Mandy was singing along to Roxy Music, then twisted in her chair suddenly. 'Look! Is that Marie Helvin? You know, the model?' The woman she was pointing to did look a bit familiar. Maybe I'd seen her in *19*, advertising Miners makeup, with her black hair and heart-shaped face, like a sort of porcelain doll.

'I just feel – self-conscious, you know,' I bellowed, over the music, as Neville came back to our table, sat astride a little stool and placed three glasses of fizz in front of us. You could tell he worked in a bar, the way he did it. An old gent was making his way towards me, sweaty forehead, beady blue eyes too small for his face . . .

'We're taken!' I shouted, and he retreated, like an old tortoise drawing its head in, melting back into the crowd.

'Do you think it's a rule that men have to wear jackets?' Mandy asked, looking around at all the men in dinner suits. 'It's so formal, isn't it, for a nightclub?'

Neville moved his stool closer to Mandy and draped an arm around her shoulders, pulling her towards him.

'Oh, my God!' Mandy suddenly shrieked. 'That's him!'

A man with a wopping moustache and slicked-down hair was surveying the room. He wore a fierce suit and a blonde, like a froth of bubbles, on his arm. Mandy leaned in to whisper but I couldn't hear so she had to shout. 'The Earl of Morven. Dickie! What's he doing here when he's got the kids for the weekend?'

'Didn't you say he has a nanny?'

Mandy looked affronted or crestfallen or something, swigging her champagne and throwing her head back. 'He only has them two days in every fourteen. He's made a huge fuss to win that. He's watching the house to make sure she's – oh, I don't know – a fit mother or something. Why wouldn't he spend more time with them?'

'It's evening, Mandy. He can go out, surely.'

She crossed her legs and drew on her cigarette, pursing her mouth.

'He's good-looking, though,' I added, staring at Dickie. He was so old-fashioned, compared to Neville, with his beads and

64

his hair and his wide lapels. Dickie was slick and grown-up and smart and noticeable, like men in films in the old days. Cary Grant and Gary Cooper. When Dr Ryan asked me who I fancied, what my type was, I suppose it was that. Men who gave me the same feeling Dad did, that they could cope in a crisis and never acted young or uncertain. That they weren't like me.

It was clear that Dickie knew everyone, though he didn't glance at our corner. He smiled and clapped some bloke on the back, then accepted a cigar from another. He and the girlfriend disappeared into another room and it was Isaac Hayes's 'Shaft' on the turntable and Neville wanted Mandy to dance. They leaped up and tried to squeeze into the tiny space. He left his hat on the table.

I watched them for a while. Neville was so tall, leaning in towards her, his hair splaying out. He looked like a stick of sedge bending towards the dyke. Then I thought again about Dickie. You wouldn't forget him. He wouldn't let you: he had the face of a bloodhound somehow. Jowly. I wondered how old he was. Older than Katharine. Maybe a hint that one day those handsome lines around his eyes would droop. His expression was so serious. You'd want to get him to smile, see if you couldn't lighten him up a bit. The same feeling I'd always had about Dad, who didn't smile often. But when he did, a fabulous feeling would break over me, like a wave.

Dr Ryan was grown-up like Dad; he had old-fashioned looks; he was smooth and properly manly, but he smiled easily. One time, when I was most dreading the therapy ending, I blurted out, 'How will I cope without you?'

'I'll be inside you,' he said, 'like one of your voices. You can ask me anything you like.' And he'd spluttered into a burst of laughter. As well as smiling, Dr Ryan laughed easily, often at nothing at all. It was the thing I loved best about him.

At seven o'clock on Sunday Mandy dried her hair with a towel, then tentatively switched on the blow-dryer. She'd been trying out a colour (copper-red) but she didn't want to miss the sound of the doorbell with the dryer on so she kept switching it off and listening. Seven thirty and no doorbell had sounded.

The telephone had been ringing on and off all day. She'd answered it once (Katharine seemed to be asleep and had hardly emerged from her room) and a man's voice had politely asked for 'Charlotte'. When she'd replied that there was no Charlotte there, he said nothing but replaced the receiver with a little click, like a snap of the fingers. Mandy felt as she used to in school when boys would try to produce an electric shock by sliding their shoes along the new carpet, then putting out their fingers to touch her.

At eight o'clock, Katharine appeared in the kitchen where Mandy was making a cup of tea. Katharine was lifting her hair from her neck and tying it with a ribbon, then letting it fall again, agitated.

'Didn't he say seven?' Katharine asked, winding the ribbon tighter and pulling it into a fierce knot.

'Would you like a cup of tea? I'm sure they're . . . caught in traffic.'

'It's the courts, the bloody courts, who insist on him having them. He doesn't want them. He does it to get at me. In the end, he's going for custody, just to hurt me. He spends the whole weekend quizzing James – does she have any boyfriends, do men visit the house, is she taking her pills. He's such a bastard, an out-and-out bastard, and he won't stop until he's finished me off.'

She was pacing the room. She reached for a packet of cigarettes on the windowsill and snatched at it, then sighed, dismayed that there was only one left.

'You have it,' Mandy said politely. 'I can pop to the pub and get some more.'

'Don't leave me here! I don't want to be on my own when he comes back.'

Mandy put teabags in the pot and tried not to notice Katharine's agitation, the panicky tone in her voice. 'I could ring him if you like,' Mandy said. 'You know, find out what time they'll be back.'

Katharine plonked down. She was picking at the skin along her nails, making them bleed, then biting at the flesh. 'I was depressed. After James. And he used it against me. It was perfect for him. When Pamela came along he tried to put me in there again and I ran away and he said that was a sure sign. And then there was Oliver. He was kind. I suppose I let myself fall a little. Just someone who talked to me sometimes, as if I was a human being. I didn't realise he'd warned him off. I wondered why he never called me. That did it. That was when I took to my bed. Lay doggo, as Dickie would say. I just wondered why Oliver didn't ring me, you know. But I had to pull myself together. I'd never get out once he started telling people I was bonkers. All his gambling chums. They were all against me, all of them. They'd have happily helped him lock me up and thrown away the key. You've no idea how *utterly ghastly* such places are—'

'I do. I do have an idea,' Mandy interrupted, but Katharine did not respond.

'Oh, do ring him, yes, do!' Katharine suddenly wailed. 'Heaven knows what he might have done!'

It was eight fifteen by Mandy's watch. James liked to watch *Alias Smith and Jones* on the telly on a Sunday night, he'd told her. She knew it finished at twenty to six, hours ago. Still, there must be an explanation. Maybe James hadn't wanted to come back in the middle of the show, or Pamela needed changing just as they left the house.

She went to the telephone and dialled the number Katharine gave her. She had no idea why her finger felt slippery in the dial. There was a long ringing sound and nothing more. Mandy put the receiver down, saying, 'They're probably on their way.' She poured Katharine a cup of tea and pushed it gently towards her, the cup – white porcelain with a pattern of bamboo leaves – wobbling on its saucer.

Katharine stared at her with big brown eyes, beautiful eyes, the whites shockingly healthy and dazzling. So, Katharine had, what, fallen for someone else? This Oliver person. That was new. Mandy felt as if she'd seen her employer for the first time.

Katharine sipped her tea, then said, 'You're kind, aren't you? One of those women who like to help others. But probably you do it because – you – it helps you feel in control. You feel kind, nurturing, and you can tell others what to do. You feel superior.'

Mandy was astonished, then affronted. She didn't know what to say. What was she *allowed* to say? Finally she tried, 'I had a difficult mother. It was my role. Listening, advising. But mostly I just longed for her to be happier.'

'What would have made her happier?'

'That's the problem. Not sure I knew. Not sure she knows. She – she likes looking after children, I suppose. So perhaps if I'd never grown up . . .'

'Didn't you say you had a younger brother? Much younger?'

'Yes. Peter. He's just a bit older than James. Fifteen years between us.'

'Well, something of a surprise, then. For your parents, I mean. Or does he have a different father?'

Mandy was shocked. How direct Katharine was. She wasn't used to being asked such questions but she supposed Katharine thought her something less than human, a curiosity, perhaps. Of the underclasses.

'Does he seem disturbed to you?' Katharine shot at her, suddenly.

'Who, James?'

'Dickie. Does Dickie seem . . . disturbed?'

Where was this leading? Was it better just to agree? Was that what Katharine wanted? The countess had drunk the scalding tea in almost one gulp – the cups were ridiculously dainty, like a child's tea set – and was biting at the skin on her fingers again.

'I know you think this is extreme – you probably don't believe me at all. But I wouldn't put it past him to gas them all. Or in his car. You know that thing men do? When they want to kill themselves, they always take their children with them. Drive them off a cliff. Jump off Beachy Head. I don't know why they do it! Inflict the most pain possible, I suppose. Oh, God, they're such monsters! Or maybe a shotgun – Lord knows he's a good enough shot. Oh, where the hell is he? Do ring again, won't you? Or, should we go round there, do you think? Or ring the police?'

'Oh, no, I don't think – no need to ring the police just yet.'

The truth was, Katharine's panic was contagious. A little image of James's worried face as he'd joined his father and the nanny in the car slipped into Mandy's mind: he'd bitten his bottom lip, widened his eyes and seemed to plead with her.

Could Katharine be right? What did she know about this Dickie beyond a couple of brief sightings?

Katharine had leaped up and was looking for her car keys. 'I should never have agreed to it, these visits. The God-awful judge – what does he know? What does any man know about what's good for children? But if I'd said no, they would have used that against me too. Unreasonable. Unreasonably biased against Dickie. Dickie. The charming man who can do no wrong. Who brought whores to my house – bastards they are, bastards all of them.'

Her voice was loud and at a strange pitch, as if she wasn't talking to anyone at all. Or perhaps someone invisible just a few inches in front of her. Mandy thought again about Katharine's eyes. Was this the medication? Was Katharine well? Should she believe her? And as she was wondering, there was a tap on the closed kitchen door, and there he was, the same smell of cigar smoke and hair-cream and tweed; Dickie, gently stepping into the room. He'd let himself in, a sleeping baby against his chest, James just behind him, his arms cradling the kitten basket.

'Daddy's given it to me to keep,' James said, beaming. 'Her name's Bengo.' The kitten stared at them all, startled.

'Sorry we're late,' Dickie said, to Mandy. He was whispering, inclining his head towards Pamela and carefully unloading her into Mandy's arms. He ignored his wife, who was sniffing loudly and had flattened herself theatrically against the kitchen wall.

'You all right, old girl? Like I say, sorry – I took them to Howlett's to see the animals and, of course, we went and got a rotten puncture and had to get Old Rogers to come and help us out.'

He beamed at Mandy. She found it impossible not to smile right back, but Katharine had pushed past her, hastening up the stairs, stumbling against the kitten in the basket as she did so. It hissed and reared up.

'That's OK,' Mandy said to Dickie, over the head of the baby in her arms. 'I'll take her up to her bed. James, did you have anything to eat? Would you like some beans on toast when I come down?'

James said he was full. She carried the baby up to the third-floor nursery. Somehow she could feel that Katharine had run up there ahead of her, was hovering, listening. Why didn't she come out to kiss the baby goodnight, or put her to bed? The house was cloaked in the strange atmosphere that Katharine always seemed to conjure: torpor, stupor.

She thought again about Katharine's behaviour in the kitchen when Dickie had been late. Frantic pacing, talking at a super-pitch. The revelation about Oliver: what was she to make of that? Had Katharine had an affair? All that stuff about Dickie topping himself and the children when Mandy felt sure the real danger of that was closer to home. She'd seen that kind of animated, heightened talk before and she knew where: The Poplars. Perhaps it was the pills she was on. Her torpor and her wakefulness both had an unnatural quality: there were those blasts of sudden clarity where Katharine broke through with a burst. The comment about Mandy liking to help and feeling superior when she did: there was some horrible truth in that, and it had startled her.

The nursery was snug. Pamela, exhausted by her day out, allowed Mandy to lay her in her cot; she fell into a deeper sleep without protest.

When Mandy came back down to the basement kitchen, Dickie had gone and James was simply standing, arms by his sides, as if the key in his back needed winding.

She felt that James needed some time with her: it would be unfair to make him go straight to bed. Katharine had not reappeared so she suggested they let Bengo have a little play in the garden. James picked up the basket eagerly, found a key to the kitchen door: it was the first time she'd been out here. Pretty small, just a courtyard, really, with an ivy-covered wall, which in daytime blocked the light.

'Daddy tried to climb up there once,' James said, crouching over his kitten, delicately unpacking the folds of blanket it was wrapped in, releasing the sour, grassy cat smell that somehow reminded her of her father's long-ago greenhouse, the tomato plants.

Mandy had already learned that James would often tell her the most interesting things when he wasn't looking at her, when his attention was seemingly elsewhere, so she waited.

'You can't climb it. It's too straight. And too high. He said he was Spider-Man – he did it to make me laugh. But he couldn't and he just fell back down again.'

Mandy stared at the darkened grey wall and could just about make out a trellis, and black roses.

The kitten was making mewing sounds but refusing to come out of the basket, and when James reached towards her she hissed and spat at him.

'Isn't Bengo a dog's name? Maybe she'd like a nicer one.' She fetched a saucer of milk and James put it in the kitten's basket, but as his hand went in the little creature stretched out a paw and scratched him, drawing blood.

'She's scared, poor thing,' Mandy said, catching hold of James's arm to examine the scratch in the semi-dark. A tiny pattern of pricks, like black stars. 'Come in and I'll put some Cuticura on that.'

'She wasn't scared. It was *my* fault. I put the saucer in the wrong place.'

Her calves were aching, crouching beside them both. The top of James's head, intent over the kitten, reminded her of Peter, the absolutely fixed attention that boys were capable of, when you knew you didn't exist and wouldn't even if you spoke.

Her voice was an oddness in the dark, meaningless. 'Bring Bengo in now, she just needs to be on her own.' As predicted, James didn't move. 'Or you could leave her. Nothing can harm her out here. She could sleep in her basket, if you like.'

At last James heard her, moved. Straightened up. The garden seemed to bristle. Little things – mice, birds, leaves, insects – rustled and flickered into life. James placed the basket closer to the back door and reluctantly followed her in.

She remembered then Katharine saying, 'I should have watered the lawn.' There was no lawn, just the flagstones, a few pots, ivy crinkling along the wall. What had she meant?

And for the first time since she'd arrived Mandy had a powerful doubt. She wanted to telephone Mum – surely these last few days were the longest she'd ever gone without speaking to her. Suddenly, she wanted to talk to Dad too, or to Peter. The phrase 'out of the frying pan' kept floating up, and she knew Rosemary would have been the first to say it. What strange life had she stepped into, just when she'd believed her own was finally starting?

The earl telephoned me. I was just eating some toast with this fab honey on it that comes from Fortnum & Mason. Lord Morven – Dickie – had such a deep and plummy voice on the phone, my heart was skittering, listening to him. He said the agency had given my number as a reference for Mandy. That his wife hadn't bothered to take up references but he was more thorough. And he knew Lady Jane, it seemed.

'Rosemary, didn't I see you in Annabel's with her?' he asked.

'Yes, m'lord,' I said. So he *had* seen us but not come over or acknowledged us. I suppose men like him didn't say hello to the nanny in that kind of place. A strand of honey was glistening from my finger and I was trying to lick it. I remembered him with the bubble-perm blonde. Standing there, surveying.

'Oh, do call me *Dickie*,' he said.

And then: when could I meet him? he asked. At his club. He gave an address.

'I'm sorry, I have the children. I'm on duty here,' I said, chasing the honey round my finger with my tongue. We batted some dates and times to and fro, then struck upon Friday morning, when Snaggy and Clemmie were at their grandmother's with Lady Jane for a birthday visit.

Mandy had said that first week about private detectives watching the house. She'd said that the bloody phone went all the bloody time, and no one ever answered when she picked up but if Katharine did an unholy row would always go on. But Dickie sounded reasonable on the phone and, well, worried. Kind, sort of. A new girl had come to look after his kids. Kids he wasn't allowed to see for two weeks at a time. Painful, that. Surely he was within his rights to find out more about her. I mean, I did give her a reference and I was the one who was a Norland nanny so it would look really bad if I got it wrong in some way.

I knew the minute I put the receiver down that I wasn't going to tell Mandy. I had the same sulky feeling I'd had watching her dancing with Neville at Annabel's. She's not bothered about me, is she? She's already obsessed with *him*. And so my conversation with Dickie, well, usually I would have been on the phone straight away to tell her, but this time I wasn't.

The club intimidated me. I wished Dickie had suggested somewhere else. I'd never been in a place like that. I wondered how on earth I should dress. I even thought of wearing my nanny's uniform – Lady Jane liked me to wear it as much as possible – but I'd have stuck out, even more of a sore thumb in it. I wore bell-bottom jeans with embroidered flowers round the hem and a white smock top. I tied my hair up with a big red scarf and put on red lipstick. Then I wiped it off and my mouth ended up stained – he'd think I'd been eating a lolly.

Mandy said, 'Have you got a bit of time off, then? The kids are at their granny's – you could come over here and spend it with me,' and I said, 'Oh, no. I have a dentist appointment, *soooo* boring.' A lie. It popped out so easily that I surprised myself.

The club was just as bad as I'd expected. A tiny shiny girl in a black evening dress and pearls sat at a little desk and I had to give my name. When that got no response, I had to give his, and I stumbled a bit: 'His lordship, the Earl of Morven,' I said. The girl put her fingers to her mouth, as I spoke, like she was hiding something. A powerful smell of perfume I recognised came off her. What was it? Mary Quant's Havoc. I saw at once that I was wearing the wrong things and my only hope was Dickie's name. But it seemed to do the trick.

She wrote something down and nodded towards a door. It was daytime but the place was dark. I'd had to come down some stairs to reach the entrance desk. It smelt of cigarettes and floor polish and the Havoc perfume; it was all paintings of old farts and dark-wood panelling. The second I stepped forward some bloke in a suit was asking me if I wanted to leave anything in the cloakroom and then I had to say I didn't have a coat and wonder why he couldn't see that, and what else could he possibly mean? My shoes clicked on the floor. Everything here was polished and ready to smash. Gold-framed mirrors lined the walls among the pictures of big country houses. There was red and green and tartan everywhere – like being inside a tin of Scottish shortbread.

It was clear I didn't know which way to go. The door he was gesturing towards looked like a kitchen to me, like it might lead to the lavatories, but I thought I'd better just hold my head up and walk through it so I did. The bloke followed me. A bigger room – green walls, brown leather seats, rugs, a kind of lounge with a bar – opened up in front of me and there was the earl, waiting and standing up as I arrived, and giving me a short smile.

'What would you like to drink?' he asked. He had a glass of whisky or something with ice on a coaster on the table in front of him. The coaster had another picture of a country house on it.

I said, 'A Dubonnet and lemonade, please,' and the silent man who had accompanied me to the table and offered to take my coat was sent away to get it.

I sat down on the leather seat opposite him. I felt ridiculous in my white gypsy blouse and jeans, like a piece of white linen that had floated into a dark brown and green room, a masculine room, and I was like a piece of laundry that had ended up there.

'So did you train at Norland College with Mandy? Is that how you know her?'

I wondered for a moment what Mandy had said at her interview, then remembered the conversation with her, the Bowlby book I'd brought her that first night. Surely she'd told the truth about Norland – how could you fake it? – and only lied about training as a nursery nurse.

'No. Mandy's not Norland-trained. She's a nursery nurse. Lots of experience, though.'

'She seems a nice girl,' Dickie said, leaning forward to sip from his drink. Mine appeared. The slimy bloke was suddenly there again, holding a tray. He put my glass on a coaster, over a picture of – well, it looked like Balmoral Castle to me.

'So how did you two meet?' Dickie said, the moment he'd gone.

'Oh, well, I was a nurse, you see. Before I was a nanny. And Mandy was a patient for a while.'

Why did I say that? I sipped my drink, gulping, playing for time.

'Nothing serious, I hope?'

'No. Just a brief stay. That was about four years ago. Then we became friends and I went to Norland College. And I came to London to work for her ladyship. And Mandy wanted to come down here . . . so I encouraged her. Yes, I encouraged her.'

'My wife didn't see fit to take up Mandy's references. I hope you don't mind that I've been more vigilant?'

I shook my head vigorously. No, no, of course not.

'But, you see, she's had some rather disastrous earlier nannies. So her rather whimsical approach hasn't always been in the children's interests. And it's a requirement. She's not quite fit. The court decreed. Katharine has to employ a full-time nanny in order to keep the children.'

'Yes.' I was glugging too quickly. There was something I liked about him, despite my nervousness, despite my self-consciousness in the posh surroundings. He was trying to put me at ease, I could see that. He offered me an olive from a little bowl, brought with the drinks, but I didn't trust myself to try one: what to do if there was a stone in it?

'So, one wonders about your friend Mandy. Is she kind? Is she good with babies? Pamela is a little slow to walk. We're worried about her.'

'Oh, yes, she's very kind. She's warm. She's lovely with babies, very good with them. She's—'

'And James? Older children? Is she firm with him? Does she give him her attention? You might have noticed he rather *craves* attention.'

'Yes, yes, she's good with him, too. She has a brother around the same age. She likes boys. I think James likes her. Though, of course, I've only been there a couple of times, seen her with him once or twice.'

'And she's reliable? Does she drink? Does she . . . Well, what about gentleman friends?'

He went on like this for some time. The questions just kept coming. Was she practical in a crisis? Was she a sensible driver? Did she think about the children's safety? Did she smoke around them? I answered as favourably as I could. I was aware not only of wanting to be helpful to Mandy, wanting to protect my own reputation (after all, I'd vouched for her), but also, strangely, of wanting to reassure him. He was very polished. The moustache was clipped, the suit sharp, the handkerchief in his pocket expertly ironed. The parting in his hair showed a tiny bit of pink scalp. That was something vulnerable. And under his eyes there were dark shadows, a little baggy. His concern was real. He suddenly downed his whisky, sat back and said, 'It's a kind of *torture*. No one can imagine. Being away from one's own children. Being forbidden . . . all the little things one took for granted . . .'

'Yes,' I said quietly.

He ran his tongue over his lip, signalled for another drink and, without asking, one for me, too. Then he glanced from left to right, leaned in a little. 'And Katharine. Of course you've noticed Katharine is . . . well . . . One is very worried. About the children's safety. I've employed some people to watch. One never really knows what she's capable of, and I can't quite express it to you, my dear. One's fears are pretty dreadful when they involve the safety of one's children.'

I saw something in his eyes: what did he fear exactly? *What?* My heart pinched, looking at him. I had to glance away, down at my drink.

'She doesn't drive them anywhere, does she? Could you make sure that Mandy's the one doing any driving or running around?' he asked, trying to get me to look directly at him. His eyes were blue, a lovely blue, and he looked like James for a moment. The first time I'd seen the resemblance.

'Well . . .'

'Oh, in time I'll talk to Mandy myself. But I thought first I needed to be sure what kind of girl she is. My wife does seem to get the nannies rather on her side and then one can't get through to them. The last one, Louise, well, the least said about that the better. Katharine has her own version of things, you know. Not entirely reliable. She spent some time, several months . . . Well, what can one say? An ugly business. She refuses to go for help again and that's why one must be vigilant. Keep an eye on things. I shan't say more.'

After that, he sat back. The intensity seemed to seep out of him, but my mind was racing. Wow! We'd fallen for it, hook, line and sinker. We'd thought him the bad guy, even while we'd seen that Katharine was in a dreamy stupor most of the time. Well, Mandy would be naturally biased, sympathetic to her boss: that was the problem. Mandy, of course, with her own experiences, wouldn't see things from my point of view. But I'd explain.

Dickie was standing up, signalling the meeting was over. He shook my hand. His last comment, leaning in a little to say it, was beseeching. His tone was, in any case. 'Do you think that Mandy might meet me like this? Would you put in a good word, eh? I rather feel that once Katharine gets her claws into them, the girls take her side and, well, collude in her mania, you know. The dream of paranoia? Not everyone understands it. But I see that you do, Rosemary – if I may? I see that you do.'

He trusted me. He saw somehow, though I'd disguised it, my professional standing, my years of experience with the hopeless and the delusional. I'd hoped to have shaken it off. I'd refused to tell him about it, about Mandy, how we really met but even so . . . Mandy and I never agreed about men. She liked the ones I thought were losers: look at that new bloke, Neville! And I, well, I have my training at Norland. I have something else too – my gift – but I try not to claim that one too much. Mandy always laughs at me if I mention it.

Dickie was a very clever man, an impressive man, and devoted to his children. Anyone could see that.

August slid to September. There was mention of James going up to Eton – Daddy's old school, he'd been down for it since birth – but James said that wasn't until he was thirteen, and Mandy wasn't sure where he went in the meantime. It felt like the end of the summer. Mandy knew that inky violet blots from the blackberries would be splatting the caravan at home, where the birds had dashed them, like the tiny heads of enemies.

She thought that perhaps James was in the middle of a change in school, something about the fees, she supposed. There had been a heated telephone conversation in the hall, Katharine hissing things into the receiver, one hand over her mouth.

'Your bloody father,' Katharine had muttered to James afterwards. 'Don't blame me if they won't have you this year.' James had looked worried, so Mandy had rushed to reassure him. Mandy couldn't figure out when he should start and, not wanting to seem ignorant – did these schools operate their own terms outside the normal ones? – she didn't like to ask.

She had been at the house long enough now to have established a routine. She learned that Katharine barely appeared from her bedroom but that this couldn't be relied upon and she must be vigilant; if she'd got Pamela off to sleep Katharine might wander up there and wake her, then drift back to her own bedroom, calling to Mandy that the baby needed changing. There was a television set in Katharine's bedroom; Mandy could hear it softly chuntering. The door was closed but she pictured Katharine lying on her bed.

A char came twice a week, a chatty West Indian woman called Gladys, who carried a transistor radio and moved it from room to room as she worked. On Friday mornings a Harrods delivery arrived, with a cheery bloke who looked her up and down, and said, 'You're the new one, are you? *Very* nice,' in a Cockney accent unlike any she'd ever heard. Mandy didn't know if she was supposed to pay so there was an awkward moment where they looked at one another, him seeming to expect something from her, and then she realised he was just a chancer, a flirt, and she said, 'I must get on. I think I can hear the baby.'

The weekend was not one of Dickie's, so Mandy wondered what the routine would be. Perhaps Katharine would want to do something with the children. But on Saturday morning there was no sign of her emerging from her room. James was dressed and drifting around the house, standing close to Mandy while she stirred warm milk for porridge.

She suggested they go out to buy cat food and toys for Bengo. She pushed Pamela in the grand pram; the baby sat up, queenly, strapped in, wearing a yellow knitted cardigan and chewing happily on the pom-poms dangling on yellow wool. As soon as she left the house, Mandy's mood lifted. She felt deliciously aware of the picture she made: a young mum with her two lovely, well-turned-out children, just as she'd imagined them when applying for this job. James walked beside her, sucking a lolly she'd made him on a Tupperware stick, breaking off to talk animatedly about Bengo and about bending spoons using only mind-power, which he was going to demonstrate later; he was sure he could do it. Pamela was sitting up, prattling her baby nonsense, bouncing, patting the ducks on elastic in front of her and laughing when they rattled and spun.

Katharine had opened her bedroom door as they left. 'Bye-bye!' she'd said to the baby, in the sing-song voice she reserved for her, and Pamela had waved and said something back that sounded remarkably close to 'Bye!'

Last night Katharine had eaten with them, downstairs in the kitchen. Mandy had cooked a simple risotto and Katharine declared it 'yummy', sitting in her dressing-gown with a black velvet Alice band holding back her fringe. She'd even laughed once, when James had tried to coax Bengo out and the little kitten had simply buried her face further in her blankets in a pointed retreat. Mandy felt a surge of pride when Katharine laughed. She'd done this: she'd lightened the whole household. She *was* a good person, no matter what Mum might think.

How accurately Mandy had pictured this! Her new life: sunny, purposeful. She now remembered her vision of the job she wanted had even involved a big pram, a crocheted bonnet and toy ducks. Hadn't she been thinking of that on the way to the interview? And the colour yellow. Not in that particular combination (she hadn't imagined James, and the baby in the mental picture had been indistinct) but close enough.

'You know,' she said to James, 'my friend Rosemary thinks she's psychic. That she gets these messages sometimes. Her family was religious and . . . it's a bit weird. But me, I'm great at *imagining* the future and making it happen, like a kind of magic. When I was in Ely, I wasn't very happy. I wanted a different life, and now I have it! That's really something, isn't it, to be able to shape your life? Better than messages from God! Or curving forks. You just get a lot of bent cutlery.'

Mandy found London pavements baffling. She was surprised at the way trees abruptly arose from the dry squares of soil, how trapped they always looked; sometimes they actually had cages around them. The vivid splash of the red bus against grey, the familiar proprietorial gull sitting atop a chimney. Scaffolding framed a building and she had to manoeuvre the pram off the pavement and on again. James immediately helped her, pressing down on the pram handle and smiling as they managed it together.

'All right, doll?' A workman grinned at her. On the wall next to him someone had painted *Keep Britain White*. The man's eyes flicked over her, top to bottom, in a way that she was used to. She was glad she wasn't wearing a nanny's uniform. She stared up at him for a second in his orange hat on the platform above her, but her eyes slid to the sky and the rooftops and a skinny bird with a long beak – a long wire coat-hanger – flying past.

'It's just imagination.' She began walking on again. 'Maybe we make the life we want by imagining it first. Remember that. When you're grown-up, I mean. Don't keep imagining more of the same. Picture something else. The thing you really want, not the way things are, and then you sort of grow towards it.'

He was still prattling about the TV programmes he'd seen last night, a cowboy thing – *The Virginian* – and this man eating a giant amount of baked beans in *Record Breakers*. He watched too much television in Mandy's opinion. In her ideal job – the version she'd conjured in her head – she would address this firmly with the lady of the house, suggest in an authoritative way that a regular hour a day was enough for any growing boy.

That would be hopeless. The reason he watched television all the time was because Katharine did, and when she was feeling maternal, or when she noticed him, she beckoned him to join her. It was the only time he got to spend with his mother, so of course he said yes. He'd drop whatever he was doing – playing Mastermind with Mandy, reading about Bleep and Booster – and rush to his mother's room, where Katharine would be doing a wobbly yoga alongside Cheryl and Lyn in Richard Hittleman's yoga programme. The door would close on the two of them, mid-pose, mother and son in a sad ballet.

And then, from nowhere, a man fell into step beside them. He must have been following. Dickie. He wore a powder blue polo neck, grey slacks. His hair was gleaming, slicked down, and a waft of smoke – he threw his cigar to one side to speak to her – billowed at her face.

'All right, old chap?' He ruffled James's hair and the boy ducked shyly, then beamed at him.

'But we only saw you last weekend! It's not your turn,' James said uncertainly.

Mandy stopped the pram outside a grocer's shop and put the brake on with her foot. Somehow she knew Lord Morven was breaking the rules by being there beside them but he was so friendly. It was only his detectives – his private investigators or whoever those other blokes were – who seemed sinister. Dickie had a playful air, the sort of father who threw a child in the air and tickled him until he squealed. She waited for a moment, but no explanation was offered.

She said she was going to pop in for cat food. She would buy James a comic. James hesitated, unsure whether to go into the shop with her. His father leaned towards her, speaking conspiratorially. 'I wondered if we could talk, my dear. Not here, of course. But, frankly, if I telephone the house, the old girl puts the phone down on me. I've had a word with your friend Rosemary, heard the reference, nothing but praise, so there's no reason to feel alarmed. I'd just like a little more information. You know. James's rugger practice, whether little Pammie here is any closer to walking . . .' He bent into the pram to tickle Pamela under the chin and spin her ducks for her. She bounced appreciatively.

'The truth is – I miss them, horribly. Katharine is . . . rather a worry. And then . . .' He glanced at James, and seemed to think better of whatever he was going to say.

'Are you off for a jaunt in the park? Perhaps we could walk along there together. James might feed the ducks or some such and we might . . . *talk*. No need to mention it to Katharine.'

Mandy didn't answer. She slipped into the shop, bought a loaf of Mother's Pride for the ducks, a copy of *Whizzer and Chips* for James, two Freddo bars and three tins of cat food. She'd left Dickie and the children outside but she could see them through the open shop door. They were just talking. James was smiling. Dickie was making a gesture – like a bow and arrow – and slapping his son on the back. The affection and James's joy at seeing his father were unmistakable. She came out again, popped the shopping into a tray under the pram and nodded her assent.

They headed for the park.

Walking beside him, Mandy tried to study him, without turning her head or letting him know. She pushed the pram and he fell into step beside her. What was it that would have made her father certain Dickie was a 'nancy boy' or 'poofter'? The polo neck, perhaps. The smell of cigars and cologne that wafted around him: a spicy, sandalwood tang. The neat eyebrows, which looked as if someone tweezered them for him. The slicked-down hair. Katharine had mentioned that Dickie had once tried out for a film. He did remind her a little of the Saint. It was his smoothness. The firm lines of the jaw and the nose, a straight nose that was – well, his nose was surely masculine enough, even for Dad. She glanced at his profile, pretended to be saying something over her shoulder to James, who was dawdling.

Dickie had blue eyes and there was something dazzling and intense about him, something she hadn't come across before. The rumour was surely right: she felt he belonged in the world of films or television. Different from other men. Like a present wrapped in shiny paper. He could be James Bond – he was that indisputably handsome (and Dad always said that Roger Moore was a raving poof too, any bugger could see that). The sense that he cared for his appearance, had clean, filed nails, and a smoothly shaven jaw. A real man was supposed not to care about cleanliness, or whether he was appealing to the ladies or not. Or was it simply that Dickie was handsome, blindingly handsome, and handsomeness was always suspect in Dad's world?

They reached the park and Dickie helped her push the pram over the gravel, which suddenly made it difficult to wheel. They stopped at the first bench next to the lake and she opened the packaging on the Mother's Pride and began breaking off the soapy bread for James to throw to the ducks.

'Look there, over where the boats are. Those ones look hungry,' Dickie said, hastily rescuing a packet of cigarettes from his trouser pocket, the wood creaking as he sat down on the bench beside her. James glanced at them. He clearly understood the message: go further away from us. Mandy watched as he grappled with himself, kicking the ground and mumbling, 'There's so much goose dirt here. It's horrid.' But he went, with a small backward glance.

Dickie stretched out his legs, adjusted the hood of the pram, so that the sleeping Pamela was shaded from the sun. A bird peeped and she became aware of the quiet. She could hear Dickie breathing. He offered her a cigarette and lit it for her, then smiled.

'Well, you've been there long enough. Bit of a rum do, would you say?'

She didn't know how to answer this. A child to her right was flying a kite, the string so drawn-out it looked as if it might whisk her into the sky. Mandy pretended to watch, drawing on her cigarette, playing for time. 'I'm a bit unsure when James is due back at school. It's September now, so soon, surely.'

He nodded, swept away her concern with a gesture. 'Katharine come out of her room at all? The last girl said she barely bothered to feed them. Pammie had been in the same nappy for twenty-four hours and her damn backside was red raw. I ask you! Hardly the world's most devoted mother now, is she? And yet . . .' he took a deep drag, blew smoke, turning his head politely away from her '. . . in his wisdom the judge awarded her custody, whereas I— Well, you know the rest. I do intend to get them back, though, and remedy this ridiculous situation. Only fair I should let you know. The old girl is against it and will tell you a cock-and-bull story about me.'

He was waiting for her to speak. She had the impression he was nervous. That his confident talk masked something. He finished the cigarette quickly and lit another, forgetting to offer her one.

'Yes, her ladyship is . . . depressed. She does seem . . . She joins us for meals. She's very affectionate with Pamela. She lets James watch the television with her.'

'Bah! Television! A boy needs rugby, he needs tree-climbing, he needs other boys. Has she had a single child to visit? The Palmerstons? The Delawares? Even her own sister Amelia and her nephews? No? My heart *aches* for the boy, spending an entire summer holed up in a bedroom with a neurotic woman feeding him all kinds of baloney.'

Dickie was trembling, and had raised his voice. Sweat appeared on his brow and he finished his cigarette with an angry tug and threw it on the grass, to join the first.

'I suppose you've noticed the surveillance I've organised? One can hardly avoid noticing. I'm building a case. I'm worried for my son. For both my children. Quite frankly, the unhealthy atmosphere that my wife – my soon-to-be-*ex*-wife – is creating is not conducive to a happy childhood or a healthy upbringing. I believe that her stint – well, you must know about this – her stint in an institution should have been all the evidence the learned bastard needed but apparently not.'

Mandy was silent again.

He glanced at her, his blue eyes searching. 'You knew about that? I don't suppose she told you about Lover-boy either, did she? Soon ran a mile once I'd seen him off. Her doctor has prescribed something. I'd like to know what. I'd like it if you could get me a couple of them so I can have them analysed and see if it's the pills that are, well, making her unavailable to the children. To her duties. Unavailable—'

'Daddy.' James appeared. 'Daddy, I can bend forks, using the power of my mind. Shall I show you?' He'd found a fork lying on the grass, a dirty one, and was dangling it in front of his father.

'I'm talking at the moment. It's rather important, I'm afraid. Run along and – um – show me later this astonishing power of yours.'

James sloped away but stopped only a few feet from their bench. Mandy felt sure he was trying to listen. That he had a super-sensitivity to any atmosphere that hummed with feelings, with anxiety or distress. Such a mood drew him – she'd noticed that already. As if he believed he could ward things off, prevent things exploding. Perhaps he could sometimes. Perhaps this had been his role between his parents. Seeing his reluctance to leave, Mandy produced a Freddo chocolate bar from the tray at the bottom of the pram.

'This will melt if you don't eat it soon.' She handed it to James with a little brushing-off gesture with her other hand. She felt guilty, as if she was shooing away one of the ducks.

Dickie leaned in a little. 'I don't suppose she's said anything to you about her time in the . . . hospital?' When Mandy shook her head, he sat up straight again, seemingly rebuffed. 'She's fragile, you know. One can hardly blame her. She'd already been sent to a psychiatrist as a child. Bullied in school. Meningitis. A fragile little thing. She's simply . . . not up to it.'

Mandy gazed at James, not trusting herself to reply. He was standing stiffly with his back to them in front of the lake. She imagined he was still engrossed with his fork, or perhaps he was eating the small chocolate bar. She thought of Peter then, and imagined him leaping and springing as he always did, or screaming with his arms out, pretending to be an aeroplane. Peter so active, so jumpy, a little wiry monkey, while James . . . James had a watchful-as-a-lizard stillness.

'I mean, don't get me wrong. One understands that gambling will test a woman's patience. I told her when we married that this was how I would make my living.'

That surprised Mandy: it was the first she'd heard of gambling as a profession. Could you actually 'make a living' as a gambler? She wondered if her expression was now surprised, or doubtful, and struggled to make herself look neutral again.

'I'd thought at first she'd be lucky. She was my lucky charm.' His voice had grown quiet. Mandy tried to read it: surely he sounded affectionate, wistful, rather than anything else. 'Lord knows she was tiny enough. I could practically fit her in my pocket. And then I lost. Rather bloody spectacularly. And afterwards, well, we're a suspicious lot, gamblers. I thought Katharine unlucky, I must confess. I couldn't shake the idea. I didn't want her to come to my club. I – I felt irrationally angry with her, to be frank. Ha! Eight thousand pounds. Just like that. I suppose that might seem – one might find that a rather extraordinary sum?'

Eight thousand pounds. Mandy tried to imagine this amount of money. All she could think was the house, on which her parents could no longer pay the mortgage – it had been repossessed when they moved into the caravan. The house had cost them £2500 when they'd bought it and £2000 remained owing to the bank. Dickie was staring expectantly at her and, for a second, she had the same feeling she had occasionally with Katharine: he actually *wants* my opinion. He's asking me for something. He wants me to say: That's an outrageous sum. She felt that he was experimenting somehow. That he wanted to understand his loss, his money problems, see it through 'ordinary' eyes: the eyes of someone who doesn't have an earl for a father to die and bail them out.

The baby was stirring, making whimpering sounds and ruffling the covers. Mandy leaped up to peep into the pram, and popped the dummy into Pamela's mouth. 'Well, I . . .' She turned towards him but found he was no longer looking at her, or expecting an answer, but instead was staring out at the lake, towards his son. 'It's very sad,' she said carefully. 'Lady Morven hasn't told me much. Honestly, I'm doing my best for the children, I really am. And if I ever thought they were in, you know, danger . . .'

He stood up. He peered into the pram where Pamela was sucking noisily, big eyes open. He smiled as he turned back to Mandy. 'Dummies! I suppose that's Katharine's idea?' Mandy didn't reply. He coughed, seemed to hear what she'd said, belatedly. 'Thank you. Yes, I can see that. I hope you won't mind if I – perhaps – walk with you like this? To see them more often than I'm allowed? And we might not mention it to Katharine? Would that be – all right with you?'

He seemed – somehow his blue eyes looked just like Peter's. Such an expression. *Help me. Only you can.*

She didn't know where to look. He was so tall and intense, he made her feel exaggeratedly little, as if she were miniature. She nodded dumbly, then said, 'I will. But I – I really don't think you need to worry. Not when I'm in the house in any case.'

'And which are your evenings off?'

'Thursday. I see a friend of mine, another nanny. Rosemary.'

'Ah, yes. I've met her. Charming. Katharine is on her own with the children on a Thursday?' he persisted gently.

'Yes, but I've given them tea. I always make sure the baby is asleep before I go out.'

'Where is James at those times?'

'James tends to be watching telly with his mother.'

Dickie sighed, then shrugged. 'Cost an arm and a leg, that place. One thought it might help. But she ran away and, well, sometimes in my darkest moments I worry that . . . she might do something. And, quite frankly . . . Well, this is a ghastly thought, one doesn't like to voice it, but the children . . .'

'No! No, really, it's not that bad.' She could hardly let on that she had worried about exactly the same thing, more than once. 'She's a little . . . I'm sure it's just the pills. Perhaps I could help her to reduce the dose. I know a bit—'

'Did you train as a nurse? I gather Rosemary did.'

'Rosemary?' She tried not to show her surprise. What had Rosemary said? Was this the moment to reveal that both of them had been in a similar place to Katharine a few years back – in fact, had met there? She thought not. That would *not* reassure him. And Rosemary had never trained as a nurse! But it was an ingenious way to account for knowledge of such places, Mandy could see that.

'I began, then changed my mind. I'm not, you know, a Norland nanny.'

James materialised in front of them, holding the fork. The handle had warped in a dramatic nose-dive. 'I did that,' James said. 'Just with the astonishing power of my mind.'

'Very impressive.' Mandy took the fork from him and scrutinised it. She handed it back, smiling, and Dickie joined her, slapped his son on the back.

'We'll have to watch you next time, make sure no other implements, a Swiss army knife, that sort of thing, were involved.'

James pulled a face and slid the fork into his pocket. Dickie was lifting the brake off the pram with his foot and wheeling it towards her, whistling. His mood had lifted. Mandy thought it could only be the relief of talking about it, since nothing had altered.

'I'll take off now. Chemmy calls. Wouldn't do to be seen. Does your mother ever look *out* of the window, James? Can't say I've seen her. Curtains are always closed.'

James appeared startled at being asked a direct question. He was sulking. His face said: Why the blazes should he care if his mother looked out of the window? He blinked a few times, scuffed at a stone with his shoe.

'Toodle pip! See you tomorrow at the same time? Here by the lake?' Dickie put out his hand to ruffle James's hair but James ducked and adroitly avoided being touched. Mandy nodded. It seemed she'd agreed to meet up without her employer's knowledge. She wondered if she ought to feel worried. It was a new sensation to see a man express regret about his children growing up without him. A memory – a shadow – flitted across her mind as that thought formed. A man of such glamour and worldliness, who would have imagined him as she had just seen him, cooing at a baby in a pram, and tearing himself away with a stricken look?

Later, Mandy tried to get James to tidy his room. He was already in his pyjamas, distracted by an Airfix helicopter, studying a tiny part that had fallen off. He started worming his way under the bed, searching for it. 'It's the Sea King. They used it to rescue astronauts from the sea after the Apollo missions,' James said.

'I can buy you some new glue on Monday. Here you are.' Mandy had miraculously found the tiny piece of grey plastic, and also the little astronaut, dangling from string, ready to winch on board. She sat back on her heels in satisfaction, thinking, Now he can go to bed and I can make myself a cup of tea.

'Where are *your* children?' James said, backing out from under the bed, taking the pieces from her.

Mandy felt like a clockwork toy that had just tumbled to a halt. A surprised stillness before toppling over. He was waiting for the answer. The terrible innocence of childhood. How simple things are, how open the force field you gaily step into. 'Away,' she said quietly.

'Boys or girls?'

She didn't know how to answer.

Now he was pushing the broken part of the Airfix helicopter into place, testing whether any other little part was missing. He was absorbed. 'Where are they?' he said, without looking up from the toy.

'I don't know.'

Now he looked up. 'You don't know?'

Yes, Mandy could hear the strangeness of her answer to a child's ear. And, having come this far, there was no point in going back. A relief.

'Peter lives with his grandparents. My mum and dad. They adopted him when he was a baby.'

James was whistling. He put the Sea King back on a shelf, started flicking through his *Blue Peter* annual. He slid into bed, taking the book with him, shivering a little at the cool sheet. He smiled at Mandy over the covers. His expression – did he know, really, what he was saying? – was exactly like his father's. 'I wish we could play one last game of Mastermind.'

'It's late, James. Tomorrow. I'll beat you for sure!'

'Shall we go and visit him?'

'Who?'

'Your Peter. We could go and play with him.'

'No, I—'

'I don't have many friends,' James said, folding his arms behind his head, wide awake.

'No, I don't think so.'

Now was the moment to say, surely, Don't tell your parents. Don't tell Mummy or Daddy. Because she had never mentioned Peter at the interview or at the agency and it would be strange to mention it now. What do people think of a nanny who has a child so young and whose parents are raising him as their own? Stupid? Wicked? She didn't understand it herself. She could barely see that girl, that young woman, who allowed herself to be shaped, passed through different hands, pressed and moulded, like a wax voodoo doll.

But, no, that was too easy. Blaming Beattie, blaming anyone else. Blaming poor judgements. Courage: she'd prided herself on that but, in the end, it had failed her. She had been afraid. She had wanted things sealing up, things back as they were. Your body opens up, like the sea expelling a whale – an enormous, catastrophic explosion – and the creature smashes back into the water and you want it all as it was: you want the surface unruffled, as if it had never been breached.

'You were a child yourself,' Dr Ryan said. 'You were so young. Your mother was prepared to step in, and who is to say that was such a bad solution? It's what's done in many other cultures throughout the world. Children who are loved by adoptive parents will usually flourish. Can't you let yourself off the hook?'

Dr Ryan was unusual. The nurses hadn't said this. The other doctors hadn't. Dr Ryan had a beard and coloured socks and was prone to saying shocking things.

Yes, she had been young. Yes, perhaps she could find it in her heart to forgive herself, once. Because Beattie was forceful. Beattie had been a good solution. Mandy had been young and ignorant.

'You don't have to be completely blameless to deserve forgiveness,' Dr Ryan said.

Rosemary had tried to persuade her, too. After her session, after Mandy had come back to the bed beside her and told her some of it, Rosemary had listened and nodded and said, 'Let he who is innocent cast the first stone.'

But then, just when she might have convinced her, Rosemary glanced at the hospital window and said, 'Listen to that blackbird singing out there. Can you hear him? He's singing, *Ha ha ha, Mandy is such a saucy, saucy girl*,' and Mandy thought, The birds are the only time Rosemary tells the truth. Or, perhaps simply, the birds tell the truth.

Now Mandy stared at James, innocently reading his *Blue Peter* annual by lamplight. She was backing out of his room, but suddenly had to put out her hand, hold onto a surface, the top of his chest of drawers. She had to touch something because a dark space was opening right in front of her. Scolding, scolding: *You don't deserve to feel sadness, pity. This is just self-pity. This is for you and you need to stop it. Think of what you did: the shocking thing, the worst thing. You deserve nothing. Nothing is what you've got.*

And then it sealed up, like a shell snapping shut. Just do your job. *This boy* needs you. This is what you have. Mandy took a deep breath, one hand on her ribs. 'Night night, James.'

As she closed the door a strange coat-hanger mobile, moons and planets, cut from magazines, made by James, was caught in a puff of air, whirling and tangling on its string. I should make Peter one of those, she thought, and felt a stab: a knife prising open the shell, just a tiny bit, before the shell sprang shut again.

Mandy nestled into the rhythms of the household. She liked it. They were all of her own making: egg and soldiers in the morning for James and Pamela, a cup of tea for Katharine; a list of things to do, things to keep them occupied and give the children some fresh air. She had never been mistress of her own time in Beattie's house. If she'd been idle Beattie would have rolled her eyes and called her a 'lady of leisure' or thrown her a broom. On the calendar in the kitchen – scenes of Scottish castles – there were only two things marked: the wedding of David René de Rothschild and the dates when Dickie had the children. The next weekend was his turn again. Mandy added in biro – boldly – that she was also going home, to see her parents.

Just for a visit. Mandy had written to them, she'd telephoned, running the gauntlet of Beattie's disapproval ('You're taking care of other people's children? What about *me*? What about the people who need you *here*?'), and Beattie hadn't even mentioned Peter, but the plain logic of her plea was unmistakable. What *was* the difference? Why would Mandy want to work for this strange, dreamy countess, this high and mighty whoever she was, when she should be at home helping look after Peter? It was a question Mandy couldn't answer, an argument she'd never win. She'd once, in an off-guard moment, when she came back from The Poplars, tried to tell her mother about talking to Dr Ryan, about how the things he'd said to her had helped. And her mother had said, 'Oh, yes, it's fine for you to have feelings, oh, lucky you with your *feelings*, but what about *me*?'

There was a delicious sense in Katharine's home that there was space for Mandy's feelings. Mandy could stretch and change shape there. She could impose her own routines, be competent. She could have thoughts that she did not need to say aloud: no one could suddenly demand she explain herself. She could be kind sometimes and cook a meal and it didn't threaten anyone.

'I can send money home to you,' Mandy said. 'Peter needs things for his new school, doesn't he?'

'Your dad's got some work,' Beattie spat. 'Over at Martin's. He's doing their lawns. Though why on earth someone of your dad's qualifications and *extensive* experience should be reduced to sitting on one of those mower things, God only knows.'

Mandy gave up. Nothing she could say would have pleased Beattie. She had long ago got used to Beattie's rages but she had honestly thought that since she was the one to provoke them, her leaving might have allowed the fury to ease off, dry to a trickle. It had been pleasing to Mandy to think that, while she was making herself at home at Katharine's, Dad and Peter were having an easier time of it back at the caravan.

Once, aged eleven, she'd sent off for a booklet about periods advertised in a girls' magazine. She'd known that Beattie wouldn't tell her about them so she'd bought a postal order and a stamp and filled in the form. When the booklet came she loved it: the strange gynaecological interiors – did she really have all those wondrous sea-creature shapes inside her?

When Beattie found it she waved the booklet in Mandy's face. 'This! What's this, Missy? Too curious for your own good! Where did you get this?' Mandy had been startled, reading a comic, hunched down on the sofa. Beattie had appeared around the arm, like a terrifying glove puppet, so that her sudden appearance, in full flow, made Mandy jump.

'You want to know so much! That's *your* trouble.'

And, of course, the shame of that, of wanting to know too much, bled into the later shame of falling pregnant, as one must surely lead to the other.

The attacks on Mandy were like a radio that was constantly on in the background. 'What are all those crumbs on the bread-board? What is it with you? You can't even make a sandwich without making an almighty mess!'; 'Look at all these hairs in the sink! Can't you rinse them out? You're moulting, for God's sake. Look at you!' (Mandy's physicality, the evidence of her existence, eating or brushing her hair, caused Beattie particular despair.) And when Mandy came home from school with good reports or results, Beattie would look at them for a moment, then fling the offending paper down with 'That Mr Jones! What does he know? You're such a show-off.' Mandy puzzled and puzzled over what might please her mother. Perhaps she could be silent for days, stay in her room.

Perhaps she could run away to London and leave them all to it.

Beattie would never visit her in London. That thought had occurred to Mandy. London (Beattie had never been) was too frightening. Beattie listened to the news. It wasn't that she liked Enoch Powell, even she could see that he was a horrid man, it was just the gist of it: that was what she agreed with. House prices zooming – well, that's right, isn't it? Isn't that why she and Dad couldn't afford another? And jobs vanishing too. All going to the immigrants. (No use pointing out to her that there were very few immigrants in Little Thetford: logic wasn't her strength.) West Indians, with their frizzy hair and their calypso music, and all this stuff about the Brockwell Three. Why should *they* escape the law? She never said this: she didn't have to. It was all head-shakes and tutting and the odd 'Well, bloody fools, what did they expect?' directed at the television.

'Where do you think her rage comes from?' Dr Ryan had asked Mandy, once.

She shrugged. She didn't know. Beattie was a force of nature, her father had sometimes said. He'd implied that this rage had saved Beattie in some way. Her upbringing had been hard, she'd needed the energy – the power, the venom of it: she drew on it to survive. But as Beattie had said so little about her own life (Mandy could barely remember her grandparents, who'd died when she was small), this could only be guesswork.

For the journey home she had taken care over her appearance, washing and leaving curlers in her hair the night before, knowing that this would be the first thing Beattie would comment on. A feeling of dread settled in her, but there was pleasure, too, at the thought of seeing Peter and Dad. She had brought only the smallest of weekend bags with her so there could be no confusion about her intentions. A present for Peter: a kite they could fly together at the park. Her first wage was in her purse: neat notes, folded very small, produced from Katharine's dressing-gown pocket and given with a smile.

'I'll only stay one night. Saturday night. I'll be back Sunday around the same time Dickie brings the children back.' Mandy stared at her boss, watching the way she gathered herself up, seemed to be trying to think of what to do next. As Mandy left, the private detective was sitting opposite the house in a black car, and Katharine gave a cheeky wave, which he didn't return. There was always, Mandy thought, a sense that something was about to happen on the threshold of that house. The street seemed to expect it behind the still curtains and the solid tubs of flowers. Those men, those cars, occasionally Dickie himself, planted there with binoculars. It was horrible, it was menacing: how could Katharine simply ignore it, or even give a playful wave?

'Just one night. I'll be back tomorrow,' Mandy had said firmly, not sure whether Katharine was listening. On impulse she had given Katharine a little kiss on her cheek. Katharine had smelt of Anne French cleansing milk.

The train tugged away from King's Cross. As it went through a tunnel the men – they were mostly men – fell asleep, as if someone had waved a hand and they were all in a sudden deep trance, a spell cast over them. A grey head nodded over a newspaper; another's head was flung back, mouth open, snoring. Mandy stared at her reflection in the train window and thought of a doll she'd once watched Beattie smack down on the bed, over and over, holding it by its feet and shouting, 'You've no respect for me, this house, or your father,' and when she'd finished Mandy had crept back and turned the doll over, expecting to see her face mashed, but it was unmarked, just as it was before.

The gasworks and grey buildings slid past, replaced by green: old men advancing their golf trollies. Then another warmer, more variegated green, then the trees disappeared and the plain neat landscape of the Fens, the space and emptiness took over. Deer leaping a ditch, flagging their white tails. Despite the dread feeling, the pain like a stone lying just under her ribs, the swept skies, the fresh, clean Fens rinsed through her like water.

Dad was waiting for her at the station, cap pulled low, collar high. He must be boiling in that heavy waterproof, but at least he could be sure he wouldn't see a spot of sun, get so much as a freckle. He, too, had grown in the shape Beattie wanted for him: she couldn't abide freckles. The years he worked outdoors, she was forever screaming at him to keep his shirt on.

He climbed out to put his daughter's case in the back, and wrapped his arms around her. She saw that he noted it was only the tiny weekend bag and looked disappointed.

'Dad. It's just a visit, OK?' Mandy said.

The car smelt of chippings: grass cuttings, sweet and a little high. She closed her eyes and breathed it in. No Peter, though, bouncing around in the back. She opened them again. 'Where's Peter?'

'Football practice. We'll go and get him at three.'

Mandy sank back into the seat. Outdoors, running, other boys, that was what Peter needed. So they haven't forgotten. He has a better life than James, doesn't he, in the end? Was she wrong about that?

Her father asked her to pass him his 'driving sunglasses' and she reached for the glove compartment. He switched on the car radio and, as it was Tom Jones, he immediately began singing along, belting out the number with no self-consciousness. He'd always been a singer. He had a rich baritone. Sometimes Beattie would tell him to 'leave off', but the songs he sang were so romantic and heartfelt even she sometimes enjoyed them.

He was devoted to Beattie; that was the strange part. He'd loved her since he'd first met her at the age of nineteen. In those days he'd sung in a local band. Beattie never realised how lucky she was with Brian, how faithful and unwavering he was. Mandy wanted to ask him: did you absorb the full force, once I'd left? She should apologise. Beattie's squalls were as natural as the weather; they would never abate. Both knew that: they had endured them together until then. And now Mandy felt she had deserted him.

The routine at the caravan park: the slow parting of the gates, Snifter, the dog that bounded out to greet their car, quickly followed by a hostile yell from its owner – Bill, a fat guy in a flapping vest – as he emerged from the site manager's caravan and then a grudging 'Oh, it's you, Flanders. Mandy, is it?'

Flanders. The nickname for her father since schooldays that only the old people could use. She'd been away a matter of weeks and Bill was acting like he didn't recognise her. That's the Fens for you. You've left now. Gone to the big city. Never been there himself, why would he? Only been to Cambridge once: what's there? Dad just nodded, replaced the Ray Charles-style glasses in their case, snapped closed the glove compartment. Everything done carefully, perhaps warily, with deliberation. He had the movements of a man who expected to be startled, frequently. He pulled the handbrake on. Switched off the ignition. Sighed. Leaned over, gave his daughter another grin and a little nudge.

'In you go. She's all spent. I got all of that. In you go.'

And Beattie greeted Mandy with a hug, and had her old pinny on, great blathering red and blue flowers on a white background. She was cooking a roast, and the greasy radio was crackling out a tune. She'd made her own Yorkshires and they'd have dinner, later, at tea-time. 'When you and your dad have collected Peter.' She smiled at her daughter. Dad was right: the squall had entirely passed.

Later, Mandy went with Peter to the shower block, to hold his towel and nag him while he scrubbed off the mud. She talked to him through the cubicle door. He told her who had done what, who'd scored goals, who was rubbish in defence. He was excited, red-faced, breathless and healthy: the animation that always happened after outdoor activity. She found herself feeling pleased, and remembering Dickie's comment: 'A boy needs rugby, he needs tree-climbing, he needs other boys.'

Peter's life: the caravan, the meals cooked on the tiny hob, the foldaway bed, the lack of space, the elderly parents, the absence of a garden or an indoor shower. A twist in her stomach as she thought of it. But a stubbornness – another dimly formed idea – had driven her to London, away from him. It would be better, in the end, for Peter to grow up accepting the story Beattie wanted him to have, to stop fighting it.

At first, Mandy had been all for the truth. She had pictured herself explaining it when Peter was a toddler, when such things would surely be natural. No two-year-old child is shocked that his mother had a baby without a husband. But the moment never came. Beattie took over while Mandy was at the hairdresser's, working, and the first person Peter held out his arms to, the first time he said, 'Mama', it was Beattie who reached for him.

Peter started nursery and it was Beattie who dropped him off, picked him up. Beattie got the cardboard card with the daffodil on it, the Mother's Day card. Beattie was the one the nursery worker told about his scrapes, that time when he tumbled from his trike and had to go in the Accident Book. They'd moved from Soham, and the Fens was small enough that people in Little Thetford didn't know.

'*I'm* your mum, Peter. It's *me*. Beattie is your granny.'

She never said it. She imagined it. She lay in bed beside him, rehearsing it. For years she did this. Through working at the hairdresser's. Through dating Thomas. When would she tell Peter? When would be the right time? When would she ever be sure that this would be welcome news, not a loss? Because one thing she did know: Peter adored Beattie. Real love, not a stand-in. And it was mutual. All that dammed-up mothering that had seemed to come so grudgingly where she herself was concerned: for Peter it was a simple flow. Peter was blond, affectionate, playful, giggly – Peter would fling his arms around you, jump on you, snuggle up. Loving Peter was easy, anyone could see that. It was loving prickly, clever-clogs-wanting-to-know-too-much *Mandy* that was hard.

Dr Ryan had said that Beattie had got inside her. That there were usually boundaries between a mother and her child, but Beattie was always breaching them. She pictured Beattie armed with giant spears, appearing above a rampart.

'Let's go to the park after dinner. I've got something to tell you,' Mandy called now, to Peter.

The floor in the shower block was spattered with wet grass. Outside she heard a dog yelp, a car backfire, and she smelt chicken frying. She called through the cubicle door. She saw his soapy feet: lovely strong white toes, beautiful, perfectly formed feet. Her heart hammered in her chest. Today she would tell him. (She saw Beattie retreating, running, abandoning swords on the grass.) *Today.*

Dr Ryan had said (he was a vain man, in Mandy's view, though Rosemary did not agree), 'You were lucky you got me. Most others here would have given you ECT treatment by now. But I think you've had enough shocks, enough surprise onslaughts to last you a lifetime.'

She didn't know if Peter had heard her. He was singing the jingle to the Cadbury's Fruit and Nut advert. There were great suds everywhere. He'd used too much Matey-bubbles again.

It was an effort to play with Peter; Mandy wondered if he knew. She was constitutionally unsuited to playing, had barely done it herself as a child: only the minimum, only the dolls, and those really in defiance of Beattie, who found them so unruly and vulgar. She walked with him to the park, he hopping beside her, still talking excitedly about the football he'd just played. She chose a spot without trees, and started it for him, tossing the kite into the air, handing the control to Peter once the line was taut. The kite was supposed to look like an eagle – it had two big eyes. It made a satisfying sound, like a snaffling crisps packet, as it took off.

Peter squealed, ran about, whooped and hollered until the kite swooped to the ground, collapsed. Then she walked towards him, tugged at the string, whipped up the wounded kite, propped its arms back into the corners, wound the string round her hand. One great flick, the catch of the wind, and it was up and alive again, flying.

What she'd prefer would be to sit on the grass by the river, stare happily into space, say nothing. If only he would sit beside her, also staring, perhaps making the odd comment about a swan or a boat passing, but Mandy understood that children didn't usually do that.

When he was littler, it had been even harder. She loved the interiority of adulthood and felt resentful that, just as she was reaching it, she had to drag herself back to the silly play of children. Story-books and Matchbox toys and cars and garages and running about shouting, 'Exterminate! Exterminate!' Thank God for her dad. He would take Peter to crazy golf, kick a ball, teach him things: carving, Lego, Meccano, Airfix, all of it. Chess, Snakes and Ladders, Beetle, board games – those, too. She didn't remember her father playing with her, as a girl. But she didn't resent him playing with Peter. Seemed like he'd been waiting all this time for a boy to take fishing at the dykes, a boy to make goal posts for with his jumper and T-shirt, and play with until dusk.

Such a painful feeling that had dominated her childhood and adolescence and that she knew, she could tell, Peter didn't feel. She was the wrong child, that was all, for Beattie and Brian River. They'd wanted someone more like themselves; they'd wanted someone else. And that someone was Peter.

The curious thing was that once they got over the shock of her pregnancy, the shame of it being Mr Barr from the community choir who had 'seduced' her, the shame of her being fifteen and having to give up school, once all of that was out of the way, she couldn't help but feel that producing Peter, lovely Peter, the son they had wanted, the sunny open Fens boy, who seemed more like them than their own daughter, was the only thing she had ever done right.

Over and over the kite went up, soared for a while, plummeted, had to be untangled, put right. Her hand felt sore. She ran beside Peter, trying to keep up. And, breathlessly, she tried again: 'I've something to tell you, Peter. Can we sit down?'

She bought him an ice-cream from Mr Todd's van: a 99 Flake. And he wanted Monkey Juice and nut sprinkles as well. Mandy felt a surge of pleasure that she could afford it, that she had the money in her pocket. Mr Todd told her she was looking well, that she looked 'bonny'. She said thank you she *was* well, and thought of the money she intended to give Mum and Dad. Wasn't that part of why she was doing this, why she was away? They went to sit on a bench near the weeping willow at the river's edge. The cathedral loomed behind them, powerful and dominating, as it had always been. Now was the moment. Peter was licking intently. His face was flushed with the happiness that came with exhaustion.

'Do you miss me?' Mandy asked.

Wrong start. That was a Beattie kind of remark, self-centred. She tried again: 'So . . . it's big school for you soon. Are you excited? Have you got your uniform yet?'

'Yeah, I've got the rugby shirt. Dad said he'd take me to Ely for the rest.'

'There's more room in your bedroom for your models when I'm not there.' That was her way of asking: do you like it better without me?

What to say, really? How could she ask? She knew Peter loved her – but as a sister. How could she insert herself into his life? Wasn't it too late, too selfish, to insist he knew the 'truth' if he was perfectly happy with the truth as he understood it? Rather than offering him a mother, wouldn't she be taking away Beattie, the one he had?

'Yeah – Mum said I can have Timmy Threadgold over. For tea.' He ate the Flake last, licked the ice-cream from the bottom, crumbled the rest into his mouth. Smiled at her with chocolate on his teeth. He had no interest in the children she took care of. He didn't ask her about James and Pamela, and she didn't volunteer. But if he'd asked, if he had, she thought (later, in bed, lying beside him in the caravan, hearing Dad creak down the tinny steps to go outside to the toilet), she would have said, 'The thing is, Peter, Beattie and Brian love you and they're good at taking care of you. James only has me.'

He was a child: he didn't make small-talk about her life in London. Instead he said: 'Best of all is a Fab with all those coloured sprinkles. But I like those ones with a bubble gum at the bottom too.'

And she said: 'What about a toffee split? That used to be your favourite.'

Nah, he'd gone off those, he said. He picked up the injured kite, began winding the line again, and then they walked back to the caravan site.

When she'd passed her driving test, first time and she could barely believe it, Dad had lent her the car. It was a yellow

Renault 4; he'd been teaching her in it, so the gear lever sticking out from the dashboard was second nature to her. 'Let's go for a drive,' she'd said to Peter. 'Just me and you.'

He'd wanted to go to the seaside. He'd never been. Now I'll tell him, she'd thought. He was six: surely that was old enough. It won't be such a big deal. I won't say, 'Beattie's not your mum.' That would hurt. I'll say, 'We're both your mum.' No, that would confuse him. No child has two mums.

Peter had sat beside her in the passenger seat, piping out instructions. Change down a gear. Take the next left. He was pretending to be the driving instructor. 'Now, in just a moment, when I tap the dashboard . . .'

'You're driving!' Peter had shouted, as they reached Brancaster, its houses studded with a special kind of stone, the roads narrow and knotted, so different from the Fens they could both hardly believe it. The cottages had names like Stoneygate and Dune House, and the route to the sea was fringed by reeds so high they formed a honey-coloured barricade, like the soft bristles of an upturned hairbrush. Or no: Peter said it was like an Indian chief's feather headdress. He wanted to open the car window and touch the reeds; they couldn't see past them to the beach or the sea at all. Mandy was nervous. What if another car came along this narrow lane – only room for one car – and she misjudged, didn't move over in time, had to reverse? She could hardly believe she was driving alone. It seemed fantastical, being in charge of the car. Did this mean she was an adult now? What if she toppled them both off the road? The power was intoxicating. Surely she should tell him, surely now.

Then the dunes appeared and the little scattering of caravans strung out like rows of washing, and the ugly golf-club beyond, and further than that (though unseen) she knew it was there, the sea, the great wide sea that went on for ever, poured out into the world, the world beyond Norfolk that she and Peter had never seen. She was breathless. She closed the stiff window, locked the car and the wind flicked their hair and lashed sand at their ankles. Now she should tell him, *now, now*.

They lingered at the little stall: cockles, lurid-coloured fishing nets on sticks, yellow and red plastic windmills. Peter wanted them all, but she just had enough for cockles, promised him he could have some on the way back. They strode along the beach and their feet dug into the sand, the razor-clam shells crunching underneath them. Peter marvelled, lingered over everything: bladderwrack, a mermaid's purse, a little cache of mussels, the prints of dogs in the sand – 'Look at their claws, Mandy. You can see their claw prints!'

Mandy. Not Mandy. I'm your *mum*.

They ran along the beach, whooping. The sea oiled the mud flats, like fat in a frying pan, brown and ordinary, after all, only the white foam curling back and forth like the tongue of a great beast. Was it deep at all? What was in it? Peter wanted to know. Monsters? Dead boats? He ran up to the frill, let the sea lick at his shoes; he startled a busy mob of oyster-catchers, which took off in a flurry. He looped around and around, his arms spread like the toy windmills: 'The earth is round!' he shouted. 'I'm in the middle of the world!'

'I brought you *into* this world!' Mandy wanted to shout back, and 'Are you sorry?' or perhaps, 'Should I be sorry?' There was so much she wanted to say to Peter: look at the sea and the birds and the big world out there; the sea is inside you, you have begun, I began you, I made you! I set you going, like those oyster-catchers' scurrying feet, like their orange beaks stabbing and stabbing, and now you're started up you can run, go on, as you like. Off you go, right up to that white edge there and straight on through it. Good luck, *bon voyage*, I love you!

The sky was a bowl of blue and Mandy had flung her heart up, up in the air and out towards her son, like the kite; she felt the tug, the wind whip her along – sadness, happiness, she didn't know which. 'Peter, Peter, come here, there's something I want to tell you!' and she sprinted after him and her heart ballooned and the words soared out but she knew he couldn't hear: the words were snatched by the wind, lost.

Beattie had always said he should know when he was eighteen, and not before. Beattie would deliver the news, when the lad was good and ready. And not a moment sooner.

They had banana sandwiches and a game of Cheat before bed. She would be catching a train from Ely on Sunday morning. She wanted to be back in time for Dickie returning the children, though she didn't say this. She tried to make her answers as vague as possible. Somehow she didn't want her life in London to take shape for them. Its existence depended on her hugging it to herself.

On Sunday morning Beattie was off to do the flowers in church. Peter could come with her and have a 'knockabout' with the minister's son, Jonnie. He said yes, and that was that. 'See you soon,' Mandy said, kissing his head. He smelt of vinegar toffee, the home-made dark brittle toffee that Beattie still made and Mandy had loved when she was his age: testing it by dropping a blob from a spoon into a saucer of cold water, the heated sugar hardening to a dark bead of amber. Beattie's rages came in like weather, and the day was currently calm and fine. There would be another storm one day soon, and Mandy hoped she'd be ready.

On the train home Mandy read the Norland College textbook that Rosemary had brought her: 'It is sufficient to say that what is essential for mental health is that an infant and young child should experience a warm, intimate and continuous relationship with his mother (or permanent mother-substitute – one person who steadily "mothers" him).'

She turned her face to look out of the train window to hide her tears: two red deer raised their heads from the grass beside the track and stared back at her.

*   *   *

She arrived at the station. The noise of London engulfed her. A sea of children in blue uniforms and black berets passed her on their way home from an outing, chattering so noisily that the babble surged and fell over her, like a wave. It unnerved her. She realised she'd only heard birds for the last two days. Birds and the odd plane from the RAF base at Mildenhall.

The sight of trees in full bloom, caged and contained in spiked fences, surprised her anew. A squirrel sped along a branch and paused, frisking its tail back and forth as if counting time, before disappearing. She wondered how it survived the racket: London was all motorbikes revving and car horns honking and men shouting, *Give us a smile, doll*, or *Nice knockers*, and even on a Sunday there seemed to be building work going on. Scaffolding clanked, like the chiming of a huge church bell; she could hear hammering and drilling as a man in an orange vest fixed a door to a shabby King's Cross hotel. On York Way a sign said 'GIRLS' and another said 'DENTIST'. She walked quickly, aiming for the tube station.

Two men with Afros and jackets embroidered with flowers passed her, and she thought of Neville. She'd been trying not to think of him, but London brought him. And then she had another strange thought: those men were nothing like Neville because she already knew his walk *exactly*, could pick it out in a crowd, at a distance, the exact swing of his legs, the way his arms pumped a little. When had she taken all of this in, filed it deeply away?

Then she worried: Had she been too cold that first evening? Why had she not seen him since the night in Annabel's? Neville had left them in the end, after she'd danced a few times with him – he'd gone to talk to the man who'd got them in as his guests, some bigwig racehorse owner, a red-faced Englishman who bred horses. He had a whole plantation in Jamaica at Montego Bay and she caught snatches of this conversation before they moved into a huddle in the corner.

She'd seen an ad in a window on Berkeley Street. *Ian Fleming, Noël Coward. Now you too can have a villa in Jamaica. Fully staffed with beautiful views* ... Somehow this and the fat Englishman did not fit at all with the Jamaica she pictured, but she gathered that there were two very distinct ones, just like everywhere else.

She caught the tube to Fulham, squashed beside other passengers in a fog of cigarette smoke. Beneath that she could smell hair spray. Two women opposite held beer glasses on their laps, sipped intermittently, giggling.

And back at the house, she saw things differently. She let herself in, with her own key, and went straight down to the basement kitchen. It was half past seven – she was worried: would the earl be late again, would Katharine be all right? But there they all were, in the kitchen, under the light bulb like some tableau of a happy family. Pamela was in her high-chair and someone had boiled an egg and squished it up for her, and made her toast soldiers, which she was waving like a conductor. True, most of the egg yolk was in her hair but it was the first time in weeks that someone other than Mandy had cooked her something. And Dickie and Katharine ... Two glasses were on the table and an open bottle. Dickie waved it at her. Mandy looked from one to the other, shook her head. She was still wearing her coat: a raincoat with a raccoon fur collar that Katharine had lent her when she realised Mandy had no clothes for wet weather.

'You used to wear that, didn't you, darling?' Dickie smiled at Katharine. Mandy could hardly believe it. The friendliness: what had happened?

' "Real people wear fake fur." ' Katharine giggled. Mandy knew what she meant; she wondered if Dickie did. It was a magazine advert. Katharine had pointed out the model to her. 'She's the wife of Dickie's horrible friend with the zoo.' The woman in the ad apparently took 'a great interest in the breeding of nature's beautiful fur-bearing animals'.

James was at the kitchen table too, and a game of chess was being conducted between him and his father, set out among the baby bowls and baby beaker and juice bottles. Katharine looked happily from Dickie to Mandy and said, in a tinkling voice, 'Here's Nanny – "home again, home again jiggety-jig". Did you have a nice weekend?'

Katharine's cheeks were flushed and she sat very close to Dickie, like a flame guttering in a strong wind. She was close enough to touch him, put out a hand, rest it on his arm. One second more and she would. Mandy took off the coat and hung it on a hook by the door. She turned back to the room. It was sad, suddenly: chilling. It was temporary. He would leave: he was pushing his chair back right now, he was standing up. The baby waved frantic arms; a splat of egg landed on the floor. James protested: 'But it's not check mate! You can't stop it there.' Katharine slumped.

Dickie said he had to go and see a man about a dog. James protested and said they didn't need a dog, they had Bengo, and Dickie explained it wasn't a real dog, it was an expression.

Katharine nodded. She didn't seek her son's eyes. Hers were only on Dickie. She finished her wine and scraped her chair back as if to get up, but slumped down again. She was melted into the chair, like wax inside a jar. She seemed to Mandy incapable of movement, or of good judgement.

Mandy felt furious with her, then guilty, wondering where her fury had come from. She accidentally called James 'Peter' when she spoke to him. No one noticed, except James, who answered anyway, as if he understood. She told James she'd play chess later with him. And James, brushing past her, running upstairs, said quietly, through gritted teeth, 'No, thanks. I'd beat you easily.'

Mandy lifted Pamela from the high-chair – the baby happily slapping a wooden spoon at her, she had to prise it out of the tight fist – to get her ready for bed. A laundry basket of clean clothing, bedding, muslin squares and nappies had appeared in the nursery. The laundry was sent out somewhere. Mandy had never seen a washing-machine in the house and all the folded things, the little vests and nighties, had come back with tags on them – it reminded her of something: terry nappies, long ago, folding and folding them. Wasn't that the final straw, the thing that had done it? But two days with her family had drained her. She couldn't think about all that, now.

It took Mandy a long time to fall asleep. Her bedroom felt strange. She hadn't heard Dickie leave and the house crackled with his presence, with the waft of his cigars and the smell of rain clinging to the suede of his coat. She flitted into some kind of light sleep, dreaming she was a kite sailing higher and higher, but when she looked down, expecting to see a hand holding her to the earth, there was nothing. Peter ran beneath her and she soared away from him, untethered.

Oh, Peter – help me! Come back, she called.

There was a commotion, a lot of noise. She had been asleep longer than she thought, she realised. Voices, upstairs. Loud voices: was it shouting? She was awake, and her breathing coming fast, as if she'd been running (as if she'd been running on a beach, chasing a kite). She slid her feet into the sheepskin slippers at the bottom of her bed, tiptoed to the bedroom door but hesitated, her hand on the handle. One of the voices was Dickie's.

'Bloody ridiculous. At this hour.'

'It does.' That was James. Relieved, Mandy wrapped her dressing-gown around her, pushed open the door. They were on her landing. James was in pyjamas, lying on the stairs that led to the top floor, foetal position. For a horrible moment she thought someone had pushed him. Dickie was sitting on the step above him, awkwardly rubbing his son's shoulders.

'It does! It does!' James moaned.

Her eyes met Dickie's and she took in that he, too, was in pyjamas.

'Boy says his stomach hurts. He's in agony, he says. But between you and me,' he made a shrug, 'we've been here before. This is what he does.'

Mandy went to James. His face was red, very hot. He was clutching his stomach, curled up, eyes shut. He wouldn't let her touch him. Mandy sat beside him, stroked his head. 'Shall we call the doctor? When did it start, James? Can you tell me?' She put her face close to the boy's, smelt his toothpaste – she thought, with a little pinch in her chest, of how obedient he was, how he had brushed his teeth without being told to – felt his warm breath on her face, but he still said nothing.

Dickie went reluctantly towards the phone, muttering, 'I'm not sure one should be *too* alarmed. He does this sometimes. I'm surprised you haven't come across it yet.'

A door opened from the bedroom opposite Mandy's, and Katharine's slurred voice called, 'Dickie?' Mandy was amazed that this was her first appearance, that apparently she had heard nothing until now. But, in an instant, Mandy had put it all together. Dickie had been in Katharine's bedroom – his shoes were neatly outside the door. So Mandy *had* heard voices: an argument. James must have heard them, too, from his bedroom above theirs. Did he really have a dreadful pain? Or had he come downstairs to try to stop them fighting? She stroked his back more tenderly, whispered, close to his ear, 'Don't worry, poppet. Everything's going to be OK . . .'

'It's attention-seeking, that's what. But if you insist . . .'

Dickie was talking quietly into the telephone. Whoever it was had answered quickly and was asking questions about locating the pain. 'Mandy – can you apply some pressure? Lower right-hand side.'

Dickie left the phone dangling, came back to join her beside James. Now he seemed more concerned, gentler, as he tried to unclasp James's clamped arms. The boy's screeches rose in pitch and he resisted any attempt to touch his stomach.

'Oh, my God! What's wrong with him? Oh, my baby, my baby!' Katharine shrieked, rushing to the stairs to try to kneel by James's side.

Dickie put his arm around her shoulders and guided her to the chair by the telephone. 'My dear – don't crowd him. We're trying to find something out here. Why don't you talk to Dr Webb? See if the good fellow might pop in.' He turned back to his son: 'Where does it hurt, eh? Is it here? Here?'

Mandy cradled James's head on her lap while Dickie prodded and the child screamed and doubled up, knees to chest. Mandy tried to open his dressing-gown and pyjama jacket so that Dickie could gently press the bare skin on his stomach: James's screams hit the highest note. Soon Katharine was crying, too. She sat where Dickie had put her on the landing chair but she did not pick up the phone, which still dangled. She put her head into her hands. 'Oh, my baby, my *baby*! What if my baby is dying? Why won't anybody help us?'

James whimpered afresh. Mandy stroked the hair back from his forehead, put her face close. 'Don't worry, love. Daddy's got hold of the doctor now,' she whispered, and James's eyes flew open. What Mandy saw there was real. She lifted her mouth from his head, trying to summon some authority in her voice: 'Oh, do try to be calm and talk to the doctor, m'lady.' If Mandy hadn't been trapped on the stairs, James's head heavily and hotly in her lap . . . She felt her temper rising. What use to a child was hysteria?

Dickie went back to the phone, spoke quietly and replaced the receiver on the cradle. Mandy thought he seemed worried now, genuinely so. The boy had cried wolf, perhaps, but who could ever tell what pain another was feeling?

And again, waiting for the doctor, on the stairs, Dickie sitting behind her, Katharine wailing in her chair, in her mind she was elsewhere. Peter. What if Peter woke in pain in the middle of the night and needed a doctor? Would her parents get it right? Would he be OK? There wasn't a phone in the caravan: they would have to run outside to the kiosk. Had she caused her son infinite, ungovernable, unmeasurable pain of the most ghastly inexplicable kind, never to be appeased, never to be apologised for, just by not admitting to being his mother? She could hardly breathe. Peter's blond head swam into view. Peter running, leaping, hanging from the monkey bars, grinning at her. Peter crunching the crackling dark toffee in a bulging mouth. Peter, when she'd left earlier that day – his casualness about her leaving: was it feigned, defensive? It had seemed real. He was happy with her parents, surely. They were practical, they would do the right thing.

James's little cries rose and fell, like a kitten's. Dickie sighed and fumbled for a cigarette, muttered towards James, 'The ambulance is on its way, actually. Don't worry, boy. Tickety-boo. We'll get you sorted out. No need to worry, little chap.'

There was a kerfuffle at the door: the ambulance men had arrived. Mandy wanted to go with James – she knew that Dickie would prefer her to be with him – but Katharine assumed that she was the one accompanying her son. Dickie went into Katharine's room and reappeared fully dressed. James was carried, cradled like a much smaller child, by a portly, tired-look-ing man, who seemed overawed to find himself in such elegant surroundings. When Dickie suggested that Mandy should come too, Katharine shrieked, 'What about the baby?' and that was that: Mandy must stay and mind Pamela. Katharine had thrown a coat on over her pyjamas and already had her shoes on and, after all, she was the boss – there was no point in trying to over-rule her. Dickie glanced beseechingly at Mandy and touched her arm, murmuring, 'Hold the fort here, won't you, and we'll call from the hospital.' And with that, the three of them disappeared.

The house was strange without them. Mandy went to check on Pamela in the nursery. The room was muggy and filled with the smell of a baby: wheaty and warm, like a nest. Pamela's face had that sealed look, slightly oiled by sleep. She wouldn't wake for hours.

Mandy slipped down to the basement to make herself a cup of tea, feeling wide awake; it would be pointless to go back to bed. The telephone in the hall startled her and she belted up the stairs to pick it up.

'Mandy? We're at the hospital,' Dickie said. 'It is indeed appendicitis.'

'Oh, poor James!' she said.

'Yes. Little fella needs an op. They have to whip the damn thing out straight away. So we'll lie doggo here for a while. They'll find us a private room at the hospital. We'll see you tomorrow – not sure quite when. Afternoon, perhaps. I know you can cope, my dear. Just bringing you up to date.'

'Yes, of course,' she said.

'Off you go, back to the Land of Nod. Pammie will have you up at the crack of dawn, I'm sure,' he said. His voice was kind. He was good in a crisis. And she could tell he was grateful to her, that he found it reassuring to have her in the house. She told him to give her love to James, and put the receiver down.

Now the house seemed stranger still. Quiet and poised, waiting for something. Where was the cat? Asleep, like Pamela. She picked out a long-stemmed white rose from the vase in the hall and sniffed it. She'd take it to her room, along with another cup of tea. She might even pour herself a tiny glass of port, from a bottle she'd noticed downstairs. She'd be mistress of this delicious house, alone for the rest of the night. She shivered a little, and couldn't tell if she was chilly or just too wakeful, too alert, stretched and pinged by the evening's odd events.

Last week Rosemary had said (they were drunk, of course, slightly drunk), 'What's the best sex you ever had? Thomas? That other bloke – Mr Barr, Peter's dad?'

God, no.

Mandy just blushed and thought, It hasn't happened yet. It wasn't that she hadn't experienced climax. She'd discovered that by herself – she'd thought she might be about to explode the first time it had happened. But sex with men was painful. Her body clamped against it. She didn't mind them kissing her or stroking her, all of that, but when they tried to get inside her – that was when the trouble started. She was resistant. She found their bodies, the male anatomy . . . disturbing. Put that great thing inside her? How could that happen?

Mr Barr had insisted he demonstrate, after asking her a few leading questions and remarking that she was very 'well developed' for a girl of fourteen. She'd been babysitting for him. His wife was in hospital. He'd come back and the children were asleep, and he'd insisted on pouring himself a big gin and tonic and making her one, too, before calling her a taxi. They were downstairs and she couldn't remember how that subject – of her being well developed – had possibly come up. When she'd screwed up her face, grimaced, he'd said she was being very silly and the human body was designed for intercourse to occur. In other tribes, other cultures, she'd be married with a child by now.

He had invited her upstairs to lie down on his wife's bed. She followed him up the carpeted stairs, past the pictures of Spanish ladies, gold-framed, wondering how she would say, 'Could you phone me the taxi now?' She felt a little shocked at the pink and cream room, the silver hairbrushes on the dresser and the cold-cream jar with the lid off. He said, 'Just pull up your dress for a moment,' and then he lay heavily on top of her in a sort of panic, trying to unbutton his flies, like someone rushing to go to the toilet, and in fact, after one fierce jerk, he'd more or less wet himself. That was what it felt like, in any case. A great flood of liquid all over the bed. She didn't think he'd quite succeeded in making the point he'd wanted to demonstrate; it felt to Mandy like he'd knocked at her, rather than entered. He'd offered her tissues from a box next to the bed and then a pink towel with 'GUEST' on it, and kissed her and said, 'There, that's nice after all, isn't it?' And he'd been very upset about the bed and had begun tearing off the sheets right away, bustling them into the linen basket, finding clean ones.

She'd nodded, pulling her dress down, not wanting to hurt his feelings, and said it was nice. She couldn't very well say that it was nothing much, only mildly unpleasant, like a visit to the dentist, because Mr Barr was in such a stew about it.

After that, and after the disaster of discovery that this one small act on Mr Barr's part could result in the extraordinary, enormous drama of Peter, she hadn't really wanted to be *entered*, or penetrated, as the popular magazines called it, she realised she'd lost her virginity while barely noticing and that seemed negligent. And getting pregnant the way she had, it was almost like that old joke of getting pregnant from sitting on a lavatory seat. It was a foolish secret. It was like everything else about her: wrong.

She said nothing to Rosemary. They were in the pub, nursing their drinks, hoping Neville would show up. She couldn't think of a reply, so silence was best.

'I've got this magazine,' Rosemary had said, giggling. '*Forum*. It's got that woman we saw at Annabel's on the front.' She was rummaging in her suede bag, her favourite patchwork one, all brown and cream and tassels.

'Marie Helvin? The model?'

'No. Molly Parkin. She's really weird. She likes sex with old men apparently. Can you believe that?'

No, Mandy couldn't believe it. She wondered if Molly Parkin was like she herself had been at fourteen and didn't want to hurt men's feelings.

'Aha!' Rosemary flourished the magazine. Mandy shrieked and nearly spilled her drink, trying to flap it away. A barmaid walked past carrying glasses on a tray and glanced their way.

'Well, take it home with you. It's fascinating,' Rosemary had persisted, opening it first, leaning in to read her some of it: a letter from the problem page. ' "My husband's penis is very large: about eight inches long and five inches circumference." Is that possible? Like a bulbous leek!' Rosemary squealed and Mandy spluttered out half of her Babycham. Mandy hid the magazine in her own bag and they put their heads together, laughing. Rosemary told her she had started going to a women's group. She wanted Mandy to come, too, but Mandy wasn't sure.

'What on earth do you do there?'

Rosemary had looked sheepish, then. 'It's actually a conscious-ness-raising group. We go to this woman's home in Barnes and we sit around saying why we think our bodies are too much like our mothers' . . .'

Mandy stared at her friend, at Rosemary's grey eyes that she knew in a certain light, if Rosemary was wearing her favourite emerald sweater, would change colour, appear a deep sea-green. Rosemary expressed a great deal of self-dislike about her own body. Everything was just a bit too much: her boobs over the top of her bra, her tummy over her pants. She wished she was better contained.

'What does it mean? I don't get it. You just talk about things? How is that— Well, why would that be different from you and me talking about things?' Mandy asked.

Rosemary fell silent. Mandy wondered if she was missing The Poplars, and the sessions with Dr Ryan. There had been two Dr Ryans, one for each of them. They had both believed he was theirs alone. For Rosemary he was a maverick, a radical who hadn't questioned her psychic abilities or her voices, though he had never claimed to hear them himself. For Mandy he was something more conventional and kindly: a father figure, like Brian but stronger than Brian, one who was more able to stand up to her mother. They both knew how extraordinarily lucky they had been to have him, even briefly. The long hair, the elegant ankles and colourful socks, the Glaswegian accent and the cater-pillar eyebrows all hid something so unusual, so intelligent: he might have been a god. He might even have been one of Rosemary's own inventions if Mandy hadn't experienced him too.

The girls had been able to intuit the dissent at The Poplars about Dr Ryan, and had known he wouldn't last long there. Ely wasn't big enough for him and his ideas. They both had the good sense or survival instinct to make sure they had left The Poplars before what had gone on in those discussions with Dr Ryan was uncovered and the old forces, the old ways, came flooding back in, like water breaking banks when the sandbags were removed.

Mandy hesitated with her glass of port outside the door to her bedroom. She absent-mindedly sipped it and put her hand in the pocket of her dressing-gown: Neville's telephone number, written on a scrap of paper.

It was two a.m. She thought he wouldn't answer, that the lateness of the hour would rescue her from her own daring, but he did. The pub had had a lock-in; he was just clearing glasses. He asked if he should come over. She wondered if he could hear the desire in her voice. She said she'd been told they wouldn't be back until tomorrow morning, the earl and countess (that was how she referred to them with Neville: she felt a degree of formality about her employers was required), but if they came back unexpectedly, he'd have to sneak out. He laughed. He said something that sounded like 'I never know you want it so bad,' but Mandy couldn't quite understand: did he mean 'I didn't know you felt that way about me'? Or 'I've never known you be that direct before' (both of which were true)? She put the phone down and ran to the bathroom to have a quick wash.

He was on the doorstep in five minutes. She heard his knock, light – he didn't bother with the bell. It was an erotic sound. She listened for a second, noting her body respond to it, the tightening feeling inside her as if someone was pulling a drawstring, and wondered – a bit too late – if the private detective was still outside and what he would make of this. But when she opened the door there again was the shock of Neville, lit by a streetlamp, hair wild, wide smile on his face. There was no one and nothing in the streets behind him, only him.

He began kissing her straight away. He seemed to think he had a green light. 'Well, a girl call you in the hours before dawn she don't really want to chat now,' he said, when she put her hand on his chest, tried to hold him a little at arm's length. He whistled through his teeth at the house. He ran his fingers along the sides of the large round table in the hall. He had taken off his shoes. He wore navy socks; they looked new. Glancing at them, Mandy had a stab of fondness, of delight. She'd washed with a flannel in the bathroom with the pink shell-shaped soap; he'd put new socks on. She let him kiss her more ardently, pressing his tongue against hers, cuddling her and wrapping her in his arms. They stumbled towards her bedroom.

He took a moment to admire her room. The swathes on the four-poster bed, the furniture, the wallpaper – he said it was like one of those stately homes or a hotel. He sat on the bed and took every piece of clothing off, while she watched, amazed at his confidence. She didn't know where to look as the last sock came off and he leaned back against her pillows, arms behind his head. She pictured him posing in the art class. He must know – with a lazy indifference – his own beauty. Why shouldn't he enjoy showing it off?

It was the most giant leap, she thought. The four steps between her and the bed. One small step for a man . . .

'I'm a genius,' he said. 'I lock off from you and I knew it would make you come running.'

Her heart beat a tattoo in her chest, her breath came in short gasps – she might be dying. The great gorgeous warmth of him flowed towards her, his hair framing his profile, his skin tinged gold in the lamplight in her room. Could she do it? The last forty-eight hours had been strange in every way. First Peter, and failing to tell Peter, then returning to find Dickie, then the drama with James. What was happening with James: was he all right? There was nothing she could do to help. Nothing felt ordinary and this was just one small extension of that. All she had to do was step towards him, let him embrace her. He would do the rest.

'Open your eyes,' he said, as she lay beside him, fully dressed, shyly kissing his chin, his chest, anywhere but his mouth. He turned on his side, propping his head up on one hand, using the other to unbutton her shirt. It was almost unbearable, him looking into her eyes while she was feeling such things. She didn't want him to see her so plainly. She didn't know if she could bear him to know. 'Why you closing your eyes?' he said.

She was woken by the telephone and the baby, both howling at once. She ran to the phone and Dickie's voice said reassuringly, 'James is fine. He's had an operation.' Pamela wailed from the nursery upstairs but, if he heard, Dickie said nothing about that. Thank God Neville had left at five: he was expecting an early-morning cellar delivery for the pub.

Dickie said that James had had his appendix removed. He and Katharine had spent the night at the hospital in a private room. James would be fine, but would have to stay there for around a week to convalesce. 'He's sitting up in bed and asking for *Whizzer and Chips*,' Dickie said.

The baby's howls distressed her. Mandy tried to get off the phone without seeming rude. She was surprised at how relieved she felt by the news of James. When James had been on the stairs, crying, she'd assumed he was faking, as Dickie had suggested, but in another part of her, somewhere not quite accessible, she'd also believed he was in pain, and been frightened. She said to give James her love, then Dickie said he'd put Katharine in a taxi and she'd be on her way home. The phone went down with a click and she bolted upstairs – two steps at a time – to the baby.

She had hardly slept and her body – her insides – felt tender and bruised. Whenever she remembered a detail, the things Neville had said – *skinny girl, fat bottom*, him asking her to get up on all fours, the sweep of his hair on her bare shoulders – a flare of desire shot up her again. A soak in Badedas in the mirror-tiled pink bathroom, right after he'd left, among the dozens of bottles of lemon and verbena from Mayfair Pharmacy, had not returned her body to her: it still felt strangely perky and new.

Katharine would be on her way home: she must have everything calm and presentable.

Pamela's cries swarmed around the nursery. She was angry: red-faced and hungry. Mandy picked her up and began patting and jogging her against her shoulder, murmuring cooing sounds. Had she been crying long? Poor little thing. Always the last consideration on everybody's list, including hers. Dickie hadn't even asked about her. She changed her nappy and found some fresh plastic pants and a clean dummy to keep her quiet so that she could make her some breakfast downstairs.

By the time Katharine's key turned in the lock, all *was* calm and presentable. Pamela was sitting in her high-chair, a yellow bib round her neck, eyes huge and enquiring as she chewed on a rusk. The kitchen was spotless. Bengo had scoffed a whole tin of Whiskas and was now licking her paws, about to escape through the cat flap. Coffee bubbled in a silver pot on the stove. Katharine was awfully shattered, she said. That must have been one of the most ghastly nights of her life, not counting the night that Dickie had left her.

Mandy poured the treacle-like coffee into a porcelain cup, surprised at the easy mention of Dickie's departure. Once again, she was startled by the curious intimacy that her boss seemed to insist on bringing to their encounters. Mandy could not imagine saying something as personal to anyone, not even Rosemary. Again, she wondered if it was because Katharine thought of her as a non-person, a sort of listening wall. Or was it something in Katharine's background – her lack of friends (none had ever telephoned or come to the house) so perhaps she was simply lonely and used to confiding in the servants.

'Nanny doesn't approve of me, does she?' Katharine said archly, when the steaming cup was placed in front of her, as if reading Mandy's mind.

When Mandy said nothing, she went on, 'I had an awfully fierce nanny as a girl. Nanny Boom I called her – can't remember why. Once went to a party and all the nannies lined up at the table behind their charges. We had those party frocks on, you know, with white socks and white shoes. I showed her up something rotten by grabbing a cake before we were meant to – fifty whacks with the hairbrush when I got home. Quite turned me on it did, by the time she'd finished.'

Mandy blushed. She turned away to pour herself a coffee, but she felt conscious of Katharine's eyes on her back. Did Katharine know what she had been doing only hours before? Did a smell of sex or a vibe or something hang around her?

Katharine was reaching into her handbag for a cigarette. 'He hasn't called his dogs off. Did you notice? All sweetness and light he was yesterday, but the ruddy Rottweiler was still outside, watching the house when I got back. I went to tell him to bugger off but he did counter with something quite interesting.'

Now Mandy's blush deepened. Her heartbeat quickening, she tried to compose her face for the rebuke, perhaps even dismissal, she feared was about to come.

'He told me Dickie had said his services were only required for another week. That I could rest easy after that as he had "all he needed". Now, what can that possibly mean? Has Dickie got something he can use against me? Or is he having second thoughts?'

Mandy sat down at the breakfast table and unwrapped another rusk for Pamela. The baby was cooing happily and, having finished her breakfast, banging her plastic spoon on the tray of her high-chair. The noisy distraction allowed Mandy time to think. So it seemed that Neville had not been seen. Or, if he had, the detective wasn't going to reveal it at this stage. Did that mean the horrid man had it up his sleeve for later? Why had she risked it? No need to answer that. A picture of Neville, naked in her bedroom, his hair springing out like a huge mane – already she knew she would risk things for Neville.

'I don't know,' was all Mandy could muster.

Katharine sighed. A large tear slid down her face and over her chin. 'If only one could stop loving a man. That's the thing, wouldn't one say? I'd take him back in an instant. After everything, I would. He knows that, but he won't ask. Pride, you see.'

Mandy thought it was more than pride that was keeping Dickie away, but she knew better than to disagree.

'And he was so beastly sometimes. But . . . so dishy. How can one help loving someone? Oh, when we first met! Well, you can imagine. Daddy didn't like him. It wasn't a match made in Heaven – Daddy disapproved. He was cut from the same cloth, recognised a bastard when he saw one and he certainly warned me off, but I wasn't having it.' The tears continued to flow and Katharine lowered her voice but carried on: 'Dickie has peculiar tastes, you know. It's a miracle we had any children at all, the way he liked it. All that buggering at school. That's what makes them such terrible husbands, you know. Rotten retards. All that m'tutor and the sixth-form bench. It's awfully sad that James will turn out the same in time. I've tried to stop it but it's not up to me.'

Mandy's heart thumped. How to reply in a way that didn't anger her boss but was honest? She felt a surge of defensiveness for James – she wanted to say: Never mind that. It's too late for you. Can't you stop thinking of yourself and think of your son, in hospital right now? Surely you can intervene if you're serious about it. What about *him*? Mandy felt she was being asked to give her real view. Perhaps that was Katharine's unconscious desire in confessing private things: to find out how the other half lived. What did other girls, not much younger than Katharine, people with normal upbringings, raised by their own families, not whacked with a hairbrush by paid professionals, what did *they* believe about love, and sex, and raising children, and how to prevent Dickie from divorcing her?

'Yes, *James*. Perhaps we can visit him today,' Mandy ventured.

Katharine put her head on the table, abandoning her cigarette to a saucer, and wailed. Pamela looked startled, and joined in with a wail of her own.

'Sssh, sssh,' Mandy said to both.

James returned a week later, delivered by a driver to the house. He looked thinner than ever, if that were possible, less distinct. He wavered. Mandy thought she could breathe on him like a birthday candle and he'd go out. She made him banana sandwiches and butterscotch Angel Delight with pieces of walnut on top and watched him try to snuggle and kiss Bengo, who only hissed at him and showed her claws.

He asked if Mandy wanted to see his scar and she said she'd love to. He lifted up his T-shirt.

It was shocking, actually, bigger than she'd imagined, and the stitches looked like angry black crosses.

'Oh, my goodness! I think you should be in bed, really. I'll come and play Mastermind with you, if you like – take the box up with you.'

James let his T-shirt drop, pleased with her reaction. 'Where's Mummy?'

'In her bedroom. You could knock on her door and go in there if you like.'

Mandy had never before given James permission to disturb Katharine. She wasn't sure she'd be thanked for it: she hadn't seen Katharine yet that day. But James's face lit up and he immediately went to do as she suggested. He paused on the stairs, said over his shoulder, 'Daddy says we're going on holiday at halves. You, me, Pammie and your friend. Scotland. I've got to get better so I can swim in the loch.'

That was the first Mandy had heard of such a plan. Might have asked me first, she thought. And which friend did Dickie mean? But she could see how pleased James was by the idea and didn't want to disappoint him when he'd just got home.

She noticed there was no mention of Katharine in the holiday plans.

———◆———

I didn't tell Mandy about meeting Dickie and I don't know why. I meant to. I was dying to. I couldn't wait, in fact, to tell her about his club with its amazing stairway and the drink he'd bought me and how later – well, that was the second time I met him – he suggested a holiday in Scotland in October at half-term. I was so excited. He has some great big house up there on a private island – and it's really 'wild', he said. It's lovely, totally unspoilt. We could all go! Mandy, him, his kids, me and my charges, as long as Lady Jane said yes. She did, of course, but better still, she said Clemmie and Snaggy would go to Venice on a holiday with them and a temporary au pair, and I would just have Rupert. Darling Rupie adores the great outdoors, Lady Jane said. Rupert is much the easiest – a cheery, loud, sweaty kind of lad. Couldn't believe my luck in being let off the hook with the younger ones.

I knew it was just a way for Dickie to spend time with his kids, of course I understood that – I'm not daft, it wasn't about me. But who could blame him? He loved those children and he missed them. He was probably thinking that all those heathery wilds he owned could undo some of the damage the mother was doing, and have a kind of bonding time with them – you know, all that hunting and fishing, stuff that men like to do. My dad was always taking my brothers eeling, teaching them how to set traps by moonlight, and how to shoot a rabbit or a hare – they could get good money for a hare in Cambridge market. He'd send them to buy his cartridges for him. It was three shillings and sixpence for twenty-five Kilham cartridges. 'Say they're for your father,' Dad would tell them, and for years I thought it was 'Kill him cartridges' until I could read, and saw the box.

Dickie had another little task for me. I met him a third and then a fourth time – just me and him again and at his club but in the evening, my Thursday off. 'Isn't it Mandy's evening off, too?' he asked, and I didn't know whether to tell him about Neville so I just said that it was but she was washing her hair. I think when you said that men tended to think you'd got your period and didn't feel up to much so it always shut them up and they never asked more.

He was looking tired. I thought he was worried, anxious – it had all got him down so badly. My time in The Poplars had taught me the signs and I really felt for him: depressed, heartbroken about the loss of his children. He bought me a very big glass of Campari with soda and ice and a slice of orange. I'd expected lemon but it was orange. I thought he was a bit nervous too, always his eyes on the door to see who else came in. He knew everyone. Someone called Jimmy and someone called Mark and another bloke called Jonno, and they all knew him and greeted him, slapped him on the back, made some comment, what ho, that kind of thing, but they kept their distance. They could probably tell that his conversations with me were important to him. I don't know if they thought I was a new girlfriend. I had squirted myself with Lady Jane's Arpège. I'd wised up a bit to the dress code and tried to look smarter: a black dress and platform shoes, that kind of thing. The remark Lady Morven had made about me and my charms as a country girl had stuck and kept coming back to me as I wondered, all over again, how men saw me and why I could only look at myself that way, why I could never arrive at my own view, see myself from the inside out, not the other way around. Dr Ryan had been quite pressing on this point. He'd even said once, 'As if you're having a bird's-eye view of yourself.' But I'd thought of the fish fingers then, and giggled, and we hadn't got very far.

Anyway after we'd talked about the kids and I'd given him the low-down, Lord Morven, Dickie, started asking about Katharine again. What was she taking and which doctor prescribed them?

Pills, he meant. He'd seen them in her room but there hadn't been the occasion. And then there was Katharine's emotional state: she was easily disquieted. Did I go to the house in Knightsbridge often? He could get me an extra key if I needed, but probably just as easy to visit under the pretence of seeing Mandy. You know. Friendship and all that.

'Not really a pretence. She *is* my friend,' I said.

He smiled – laughed, kind of – and some of the pain in his blue eyes lifted.

'The prescription – or a package with the exact dosage and the name of the pharmacy and the doctor. If only I'd thought of it at the time. One was rather preoccupied, with James and all that. Evidence, you see. Not Dr Webb, I assume. She'd know I'd be able to ask him . . .'

He rattled on like this and I said I would and promised and nodded and wondered if we would ever get off this subject. He did seem a bit – *intense*. He asked if I'd like dinner and I said, 'Fab!' And a little ping went off in my chest – I thought I'd popped a safety pin on my blouse at first but, no, it was real, just a feeling. Would I like dinner! Here! And champagne! Before I knew it he was ordering champagne and it came in a bucket of ice, the whole bottle just for us. He only had to click his fingers and there it was. I couldn't wait to tell my dad. It was the sort of thing Dad would have pictured for me, when he imagined me working for nobs.

So after we'd drunk most of the champagne he ordered us dinner. Lamb chops and new potatoes. It all sounded a bit school-dinners to me but I trusted him: I was sure it would be a superior kind of lamb chops and it was. The mint sauce came in a little silver dish with a teeny-tiny spoon. I think it was fresh: chopped-up bits of mint, I mean, not out of a jar. And I turned the spoon over to look at the handle: it was Oneida.

We'd moved by then. A waiter had come and said the table was ready and we had stood up and gone into the dining room. A bottle of Blanc Foussy had arrived – my head was swimming a little – and he was such a good conversationalist, asking me all the time about myself, my life in the Fens, Mandy and me. Don't tell him about the birds, don't tell him about The Poplars, I was saying to myself. Don't say anything about God or Jesus. I knew my face was becoming really hot but I didn't know how to interrupt him or say: 'Excuse me, I need to powder my nose.' Then he moved on to my training, and I told him what Lady Jane had said when she offered me the job, that she didn't want a village girl, a Sairy Gamp, and I wondered if I was one of those because I'd never heard of it. But I'd had the Norland Nanny training, so I thought not.

He asked me again if I thought that Mandy's training was sufficient, given that she wasn't a Norland girl like me. This seemed to really worry him. I told him all the things I'd said last time about Mandy – I was very loyal – how warm she was, how clever and sensible, how much the children liked her, but he didn't seem a bit pleased.

'Oh she'd easily pass Norland exams,' I told him. 'She's read *Childcare and the Growth of Love*. That was our Bible. If a baby wets on you it's an honour, they said. It's given you the only gift it has. Yeah, but I've still got to go and change my uniform. Some gift!'

He laughed at that, and ordered us sherry trifle. It was very strong. Alcoholic, I mean, and it had no fresh fruit. I could have made a better one myself – amazing that such a posh place did such a bad dessert. I would have chopped up the banana really small and added a few fresh cherries with the stones out, but I didn't say so, of course. I wondered why he continued to be so worried about his kids and, well, just a tiny bit obsessed. I told him more about my training. It was such a nice feeling – him so interested in me. He had this way of looking at me, sort of drawing his brows down until his eyes darkened and turned this fabulous deep colour. No one had asked me this much about myself since Dr Ryan.

I told him about the medical part. I bumped that up a bit. The experience in the maternity ward at Farnborough Hospital, and the time I asked one of the new mothers if she wanted me to teach her how to bath her little baby and she said, 'No, thanks, love. I've got twelve at home. I'm just in here for a bit of a rest.'

He laughed again and topped up my wine glass. (The minute he leaned forward to do this, the waiter appeared and stepped in – 'Let me do that, m'lord.') So I told him I didn't agree with the training that made us hold down children who were screaming – you know, hold them on their beds when their parents left. I thought that was cruel and I could never do it, especially after we'd watched the film *A Two-year-old Goes to Hospital*. Heart-breaking, that was. I might have been a bit too soft for some families, you know. Some people wanted a strict one, an old-fashioned nanny, I mean, but I didn't think much of that.

Then he looked a bit serious. He said he'd had a 'rather bloody' experience of something similar himself. His parents had sent him away to America as a little boy. He'd been 'dreadfully unhappy' so they'd sent him to a famous analyst, a Dr Winnicott. That was why he was so concerned about his children. He knew the harm that separation can do.

'But yours was separation from both parents, wasn't it? And your nanny as well? Bowlby says that one consistent carer is fine.'

That didn't seem to reassure him.

'Bowlby was from a background like yours,' I said. (I didn't like to say 'aristocratic'. That sounded a bit rude.) 'He said that in the poorer classes, even neglect, or poverty, even if things were extreme and there was an outside lavatory, if the children were raised by a loving mother or grandmother they would still flourish.' The wine must have gone right to my head. Lecturing the Earl of Morven on child development. I was glad when the waiter came by again and Dickie nodded for him to take away our bowls and spoons. I closed my mouth. It was the only way sometimes to stop stuff coming out of it.

Dickie whipped his linen napkin off and threw it on the table with a gesture that seemed suddenly quite cross, and different.

He still had the private detectives engaged, he said. One could never be too sure. And then he asked me if Mandy was a bit like her namesake, Mandy Rice-Davies. Or Christine Keeler. Did I know that Keeler had had a thing for coloured men? He mentioned this bloke, Lucky Gordon – did I remember all of that, the trial? I was startled. Such a long time ago! Mandy would just have been a teenager then, but I did remember, a bit. My dad had gone on about it. What a tart Christine Keeler was for going with a darkie. So many men used to say that. What on earth had brought this on? Had someone mentioned Neville to Dickie? Then I remembered Dickie at Annabel's with that blonde, and though he hadn't acknowledged us he must have seen Mandy dancing with Neville. I was sure my face had gone tomato-coloured. I put my hand up to my cheeks, couldn't meet his eyes.

'Oh, that Lucky Gordon thing. I think my dad used to mention it, but we were, you know, just teenagers then. No, Mandy's . . . well, she's lovely-looking, of course, so men like her. But that's— You can see yourself, can't you? She doesn't go after them . . .' I trailed off. This was getting sticky.

He started talking then about his place in Scotland and would I like to go there at half-term with my charges, his children and Mandy? I was so glad to change the subject. My face cooled down and he relaxed, talking about how beautiful it was up there. I said I'd ask Mandy but I thought it a great idea. He ordered us brandies and coffee. He didn't ask if I wanted milk in my coffee. I did, actually. I wanted some cold milk but I didn't like to say so. And I kept worrying, reliving the blushing: how much had he noticed it? Blushing is such a horrible giveaway. It seems to last long after it's finished. I wanted to check my skin, to feel if it had properly cooled down now.

Mandy was mystified that James wasn't at school. Every time she raised the issue Katharine looked crestfallen and simply said: 'I know, we are *trying* . . .' And now it was already half-term – halves, as James called it – and Mandy was packing the children's things for the holiday. Dickie had said a car would arrive in an hour to take her to Euston, and it was late, such a curious time to catch a train, she couldn't quite imagine it, this sleeper to Glasgow, but hurrying around the house, picking up this and that, she was conscious of the loneliness that emanated from Katharine, the fragility. Was it really all right to leave her here alone? Dickie had bought the tickets for all of them, Rosemary and Rupert too, and now all Mandy had to do was find the right amount of dummies, nappies and woolly cardigans – she didn't know what she might find in the wilds of Scotland – but all the time she thought of Katharine, who was sitting at the kitchen table in the basement, as small as a child, in her oversized dressing-gown, her hands nursing her coffee cup.

Mandy risked asking her, hoping to put the idea in Katharine's head, 'Do you have any friends you might stay with or visit?'

Katharine said she had her sister, Amelia, but that she wouldn't welcome a call from Katharine.

'Oh, I'm sure that's not true,' Mandy said brightly, in the style she had adopted, the relentless cheerfulness that felt phoney even to herself, but also necessary, to counter Katharine's gloom. 'I'm sure the children will miss you,' she added, rinsing out a baby cup and filling it with fresh juice for the train journey. She wondered what on earth Katharine would do that week. There would be the char – Gladys – twice and the usual delivery from Harrods but apart from that . . . Would anyone even telephone her?

'Diddums won't miss me at all, will you, darling?' Katharine said.

Pamela was in her high-chair, chewing the ear of her doll and saying, 'Ah! Ah!'

Mandy was thinking that it was completely the wrong time for her to be awake and worried about her break in routine but, of course, Dickie had booked the tickets and considerations of a baby's routine seemed a trivial thing to mention. Right now Pamela's squeaky, bossy, annoyed sound possibly meant that she was tired beyond endurance. Or it might mean 'I want a rusk.'

Whatever it meant, Katharine ignored it and slumped further, clinging to her cup. 'But James might. Do keep an eye on Daddy, James, so that you can tell me what he's up to. Whether he has any lady friends – and whether he catches an excellent big fish!'

James raised his head a little at the mention of his name, then figured out what was being said and turned back. He was kneeling on the kitchen floor, watching Bengo eat, and trying to pat her head without the cat twisting round to snarl at his hand.

Mandy was thinking of the pills she'd seen in Katharine's room. How many there were! She had a strange, wicked thought that she would hide them, or throw them out, but Katharine could easily get more. And that might be a sacking offence, tantamount to stealing. The constraint, the sense of what she could or couldn't say, was draining. On the one hand the household was informal: Katharine seemed to say whatever she liked (yesterday she had asked Mandy if she wanted a little violet-coloured silk teddy, saying, 'Dickie used to love me in that, but who would fancy me now?'), but Mandy felt false, tongue-tied, and unable to be herself. She hardly dared to speak to her boss about the pills. She longed to say, 'Don't think no one cares about you. James cares. James needs you. Why don't you pull yourself together for him?'

Somewhere in the back of her mind was guilt, a powerful seam that ran under everything. How much she had given up. She had dreamed of a home like this one. She had looked in magazines. She'd pictured herself with a proper husband, hosting Tupperware parties and putting fresh flowers in vases. Making dinners, discussing homework. Being a proper couple, giving her child a father to be proud of, she'd thought all of that preferable to her own situation and felt heartbroken at how little she could offer her son. And now she was rethinking it, and instead of being consoled, she felt something else entirely. How it burned in her. The irony. The pain. How wrong she'd been. Peter blossomed, like a plant, under the sunlight of his grandparents' gaze. In another moment, she might say something exasperated – it might burst out.

She zipped up the duffel bag. She found a yellow knitted hat with bobbles for Pamela, folded it and placed it in one of the pockets. She contemplated saying to James that he should wear his pyjamas with a blazer over the top and thought better of it. The humiliation of travelling through London in pyjamas – she could imagine what Peter would say about that! James, she thought, would not protest, but not because he didn't feel the same way.

'Would you like me to call the doctor for you? Make an appointment?' She didn't look at Katharine as she said this. The cheery voice again.

'Whatever for?' Katharine looked up sharply.

Mandy glanced at James. 'James, do you think you could go and fetch the travel chess set? We can play on the train. I think it's in your room, or perhaps in the hall.'

James went upstairs to look. She saw how he dragged his feet, trailed his hand on the banister. Mandy felt the usual pang when she looked at him, making a mental note to give him lots of attention on the journey, play chess until he went to sleep. Pammie was shouting and banging on the plastic tray of her high-chair. Mandy handed her the newly filled cup of juice. Silence.

She moved closer to Katharine, pulled out a chair. Glanced at the clock on the cooker. 'I've left all the Whiskas lined up for Bengo. She needs some dried food too. I think there's some in the delivery coming on Wednesday.'

Katharine nodded.

'And . . . if you'd like me to ring Dr Webb? I think that perhaps . . . Well, to me it seems that I could ring him now, if you like. You're – unwell?'

Katharine repeated, 'Unwell,' in a tone that suggested she'd never heard the word before.

Mandy soldiered on. 'Look – I was in a place too. I had a kind of breakdown. I didn't want to say in case you thought badly of me. But lying in bed, not wanting to get up, do anything, that's exactly it. I didn't want to talk to anyone. Such a deep sleep. I didn't want to wake up. And they gave me Valium, and when that didn't help they gave me Largactil, Stelazine and, you know, they made me seem madder still. They affected my vision and made me mumble so that psychiatrists could say, "See! She really is mad, she needs our help, she needs more pills," and then I met a doctor – he was a bit different. He made me throw them away.'

Now Katharine was listening. She gave Mandy an arch look that seemed to say, Ah, you too. You think I'm mad too, do you? But she heard her out as Mandy stumbled through a little speech about how helpful Dr Ryan had been and perhaps Katharine might consider some kind of counselling, someone to talk to.

A car horn was hooting outside, and James was shouting, 'The driver's here!' from the hall.

'I don't think it's unusual . . . just mourning, you know,' Mandy continued. 'That's what it was with me. *Grieving*, really, a kind of grieving on such a scale that you can't do it, your foot on the pedal, squashing it all the time. People can't understand that your future's gone, along with the – with the husband and the dream of it. Honestly, I'm sorry I shouldn't have said anything but – no one else . . .'

Katharine nodded. She'd still said nothing, and it was impossible for Mandy to know what she was thinking, whether she was angry or just listening. Her eyes, chocolate-brown, so pretty, so wide now, had a glistening, dreamy expression. The room seemed to shimmer a little.

Mandy unstrapped and gathered Pamela from the high-chair and placed the hot lump of her in Katharine's lap. The baby stared at her mother with huge, surprised eyes.

'Come upstairs and say goodbye to James,' Mandy instructed, growing bolder. Katharine stood up, carrying Pamela. She brought the baby upstairs.

Katharine's mouth was in Pamela's hair, but she mumbled over the top of her daughter's head, 'You've a way with words, haven't you? What happened when you took your foot off the pedal? Did the car sail gaily into a wall?'

Mandy's foot was on the stair, just behind her boss, who had reached the landing. They both stopped to hear Mandy's reply. James was standing in the hall, partly obscured by a giant bowl of flowers, alert, holding the travel chess set.

'Here I am, aren't I?' Mandy said. Just tell the truth, she instructed herself. You started it. Her heart was struggling in her chest, as if she'd been running, pounding the streets. But why stop now? She swallowed. 'I made a friend. Rosemary – you met her. I cried a lot. I came to a decision. I was sadder than I'd ever been. It went on a long time, like a tap turned on that I couldn't turn off again. But it didn't kill me. One day I thought, God, was he worth it? All that for – well, a bit of a pasty-faced bastard starting to go bald.'

'But that's the difference,' Katharine said instantly. She seemed not to mind at all that James was listening. 'You've met Dickie. You can see he's *extraordinary*. And I love him, and he loves me. He'll come back to us. This is just – temporary.'

But not long ago you were asking me if I thought he was disturbed! You said he might do something terrible to the children! You told me your sex life was hopeless! A monster, a rotten retard!

How could she say that? The doorbell rang and James jumped, then grabbed the handle on the first of the cases. His eyes were on his mother. Mandy's shoulders fell. Trying to speak honestly to Katharine was exhausting. She glanced at her now – the pale pink dressing-gown with its chic black silk trim gaping a little, the fine white skin of her throat and collarbone exposed – and wondered why the shape of her kept shifting: one minute fragile, melting, the next something else.

Opening the door, Mandy wondered for a second at the man she glimpsed on the opposite pavement. He was looking straight in at them. Another detective? Or an innocent passer-by, stopping to light his cigarette. James hesitated, seemingly waiting for a signal from Mandy that he was allowed to go out to the waiting car. The driver had gone down the front steps and was standing beside it.

James wished his mother a formal goodbye and Katharine kissed his cheek, and ruffled the baby's hair. She handed Pamela to Mandy, and Mandy said goodbye and, on a whim, added, 'I'll ring you from Scotland if I can. I'll ring Thursday, to make sure everything is all right.'

It was a warm night, muggy, no nip of autumn in the air. 'Thursday is your day off,' Katharine said, turning back inside the house, waving the offer away.

When we got to Euston I was a bit disappointed. I'd thought we'd be travelling with Dickie. Of course I knew he'd be in first class and we wouldn't, but I hadn't realised he was already up there in Scotland at the house and we were just joining him. James and Rupert nodded to one another – so hard to believe the boys were the same age: James was spindly by comparison, Rupert *enormous* – and Mandy seemed worried about something.

We had two private carriages, which was exciting. Little beds and a sort of tray thing that flapped down. It was a bit of a squash. Tartan blankets and green curtains on the window. I thought the boys should go into their carriage and get into bed straight away, but Mandy said they could stay with us and play for an hour first. ('They need to get to know each other a bit,' she whispered to me.)

We put our luggage away. Pammie was sleeping in her carry-cot on a table by the window. The boys sat opposite us and sneaked glances at each other from under their fringes. I took my hat and gloves off and put them carefully in my case. I had my uniform on but Mandy was dressed up: black velvet bell-bottoms and a red polo neck with a slim black belt, platform boots and a black felt beret on her red hair. She looked fabulous, as usual.

Of course we couldn't talk about Dickie when the boys were there. First, Mandy played chess with James – what a weird boy: he hardly spoke and was fixed on her, as if his eyes were holding her there and she might disappear if he glanced away. She must be bored, I thought, but she didn't complain. I was starving. I'd packed sandwiches and snacks, not sure what you could buy on trains, but when I got it out for the boys I couldn't resist having some myself. Ham sandwiches, boiled eggs, Walnut Whips and orange squash. Mandy kept saying, 'Let's wait until we get a bit further – it's a long journey.' I can't imagine ever saying, 'I'm not hungry yet.' It always amazes me the way Mandy doesn't think about food. Her waist is so tiny. How can she not be hungry?

Finally, we got the boys to play a chess game with each other. They were wary. They had to put the travel set on the bed they were sitting on above ours and crane their necks under the ceiling. Rupert's fingers were big, the little chess pieces fiddly, so the tiny pawns kept falling on the floor and getting lost. James had to search for them, producing a torch from his pocket to look under the beds. The pieces were hard to find: they looked like black beetles. Rupert isn't much into things like that. James beat him easily and sat back, eating the walnut off the top of his Walnut Whip and saying that he didn't know how he'd done it, beaten someone at chess in only ten minutes! Rupert sucked the white stuff out of the middle of his and said he was bored. He's got a stamp collection. He and James did talk for about five minutes about sending stamps to *Blue Peter* for their Stampede: the Ethiopian appeal. Then that awkward little conversation dried up.

Rupert jumped up and looked out of the window, pulling the curtain to peep out. England was just a black pane and jolly boring, he said. Why did they have to go away at halves? And where were all the cars? James said they would see animals in Scotland: there would be red deer – they could shoot one.

Rupert paced the carriage, his new school shoes squeaking, like a whiny voice following him everywhere. He smelt sweaty and cooped up, like a hamster. Pamela woke up and started saying, 'Joo, joo!' Which meant juice. Mandy was thrilled because Pammie never said anything usually except 'Ah' and this was her first recognisable word. Mandy got the Tommee Tippee cup out of her bag and was suddenly happy, didn't seem so anxious. I think she'd been worrying about Katharine. She'd said, 'Can you imagine what you'd actually do all day if you didn't have any *work*? And you couldn't even do laundry or go shopping because your washing is done for you and your shopping is delivered and the cleaning is done by Gladys and your children are being looked after by nannies.'

'I wouldn't mind,' I said. 'I'd lie in the bath all day and read a book.'

Mandy said she'd never seen Katharine read a book. She only flicked through magazines like the *Lady* or *Tatler* or *Vogue*, adding, 'In the end, isn't that the worst thing in the world? To have nothing at all to do? I mean, even making a child his tea or reading them a story, doing their washing gives you something, makes you feel useful, fills up your time . . .'

'Hark at you,' I said. I'd been reading a new magazine and it had an article about 'wages for housework'. I couldn't believe Mandy was actually suggesting that Lady Morven's life was the poorer because she had no grubbing and chores to do all day.

I was about to say this when Mandy suddenly said, 'Isn't that what Dr Ryan said a person needed to be sane? Something to do and someone to love. Love and work. He was quoting Erik Erikson, or maybe it was Freud or something.'

She had to stop then because James came back from the lavatory, and he was in his pyjamas and anyone could see he was the sort of boy who listened. He took in everything. He was nice-looking – he had his mother's fine bone structure. I could see Mandy was very fond of him, but he gave me the creeps a bit, compared to Rupert, who seemed so healthy and like a big fat apple, red and sweating. James was too still, too watchful, too old for his years. We told the boys to brush their teeth at the little sink.

I felt a stab when she mentioned Dr Ryan. It made me feel funny because he hadn't said that about 'love and work' to me. He hadn't said anything about Freud either, and now I wondered why not because, after all, I was the one who'd been to Chelmsford College for a year, not Mandy. I was the one studying child development, wasn't I? But all he talked about to me was birds and the supernatural and my religious family and hearing voices. Anyhow, at least it was good to see that Mandy had given up worrying about Lady Morven. I mean, what could we do, when we were travelling so far from London? The furthest either of us had ever been. Now she was smiling and laughing with the baby, dandling her on her knee and giving her the drink and repeating, 'Juice,' just to hear Pamela put the cup to one side and say it again. It seemed a good moment for me to finish up the sandwiches. I'd brought salt in a plastic bag and a small Tupperware pot of vinegar for my cucumber. Mandy laughed when she saw that. 'God, you love your vinegar,' she said. Things were looking up.

We went to the dining carriage. We left James and Rupert in their beds – Rupert wanted the top one and we tossed a coin and he was lucky, as I'd known he would be. They weren't asleep but reading about Sid and his snake, Slippy. We thought they might bond a bit better if we left them alone. We brought Pamela with us in the strange Mothercare sling, sleeping on Mandy's chest, because we didn't dare leave her. I wished I wasn't wearing my uniform because every bloke we passed gave Mandy the eye – some beardy type with beads round his neck immediately offered to light her cigarette when she got the packet out of her handbag.

She put the sleeping Pamela, still in the denim sling, on the seat beside me, then went and sat away from her, so she could smoke more easily. 'Keep your hand on her,' she said, 'so she can't roll off.'

When we discussed this holiday, I'd had to tell Mandy that I'd met up with Dickie, and if she was surprised, or cross, she didn't say so. Now, she said, 'He's obsessed, isn't he? Lord Morven. Obsessed with getting the children back. That's all he talks about.' She was drawing her mouth really small as she sucked on the cigarette. 'He's come to the park with me a few times. To see them.'

'Well, yes, because he's so worried about them.'

'But,' she said, 'he could have worried all those years when he was at home and never showed a bit of interest. Spent every minute at his club, gambling. First weekend he has them, he goes out for the night. Katharine thinks it's his way to get at *her*.'

'Well, but she's totally weird, isn't she? Is she even all there?'

Mandy looked a bit cross then, I thought. I saw her do that little gesture she has, a sort of quick shrug of the shoulders when she's squashing something down that she wants to say. I'd felt a dart of surprise when she said Dickie came to the park to see her. It was the same feeling I'd had when she'd spoken of Dr Ryan. How stupid of me to think that Dickie had only wanted to talk to me.

She finished her cigarette and stubbed it out in the white china ashtray. The dining car was deserted. The curtains had been pulled against the windows but it was wobbly: you felt you were jogging side to side a little, couldn't forget you were in a train. It was midnight, and exciting, I thought, to be going so far, far away from anywhere. I put a hand on the warm Pamela. Her tummy rose, like a loaf of bread, then deflated again.

'She can be kind,' Mandy said, picking up the menu. She meant Katharine. 'She's given me loads of stuff. Things that still fit her from Biba or whatever, but she says, "What's the point?" and just flings them on my bed. She tells me such personal things, I don't know what to say. She said her father was an alcoholic. He was a viscount and, you know, some kind of womaniser. She once told me, showed me, I mean – she sort of acted it out – this huge row her parents had had when she was a little girl, and she was very funny. She took all the parts, ending with her mother coming at her father with the scissors and screaming, "You bastard, I'll cut that right off for you and you won't ever get to use the damn thing again!"'

'Crikey. I thought Fen families were bad.'

'Oh, and one time – God, this is *really* strange – she was giving me clothes and I was in her bedroom, and she was going through her dressing cupboard. And there was this long sort of stick thing, all wound down at the bottom with plaster. You know, sticking plaster that you put on kids' knees? And I said, "What's that?" and she gets it and looks at it. It's a long stick. And she goes, "Oh, Dickie. He liked to smack me with that! Can you believe it?" She sort of blushed and I knew what she meant. Blimey, eh? So kinky. The things she'll tell me . . .' and Mandy just started giggling, snuffling and hiding her mouth so she didn't wake the baby.

'There's lots of that in *Forum*,' I said. 'She should read it. People spanking each other. I bet she'd love it. Did you read the copy I gave you? I've got the latest one now. Oh, and I've got this other book, *The Joy of Sex*. You'll like that – the bloke's got a huge beard, just your type, eh?'

She was blushing then – she went absolutely scarlet. I felt bad.

I'd secretly hoped Dickie would pick us up himself but when we arrived in Scotland, there was a driver. Pigeons flipped and flittered around the station and we blinked and rubbed our eyes and there he was with a cardboard sign, Dickie's name written on it. He was a young lad with a cap and everything. Dawn was breaking over the sky and it looked a bit like a rust-coloured teabag dunked in water and flushing the pale clouds. When he led us to the Bentley parked just behind the station – he was carrying our cases – I couldn't believe it. Shiny, black and new. If only Dad could see it! James and Rupert lugged the carry-cot between them. The boys weren't impressed by the car. I suppose both of them had been on holidays before and knew to expect it. Rupert did want to sit up front with the driver, though, so he could look at the dashboard and pretend to drive.

There was a smell of polish and new leather when the driver opened the doors for us. It was cool and dark and he was keen to show us how to strap Pamela's carry-cot into it. Well, Mandy and I felt like royalty. 'This must be exactly how the Queen travels,' I whispered. He wore leather driving gloves and he had this walnut dashboard and he never took his cap off and he called Mandy 'm'lady' in a Scottish accent. We tried not to laugh. It made me think of *Thunderbirds Are Go* – Lady Penelope.

Then I wondered if actually he'd mistaken Mandy for Katharine. I mean, I had my nanny's uniform on, the N over my breast (reminds me always of Dad saying when he first saw me in uniform, 'If that one's "N", what's the other one called?'). I had even put my hat and gloves back on when we arrived, but Mandy had changed into a suede patchwork midi skirt in tan and chocolate brown, and a brown ribbed polo neck. She looked like a model – she was always confident somehow in the way she walked and held herself. She *could* have been a lady, and maybe he'd never seen photos of Katharine. Even if he had, there was a resemblance. They were both petite, with lovely figures and dark wavy hair – Mandy's more red than brown, but still.

He knew where he was going, we didn't need to tell him. There was still a long way to go to the bit of the mainland where we would catch a ferry and then another little boat. He said, aye, it would be a grand trip through the Highlands, had we ever been before? We said we hadn't and he said we ladies were in for a treat. Then he fell silent, as if maybe he'd been too cheeky, too familiar. The back of his neck was newly shaved and had two tiny spots. He was right in front of me and I thought, He's young. Maybe he hasn't had this responsibility before and is secretly as overexcited as I am.

We turned our attention to amusing Pamela with the pictures in a Miffy book. The driver offered the boys Murray Mints. I thought, This is heaven. Imagine a life where you just turn up and a chauffeur is waiting. You don't have to carry your own bags or buy your own tickets or organise your route or struggle up and down stairs, lugging sweaty babies and cases and carry-cots. And never, not once, do you have to think: How do I find the money?

So we arrived at this old jetty, unfolded our legs and got out. The ferry journey was short and now we were at a bay, waiting for the boat to take us out to the island. The sun glittered, making it look like a thousand silver fish were jumping from the sea. I got my camera and took a picture. Dad would love this one. A private island! Rupert was crouching, trying to pick up a tiny green crab. Mandy was kissing the baby's head, pointing out to James the slippery moss on the jetty, shining green and wet. She was saying to him to take care because it's easy to slip when you're getting on a boat. Once again we weren't expected to carry our bags. The young lad in the cap brought them to the jetty, pointing out the boat across the other side making its way to us. He told us he'd radioed it: it would only be a ten-minute journey.

We were helped onto the boat. The driver actually held out his hand to us. We passed Pamela across first in her carry-cot and he settled her, then helped each of us in. The other chap untied it from the hook he'd roped it to. Mandy trailed her hand in the water. The surface looked metallic and dimpled, a bit like the wrong side of a cheese-grater.

The house could soon be seen on the other bank. There was only one so that must be it. And a man in the grounds – was it Dickie? – a man striding with green wellies on and a long coat and a gun? I tried not to stare at him. Spray hit our faces. The older chap was driving. 'Herons,' he said, pointing. 'They're juveniles.' Five of them, lined up along a bank like a row of knives.

Maybe that was a sign. They were too silent. They said nothing; they didn't even raise their heads to me. Now I think I should have known. Granny said you only ever see a heron on its own. More than one, you need to worry.

Delivered to the deck at the other side, their hair damp from the drizzling spray, the boys now discussed whether the water they had just crossed had been loch or sea (James was convinced it was the sea because he'd seen spongy orange seaweed at the bottom) while Mandy and Rosemary swung Pamela in her carry-cot between them to keep her amused. James excitedly pointed things out: 'A pirate's island over there with one tree on it! That's where J. M. Barrie came long ago with his Lost Boys! That's a little studio near the water – it's for artists and my dad says I can do some painting there if I want. Look at those tennis courts! Look – up there on the hill – isn't that a deer with its antlers?'

The sound of wood being chopped came from somewhere. There was no sign of Dickie.

A gardener came to carry their cases up the sweep of lawn to the house. First he tried to carry the baby for them. She and Rosemary said they were fine carrying Pamela and there was a little tussle while each clung to a leather handle of the carry-cot. Mandy sensed that this wasn't quite the done thing but she was reluctant to give up her charge so easily.

'It sounds as if she's shouting, "Jew"!' whispered Rosemary, worriedly, the fourth time Pamela emitted her favourite new word. Mandy laughed and gave Pamela her cup to drink from and pointed out a pied wagtail on the curved gravel driveway they were now crunching along. Rosemary eyed the bird warily. The Scottish colours were deep and vivid: the grass spongy and well watered, bright crimson splashes of rhododendron bushes lining the route, two richly coloured copper beeches. A squirrel scampered up the lawn ahead of them, as if leading the way.

They fell silent as the house loomed, flanked by giant red cedars, intimidation casting its spell. As they approached there was the sound of the old plumbing rattling its way through the building.

The door was opened by a woman of about forty, with red cheeks and an inscrutable expression, who offered at once to take the carry-cot off their hands. This time they relinquished it immediately: the woman inspired that kind of obedience. She placed it on the floor beside her with barely a look at the surprised Pamela, pausing mid-glug to survey her new surroundings. No one explained who the woman was and no introductions were made so Mandy and Rosemary politely held out their hands for shaking, and Rosemary presented the small gift of chocolates from Fortnum & Mason that she'd bought for 'the lady of the house'. These were accepted wordlessly.

'You can take off your wellies there,' the woman told the boys, in a strong Scots accent, and Rupert and James dutifully went to the boot room, next to a green urn full of umbrellas and a wall lined with guns. This room had a marble fireplace, though no fire was lit. Boots were lined up in every size from small to big. A powerful smell of rubber and wet wool came from the confined space, hung with mackintoshes and tweed hunting jackets and Mandy – who had followed them – was relieved to step back into the hallway, only to find herself moving into the menacing gaze of a mounted stag, glaring at her from its stuck position on the wall opposite.

'The artwork is lovely – what a beautiful house,' Rosemary said, clearly wanting to pause and look around.

'I'll show you gels to your rooms,' the red-cheeked woman said. They could hear other voices in the house, laughter, glasses chinking, the sense of a party, possibly Dickie's voice among them. There was the masculine smell of cigars and a fire burning somewhere. They followed the woman down some stairs and towards the lower rooms.

There were six bedrooms to choose from. Mandy was offered the larger one so that she could keep Pamela with her. It had a dapple grey rocking horse with a red corduroy saddle and real white hair. The room was much bigger than her bedroom at Lady Morven's. She was beginning to understand that this Scottish woman was not the lady of the house but a housekeeper or other servant of some sort. Bathrooms were pointed out (two of them); they were led to a downstairs kitchen.

'How many rooms are there?' Rosemary asked. She had not taken off her hat or gloves. It seemed to Mandy that Rosemary always kept her uniform on when she was feeling unsure of herself, which somehow made Mandy feel worse.

'Twenty-four bedrooms,' the housekeeper replied. 'You'll be mostly down here, though, with the bairn.'

If only she would leave them alone to get their bearings and relax! Rupert and James had run off and were making themselves at home elsewhere. How galling that even a ten-year-old child felt more at ease in these surroundings than she did. Mandy was annoyed with herself. What on earth produced this feeling – how could a mere house do it?

'And where will we have dinner?' Rosemary said, kicking off her shoes and sitting on the blue-flowered counterpane in the bedroom she'd chosen.

'You'll eat here, or upstairs if his lordship asks you to. I hope you brought a dress, Miss?'

This was directed at Mandy in her ribbed polo neck and suede midi-skirt. Clearly this wasn't at all the kind of thing a girl should be wearing in this house. Mandy looked startled, but composed herself quickly and replied, 'Lady Morven has lent me a few things, yes, but I think we – we'll mostly be happy down here.'

Mandy and Rosemary did not dare to look at one another to find out which of them was feeling worst.

'Shall we go to the kitchen and I'll make you a cup of tea, then? We can put a splash of whisky in it, if you like.'

Rosemary took off her hat and gloves and smiled for the first time. 'Whisky would be lovely,' she said, getting up and following the housekeeper. Mandy listened to the heels on the floor above them. How naive they'd been to assume it would just be them here – well, just them, Dickie and the kids – and that they'd be in the main part of the house with him, not the servants' quarters. She felt horribly shy suddenly and thought with a pang of Neville, saw him, for a moment, drumming on her naked tummy with his fingers and smiling at her, as if playing an imaginary piano. She could cope with Katharine. And Dickie too, come to that. But one at a time – not a great braying pack of them. She reached for her cigarettes. She wondered how many people were here and what on earth she and Rosemary had let themselves in for.

Later that first afternoon I heard Dickie's voice and he was calling my name! And I wasn't imagining it, he really was!

'Rosemary! Rosemary! Mandy! Look at this . . .'

I don't know where Mandy was but I rushed upstairs from our below-stairs part of the house – I'd been in the bedroom, unpacking – to the huge hall with the wooden floor and the giant stag stuck in the wall (hard not to imagine its hindquarters sticking out the other side of the house). There was Dickie squatting on the floor. And Pammie a few yards from him, sitting on her bum.

'Look, look!' he said, and rushed to pick her up. She was wearing pink tights and a little purple corduroy pinafore. He lifted her from behind under her arms and set her feet in their tights gently on the polished floor. Her fat bottom seemed to weight her. And then let her go with a theatrical gesture, saying, 'Da-dah!'

Pamela took a few wobbly steps across the floor and then, seemingly surprised to find herself doing it, plonked herself down on her bottom again.

'Again, again!' Dickie laughed and set her on her feet, gently holding one hand and then letting it go. She giggled and tottered a few more steps before falling.

By now his mother had appeared in the hallway with her specs dangling round her neck, a droopy old man's cardigan and a fierce, watchful expression. Mandy and I had been told by the housekeeper over the tea and whisky that the house was Dickie's childhood home and belonged now to his widowed mother, 'her ladyship, the dowager countess'. Moments later, confusingly, the housekeeper had called her Lady Morven, and Mandy, startled, had said, 'What – are there *two*?' and the housekeeper painstakingly explained that, yes, of course there were. She gave us – well, if looks could kill. Now Lady Morven was in front of me and we had not been introduced. She put her glasses on to stare at her granddaughter.

'How old is she *exactly*?' Lady Morven asked.

'About fourteen months, m'lady,' I said.

'About bloody time.' And that was it. She turned and went back into the drawing room.

But Dickie was delighted. I felt he wanted to twirl me around and kiss me. He picked Pamela up and set her going again. 'Clever girl,' he said, lifting her and burying his face in her hair. 'Who is Daddy's gorgeous, clever girlie? Wait till we tell Mummy, eh? Naughty Mummy doesn't care, though, does she? She hasn't realised what a clever little poppet you are.'

Mandy appeared then, and Dickie got Pamela to repeat the performance for her. It was hard not to smile and shriek too: his excitement was infectious. Each time she walked a little further before falling and was thrilled with her audience. On the fifth go Mandy swept her up and said, 'Pooh! Someone needs their nappy changed,' and whipped her off. Dickie gave me a strange little pat on the back and went into the drawing room to join his mother. That was my signal to go back downstairs.

In the middle of the night I got up to go to the lavatory. I remembered where the bathroom was in our corridor so made my way without switching on the hall light. Once inside the door I felt for the switch on the wall – was it a long, dangling one, perhaps? My hand found scallop-shaped wall lights but not the means to turn them on. The sound of tinkling pipes was growing louder as I stumbled into some bloody free-standing chrome towel rail, the lavatory I remembered being at the far end of this ginormous room with its deep blue carpet, its claw-footed bath bigger than any I'd ever seen, as big as a coffin, actually, and this dark oil painting of a skull and then a great big urn filled with lilies. Why would you put lilies in a bathroom? Anyway, my eyes were adjusting a bit and I made out a window at one end: a square of grey moonlight and the skeletons of trees. I sat on the lavatory seat, my back to the window. I turned only once, feeling for the long ball on a chain to flush. The crash of old pipes filled the room.

I had tried not to glance at the moonlit square of window. But, accidentally, I did. And something moved.

I looked again. The chuntering in the pipes was crazily loud. The whole house must be awake now. Even as the sound ebbed I felt it had moved inside me, humming in my veins. *Dear God, please help me.* What had I seen at the window? A white sweep of an owl? Did it have something to tell me? I moved closer to the glass, peered out, my heartbeat quickening, a feeling of something familiar, sticky, stealing up my spine. Then I knew: it wasn't out there, but here with me, in the bathroom. If I twirled around now I'd catch it, see it at last, maybe feel it tapping my shoulder.

But I didn't dare – I couldn't: I was rooted. My lungs were braced with tight fingers. I was afraid to put my face close, feel the cold glass on my cheek.

The housekeeper. We should never have talked about it. Thank God the boys didn't hear! Last night, in the kitchen, over the coffee and whisky. She'd said that the author J. M. Barrie had brought his Lost Boys here – Michael, a handsome wee man. Barrie had played tennis with him over there on the courts, and Michael had painted his foster-father right there in the little studio by the loch and a year later he was gone. Who? Michael. The one Barrie loved best. Drowned in a lake at Oxford, his foot, his ankle – here she lowered her voice – tied to another boy's. Her mouth closed tightly, and she tipped more of the single malt into our glasses. Dead within the year of his visit here. It's a curse, you know. It picks you out. Dead within the year. When you enter a room you feel it. Someone waiting for you there.

And I felt it. I couldn't walk past it or through it. It – the feeling – was gathered in the one place at the centre of me: thudding, thudding in my blood, like those pipes, gushing, gurgling, going crazy. *Oh, you're here, you're here, after all. You never left me, did you?* Things only the birds saw – always pigeons in the roof of the church – always birds, when the vicar took the children aside, one by one, only the birds flying over, peeping in, tapping at windows, looking, *looking* but never telling, sending their messages like starlings, their shapes shifting, one minute a cloud, the next a letter, the next a sweep of iron filings pulled by a magnet, but you had to be fast, so fast to understand them. Maybe they were God, angels. I had such a strong feeling they had something to tell me, they were trying to help me . . .

I saw this: a sea, a black sea, crested with white. And a boat, a small one, bobbing on the squally dark waves. Two men were on it. One was standing up and the other was hanging something around his own neck: weights, chains. He was swaggering. He must have been crazy, or drunk. He was stepping towards the edge of the boat. And now he's got one leg over and the other man is dark, turned away, and perhaps doesn't look as the one in chains bundles himself over the edge. Tipping, a light spot in that flapping coat, and gone. Not even a splash as the black sea closed around him, like a dark flower pulling in its petals.

I couldn't understand what was playing out in front of me. *You're a weird girl, Rosemary. You're not normal, you never will be!* I know, I know, but . . . Who is here now? Who is showing me this picture, what is it, what can it mean? I can hear humming. Voices. I know you're here. Tell me, please. Are you trying to warn me? Or simply show me? Not out there but in here, in the end, always in here. A hand clamping my mouth. *Little bird, I have heard . . . what a merry song you sing.* What is it – a warning? Something it wants to show me but so dark, so unformed, so out of reach. How can I know what to understand, *what*?

Soaring high in the sky, on your tiny wing . . .

My mind roamed over the house, sweeping in and out of rooms: Mandy, James, Rupert, Dickie . . . all of them sleeping, quietly, or was someone awake, someone out there? Who do they want to take me to?

I hadn't switched on the light. I couldn't see anything, not exactly. Perhaps if I strained I might make out the dark shape of the bathroom door, the smooth round handle. If only I could grasp it. There was nothing. Nothing to smell, nothing to hear. The old song from church running in my head: *Jesus loves me this I know, for the Bible tells me so . . .* but still at the limit of my senses, at the edge, I could feel it. Its eyes perhaps. A carved space where nothing was but everything hummed. Throbbing, an air pocket. Something. Please, I begged it silently. Please, go away . . .

Once Dr Ryan said to me, 'So you believe in evil, Rosemary, and sometimes you feel sure of its presence. Is that it?'

And I'd said, 'Of course, of course. What else is there? The devil is as powerful as God and you have to acknowledge both or neither.'

And then there was a rattle on the door-knob, dragging me back. Knuckles tapped at the bathroom door and Mandy's voice, oh, Lord, such a relief, the sweetest sound I'd ever heard: 'Rosy! Is that you in there? Hurry up, I'm bursting!'

A flap, a hiss in the air, a gathering of the molecules, as the thing – whatever it was – left.

'You OK?' Mandy said, gawping at me, as I opened the door. I passed her wordlessly. She doesn't believe in evil. We've talked about it many times. She believes in damage to a healthy thing, a plant unfed, or poisoned.

There we differ – after all, she didn't see the herons lining up and I never told her about the man on the boat. I couldn't explain who he was, how close I felt to him in that unlit bathroom. I felt the force but not the form of it. I'm sorry now. So sorry that we were moving so much closer to the moment when evil would show itself in all its colours and I didn't tune in properly: I couldn't quite catch the proper shape of it.

———— ◆ ————

Mostly they lived an upstairs downstairs life in the big house in Scotland. Rosemary and Mandy tended the children, made them breakfast in the kitchen, the smell of kippers smoking out the entire corridor, laughter and shrieking from Pamela as she banged a new toy against the table: dink! Dink! Kip-per! A riot of them, new sounds, like branches endlessly tapping against glass. 'Tip, tip, tip!' (This was her Tommee Tippee cup.)

They took the boys kayaking, and the men came too. Dickie and this man Jimmy, a balding man who had arrived in a helicopter, six foot four and famous, Mandy remembered dimly, and somehow terrifying. He hadn't bothered to acknowledge her. She could feel that she was invisible to him. Nannies peopled his world the way dogs or babies did: not quite real, a backdrop.

The day was holding back, damp behind drizzle, as they pushed the boats out from the orange boat-shed, Rupert shouting happily, James pushing out the smaller of the boats, Mandy standing on the shore with the baby, breeze lifting her hair and whipping it against her cheeks.

The loch was the colour of green tea, the colour of bracken, of elderflower wine; Mandy was waving to James, waving to Rosemary, confident in her own small boat, her lifejacket standing proud from her shoulders.

'Let me take the bairn,' Mrs Mackay, the housekeeper, said, appearing at Mandy's side in her wellies and green coat. 'I'll take her for a wee nap.' Pamela was lifted from her arms before she could protest, and a kayak found for Mandy, too, along with a lifejacket. There was never the moment to say that she was afraid of water.

Dickie held the boat in the shallow water for her to step into. It tipped as she wedged herself in, and it felt terribly small. Mandy stared back at the red cedar tree near the house, thinking how its old trunk swelled like a pot belly, and then at the wooden boat-shed with its solid stone base, as old as the landscape itself, and at the path taking Mrs Mackay away and back to the house, carrying Pamela against her chest, like some kind of pupa inside a cocoon.

Dickie strode into the water, knee deep in his wellies, a cigarette between his teeth, and his eyes flashed good humour at her as he leaned in and pushed at the boat. It wobbled and freed itself from the stones, drifted towards the others. She could hear James shouting, 'Mandy's coming too! Look! Mandy's in a boat – Mandy's coming!' She didn't want to be a kill-joy.

The sun appeared; the water came out in a rash of silver spots for a moment. Mandy tried to manoeuvre her kayak to catch up with the others, but felt herself disadvantaged. They were strong rowers, all of them. Even Rosemary had better command of her little boat and, without meaning to, the others were widening the stretch between her and them. The water's colour deepened. The four other kayaks raced ahead. The loch loomed deep and green. A bird, a tern – fine, chiselled like a newly sharpened pencil – dipped into the water beside her. She could no longer see Dickie on the shore – had he gone back up to the house? A squally wind was getting up.

Mandy worked a little harder, made an effort to paddle more forcefully. She lifted, plunged, trying to remember what she'd been taught. Her hands were wet, the paddle slippery. The boat's nose turned this way and that; steering it felt impossible. It was cramped and flimsy, and she was trapped inside it. She didn't seem to cover much distance, and the water – moments ago she'd thought it peaceful – was now choppy, and fighting her. She could never catch up with the others. The four orange dots were getting smaller. Her heart began to thump. Perhaps she should give up trying to catch them and instead make her way to the shore. She looked back towards the house, at the mountains flanking it. The little boat-shed. How far they all seemed now. She turned to look for the other kayaks and they were far, too far to reach. The calm had turned treacherous.

'Rosemary!' she called. The wind batted her voice back to her, snipped at her cheeks. How could she admit to the others – to the children – that she hadn't the strength to keep up, and couldn't seem to steer the kayak in the right direction (it was so rickety, and ungovernable, like a leaf being propelled by a jet of tap water: for a moment it twirled round in a circle, so she tried to paddle harder on the left side to get it pointing the right way again), and that she was frightened. 'Help me!' Was the wind picking up? The kayak was rocking alarmingly. Surely in an instant she'd be tipped into the icy loch. The others were going to search for sea-otters led by this bloke Jimmy; they wouldn't be waiting for her.

The mountains glowered in their dark violet colours. Her shoulders were aching with the effort, but still her kayak tilted alarmingly, and barely moved from where she was. What if she capsized here? Would she be able to swim to the jetty? She was wearing a lifejacket but the stupid bulky thing would get in the way, surely, make swimming harder. She'd never be able to climb back into the kayak. A cold terror gripped her ribs as the boat rocked from side to side while she tried to stab the water with her paddle without tipping herself in. Her fingers were icy, and in a moment she would put her head in her hands and give up. Then she saw a flash of orange and realised Dickie had appeared from somewhere – he must have been in the boat-shed and noticed she wasn't with the others. He was on the water now and slid his kayak alongside her.

'Bring your right elbow up until the paddle is level with your nose . . . That's right. Keep the paddle vertical.'

'I can't!' she wailed.

No doubt he had assumed that, like James and Rupert (Rosemary, too, as it turned out), she'd done this before.

'I want to go back!' She was ashamed of the babyish whine in her voice and expected him to admonish her. Oh, the things posh people took for granted! That you'd ridden a horse, or paddled a kayak, or played golf, or eaten squid, or been abroad – so many hazards and embarrassments, so much evidence that your life had been small. You had done the same things as your class-mates, give or take a few exceptions! That didn't amount to much.

Dickie smiled. The wind lifted his hair from his forehead and she was reminded, absurdly, of a cockerel. His voice became warm and commanding: 'That's fine. Let's head back towards the shore, then, shall we? Right-ho, pull there on the left side – that's it – and now again, keep the body upright, push your feet against the toe-pegs and now in . . . Yes, that's it.'

She knew he was doing it deliberately – he had gone into officer mode, how to keep the troops from mutinying – but there was no point in resisting. Mandy screwed up her courage and tried to concentrate, to obey his instructions. *I'm like one of his horses, one of his gun-dogs.* That voice. It was like having a large calm hand on her back.

In this way he guided her. She cleaved to his voice, only plung-ing the paddle into the water when he told her to, paying no attention to anything except the sound of the next stroke, the wood smacking water, the next instruction. She was only dimly aware of other voices, of splashes. Rosemary and the boys were perhaps not far away, were possibly even enjoying themselves – Rosemary had gone out many an evening on the river Lark, fishing or eeling with her father; Rosemary was at home on water. Mandy didn't twist around to find out.

'That's it,' Dickie said again, then: 'Left side this time, that's right, keep your eyes on the shore.'

The shore barrelled towards them. The sight of it calmed her breathing, and her heart ceased its untethered bobbing in her ribcage. As the kayak finally touched gravel and the smell of wood-smoke from the house floated towards her Mandy felt a surge of euphoria. 'Oh, thank you, thank you,' she muttered, and clambered from the boat, almost toppling into the shallow water in her haste. She smeared tears from her cheeks. 'I'm sorry, I'm sorry, I—'

'Don't worry, my dear,' Dickie said kindly. 'Shall we go back to the house and have a brandy? The boys – the others – will be fine with Jimmy.'

The kayaks were abandoned, upturned like orange corn husks. Dickie helped her out of the wet lifejacket (she watched, helpless, as his masculine fingers undid the catches for her as if she were a child), then draped his arm round her shivering shoulders, leading her back to the main house. The gillie materialised – he must have been watching them, Mandy realised, with a further stab of humiliation. He began packing the boats away.

Back at the house, upstairs, Dickie demanded that a fire be made up in the drawing room. He handed her a towel for her hair and a blanket for her shoulders and ushered her into the beautiful room she'd only glimpsed a few times that week, when coming in with James to wish his father goodnight. There was a grand piano and a tartan sofa, a huge fireplace with a hairy white rug in front of it. The walls were all gilded mirrors and strange modern art – on the mantelpiece there was a sculpture made of driftwood and rope that, on seeing it from the threshold to the room, Mandy had assumed a child had put together until she heard Mrs Mackay complaining about having to dust all the artworks and understood that this was one of them.

Usually when she had passed the open door of this room there was the sound of laughter, the crackle of a fire and the slap of cards on a table. Dickie, Jimmy and a woman called Susan, with a beaky nose and the look of a librarian, would be there. Also, not playing cards but reading, glasses on a chain around her neck, in a leather armchair, there would be a tall woman with long, slightly out-of-control grey hair: the first Lady Morven. Dickie's mother. Rosemary had somehow uncovered that Dickie's mother's first name was Elizabeth.

The upstairs part of the house had felt largely out of bounds to Mandy and Rosemary since their arrival. There was a billiard room, a huge dining room, this drawing room and a gun room; their time had been spent downstairs in the kitchen and servants' bedrooms. They were not expected to do anything other than be with the children – their meals were cooked, their towels folded, their cups and plates cleared away. But to mingle upstairs with the guests was out of the question.

Dickie lit himself a new cigar and the brandies were brought on a tray by Mrs Mackay, who glanced at Mandy towelling her hair, then left. Dickie was staring at her. Was her blouse clinging to her? She sipped her brandy – a huge, heavy glassful – and it burned her throat. She wondered what to say.

'I'm sorry,' she tried. 'I'm not normally so feeble. I'm not good on water. I felt a bit sick.'

'Don't mention it, my dear. James is having a fine old time. So good to see him not stuck in front of the goggle box, the way his mother always has him.'

Mandy sipped again, wary of the direction the discussion was going. The way it always went. She saw how his eyes had narrowed, the intensity that gathered around him whenever he talked about Katharine. Not for the first time she had the feeling that this was *all* he really wanted to talk about. That, despite his urbane, calm appearance, something fermented inside him. He downed his brandy in one slug and topped up both their glasses from the decanter. He was not *over* Katharine, not one bit. He was sick with it.

But he's just saved you from drowning. At the very least, from making a fool of yourself. He was kind to you. That was how Rosemary would see it. Rosemary would be extraordinarily impressed that he wanted to spend time with her like this. That Mandy and Dickie should sit alone together in front of the smouldering fire, enveloped in a fug of cigar smoke and sipping brandy from crystal glasses. As if they were equals.

'I hope you'll tell my dear wife. Let her know how much he has enjoyed his time with me. How good it is for a boy to spend time with a father.'

Mandy couldn't say, But you're not with him now. You've hardly seen him. He's only been upstairs with you a few times. Instead she nodded, and took another, deeper, glug of brandy. No doubt it was very good brandy. In any case it flooded through her from her throat to her toes and a hot, liquid feeling snaked through her.

Dickie stood up, found another log in the basket on the hearth and shoved it onto the fire, hard. He had his back to her: broad shoulders in a fisherman's-style sweater, a slight reddening of his neck in the heat. She had the sudden feeling he wanted to hide his face from her, hide his thoughts about Katharine. From nowhere the strange, plaster-covered stick that Katharine had shown her popped into her head. Heat crept up her face. She had drunk the brandy too quickly: she might be sick.

Dickie turned back towards her with a smile. 'One does rather take for granted certain skills. I always did love boats. Hard to remember that others don't. I was sent away as a boy – lived with some relatives in America during the war and they had a rather splendid yacht. Tried to send me to summer camp and I— Well,

I'm afraid I behaved rather badly so that they'd have to send me back. I loved that yacht.'

Mandy could think of nothing to say about a yacht. After a moment he tried again: 'I hope you've enjoyed your little holiday with us. Beautiful part of the world, isn't it?'

'Yes,' Mandy said. She didn't say: it hasn't felt like much of a holiday. Or: I was up most of last night with Pamela, who seems to be teething or colicky or missing her old routine or something. Somehow she understood that he didn't think of the work she did as work, and she mustn't mention that it was. People who had been raised by nannies clung to the belief that it was not work at all, but love.

He seemed to be waiting for a further reply. After a moment he said, 'May I just say – how glad I am that my wife has found a decent nanny at last?' He raised his glass to her, and she chinked hers against his. 'Nanny Friend,' he said. 'She was *my* nanny. When I was a very little chap, before my family sent us to America. It had been my fond imagining that one might employ her some day for my own children but Katharine wouldn't hear of it. Too old school, you know.'

Mandy didn't know how to reply to this. The revelation that he longed for his own boyhood nanny did not surprise her. 'She must be quite old by now,' she finally offered.

'Oh, I've no idea. One doesn't keep in touch,' he replied swiftly. It was a fantasy then, the idea of employing her, Katharine's objection immaterial.

As if on cue, they heard the sounds of a baby crying downstairs. Mandy wondered how long Mrs Mackay's patience with her unasked-for new duty would last. She moved to get up.

'Oh, Sheila will be fine with her. Old biddy's been longing for a new baby to play with. Feeling a little better now, I hope? That fire should be just the ticket. Would you like a cigarette? Something to eat perhaps?'

She said no thank you to food but yes to the cigarette, and he found one in a silver case on the coffee-table. He came forward to light it for her. The baby's cries had died down. Their eyes were only inches apart.

His eyes were a vivid blue, the colour of the harebells on the hills surrounding the house. The exact same colour of James's eyes. She remembered, before she could stop herself, Katharine blushing when she had said that, after he had beaten her with his strange plaster stick, he had liked to touch the welts he had made on her buttocks and kiss them, turn her over, and make love to her.

He's completely uneasy. He has no idea what to say to a girl like me. She scrolled through possible topics and found none. She couldn't make conversation about horse-racing, or gambling, or politics. Men, these days. They mostly wanted to talk about the IRA.

There was a noise in the hall: a door dragging across the wooden floor and the voices of the children: Rupert laughing, James, she thought, protesting about something. From his reaction Mandy noticed that Dickie must have hurt his neck: it was stiff. He turned very gingerly, seeming to move only his eyes and his chin, rather than his neck. It gave him the same look James had: the look of a lizard.

The others burst into the room and Dickie backed towards the fireplace, as if caught out. He had a fine military bearing, when he chose, her dad would have said, all references to cissies who wore blue polo necks forgotten. Mostly, when she had seen him, he was slouching, leaning back in his chair, cards in front of him: the pose of an insolent teenager. Now he had squared his shoulders, smoothed down his hair. That's his appeal, Mandy thought. It's as if he gathers himself, pulls all that strength and maleness together when required. There was a portrait of him back in the lounge – a room she rarely entered – in the Knightsbridge house. In it he was wearing a robe, an ermine collar, his jaw-line settling into jowly age. He was solidifying into his father, the sixth earl. Or the man he would one day be.

Yet the side of him she responded to was underneath that. It was the same way with James, when he was intent on playing with his Airfix, affecting unconcern. Or Peter, telling her about going up to big school, never able to say, as a girl might: I'm a bit scared. What if I don't like it or don't make friends or no one wants to play with me? Her own tender spot always flared then. Dickie's hairline was receding in two strong lines – a Cary Grant shape – and his top teeth rested on his bottom lip when he was thinking, or trying not to say something. She saw that he had enormous self-control; that something was contained.

But he stood by the fire and greeted the noisy arrival of the others. He was as polished as a copper shield, and the room glowed and the fire snapped and she smiled back at him.

'Oh, he's dishy, though, don't you think?' Rosemary giggled. They were back in the kitchen. Rupert and James were playing upstairs in the billiard room. Mandy had persuaded Mrs Mackay to allow her to cook and was making them a macaroni-cheese tea. Rosemary had opened a bottle of white wine she'd found in the fridge and was already half cut. 'He's an Excellent Specimen. Isn't that what Katharine said about him?'

'He's not my type,' Mandy said, putting a flake of grated cheese into her mouth. She was thinking suddenly of Neville. Lust leaped in her, like a salmon, when she remembered their night together. She had loved that he had asked her to keep her eyes open. He wanted to look into her eyes while stroking her with skilled fingers, before rolling her onto her back and lowering himself into her; he was testing. Every inch of her was receptive, was alive and singing, every place he touched pinged, went off like a cracker. The way he watched her, the way he properly *looked* at her, it was almost too much to be *seen* like that while experiencing such things. But his eyes told her that if she didn't like it, he would stop. Neville had made them a drink – he'd brought ingredients with him from the bar. Sweet milk in a tin that he mixed with Guinness. Grated nutmeg. Nutmeg, he said, to stiffen his wood. He laughed, and because he'd told her it was an aphrodisiac, Mandy had felt at once that everything altered, that she'd taken a drug – perhaps she had – and twisted the dial on the pleasure, turned it up to a new frequency.

Afterwards, she had lain in the crook of his arm and talked in a way that she had never talked to anyone. He had asked her without embarrassment about her pregnancy; he knew about childbirth. After all, he had his own son. She was astonished, too, that he was interested in this most secret and dangerous part of her, that he had a name for it (several as it turned out). He spoke without coyness – even the midwives hadn't managed that.

With Neville, lying in the dark cradle of her new life, how fascinated she had been with the discovery that instead of an emptiness, a mystery, a place that couldn't be named at the centre of her, to him she had something walled and variable, something active. She had made the same discovery when giving birth: that her mysterious internal self was not an absence, a 'hole', as the rudest boys at school had said, but a fierce, muscled animal. She had strength and could retreat, close like a fist or expand like a flower – she knew this from Mr Barr and, later, from Thomas. What she hadn't known for sure was that men knew.

Neville told her, too, how sad he was about the father he never found, his own 'cock-ups', as he called them, his son Mark, with whom he used to make balsawood planes, but these days only received the odd short letter from; as they talked, Neville's strange accent meant she had to listen carefully to every word. Something like a glow of light was shining from him whenever he kissed her, or moved onto his back to score the air with his extraordinary profile. His face was a shadowy landscape in the bedroom darkness: his nose, his chin, his beard jutting, like a mountain range. His skin was gleaming gold with a sheen that dazzled her, something real and also something only she could see or feel, so that as she climbed onto him again and took him once more inside her, sinking heavily into the fullness of him, growing wilder and wilder, wanting to yell and scream and somehow burst with this feeling of all the world filling her up, ah, yes, she knew. This was Neville. This was unlike other men. This was love.

Now Mandy kept her back to Rosemary and her voice steady, crouching with oven gloves muffling her hands to place the Pyrex dish of macaroni cheese in the oven, saying only, 'I'd like to see more of . . . Neville. You know. I think he's my type.'

And Rosemary's mouth snapped shut and Mrs Mackay came into the kitchen and the topic of Dickie's sexual appeal or lack of it was abruptly halted.

Later that night, tiptoeing to the kitchen to warm some milk for Pamela, Mandy overheard a heated discussion upstairs. The voices were Dickie's and Jimmy's. There was no female voice. 'Twenty fucking thousand, it cost me . . .'

Then Jimmy's reply: 'Your own flesh and blood. Of course you should! I won, remember? Isobel would have been with her fucking grandparents . . .'

The anger crackled. There was a smell of it, along with the lingering wood-smoke, the cigars, and that sandalwood after-shave Dickie wore. The floorboards creaked: someone was pacing.

Mandy trembled a little as she poured milk into the bottle, screwed on the teat. Her feet were cold on the bare kitchen tiles. Beattie and Dad had quarrelled a lot; she always hated hearing others argue. Her own heart hammered in sympathy. All Dickie's ease, his smoothness from earlier, was gone. She wouldn't have been surprised if she'd heard the sound of glass smashing. Jimmy's voice was now murmuring, possibly trying to soothe him or change the subject. She knew that Dickie was referring to the court case with Katharine for custody of the children: it had cost him exactly that sum. Once he started on the subject it would be difficult to stop him.

'Fucking crazy bitch,' she heard. Then, after an interjection of Jimmy's, 'I *ask* you.'

She scuttled back to her bedroom, where Pamela was not crying but wide awake, lit only by the lurid green from a nursery night-light, standing up in her cot, in her little white nightdress, gripping the bars. When Mandy returned she held out one hand for the milk, wobbling a little: 'Dink! Dink!' she said plaintively.

Mandy picked her up and brought her into her own bed. She nuzzled the baby's sweet-smelling head as she fed her and watched with pleasure as Pamela grew satiated and heavy and slipped across the magical border into sleep. She laid the baby down beside her and decided against putting her back in her cot. She loved the warm spot in the bed and the sound of Pamela's hot breathing.

Maybe she should look for another job. Katharine had said that Dickie was in 'rather a fix' about money and that week hadn't paid her the forty pounds the judge had ordered. 'But then I noticed he had a Savile Row shirt the other day and that won't have been cheap,' Katharine had added. 'Nothing but the best for Dickie.'

Mandy didn't want another job. The children need me, she told herself. It was more than that: the children, her beautiful bedroom, Neville, escape. She didn't want to give any of it up. She was growing sleepy, pulled down by the plumb weight of Pamela into the same rhythmic breathing.

Tomorrow was Thursday and she would find a moment when Dickie wasn't around to telephone Katharine. She knew she would feel better about herself if she stuck to her promise.

Katharine sounded alert, alive, her voice crisp on the line, more awake than she'd been for weeks – certainly than she'd been when Mandy had left the house. 'I spoke to a friend of mine,' Katharine said. 'I went to see a friend. He told me – he said he was worried about me. Dickie has been saying such awful things at his club. The friend said he was worried for my safety.'

'Did – this friend – say why?' Instinctively Mandy cradled the phone, put her hand over the receiver. Rosemary was with the children, playing outside on the tennis courts with them. This was not a conversation you wanted your children to hear. Such a surprise to discover Katharine had a friend, after all.

'Oh, he was shocked, my friend! He was *shocked*. Dickie's fix is worse than I thought. He has no money. He won't file for bankruptcy. The things Dickie told my friend he was going to do to us – to me. Dump me in the Solent!'

Mandy's heart was sputtering and a war of impulses was playing out. She thought of Dickie yesterday, the moment the orange kayak sidled up beside her, her great wave of relief, from head to toe, to be rescued. How kind he had been, later. His blue eyes. His wistful remarks about Nanny Friend. And yet, and yet. Katharine sounded coherent and her fear felt real. It sizzled down the line.

Mandy found herself whispering: 'Have you been to the police?'

'Oh, it's hopeless. They'll drag up my – episodes. They'll say I'm being hysterical.'

'Well, you have this friend to back you up.'

The front door opened and Katharine said something then that Mandy didn't hear. Rupert was saying loudly, 'He's useless! He can't serve for toffee, can he, Rosemary?' and Rosemary saying, 'Now, now, he's had a recent operation and he's still a bit weak, you know,' and Rupert striding past Mandy in the hallway, his face red, angry.

Rosemary and Mandy exchanged a look; the phone conversation was cut short. Katharine hadn't asked about the children but Mandy gave her an update – they were having a lovely time, Pamela had said loads of new words – and told her they'd all be home very late tomorrow.

'Where's James and the baby?' Mandy asked Rosemary, as she put the phone down, still distracted by what Katharine had said. Katharine having something tangible to fear had firmed her up, made her seem more solid than she had for weeks. But what should Mandy do with the information? How seriously should she take it?

'Oh, Dickie took them out on the boat. Not a kayak, the little motor-boat.'

'He took them in a motor-boat?'

'Yes. I think he said he was going to one of the other islands.'

'Was Jimmy with him? The gillie? Susan? Anyone else?'

'No – why are you asking? He can drive a motor-boat, you know. He used to race powerboats.'

He had taken both of the children out on a motor-boat, alone. *He wants to dump me in the Solent.*

Mandy fetched her wellies from the gun room and began running to the jetty. Rosemary watched her for a moment, then followed. Rosemary's pace was slower, no need to be undignified, or panicky. Mandy crunched down the gravel path and over the fine lawns towards the water's edge.

'I think it's good – it's a good thing when a father wants to spend more time with his children. In the women's group they're all for . . .' Rosemary said, a little breathless, once she caught her up.

Mandy wasn't listening. They both stood on the jetty, listening for the engine of the boat. Mandy was panting, too, one hand on her ribcage.

'He's an expert boatman,' Rosemary said. 'He'll be fine.' Her tone was defensive.

Mandy felt some unspoken accusation. Was she overreacting? 'Katharine just said something. He's angry and he's bankrupt and – I don't know. I don't know what he might do,' Mandy said. A pain grabbed at her chest. 'Doesn't he seem angry to you? He's intense, it's all he talks about – he's obsessed.'

'He seems like a man who's lost custody of his children to a useless mother. *I*'d be angry,' Rosemary replied.

The water was calm. Stones glowed orange in the shallows; the deeper water further out was green and inscrutable. No sound or sight of a boat. There were birds, terns and gulls and herons, and (Rosemary was shading her eyes with her hand) the menacing circling of an eagle. Mandy's eyes dropped to the loch, as if she might spy the eagle's prey there.

'Oh, God,' Mandy said quietly. 'You know he watches the house all the time? Or he sends men to do it? That's not normal, is it?'

Rosemary tutted. 'It's not a crime, though. It doesn't mean anything. Having your wife watched because you don't trust her isn't against the law.'

They stood for a while in silence, straining to hear the boat's engine. Mandy's stomach was plummeting. Ice trickled through her veins. Dickie's voice last night: quite unlike anything she'd heard before; unmistakably angry. Katharine's infectious fear. But what did it take to make someone cross such a border, damn themselves for all time in actions like the ones she was imagining? When should you *really* worry? When should you understand you were crazy and these were extreme thoughts, a dream, paranoia, based on nothing?

'You know that time at Ely station, when you came back from Chelmsford . . .' Mandy began.

They had never spoken of it again. Mandy knew the details. She knew it was shortly before Rosemary's mother had died. Now Rosemary didn't look at her or acknowledge the comment. The wind whipped her hair around her face, hiding it. She continued to stare out at the loch.

Mandy persisted: 'If the station master hadn't come along—'

'Oh, there! *There!* Look! There's the boat!' Rosemary burst out, pointing.

And there it was. The tiny white form carving a foaming V in the loch and coming their way, the growl of the engine. One figure, James, was standing up; Dickie, wearing a cap, was driving. They couldn't see Pamela but Mandy's lungs expanded, her chest filled again with air: she must be in the boat. Everything looked so normal; Pamela was strapped in, perhaps, somewhere out of sight.

'See,' Rosemary said. Smug, delighted. 'You're letting her get to you. Poor Dickie! Can't even take his own kids out for a boat trip.'

But men *did* do it sometimes, didn't they? And wives, ex-wives, were right to fear it, fear for their children's lives. It wasn't madness or misjudgement because it did happen – you read about it in newspapers. Mandy wanted her question answered. She stood her ground and repeated it: 'What would you have done, though, that day, if you hadn't been – stopped?'

'I don't know. I think it was just what they said. A cry for help.' But Rosemary didn't look her in the eyes as she said it.

A pied wagtail appeared on the jetty beside them, tapping a little pattern with its tail. 'The birds like this island more than is seemly,' Mrs Mackay had said that morning. She seemed to be quoting something – J. M. Barrie again, perhaps. Rosemary had said it was a bad omen.

They waved to the figures on the boat, pretending casual friendliness, then turning back towards the house. Panic leached away. Rosemary and Mandy walked side by side, as if they were strangers. Mandy stared down at her feet, at the wellingtons squashing down the springy pink low-lying flower that Mrs Mackay had called sea thrift. She was left with the curious sensation that Rosemary hadn't lied to her about that day at Ely station. It was more disturbing than that. Rosemary hadn't known the answer. Maybe no one knew what they were capable of until they did it.

The night I came back from Chelmsford, the night the pigeons told me to finish myself off, to throw myself on the track, the one Mandy asked me about, it was about my mother. I'd spoken to her by phone earlier that day, in her hospital bed, and I knew. 'Look after your father,' she said.

I sobbed. I covered my mouth.

'Don't be sad,' she croaked. 'I'll be seeing you. I'll always be with you, Rosy. Be a brave girl, be Mummy's good girl . . .'

The baby voice, the childish phrases she'd used for me, long ago. I knew then, I knew, I knew, and a sweeping, wailing world opened up. It was like a big scooped-out sky. I was on my own there. Who would care for me now? Who would I do anything good for? What would be the point? When would I get the chance to tell her all the things I'd meant to tell her, I'd been waiting to tell her? Oh, Mother. I'm so sorry for everything. For being big and clumsy with stupid hair that won't lie flat, and for being noisy when you were ill and slamming the door too loudly and sometimes annoying you and not being the Rosy you wanted. Or *was I*? Was I sometimes that girl? I tried so hard: I so wanted to be.

Birds were squawking. They were swooping down at me. They were calling things. *Throw yourself under a train! What's the point? Why not? Give up, she's gone. She didn't even say goodbye. Give up, go on.* The station master took me to the police station; the police station called my father. Between them they took me to The Poplars.

Then, soon after, Dad came to The Poplars to tell me. She'd died on the Monday. So I'd been right. She'd died a few days after she'd telephoned me. The funeral would be next week but it was unlikely I'd be allowed out for that, the state I was in.

'I can do without all this, Rosy,' he said, running hands through his hair. 'I've got a funeral to organise. I've got a box to make. I can't be doing with you.'

I nodded. I understood.

And so I never saw Mother again, but I dreamed of her. She was rocking me in her arms. It wasn't so much a dream as a memory, really. You might say, How can anyone remember being a baby, being sung to and cradled like that, flying through the air?

Speed, bonnie boat, like a bird on the wing ... but I could, I could, I could feel her heartbeat next to mine. I could smell her and feel her warm arms around me. I could feel my cells growing, I could feel myself forming: that was what the dream told me. Love made me; this is who I am; this is how I came to be. I was so grateful, it swelled up inside me: I knew she was slipping away.

I never got to thank her, or say goodbye, that was all. I think I said it in my sleep. Perhaps I said it. And then, miraculously, I felt her kneeling right beside me. I reached out my hand and clasped hers. A voice, a strange young voice out of nowhere, said, 'It's me, Mandy. In the bed opposite yours. Are you OK? You were having a nightmare.'

The world sank right back to a normal, yellow-lit ward. No singing. Mother had gone for good. This red-haired young woman next to me, I hardly knew her – we only began talking yesterday – but how kind she was. She'd shot across the ward to stroke my hair, to offer me her hand.

'Are you all right now?' she asked. She had lovely big eyes. She was wearing an odd, shapeless smock. Now she was offering me a glass of water and saying she could go and get the night sister if I needed her. I didn't. I shook my head. We smiled at each other, a bit embarrassed to be whispering together like that in the middle of the night.

'You were singing, sort of,' she said, and we giggled. 'Or kind of shouting.'

'I had a dream about my mother,' I said.

'Oh. *Mothers*,' Mandy said. She stood up and her knees creaked. We nodded to one another and she went back to her own bed. I liked the way she said it. Her voice was *luxurious*, or big, or something, a little husky, I remember thinking, with a lot of air in it. I felt better after that and I closed my eyes and sleep came back.

On the train back to London Mandy could think of nothing but Neville. The rhythm of the train muttered *back to Neville back to Neville* over and over. She was wrung out by the so-called holiday. James and Rupert had not got along – Rupert was bigger, stronger and faster but with far less sweetness than James – and she'd spent a lot of time jiggling Pamela in one arm, saying to James, 'He's a bit of a bully, might be better to play on your own.' Advice that James was unwilling to follow.

Now she longed for Neville. She planned to telephone him straight away, arrange to see him the first chance she got. That she could talk to Neville so easily was part of his draw; it was as if a brace was lifted from her ribs when she was with him. But she wouldn't tell him she loved him. That would jinx things. She would keep it to herself, hold something back. In the end, saying it had been her mistake with Thomas, and on that occasion, no sooner spoken than, in a puff, *love* – whatever that meant – had evaporated.

Even Rosemary had tired her. Rosemary had not shucked her old self, like an empty wheat husk, and left it at The Poplars, as she had. Rosemary's fascination with Dickie, that strange moment in the middle of the night, just outside the bathroom, when Mandy had seen that old look come across her face. It had frightened her. It was a glimpse of something Mandy had thought they'd both left behind.

You're kind, aren't you? One of those women who like to help others. But probably you do it because – you – it helps you feel in control. She'd been stung by that remark of Katharine's but she remembered it and knew there was truth in it. She'd wanted to help Rosemary, just as she did Katharine, or her mother. But now she felt tired. Katharine wasn't her responsibility, neither was Rosemary: why couldn't she stop?

Here was Rosemary now, bringing her a coffee from the first-class dining car. 'God, those Americans. Don't mind squeezing past you, do they? Nearly rubbed my bosoms right out, squeezing past that close!' Rosemary handed her a Club biscuit. 'They only had the orange flavour – hope that's OK?'

'I bet *he* travels first class, eh? I can't imagine *him* roughing it, can you? But second's good enough for his own kids and for us,' Mandy said, feeling disloyal. She glanced at James, to make sure he wasn't listening.

This time, they were all squashed into one compartment. It was irritating. The flimsy tray that the boys had pulled out to play chess on kept flipping up, springing the tiny pieces everywhere. Rupert, the tallest, had to sit bent like a hairpin just to fit on the top bunk. The baby's carry-cot was ready to tip off its shelf under the window any time someone's knee nudged it.

' "If you like a lot of chocolate on your biscuit join our Club," ' Rupert was singing, loudly.

'I didn't get myself one,' Rosemary said, handing the boys theirs. 'We can't all look like Mandy in our bell-bottoms. Some of us have to watch our figures.'

The remark annoyed Mandy. Too much like Beattie: an invasion of privacy. Rosemary was trying to get *inside her*. Ironic that this made her fearful when with Neville – who really was, who *literally* was – she was finally opening up. She thought again of Dr Ryan and his comments about Beattie. He'd once said, 'I don't think your mother has a fully formed sense of self. She doesn't know where she ends and you begin.' Such a curious expression. It had stayed with her.

I begin here. She accepted the coffee and the sachet of sugar that Rosemary offered. *I began when I got to London.* James had jumped down, abandoning suddenly the game of chess. He was standing by the window, staring intently at his spoon, trying to use the power of his mind to bend it. Rupert had picked up *Whizzer and Chips*, dropping his biscuit wrapper on the floor at her feet, one foot relentlessly thumping at his bunk. Pamela was sleeping. And the train crooned *back to Neville, back to Neville*. Mandy puzzled about people who believed such things were real, who heard not their own secrets but an outside voice; she thought of Rosemary, and all that she had told her, and wondered.

That night, on her little bunk, Rosemary's snores rolling through the compartment, Mandy allowed herself to remember. *Thomas.* He was tall, broad-shouldered and sunny; he had made jokes to the class that he taught (O-level English, adult evening classes in the community centre in Ely: Mandy had thought she'd be the eldest there but was consoled to find that the opposite was true). He had a trace of an accent that she later learned was Canadian; he was cultured and used words like 'Leavisite' (she hadn't dared to ask what it meant). And he'd turned his blazing gaze on her one day when she was stumbling through a clumsy response to *The Mayor of Casterbridge*: 'He's posh, this author, but he's writing about farming people and he – so he's just trying to show that their lives are hard. That's why he doesn't give Gabriel any luck . . .' and Thomas had said, 'Why are you so sure the author is posh, then?' and Mandy blurted out: 'Oh, he calls himself Thomas, rather than, you know, *Tom* . . . He must be,' and the class looked at the tutor and burst out laughing. She blushed then, realising what she'd said, but Thomas seemed only amused.

After class that day he hung back as she was packing her bag, made a polite enquiry about why she'd returned to study, and Mandy hesitated, wondering how come he didn't know, like everybody else in Ely did, about Peter? 'I dropped out of school. I'm working in a hairdresser's. I don't like it much. I thought . . . maybe a primary-school teacher or a nursery nurse. So I need maths and English. Minimum.'

'I don't know about the maths but you'll easily get the English,' he said then. 'You're one of the cleverest I've had in my class.'

It was strange how this sentence had affected her. That was when it happened, she realised later. He was the first person who had noticed what she'd always suspected: Beattie was wrong. She wasn't stupid and it wasn't evil to want to know things. In some circles it was even admired.

He asked her to go for a drink with him, the pub by the river. She'd never been on a date – she was twenty-three! – but she didn't tell him that. She shaved her legs and bought a new blouse with a Laura Ashley frill; she washed her hair with Harmony Copper Glow.

Thomas was thirty, seven years older than her, and a proper grown man, but not in the seedy way that Mr Barr was. He was separated – his wife had gone to London to join a women's theatre group and 'find herself', he said, a phrase that amused her until she saw he was serious. He had met the young wife at a conference in Vancouver. Miranda was a 'free spirit', an academic at Cambridge. He had given up everything to be with her (he was a romantic, he freely admitted) and then, once here in England, she'd dumped him and hightailed it to London with her 'lesbian friends'. He couldn't afford to live in Cambridge on his own so he had moved to Ely where rental was cheaper and where he could pick up some extra hours' tutoring without bumping into colleagues, who'd ask about Miranda.

He didn't want to talk about Miranda – she was the last thing he wanted to talk about. She'd gone! It was over. *Miranda this, Miranda that*: he wished people would stop asking him, for God's sake. The point of the matter was, she was glamorous and she was memorable. OK, he understood that. But give a man a break. After all, he had been in her shadow. She was younger than him.

He hoped Mandy hadn't minded that he'd explained all this? Mandy shook her head. After all, he said, no one could deny Miranda was beautiful, with those dramatic almond-shaped eyes and that mass of black curls. No doubt, he murmured gloomily, she'd make it big down in London with her bra-burning bunch of friends and he'd have to hear about her, see her everywhere. He confessed how much he dreaded that and suddenly, yes, he had conjured her: Mandy could see her too.

Wild black hair. Stunning beauty and *soooooo* clever. No bra either: nipples sticking through a T-shirt.

Mandy listened, eyes widening. She had never heard of anyone so exotic. Women's theatre groups, academics, conferences in Canada, women's lib, lesbians! How shocked Beattie would be if she mentioned any of those things to her. But then Beattie had met Thomas – their second date, he came to pick her up in his old banger, with its CND stickers on it and, against all probabilities, Beattie was charmed. He had looked boldly into Beattie's disapproving glare, shaking her hand. He was confident: his way of standing, really planting his feet before surveying things, weighting himself, grounding himself. He was healthy and strong and he could stand up to Beattie. 'I hope you don't mind me taking out your lovely daughter?' he said. *Lovely daughter?* Beattie's mouth opened and closed. He handed over a small gift he'd brought: darkening bluebells picked from a wood that he and Mandy had already strolled through. Peter burst out from behind Beattie's forbidding legs, on his way to play football in the caravan park, and Thomas paused. He held out his hand to the boy so that Peter laughed and said, 'Hello, Mandy's teacher!' with a cheeky grin and carried on running. (She hadn't told Thomas that Peter was hers: she was building up to it.)

Later, though, much later, he said to her, 'You're – something really special, you know that . . .' And that was the second thing. She was clever, she was special. She wanted to ask him more – could he tell her in detail in what way she was special? – but he'd moved on, his soft voice, with its occasional twang, roaming over subjects from Joni Mitchell's amazing lyrics to the best of Hardy's novels, and she was content to listen, to drink it in, and to think about that word 'special' and why it mattered. No one had said it to her before but, in her deepest, most secret childish heart, she agreed. She felt she had been waiting for someone to notice. Mr Barr hadn't said it. But, then, Mr Barr hadn't said much in their short-lived encounter and he was hardly to be compared with Thomas (though she did concede that teachers seemed to be a thing with her). Thomas took her back to his flat and kissed her, doing something funny with his tongue that felt as if he was pulling an electric wire from her groin to her mouth: she wanted him to do it again, and kissed him back enthusiastically. His hands – stroking her cheek, her hair – smelt of the thyme he'd been handling, making them something to eat in the kitchen. She didn't know what to be most astounded by: a man who could cook or one who could charm Beattie.

His bare feet – his elegant ankle bones – were thin, and vulnerable, she thought, and very white. They reminded her of the cuttlefish they used to give their budgie.

In the bathroom of Thomas's flat she spent a long time trying to insert the Dutch cap she'd got herself fitted out with at the family-planning clinic. The nurse – Mandy had gone all the way to Cambridge; she'd given her name as Mrs Price – had shown her how to smear it with ghastly jelly stuff and squeeze it into a sort of oval shape, supposedly for inserting to fan out inside her (she pictured it like a small inside-out umbrella, or a jellyfish), but though she was crouching in the correct position it kept bouncing back to its original dome shape and squirting out of her hand. Wouldn't the bizarre smell put Thomas off? Would a sophisticated man like Thomas be able to tell she'd had a baby?

Pondering this, squatting in the undignified pose on the bathroom tiles, Mandy gave one final, painful shove and staggered to a standing position. She stared at Miranda's half-used bottle of Anne French cleansing milk on a shelf in the open cabinet and a bunch of cotton-wool balls trapped in glass, and wondered. A quick check revealed Badedas bubble bath on the side of the bath, too (could be Thomas's, though). A bottle of Man Tan. Mandy thought, Miranda's ordinary then, after all. Everybody uses those, and was surprised to find herself disappointed.

In the end Thomas seemed to notice none of the things she'd feared – he buried his mouth in her hair and only raised it to shriek, after a lot of thrusting and thrashing, '*Ah, Mandy, I'm coming, I'm coming . . .*' She was grateful for the notification, though it did make her seize up a little. She couldn't stop wondering if the Dutch cap had worked and about the journey his sperm were now making and tensed still further, instinctively trying to prevent them swimming too far. Something inside her was aching and bruised; she could feel an obstruction.

'Darling, I'm sorry. Next time I'll go more slowly,' he said, kissing her, murmuring that her breasts were magnificent (she thought they looked ugly, splayed as she was on her back, but said a quiet 'Thank you'). After a while she got up to go to the bathroom to check the Dutch cap. She thrust fingers inside herself, dutifully feeling for her cervix as she'd been instructed to do (like a nose, the nurse had said) and that was when she discovered that she'd inserted it all wrong. She'd managed – she didn't know how – to shove the damn annoying cap up *alongside* her cervix. That was probably why it had hurt so much. But, worse, the mouth of her womb, that little nose-shaped protruding thing, the entrance and invitation to utter disaster, had been unguarded all the while.

With Neville she was prepared. Finally, she'd braved the clinic in Knightsbridge and come out with the magical purple packet of pills. Arming herself with copies of *Forum* that Rosemary had given her, she had learned about the clitoris (a further example of her terrible sin of wanting to know too much, no doubt, had she ever shared this extraordinary discovery with Beattie).

As an explanation for why sex was so different with Neville this anatomical detail struck her as only half the story. Yes, he stroked her; she supposed he was more experienced and less embarrassed. He wanted her to enjoy it; he lingered. That was all true. But the real reason was simple. She wanted him. And that discovery taught her that she hadn't wanted Mr Barr or even Thomas. She had been flattered to be desired, that was all. (Ridiculously flattered, in Thomas's case.) Neville was so handsome – with him, she was the one who did the fancying: he was not her mirror, reflecting her back at twice her natural sexiness. It was all about him: how gorgeous he was, how delicious he smelt, how smooth his arms were, how strong his legs, the ridge of muscle down his back. Wanting him was exhausting: it made her lower body ache, softening and melting, like the sauce at the bottom of a lemon surprise, but it was exhilarating too.

And, further, he was unknowable. She felt guilty about this, about her pleasure in it: was it because he was foreign to her? Yes, there it was. Uncomfortable, but true. No matter how much he revealed of himself – and he did, he was good at this, he was open – he would never *merge* with her, or take her over. He would always remain separate, self-contained, *fully formed*, to use Dr Ryan's words, and this problem she had – if Dr Ryan was correct – this problem of a self that had been knocked about, pummelled, set-upon by Beattie, well, that self was good and safe with Neville.

They were home by mid-morning the next day. Mandy was relieved to see Katharine sitting in the basement kitchen, flicking through a magazine, her velvet headband and black eyeliner intact, cream polo-neck sweater and camel-coloured slacks. She looked as if she had taken care with her appearance, anticipated their arrival. She even held out her arms for James and smiled. He ran into them, and then, after a moment, tore himself away to fling himself on the cat.

'We've sorted out your school,' Katharine told him. 'You'll be a day boy now. Won't that be jolly? And you really *must* go tomorrow, darling. You've missed an entire half term already.'

James focused on stroking Bengo, lying on the floor on his stomach and not looking around. Pamela was sitting in her mother's arms but squirming to return to Mandy. Katharine jogged her for a moment or two on her knee, then handed her back. 'She clearly prefers you, my dear. I shall just go and have a lie-down.'

Mandy couldn't quite think what to say to detain her, but felt a pang as she watched Katharine's mood slide. She was already halfway up the stairs. Mandy followed her, carrying Pamela, wondering how to fix things. Should she tell her that Pamela could walk now or let Katharine discover it for herself? She was puzzling over what to say but Katharine disappeared into her bedroom before she could speak.

Gladys, the char, was just leaving. She was packing the mop and bucket away in the cupboard in the hallway, taking off her checked overalls. She nodded to Mandy while Mandy searched for Katharine's purse, abandoned on the marble table top. As usual, it was stuffed with notes. Mandy knew it would be fine to pay Gladys without Katharine's permission: her employer was casual to the point of reckless where money was concerned.

'She looks well,' Mandy said shyly.

Gladys folded her arms and said, 'Oh, yes, *now* she does.'

Mandy met Gladys's large brown eyes. What? What did the other woman mean?

'Yesterday it was pink smoke. Seeing things, all sort of funny things. Men jumpin' from cars with truncheons. Scared of her own shadow. Who can blame her? I got eyes. Many a time, I *see him*. I heard him one time, shoutin'. If you ask me, the problem is *him*.'

Mandy took a step back. Pamela was chewing vigorously on her knitted toy and she was heavy, but if she put her down she'd be off and there was no stair gate to prevent her falling down to the basement, and what was this, what was it again? Why was it always so frightening round here? Why could she never relax for a moment?

'I know. Yes. I know what you mean. Thank you, Gladys,' she said. She felt she sounded panicky and took a few deep breaths to calm herself.

Gladys was buttoning up her coat, slipping the little radio into her pocket. 'Callin' her on the telephone all of the hours of the night and day!' Gladys shook her head, watching Mandy's face, then turned to the door. Her face closed.

179

As Gladys opened the door, the most extraordinary thing occurred: there was the man himself, walking briskly past. And even more extraordinary was that when Gladys grunted, 'Speak of the devil,' to him, and when Mandy said politely, 'Oh! Hello! Did you want to come in?' Dickie only stared straight ahead, rushing stiffly down the street, as if they were invisible to him or – this felt most accurate to Mandy – as if he were a child, pretending they couldn't see him.

'But it's not a crime, is it, walking past your own house?' Rosemary said.

It was the most heated argument they'd ever had. They were in the Natural History Museum, in the café part, with the smaller children. And James. James, after only two days back at school, had contrived to miss the bus, and Mandy – feeling sorry for him, as ever – had brought him along to help her with the newly walking Pamela, to help her fold up the umbrella-like pushchair, which she had persuaded Katharine to buy so that she could at least get onto buses more easily.

Ten minutes earlier, they had been waiting outside in the queue, standing by the spiked black railings when Rosemary had spied a nanny she knew from Norland, another girl in her brown uniform: Louise. She had waved her over, excitedly. 'Hey, Mandy, this is Louise. Louise used to work at your place.'

Louise looked startled. 'What – you're not working for the bloody nightmare family, are you? *Rosemary* – did you tell her?'

And then Rosemary stubbed out her cigarette on the paving stone, and whatever she said in reply was lost in the surge of traffic from Cromwell Road. Clemmie was trying to climb the black railings to get a closer look at the birds and lizards carved on the walls of the museum so Rosemary was temporarily distracted while she removed her and strapped her back in her pushchair. The queue edged forward.

'You can have an orange squash when you get inside,' Rosemary said to Clemmie. Snaggy was asleep in the double pushchair. She was never as much trouble as her sister. Rosemary asked, 'Are you coming, Louise?' Louise was in her uniform, but there was no sign of any children with her.

'Nah. I just dropped them inside with their mum and she can cope for about an hour with them on her own. Then I'll go in and rescue them. I get to have a break.'

The nanny was blonde, and young, probably only twenty, with a Midlands accent. She turned to James now and ruffled his hair with a gloved hand. 'Hi, sweetie. How come you're not at school?'

James looked at her as if they had never met. He took one tiny step back and muttered, 'Missed the bus,' then turned his attention to the same carvings of creatures on the walls that Clemmie had been admiring, running a hand over them.

'Everything all right?' Louise asked him.

James stared ahead, trying his best to block his former nanny from his sight. A tiny gold fish spun atop a weather vane against a sky the colour of milk. Louise's voice seemed kind to Mandy. Despite the children and the sense that they should try to get them inside before Clemmie erupted in protest again, she wanted to know: what should Rosemary have told her?

But the problem was James. How could the other nanny tell her if it was something awkward about the parents? Mandy offered Louise a cigarette, then a light from her pocket, edging her slightly away from the others under the pretext of getting out of the wind. Louise nodded and murmured, 'Thanks', peeling off her white gloves and stuffing them into the pocket of her coat. The two women studied one another over Louise's cupped hands. Noisy voices, foreign tongues, passed them, and the traffic made it difficult to whisper.

'Poor lad,' Louise said. 'James is sweet, isn't he? And little Diddums. But I might as well tell you. I bloody didn't like Lord Morven much. And I packed it in because they kept forgetting to pay me. It was him. He withheld her money to make things awkward because the judge had said she had to have a nanny. Do they do that to you?'

'No, no, it's pretty quick and regular. Lady Morven gives me it.'

'Hmm.' Louise was inhaling her cigarette and narrowing her eyes. She glanced across at James, Rosemary and the other children in the queue, moving closer to the entrance. They were out of earshot. 'Does he still watch the house? Are those blokes outside all the time?'

'Yes.'

'And don't you find him . . . a bit frightening? I mean, he's so tall, isn't he, and so loud? Screaming, arguments, yelling at each other. I stayed in my room with the children. It used to make James shake from head to toe. I hated it.'

'Well . . .' Mandy didn't know if she did find him frightening. No. Except for that one moment in Scotland, the answer was: probably not. But why hadn't Rosemary mentioned this to her? If Louise had left because she hated it so much, why had Rosemary been keen for her to get the job?

'Oh, well, I can see you don't agree,' Louise said, a little stiffly. 'I know his type. I'm glad I'm out of it. One time Lady Morven asked him to give his key back and he wouldn't. I didn't like that. I didn't like him having it.'

'Come on, Mandy, we're nearly at the door!' Rosemary called.

Mandy glanced over towards the stone entrance to the museum, saw that James was examining the carvings of monkeys and weasels. Was he pretending to be unbothered? She felt sure he was, somehow. He had barely acknowledged Louise and it sounded as if she'd looked after him for some weeks. A pang struck her then, as so often, where James was concerned.

'It was nice to meet you,' Mandy said. Louise nodded and gave a short wave to the others. Mandy ran to join them.

But inside, once in the café, while James was in the toilet, she couldn't stop her anger from escaping. 'Why on earth didn't you say that the previous nanny thought him a nightmare? Thought them both a nightmare.'

'I'd forgotten! I'd honestly forgotten that it was the same place Louise worked,' Rosemary replied.

'Forgotten? That makes no sense!' Mandy was furious. Her face felt hot. She remembered their scheming to get her down to London, away from Beattie. Had Rosemary been so keen to get her there that she had chosen not to tell her some vital information?

'Look, Louise did tell me. Yes, I remember now. But I don't think she mentioned the name of the family. I didn't put two and two together. I'm sorry! I mean, that isn't how I heard of the job – that was through Lady Jane.' Rosemary was pouring milk from a metal jug into her cup and stirring and stirring it. She wouldn't meet Mandy's eyes.

The little ones were strapped into high-chairs and the noise level in the café – which was just a cordoned-off bit in the draughty hall of the museum, surrounded by dinosaurs and giraffe skeletons – was extreme: children squawking like monkeys in a zoo. The interior was the colour of dirty bones, the lighting low and green, like being underwater. James was gawping up at the vaulted ceilings, the stained glass and the tiles like giant playing cards. How cold it was. Cold and intimidating and ancient and disturbing.

Mandy fell silent. She didn't like to argue with Rosemary – after all, Rosemary had helped her immensely in getting her to London, and she had much to be grateful to her for. She tried to get her temper under control.

'. . . Lady Jane said not to be intimidated by him,' Rosemary was saying. 'Inside he was a real softie. And he is, isn't he? That's true. I mean, didn't you think that when we were in Scotland? How sweet he was about Pammie walking. And he rescued you! He was so nice to you. He's just like, you know, those posh types, stiff upper lip and all that. Of course he's not going to show his nice side that easily to every new nanny who comes along.'

'Screaming. Arguments. Yelling at each other. That's what Louise said.'

'Well she didn't tell *me* that. It didn't sound that bad. And some people are a bit feeble, aren't they? Can't put up with much. You and me are made of stronger stuff.'

Mandy wondered if this was true.

Rosemary pushed on: 'Louise's moany. Maybe she just sees it everywhere, she's looking for it.'

James came back from the toilet. He sat down sulkily and accepted the cup of milk, ham sandwich and Furry Friend that Mandy had brought for him. 'I wanted a Walnut Whip,' was all he said.

Snaggy had thrown her gonk out of the pushchair. James picked it up from the floor and waved it teasingly in front of her face.

'Don't be mean – give it to her,' Rosemary said mildly. James stuck out his tongue and gave it back.

Mandy sighed. She hadn't the heart to tell him off; she couldn't help thinking that seeing Louise had upset him. If he'd been younger she'd have got him on her knee and given him a cuddle. Instead she patted his head and said, 'I'll go and swap it for a Walnut Whip.'

Rosemary frowned at her as she returned to the counter.

'She doesn't half spoil you,' Rosemary said. James grinned – the first time he'd smiled all day.

Later that week the telephone rang and it was Neville, asking if he could see her. It was Wednesday and his voice had that clogged, sexy feeling she recognised. Oh, God, she wanted to see him, yes. She would ask if she could change her night off and work Thursday instead. She felt his pleasure radiate towards her when she came back to the phone and said, 'Yes, Lady Morven says it's fine. Where shall we go?'

'Come to mine,' he said. 'Come upstairs, above the pub. Eight o'clock. I'll be waitin'.'

And when she arrived, the place smelt delicious: Neville was cooking. A man cooking! She tried to hide her surprise. He was wearing a T-shirt and jeans and had the three-bar fire on full; the room was steamy and snug, filled with the smell of frying chicken. Chicken and peas and rice with coconut and something she'd never eaten called 'ladies' fingers', which she thought a bit slippery and strange, but didn't say so. The smell was spicy, peppery. They drank Guinness from tankards that said at the bottom: 'Property of the Plumbers Arms'. He had a tiny little gas stove. He wore three bands of leather round his wrist. The room was very small and she had to sit on his bed. A single bed. A green counterpane. She could barely look at it, such was the kick in her stomach every time she thought of them there, of what he would do to her, soon.

'You've made it very nice here,' she said. It was a joke. It was so plain, so masculine. Barely a sign of habitation. A bottle of Vitalis, which she knew he used on his hair, was beside the bed. His hat, the hat he'd worn the first night they'd met, was on the wall, presumably a peg behind it, holding it there. He was neat. Above the stove – greasy, curling – was a photo of a boy. She supposed it was his son. Mark. Bare feet. She was surprised at his age. Neville must have been pretty young to have a boy of . . . thirteen? Wearing a T-shirt and shorts, and with lovely brown staring-at-the-camera eyes. Shyly she picked it up and, seeing her, Neville turned from draining the rice and smiled.

'Handsome, eh? Like him father.'

'Yes,' she said.

As he dished up, surprising her again with a neat little fold-out table, serviettes, proper glasses for wine, he said, 'You should come here more often. Your place posh with the big showing-off bed and all that stuff, but it nasty.'

'Why?'

'Them private detective or whatever the fuck them fellas are. Why does he do that?'

They had never spoken of it before. Now Mandy found she was glad to share her worries with someone who, unlike Rosemary, didn't keep defending Dickie.

'I know. He's . . . He told me he was building a case. A custody case against her. I hate them too. It's scary. And last week Katharine told me he'd been saying to a friend that he wanted to – that he was going to . . .'

Neville had the loaded spoon of rice raised above her plate.

'. . . that he was going to kill her and dump her body in the sea,' she finished quietly.

'Nobody tell the police?'

'Well. I don't know if it's a crime to threaten someone. Just something people say. You know when he's angry . . . I heard him with some mate of his when we were in Scotland and he was really shouting, and I could tell he was. It was a bit scary. I suppose he wants custody of them and he's using the detectives to watch the house and say whether she, I don't know, takes them out enough or has too many boyfriends over. Or maybe whether I do.'

They were eating now and it was delicious. Hotter than anything Mandy had ever tasted, the colours and flavours sharp and strange, a fragrance she didn't know from a herb that he sprinkled on top. She thought of how everything Neville did was designed to maximise pleasure. What a connoisseur he was of this – how seriously he took *pleasure*. That first night they'd met she'd seen he was deliberate, glittery. Determined. How much joy he liked to extract from things. As if he'd been starved and was experiencing them for the first time. In this respect she felt he was like her. She'd been starved too.

'Why him want them so bad anyway? Better off with Mum.'

'I've been wondering whether I should pack it in.'

He glanced quickly at her then, and she was gratified. It was a worried look. It was a look that said, Do I mean something to you then or not?

'But then I think there are other reasons to be here.'

He smiled. Took the plates away. He put them into the sink and, taking the glasses, the cutlery, he packed the little table away. Mandy watched wordlessly, her heart beating fast. She was swigging the last of her wine when he took the glass from her, so that he could kiss her full on the mouth. 'No Angel Delight?' she asked. She'd seen the packet on his shelves. He laughed and said the sweet course was coming now. He led her to the bed.

But what she hadn't reckoned on, the one thing she had never dreamed of, was when he was deep inside her, his locked eyes on hers, and hers wide open, when they were as close and moulded as they had ever been, rocking together, like a boat on a choppy sea, sweat slapping between them, when the pleasure was so intense, she did wonder if it was possible to die of it. Then, at that moment, his eyes on hers, he pulled his head back a little and asked, 'Anyone ever love you like this?' and once again she wasn't quite sure of his meaning: did he mean did anyone ever love you *as much* as this? Or did anyone ever *make* love to you like this? Or perhaps he meant: in this position? But now wasn't the moment to question him so she just squeaked out, '*No,*' and got up on all fours, as he'd asked her to. And when she climaxed he turned her over and kissed her, and said, 'I love you, girl.' The last thing from Neville she had ever expected to hear. She lay beneath him, pleasure scattering in her, like seeds. Her orgasm seemed to go on and on, shuddering, reverberating. She clung to his salty body and thought, No. To answer your question truthfully, no one ever did.

She thought it would be all right, she would tell him now. It would be OK to admit it. She was safe with Neville. She could tell him everything, she felt. He had been so matter-of-fact about Peter, not shocked. He seemed to think it natural. Regrettable, but not calamitous or shameful. There could be no question at all, what she felt for him. Surely he knew. She had loved him from the start.

*   *   *

And so she told Neville at last about George.

Mandy had held her baby George for just fifty minutes. She was in the mothers' home in Wisbech. She'd glanced at the clock as the nurse said awkwardly, 'I'm not supposed to do this. We're told it's not a good idea, you know, to let you, when you've decided . . .' but Mandy had begged her. Mandy had a sweetness that many found hard to resist. And so the baby was brought, wheeled in a sort of plastic box beside the bed, and the nurse – conscious that she might get into trouble for this – was quick to leave the room.

She heaved herself up, weary, bovine. She stared at the baby's small, triangle-shaped mouth. He was asleep. She reached in, scooped him out, and his downy head brushed her arm.

Mandy thought, as she lifted him, I won't feel anything. It's decided. It's done. Thomas doesn't want him and he doesn't want me.

Thomas had said, 'She's coming back. My wife. She wrote me a letter. I have to give it one last try, Mandy. I hope you understand.'

In her arms the baby's little head wobbled. He tucked his chin back into his neck in a funny movement that reminded her of a tortoise. He was warm, wrapped in a blue cotton blanket, and smelt medicinal, like the hospital detergent. His eyelids were very pink and fine as petals. He reminded her of Peter. She kissed his eyelids and his head.

When Thomas had told her, she hadn't understood. Thomas had been the first person who had called her special and spoken of his feelings. She had thought that made him different, that she could trust him.

'Miranda's been all over the place, not at all herself,' he'd said. 'And I'm not doing this because I feel sorry for her. I'm doing this because of the weight of the past.'

What a strange reason. As reasons for a break-up went, she couldn't make sense of it. She looked at Thomas, so strong, so healthy, and thought, Miranda. That's all you talked about all along. Why didn't I understand?

'What I'm getting at is—'

But there had been no point in discovering what he was getting at. No point telling him either that she was pregnant. That was her own stupid fault, surely. She was slim, the baby didn't show yet, and she knew from her experience with Peter that she could go a long while before it did. Some women's bodies were like that. She'd believed Thomas. She'd imagined them marrying once he'd divorced Miranda, as he'd said they would. She'd seen them together: he with his great brainy dome of a forehead, the glasses he sometimes had to push down to peer over the top; the child, blond like him, riding a little trike in some scene bathed in yellow light, just like a TV ad.

And as the magnitude of her mistake hit her, that world crumbled and she did too. That was the caving in. She had no means to shore herself up any more. Thomas was rambling on: 'I've worried about you so much,' he said. 'I never wanted to hurt you.' His shoulders were shaking. The fringe on his forehead flopped and flung itself about.

'It's possible that our marriage is reparable. I have to find out, Mandy! You understand that, don't you?'

Why did he so need her to understand? She'd been foolish, foolish and trusting. How could she tell Beattie? Who would help her this time? Once, maybe. Once this great drama had been forgiven: Peter was healthy; he was loved and happy; it had worked out all right. But twice – *twice*? And she felt herself falling away, all the flimsy defences against despair dissolving. I'm no good. I'm not special. I'm ridiculous. I'm the biggest fool ever. No one will ever love me, or help me . . .

And he'd been saying: 'What I felt for you was real, Mandy. It wasn't just rebound stuff, you know. I wish I could hold up a mirror for you and you could see yourself as I do. You're lovely, Mandy. You deserve better. Please forgive me – I'm in torment.'

He was in torment. And where, now, was she? Oh, yes, he had the gift of the gab, as Beattie would have said. But words were leaving Mandy. She couldn't think of a single one. Something was scattering. A wave of purple, then pink and black flooded up under her eyelids. Is this it? Is it possible to go mad from disappointment? she thought. Her hand went to her belly – how many weeks was it? There was a kind of fizz near her pubic bone, pressing on her bladder. It was too late for an abortion. She thought of the ground she stood on: was it collapsing? Was there a shift? Nothing could be trusted, and no one. And still he went on: 'I've only ever loved two women in my life, Mandy. You have to believe that. Miranda, and you.'

Now, in the mothers' home, underneath the fragrance of the detergent, the baby smelt of honey, of sweetness. He reminded her of someone: was it Dad? His little nose. It was like the eraser nib of a pencil. Perhaps he looked like her. Oh, and they were not nothing, her feelings. She'd been wrong about that. She glanced at the clock. Twenty minutes she had held her own son close to her heart, as if he was a package she was waiting to post. There would be only thirty minutes more. George, she thought. *Goodbye, little George: have a good life.* No, they were not nothing. It was done, it was done. But this – it put her feelings for Thomas in the shade. Maybe this was what men dreaded, after all. A great wild thing rose inside her, cracked at her ribs. Oh, my little boy, my darling baby, I'm so sorry.

Since the beginning of time, women had had to do this. How many women had done it? Fat tears fell on the baby's head. The nurse came back in the room, a worried expression. Perhaps she thought Mandy might have changed her mind and she would have to tell her it was too late: the papers were signed, the couple would be here soon. But Mandy said nothing. She handed the baby up to the nurse and the young woman wheeled him away and that was that.

'The thing is, I never meant to hurt you, Mandy, you have to believe me,' Thomas had said, four months earlier.

Did she *have* to believe him? She couldn't and she wouldn't because it was impossible. She'd listened, she'd tried, she'd let him talk, but then something strange had happened. The seat beneath her buttocks felt as if it was tipping over. She'd looked at her arms with their light furring of red hair, and all she could see – she wasn't sure it was real – was a little orange money spider running there. Her veins frightened her. Her hands did not look like hers. She had been flipped outside herself, like a mermaid's purse exploded on the beach. Beattie had tried but never quite managed it. Mr Barr had never come close. But this trusting, this *believing* him, oh, my God. The biggest mistake of her life. It had turned her inside out and now she was undone.

That was The Poplars. That was how she ended up there. Voluntarily too: Thomas hadn't taken her. After weeks of incoherence, weeks spent in bed, then up and running around, folding the little terry nappies that Peter had used and had been washed and saved, folding them, looking at them, then kicking the pile over. Finally, she had said nothing to Beattie about why she wouldn't go in to work and took the bus to Newmarket. She'd got there herself. She thought of Beattie bursting upon her in rages, the doll that had taken a beating and come out looking exactly the same, and thought, *Enough*. I'm not unscathed: it's a lie. I knew I'd come to this one day and here I am. She was pregnant again and she was alone. She'd tried to break out from under the siege that was being born the daughter of Beattie River. Now she thought, with ice-cold certainty, perhaps as Rosemary had, I know what to do at last. I'll give up.

The doctors at The Poplars knew Mandy was pregnant and asked her if she wanted them to tell anyone. The father? Her parents? She shook her head. And after Thomas had visited her, after she knew there was no reprieve, no changing of his mind, she told the girl in the next bed. Rosemary.

'What does Dr Ryan say?' Rosemary had asked.

'He asks what I have in mind. What plans I'm making. Where I'll live, that kind of thing. There's a maternity home near

Wisbech. You can go there and hide. He doesn't say I've been wicked or stupid at least. He asks if I've told my mum. Beattie.'

'And have you?'

'What do you think?'

'Come and live with me,' Rosemary said, just like that. 'Until you have it, I mean, and afterwards, too, if you want.'

'I'm not keeping it. I can't. I've decided.'

Rosemary was silent then while her dream – her, Mandy, a baby – shifted. Later, weeks later, Rosemary came up with her plan. 'OK, that's fine. But come and live with me. Let's try to get out of here. You're voluntary. You just have to say you want to leave, not like me. I need Dr Ryan's signature but that's OK. I'm sure he'd give it. Say you're fine now! Tell them. I'll ask Dr Ryan . . .'

And that was what they did. Theirs was only the briefest spell at The Poplars.

In their last meeting Mandy realised that Dr Ryan was leaving too. His hair was looking a little wilder, she thought. And the strange smell that clung to him, smoky, rich and sweet, was getting stronger.

'Get out while you can,' he said. 'You have no kind of madness or illness, Mandy. Life treated you cruelly and you've been betrayed. You crumbled for a while, under the onslaught. You're much too clever to make such stupid judgements. There are a lot of bastards out there, that's all.'

'But how will I know – next time, I mean?' Mandy asked. It all felt too soon. His brand of wisdom and challenge, the soft Glaswegian voice, the light cough that punctuated his sentences (she thought he smoked too much): she wanted more of them.

He stared at her for a while, sweeping a hand across the fluff on his chin, as if to wipe it away. He was staring hard, beetling his brows, contemplating her question. 'How will you know if someone is a bastard?' he repeated.

'Yes, I mean, OK Mr Barr, yes, but Thomas, he was nice, and . . .'

'You don't have birds talking to you or anything like that? Like your friend Rosemary?'

She was startled by this question. Was Dr Ryan losing it? There had been talk about him. Some said he wasn't leaving of his own accord. His jumper was unravelling, a little thread there in the corner. Maybe if she pulled it, all of him would go . . . 'No, I don't hear things. You just said I wasn't – I didn't have any kind of psychiatric condition. I'm just wondering if you could give me some guidelines for the future, in case . . .'

He stood up then. He looked tired and dismissive, and she didn't understand his expression. 'Wear a helmet on a motor-bike. Clunk-click every trip. You're a vivid person, Mandy, and that's a good thing. Crazy stuff still happens to us, no matter what. We have to be open and fully alive – don't bother with the pills, Mandy, they're not the answer. Maybe retrain, get another job, like Rosemary. Be yourself – there's only one of you. Fall in love . . .'

He was rambling, she thought. His pupils were wide, black, filling up the irises. What was happening to Dr Ryan? Who could she trust, if not him?

'You have your friend Rosemary,' he said, as if answering her unspoken question. He held out his hand. She had never touched him before: how cool it was.

'Goodbye and good luck, Mandy. Send Rosemary in to see me, would you?'

She closed the door softly behind her, a strange ache filling her. He was abandoning her, she thought. He was absenting himself. The little label with his name and the title 'Head of Clinical Psychiatry' had already been removed. In its place a blank plastic slot waited for the name of his replacement.

Mandy went to live with Rosemary for the time leading up to the birth. Rosemary's brothers ignored them both, and they lived in the draughty farmhouse with its red-tiled floor and smell of farty beets, and the flattened strip of black land beside it, like burned toast. Rosemary took a job working in the post office in the village.

Rosemary's granny came to visit them, the strange old woman called Granny Otterspoor, who, Rosemary said, was a witch. The stories she told of her own children, and her ignorance, astonished the girls. 'I nearly had one of mine in the chapel. It were the first. I just had a sharp pain and I thought, What's this? And my mother said, "The baby's coming." "Where's it coming from?" I asked. "Same place it got in," my mother said.'

When Granny Otterspoor had gone, taking her smell of cigarettes and paregoric cough sweets with her, they would shriek with laughter. But Rosemary said, 'It's shocking, isn't it? Can you imagine knowing so little about the facts of life?'

Mandy thought of how she had sent away for the booklet to explain them, and how angry Beattie had been. Maybe older women liked you to remain in ignorance, so your experience was as bad as theirs had been.

Rosemary was saying: 'She had fourteen babies. I don't think I'm ever going to have any. The nappies hanging up on the line used to go on for ever, a great line of white flags, Granny said. I want to . . . I don't mind working with them, babies, I mean, being paid for it, but not just having and raising them for nothing, and no one seeing it as a job at all.'

Sometimes Rosemary said stranger things. Once, waking from a dream, Mandy heard her murmuring from the bed next to her own: 'I can see things sometimes, you know. I always could. I knew when my mother was dying that the time had properly come. I knew the exact moment. Some people have this gift.'

Mandy thought her friend must have been dreaming, or halfway between sleep and wakefulness. But the voice coming out of the darkness chilled her, this side of Rosemary. In some ways Rosemary was so modern – the first to mention the women's liberation movement to her, wages for housework: what an extraordinary idea! They watched Miss World on their little black-and-white television set and Rosemary said, 'No better than a parade of cattle at the market in Ely.' She would shout at her brothers if they stared at Mandy: 'Get your eyes off her! She's not one of yer horses!' But sometimes Rosemary seemed older than Beattie in her strange ideas.

Mandy's mother visited her a week before the baby was due. She'd known for months, it seemed. Beattie took the bus as far as it went – to the village – and walked the rest of the way up Black Horse Drove under a fantastically strong beam of light. Mandy was standing in the farmhouse kitchen and saw her mother's small figure making its way across a landscape that shivered with movement, the wind pulling the reeds that lined the ditch, pulling her curls as she opened the kitchen door, flapping her dress. All was waving, moving, glittering at the fringes of the black fen as Beattie, in a green raincoat and a flowered scarf, approached.

'So. This is where you got to,' Beattie said.

'Hi, Mum.'

A deep breath. So hard to know with Beattie what her mood might be, what the next comment might be.

'Come in, Mum. I'll make you a coffee.'

'Is that girl here? The mad one?'

'No. She's working at the post office.'

And so Beattie had come in, and accepted coffee in the big chipped mug and glanced for a second at the great swell of Mandy's belly, and shook her head. 'Even the nice ones are bad 'uns really,' Beattie said. She could hardly look Mandy in the eye.

'Oh, don't say that! There must be some nice ones. What about Dad?'

'What are you going to do about it? Why didn't you just come home? I knew you were here. I've had to put up with so much talk. The Poplars! I ask you. Shamed us, you have. And what about Peter?'

Mandy had been worrying about Peter. She'd written him letters. She'd sent him parcels of money, comics, sweets. She'd been knitting him a jumper. But, it was true, she hadn't seen him for several months.

Beattie and Mandy met each other's eyes at last, over the coffee Mandy had made. Mandy had lowered herself gingerly onto the soggy old couch, knowing that, once she'd sunk into it, it would be impossible ever to raise herself again. And somehow the room was filling, and Mandy was thinking, The swell of it. The love you feel for a mother, even a cruel one. Where does that come from? Why, why?

'We can't afford another one,' Beattie said. Her voice was quiet. Mandy checked, but there was no anger: it was surprisingly soft. 'Your dad would, but you know he's lost his job now, don't you? We can't afford it. Not two. We've no room. Where would it sleep? We're stretched as it is. Thomas isn't giving you any money for it, then? Or no intention of marrying you?'

She couldn't bring herself to say what had happened to Thomas, so she lowered her face into her mug and sipped her coffee, the steam stealing up her nostrils. I won't cry, I won't cry.

'I'm having it at the mothers' home at Wisbech. I'm giving it up,' Mandy whispered eventually.

Beattie nodded. Her expression was not triumphant, as Mandy had expected. It was unreadable.

They could hear a tractor trundling past the cottage: harvest time. One of the brothers was following behind it, spiking the odd beet on the end of a scythe and chucking it into the trailer. Horkey: the last load from the harvest. She was due in a week. Beattie stood up, as if they'd had a full and proper conversation, leaving her coffee untouched. As she opened the door, the sounds of outside blew in: the wind like rice being shaken in a sieve. The land was raised in chocolate furrows that reminded Mandy of the crinkled black paper in a box of Milk Tray. Beets dotted the rows and a white spatter of gulls followed the tractor.

Beattie leaned forward quickly in the doorway and pecked her daughter's cheek. 'Come home. Afterwards. Come back. Peter needs you. Your dad misses you. This mad girl isn't good for you

– you don't want to hang around her. Whole family's inbred. Religious nutters. Come on, Mandy, you know you want to.'

She did want to. That was the strange part. She had been holding herself together, holding herself apart, trying to do whatever Dr Ryan said she ought to do to 'actualize', to separate, but she wanted one last time to succumb.

The smell of Beattie's cheek when she kissed her was the scent of lily-of-the-valley and sweetness: the smell of Mandy's childhood, of being tucked into hand-knitted cardigans and given sherbet lollies to suck, a childhood, which, in the end, had not been all bad.

She watched her mother pick her way over the furrowed fields, head down, no gesture of acknowledgement or wave to either the brother driving the tractor or the one walking behind it with the scythe. Dad's phrase about Beattie: a force of nature. Strength, that's what Beattie had always had. Dad loved it and finally Mandy was grateful for it. The beets lay on the ground, like scalped heads. The willows at the edges of the ditch looked burned; two horses in the next fen stood as if in a photograph, refusing to move or lift their heads to show they were alive. She felt the baby tumble inside her, lost in space, never again to have her as its home. She would go back and live with Beattie and Brian, then, after she'd given the baby up. Whatever Rosemary's protests, she would do it. She would let Beattie possess her once more.

She didn't tell Neville much. She simply said, 'Peter isn't my only child. I think once – once is understandable. But twice – now you know. I was crazy for this fellow. I was stupid. If you want to finish with me, I'll understand.'

And she cried, and he held her and then after a while he said, 'I got pins and needles in me arm,' and she let him move and he got up and made them coffee. And that seemed to be it. The secret, the terrible secret, had not cracked anything. Nothing had splintered. Dr Ryan had once suggested to her that she might be ready one day to talk about it. She hadn't believed him. She hadn't ever imagined falling for anyone again. But now she had, and Neville had remained as loving, as warm as ever. She checked his face for signs but none appeared. He did not seem to have rejected her.

She washed her coffee cup in his poky little sink and glanced again at the photo of his son, Mark. He put a cassette in the recorder for her, knowing how she loved it: Carole King. You make me feel . . .

'He looks so like you. Such a serious expression,' she said.

Neville was standing behind her, kissing her neck. He lifted his mouth away to say, 'He look like my auntie. His mum.'

You make me feel . . .

Mandy whirled around, unsure what he meant. 'His mum is . . . your auntie? How can—'

'Daphine. My dad's younger sister. She just eighteen. Me, twelve. She tell me to do it. I was riding her and I can remember I didn't understand what I was feeling so I said, "Oh, I need to pee." And she said, "No, don't get off, just keep going." So then I caan stop. She tell me afterward not to tell nobody else.' He shrugged, watching Mandy's face carefully. 'But the whole family know. Mark the spitting image of her. That another reason I came to England to find my dad. He's no good and nobody in his family neither.'

Mandy didn't know what to say. She put the photograph back above the cooker.

'See. Nobody spotless like snow. Everybody have something,' he said simply.

She made her way back to the house in the early hours. Neville walked her to the door. That night they saw no one in the shadows or lurking round the house. Mandy hugged her delight to her, picturing a net of winter mornings with Neville, extending into the future. She was exhausted. She felt as if pure water had washed through her body. She pictured the baptisms she'd seen as a girl in the river Lark. No doubt Rosemary's family had taken part in them. She felt she had been dunked under water, as if a deluge had flushed through her. Perhaps it was because she had so rarely cried. How cleansed, how blissful to have told the truth at last, to have mentioned George by name.

'Maybe he's called them off at last? Got it out of his system?' she said.

'Huh?'

'Maybe Dickie's called off his warders?'

Neville said that in his experience if a man was gentle by nature, if him the sort that never kill a fly, then him not about to start. But if he had a temper, if he had form – did Lady Morven say he had? Mandy said Katharine had told her about beatings, the sexy ones. That in Scotland she'd heard him really raging, drunk and angry one evening, and his tone had scared her. And, after all, Lady Morven had said that Dickie had threatened to kill her. That this other nanny, Louise, admitted to being really frightened by him when she'd worked there. 'Well, then. A leopard don't change him spots,' was Neville's last comment. She told him not to worry so much, and kissed him goodbye on the step.

On Thursday morning Mandy awoke with the little alarm on her bedside table trilling right next to her ear, the bell knocking from side to side, the clock vibrating, croaking its last breath and stopping. She couldn't hear sounds of James in the bathroom or any sounds of anyone else being up. She'd overslept.

She found James in his room pretending to be asleep. She crouched by the bed. 'Chop-chop! If you get up now, there's just about time to catch the bus to school,' she said, stroking his blond head. James turned towards her; she smelt his sweet-sour breath on her face.

'My stomach hurts,' he murmured.

She remembered Dickie saying, 'This is what he does,' and Katharine crying on the stairs: 'Oh, my baby, my baby! What if my baby's dying?' Between a strict father and a hysterical mother, what did James need? A tender-hearted nanny.

'All right. It's nearly the weekend. Come downstairs when you feel well enough for some breakfast, and I'll telephone the school to say you'll be in again on Monday,' she said.

James rolled eagerly onto his back, pulling the sheets up to his neck. 'Oh, I'm much too poorly to eat!' he said. The grin he gave her was perfectly understood.

At the door Mandy said, 'After Monday I'm going to be much stricter, James. Even if you don't like it, you have to go in, I'm afraid.' She didn't know if he heard.

In the basement kitchen she prepared mashed banana and baby rice for Pamela, then went to fetch her from the nursery. Coffee was bubbling in the Italian pot on the stove. No sign of Katharine but that was normal and, in fact, just as Mandy liked it. Her time, her routines were her own: bliss.

She took James some Coco Pops on a tray upstairs and he relinquished the invalid act, tucking in hungrily. She then called to Katharine that she was taking the baby for a walk in the park. She needed cigarettes.

On the street opposite two men – both in suits – were crouched by a car, changing a tyre. For a moment, struggling down the steps with the pram, she wondered if they were private detectives, if the tyre act was some kind of cover, then told herself she was becoming . . . paranoid? Was that the word? She walked quickly away from the prettified black-spiked fences, the doorsteps with their flowers in pots, towards the London she associated with Neville. How quickly the city shifted: here there were Indian shops, now two West Indian men loading crates rattling with bottles into a basement; one had a beard that looked like a huge brown mitten attached to his chin. Here, too, there were scrawled messages on billboards: Free the Brockwell 3 – Sympathy won't set them free, what we need is action . . .

Mandy knew, as she walked by the pub, she was hoping to see Neville. She couldn't stop thinking of him. Remembering the night's events made her feel as though a buzzer had gone off in her pelvis, just as she remembered a particular detail: the way he'd looked at her, the way she'd felt when she told him about George. The relief, the relief, the fluid relief, to talk about George at last.

And returning, almost at the house, the cigarettes bought, deep in thought, she didn't see where he came from, which side, how he approached her. Dickie was there and she knew at once things were not right.

He was swaying. His usually slicked-down hair sprang up in an unkempt, slept-in way. His eyes looked different: the pupils dilated, black flooding the pale blue. The air around him seemed to sizzle.

'Is that fucking bitch at home, then?' he said. He'd been drinking. Rage bubbled all around him. Gone was the gentleman, the debonair, kindly lord of their Scottish holiday. Here he was in all his glory, as Dad would have said. The man whom only Katharine had seen, Louise had glimpsed, whom no one else knew existed.

Mandy gripped the handle of the pram. Panic was making her icily calm. They were almost at the house. James mustn't see his father like this; she mustn't let Dickie inside. She couldn't think what to do – they were nearly at the front door. Keep on walking. Walk past the front door. Act normally. Be pleasant, friendly, focus. Block out everything else. How fast her heart was beating. How sweaty her hands were. The sense that she must force her way through a dark, burning cloud.

Dickie put his hand over hers on the handle of the pram. For a second she thought he was going to say, You've missed the house, that he wanted to help her, but the next moment she felt the powerful shoulder he placed between himself and her. 'Just taking my own daughter for a walk,' he said, and with that, he shouldered her aside, reached into the hood of the pram, plucked the sleeping Pamela from it, and began running.

A scream tore from her before she could stop herself. An old man with a walking stick was beside her, asking, 'Is that your husband?' Dickie raced to the end of the street – he was running so fast that he was already only a small dark shape, disappearing.

'No, no! My baby, my baby!' Mandy wailed. She had never in her life abandoned herself to fear like this, to such a sweep of terror. Whenever disaster had threatened, when Beattie had erupted in rage, Mandy's calmest, coldest self had come to her rescue, allowing her to survive, but now all she could think of was Pamela. What was he going to do? A flash of the pond at the park. Where was he taking Pamela?

The man with the stick was limping to the phone box on the other side of the road, saying over his shoulder, 'Calm down, lady, I'm calling the police, don't worry,' and there were others crowding around her, peering into the empty pram, offering her their arm, saying things to her that she couldn't really hear: it was as if something heavy was pressing on her ears, her chest, stopping her breathing. She was bent double, then her knees buckled and she plonked down, right there on the pavement. He's taken my baby away from me.

The small crowd of people surged at her. She heard Lady Morven's name mentioned, and the whisperings, 'I heard he was bankrupt' – how was it that money was being discussed? She was in a cloud of buzzing bees. Where is he taking my baby? The pavement was dusty, dirty, under her hand. Her legs in her tights seemed thin, outstretched like that. They looked like Beattie's legs.

She didn't know where he reappeared from. How he came back. Dickie was back and his hair was smoothed down and his pupils a normal size, his eyes blue again, not black. He was contained, he'd got a hold of himself. He was talking to the small crowd, saying something like: 'Yes, this is my daughter. Yes, a custody visit. That's the nanny. Just having a little turn. All fine now, folks. No need . . .' And in his commanding way he was shooing people away, and making them leave, then jiggling a howling Pamela in one arm. He pushed the cover back on the pram and laid Pamela in it. The baby's wails brought Mandy to her feet. She took one look at Pamela's face and thought: If I'm scared, she's ten times worse.

'Pull yourself together and get her inside. You're making a spectacle of us,' Dickie hissed, as if the whole thing was her fault. Mandy put one hand on the pram handle, feeling the knobbly plastic as if for the very first time. With her other she smoothed the dust from the back of her coat. This steadying action helped. She began pushing the pram towards the front steps of the house, dreading the awkward moment when she would be forced to slow down and get the wheels up each step. She didn't look back over her shoulder at him. She could feel rather than see that he was standing perfectly still, watching her, just as she could feel the simmering hatred in his heart for her, and the baby. And yet – frustration, reason, something rational – had kicked in and made him give up his plan. She should be grateful. She must get Pamela inside the house. Her heartbeat was flickering to a steady tick. Her breathing was slowing.

What should she say to Katharine? Well, what would Katharine do? Scream, cry. She would alarm James. She wouldn't do anything practical. That was Mandy's task. She should pull herself together and think of James. At least James had not witnessed his father behaving in such a frightening way. Small mercies. She needed a coffee or a lie-down. She longed to talk to Neville.

She told Katharine at lunch. James was still upstairs in bed, tray across his knees. He had a marvellous appetite for one so ill, Mandy told him, but he just laughed. Pamela was in her high-chair eating mashed carrot. Most of it was in her hair. She'd been shaky and grouchy ever since the morning. Mandy tried and failed to imagine what it had felt like to be snatched up, clutched to a chest beating in anger, and carried at speed by a running man. People thought babies forgot things easily but she was sure they remembered feelings. Terror would be indelible, surely.

Katharine's fear flickered in her eyes and then she drew on her cigarette and said, 'No point reporting it. He did it once before. When Louise was working for me. Gave us both a dreadful fright and it was one hell of a job to get them back.'

'What – just snatched them in full view in the street?'

'No. That time he got his henchmen, his detectives, to do it. Bundled them into a car. Louise was quite hysterical and refused to work for me after that. And then he issued a court order. We went to court. I got custody. It cost him a lot of money.'

'Oh, poor James. How upsetting, and confusing . . .'

'The irony was that, in those days, Dickie never saw much of them. Always at his damn club. I don't think he'd spent more than an hour with the children until the courts granted him his weekend visits. He's not a bad father, now that he makes the effort. I can see that. James is – will be – the eighth earl. That's all terribly important to men like my husband.'

Katharine pulled deeply on her cigarette, finished it, and reached for another. She had not bothered to get dressed. The navy quilted dressing-gown that Mandy had first seen her in was what she mostly wore these days. Sometimes she added jewellery – sapphires, diamonds – and fixed her hair and make-up, but the dressing-gown was always draped over her slender frame, as if she might cast it off at any moment and suddenly be back to the person she was, fully dressed, ready to spring out as the countess once more.

'You weren't hurt?' Katharine asked, turning her bright gaze on Mandy.

'No.'

'Poor Dickie. Terribly sad for him, actually. He does so miss the children.'

Never mind poor Dickie! He's a frightening loony, Mandy was thinking.

'I have a ghastly temper too. One loses all dignity. The things I said to him – they played a tape of me in court!' Katharine smiled impishly then, darting a look at Mandy. 'But I didn't used to use that kind of language. And then they use that against one . . .'

Pamela banged the high-chair table with her spoon, knocking her bowl onto the floor. A few orange splats fell. Mandy rubbed some carrot out of her hair with the tea-towel, gave her a rusk to chew, and took the plastic bowl to the sink to be washed. But she came back to the table quickly because it was clear Katharine was in reflective mood, wanting to talk.

'His friends think he's so – polished. Even when at the roulette table – huge losses sometimes – he has that marvellous stiff upper lip. I imagine that's the case with many wife-batterers. Do you know he pushed me down the stairs once? Only in his own home does he degrade himself. I wonder why no one seems to get that. It's a man only his wife sees.'

Wife-batterer. And so it was out. Katharine seemed to be challenging Mandy to say something, to counter the prickly, powerful phrase. Her hands were trembling as she tapped the ash from her cigarette into the ashtray in front of her. To ease the embarrassment, Mandy got up again and began gathering more plates to wash at the sink.

Yes. It had been degrading. Mandy, who had experienced many a verbal onslaught from Beattie, realised that this was exactly the word for what she had felt hours afterwards. Degraded. She squirted Fairy Liquid into the bowl and began washing plates with scalding hot water. Once again, she wondered, should she look for another job? Abandon Katharine, and James and Pamela? As she turned round, she saw that Katharine's eyes were full of tears.

'I wish I didn't love him,' Katharine said.

Mandy sighed and postponed her decision. What on earth would they all do without her? She would leave when she was ready and Dickie wouldn't scare her off that easily.

She remembered – there was time to think about it, at last – what Neville had told her last night about his son Mark, and the shock and sadness washed over her again. The young Neville, the child he had been. How to think of such a thing? An assault

– what was the name for it? – by an older girl. Well, at eighteen not a girl, but a woman, and his own aunt, too. Her sadness for Neville, the tenderness she felt on imagining his boyhood and its sorrows: was that the root of Katharine's love for Dickie, too? Dickie's childhood had been appalling – the wrench of being sent to America without his parents; she knew even from that one conversation that Dickie had suffered. And Katharine responded to this. It wasn't rational, but it was her nature, and Mandy's too, opening like flowers when a bee brushed past. A man you loved had been vulnerable once; he needed you.

Later that evening Mandy longed to go out. To phone Beattie or, better still, to talk to Rosemary. She wanted to go to the pub and see Neville, feel his hot chest as he drew her towards him, the beard that tickled her face, his room with its strangely sexy smells of the gas cooker, beer and spicy chicken. She felt an ache of something she couldn't name. Pamela took a long time to settle (no doubt the result of her morning's terrors), needing endless patience: dummies, an extra bottle, cuddling, singing, pacing the room, until at last she fell into a desperate, scratchy sleep. It was five to nine. She heard James padding down from his bedroom and going into Katharine's room, then the sounds of the television set: canned laughter.

Around this time Katharine usually went to the basement to make herself a cup of tea. Mandy realised she was listening out for this: how quickly she'd grown accustomed to the routines, how much she liked them. This was her home now.

'Would you like a cup of tea?' Mandy knocked on Katharine's bedroom door, glimpsed James snuggled up beside his mother in his pyjamas. Mastermind was on the telly, the black leather chair looming into view, the doomy-sounding music. Katharine said yes, and Mandy gathered up last night's tea-cups, left on a tray on Katharine's bedside table, to take them to the basement kitchen.

The night it happened, the Thursday that Mandy went down to that basement kitchen, I was in Belgravia. I was washing up and a bubble of liquid popped on a long wooden spoon and I looked at it, and I can remember standing by the window staring out at a great drooping cherry tree that Lady Jane had in her London garden, and it was dark so I couldn't really see it, just shapes. Quarter past nine. Instead I saw, I was seeing, Mandy's little navy court shoes for no reason at all, as if they were in front of me, seeing them right there in the black pane of glass. I mean, truly vivid: shiny, navy patent, small, scattered. Footless. That was the word that popped into my head because she wasn't wearing them. Then: *footloose* and fancy-free.

———————— ◆ ————————

And so Mandy went down the basement steps, wearing navy court shoes, because she couldn't find her slippers, and her feet were cold. The light switch to the basement stairs didn't work, so she put out her right hand – the other holding the tray with the cups on it – and felt the wall and the hand-rail as she edged carefully, step by step. What was she thinking of, that night? Was it Neville, the future? It wasn't in her to give up on men, on falling in love, on daring to feel. She was not afraid to fall in love again. Her heart was stretched sometimes, like a taut balloon, trying to contain all the things she felt.

And then she heard a sound in the darkness. A tiny sound from the stairs beneath her. What was it? A movement, a thump – that was all. It made her start. Was someone in the downstairs lavatory? Or perhaps crouching at the bottom of the stairs? A pinprick of alarm filled her. The cups wobbled on the tray. She couldn't see her hands in the dim light, only grey shapes, shadows. She couldn't see what awaited her, *who* awaited her. Maybe she was thinking, Where's the downstairs light switch? or maybe she was remembering Neville's eyes, or maybe something else, something ordinary, something about one of her sons.

At the first blow to her head, she dropped the cups, which splintered on the steps. A kind girl, everyone said so. Nothing could have prepared her for what came next.

At the second blow – from behind – at the pain as it reached her consciousness, her knees crumpled and blackness surged. In it she saw the Underworld, the long route down. Like staring into a narrow well: a small circle of light at the bottom. In the circle, a tiny fish swam. *Rosy! Help me!* As the pain came again. This is my end and my beginning. The tiny fish glittered. Its last spark went out.

It came at me with a slicing pain in the head and a scream and a shock, like the swan, and then a chilling, icy trickle. A lovely sweet voice, young-sounding. Saying my name, over and over. Rosemary – Rosy! she called. *Help me.*

I had to sit down. I think Lady Jane came into the kitchen. She wanted a glass for her sherry but I was untying my apron. I couldn't think straight, I couldn't hear her. My head was hurting so much I just found myself saying, 'Something . . . awful. Something's wrong, I don't know—' and putting my hands up to my head, it was hurting so much. I felt stunned by the worst headache . . .

And she was saying, 'Rosemary? Rosemary, do you need some brandy?'

And she brought me some brandy and I sat down and some time passed. I don't remember what happened, what she was saying, because I was panicky, fidgety. I felt something I hadn't since The Poplars; I could hear all my voices clamouring at me, as if a tunnel swirled in front of my eyes and threatened to drag me along it. I could hear things like Granny saying, 'Oh, herons should be just the one, on its own. Juvenile herons lining up like that, that's always a bad sign. Why didn't you see it, Rosy?' And then Mandy: 'Men! Don't they know we're on to them?'

At some point I could hear that the phone in the hallway was ringing – perhaps it had been ringing for a while. I'd drunk the brandy. More time had passed. I went to the lavatory, I picked up the telephone. Later I came back downstairs, and Lady Jane said, 'Oh, that's better, some colour back in your cheeks.' And the phone was ringing a second time and this time *she* went to answer it – it was late by then, I think around half past ten. She came back in, running her hands over her skirt and saying, in a strange voice, 'It's the dowager countess. Lady Morven. Dickie's mother. Asking for you.'

And so that icy elderly voice with no pity in it was the one to tell me.

'Something has happened. There's been a terrible accident.'

'Is it the children? Is it— What is it?' I knew, though, I knew.

'It's your friend. The other nanny. I'm so sorry to be the one— Are you sitting down?'

And I *was* sitting down by then. My legs had collapsed. The rest of me had crumpled like a paper bag. I don't remember her words. I didn't want to hear them because then they might not be true. I could only see the little shoes and hear a faint echo of Mandy. Rosy, is that you? a voice said. Lady Morven carried on talking.

I got myself to Mandy's place in Knightsbridge, like Dickie's mother asked me to. I'd put my hat on, my Norland hat – how strange was that? – my gloves. I brought the empty canvas sling to carry Pamela. When I arrived there were police everywhere, and lights and people to-ing and fro-ing and onlookers, and I suppose a gaggle of photographers too. I couldn't really take it all in but I think the uniform helped. It meant I was official.

Recognisable. This detective appeared at the door and ushered me inside.

A weird shaking had begun at the top of my thighs. I could feel it fizzling up to the base of my spine. Soon all of me was shaking. I felt as if someone had hold of me – I was like a doll in their hands. There was nothing I could do about it. The police were swarming the house, like beetles – hard pointy helmets, shiny black boots, spoiling that lovely powder-blue carpet. The smell of them, the sound of them, their uniforms and their male voices, their London accents, the bright lights, the strangeness . . . It was helping, actually, because it just made it so unreal. I couldn't believe that Mandy was there somehow, that what the dowager countess had told me in that phone call was true.

I could hear a baby crying. One of the policemen, an older, fatherly one, had picked Pamela up from her cot and was pacing with her in the hallway, pressing her soft body against the hard buttons of his police jacket. As I stepped towards him he handed the baby to me but he said quickly, 'Don't you go looking down at the basement, Miss. No need to look down there. Give us your name and where you're taking the baby.'

It was kind of him, but pointless. I could smell it. It was everywhere. It was choking. I couldn't wait to get out of there. A sob was catching in my throat but my voices were saying: *Come on, Rosy, come on, you can do this, just do your job* . . . The policeman was trying to protect me but it was hopeless: blood and death were everywhere.

'There's another child!' I said, my voice coming out squeaky. 'There's a boy, James, he must be asleep.'

It was everywhere in that house and the fear and dread of it swelled inside me, too.

James wasn't asleep. When he heard my voice, he appeared at the top of the stairs – the ones leading to his room – in his pyjamas. Poor boy ('little old boy', Dad would have called him) didn't look as if he'd slept at all. All these people in his home. The noise. The smell. He had a book in his hand.

Daddy was wearing dark trousers and an overcoat, which was full length and fawn-coloured with brown check. I was sitting on the bed as they came in the door and I didn't see them very well . . . I couldn't see if Daddy's clothes had any blood on them. I wondered what had happened, but I didn't ask. I went upstairs to the top floor of the house and read my book.

I was to take the children to Dickie's mother's. This was what Lady Morven had asked me to do on the phone. She said Dickie had rung her and said, 'Mother, the children are alone in the house. Ask the other nanny, Rosemary, to bring them to yours.'

I found a coat for James and he put it on over his pyjamas. He was rubbing his eyes, pretending he'd been asleep, but I knew. His big eyes were so frightened, I could hardly bear to look at him. He was silent. The atmosphere was strange. The trembling in me was getting worse, I felt like a piece of fen sedge in a strong wind, but I tried to be calm, for James and for Mandy.

I had to sign a paper that was wobbling in my hands and to give an address, and then the police let me go to the taxi that had been purring away outside, like a big black cat, all this time. I was worried how I would pay for this. And that I'd come so empty-handed; I'd put my Norland hat on but hardly thought to fetch a nappy, and I knew Dickie's mother wouldn't think of such a thing. I was in shock, of course. I did what was asked of me and what Mandy would have wanted. I put the children into the cab and we left that house and I never ever went inside it again.

In the car I had Pamela sleeping against my chest, huddled against me in the sling. I could feel the damp spot of her mouth. I let some hot tears slip onto her head, and then I sniffed and pulled myself together. She was too big for that awkward sling now, but it seemed the easiest way to transport her. The warmth of my body, perhaps my terrified vibrating, had sent her to sleep. I reached for James's small hand in the darkness of the cab. It was icy.

'Where's Mummy?' he whispered. He was staring straight ahead.

'Mummy's going to be all right. Mummy's in the hospital. I'm sure you'll see her soon.'

I knew this from Lady Morven. He had attacked her, too, that man. Katharine had bravely run to the pub and now she was in the hospital with some terrible head injuries but she was going to be all right.

'Where's Daddy? Why can't I go to Daddy's house?'

This one wasn't so easy to answer. The *attacker*, Lady Morven had said. As if it was a stranger. 'My son called me. He said there's been a terrible accident. A man has attacked the nanny and – and I'm afraid—'

And then this same *someone*, this *stranger*, had attacked Katharine too. And then disappeared. And Dickie had been just passing, and witnessed it all, although where he was now was anyone's guess.

'Daddy is— We're going to your granny's house. That will be nicer, won't it? It's late and Daddy's . . . he's gone away at the moment.'

'Is he in prison?'

'Oh, no, James, no.'

James never asked, but it hovered in the cab with us. *Where's Mandy? What happened to Mandy?* His icy little hand stayed clasped in mine. London flipped past us, lights and twinkles, and all the years, all those days, the laughter, lying on our beds, blowing smoke rings, turning the pages of magazines, the trying on of clothes and giggling, the walking in the Fens, the late-night conversations, all those hours flew by and it was over, it was *over*. *I would never see her again*. Inside the cab the knowing and trying not to know loomed and nearly choked us.

I said nothing. James continued to stare straight ahead.

So. Lady Morven was waiting. She opened the door at Eaton Square before I rang the bell. She had shrunk – she seemed so small suddenly. Her beaky nose, her skin so pale she looked almost yellow. The long green cardigan swamped her. She didn't say hello to me. She took her hand out of her pocket and reached for her grandson.

'Up to bed with you, my son. It's very late,' she said, with the merest brush of her hand over his head. He looked startled; I wondered if it was the first time she'd ever touched him.

I followed James to the room she indicated. A cold room with an enormous painting of a man with gun dogs, it smelt as if it had never been used. But she'd put up a travel cot in there, so in some way Lady Morven had done her best. Once I'd unloaded Pamela from the sling and laid her down, I was at a loss for what to say to James.

'What about Bengo?' he asked, sitting on the single bed, with its slippery silk counterpane, still in his coat. I helped him off with it. His little frame in his pyjamas was trembling almost as much as I was. For a moment I couldn't understand his question. I thought he meant had the cat been attacked, too. Then, understanding that he was asking who would look after her, I said, 'Oh, I'm sure one of the nice policemen has taken her. We can get her back tomorrow.'

'I don't want her,' James said. He was slipping obediently between the stiff cold sheets, pulling them up to his chin. 'I hate her,' he said quietly, and turned his back to me.

Lady Morven insisted on giving me brandy, too, before I left. She'd wanted to delay me from getting the taxi back to Belgravia: she was alone in the house with the children, and she wanted to talk.

'He was such a sweet boy,' she said, standing with her back to her fire. A two-bar fire, which was switched off, though she seemed unaware of this.

'James, m'lady?'

'No, Dickie. But he was – he had these awful headaches. Couldn't sleep at all, after he came back, you know, from America.'

I didn't know, but no point saying anything. Maybe she meant the war. Children were sent to the country in the war. Perhaps posh people sent their children to America. I sipped my brandy and tried to quell the shaking in my legs. In the end, though she didn't say I could, I had to sit down. I stared into my glass: when would she let me go home?

'We took him to a famous doctor, you know. Dr Winnicott. Paddington Green Hospital. Precious little use he was, I must say. One could have predicted the things he said. So Dickie liked string. He liked binding things and tying things. Well, he was a boy! Boys like string. And this Dr Winnicott said he wanted to attach himself to me, and to his father. I ask you!'

She didn't care if I replied. She was rambling. The room was icy and my brandy was icy. Everything was cold and shocking and all she wanted to talk about was string.

'Once, he did – such a naughty thing. Gave one a terrible shock. I came into his room and he'd – he'd rigged a rope around his neck. Can you imagine? And he was lolling with his head to one side and I honestly thought . . . I screamed. Of course. His father came running. It was just Dickie's idea of fun. A little joke. Such a sweet boy he was when he was James's age. And looked just like him, too.'

She hadn't said a word about Mandy. Only her son. That was all she talked about. We're all like that, I suppose. We just think about our own loss and this was hers. She was thinking of what he might do now. Impossible not to think like that. I'd heard a policeman mutter it too. She would probably never see her son again and she knew it. I got up without her saying I could. I switched the fire on for her. She sat down heavily on a leather chair and looked at me for the first time.

'Oh, Dickie,' she said.

I let myself out.

I went back to Lady Jane's and didn't sleep a wink. I kept trying not to know what had happened. And then it would flash up and I would think, No, impossible. But it was hard work fending it off, trying so hard to push away that quiet voice saying, 'Are you sitting down?'

In the morning I felt like a zombie. I made myself a strong coffee and told Lady Jane I was handing in my notice. She was gathering up the newspaper from the doormat. She put it on her tray to take up with her breakfast and there was no avoiding it. I hadn't wanted to look at one, to see Mandy's face, but there it was.

'Killer guard on earl's children,' I read. 'Police find body of nanny dumped in mailbag.' And then more: 'The earl's children last night were being guarded by police at a secret address following the murder of their nanny in an *Upstairs Downstairs* drama in London . . .'

Guarded by police? I hadn't noticed police at Lady Morven's. But, then again, there had been mention that today James and Pamela would go to another location. I wasn't told where but I guessed it was to be with Katharine's sister, Amelia.

One photo was of Mandy and one of Katharine with her dark hair, huge eyes, that pouty mouth. Her puff-sleeved dress and skinny arms. The paper said it was a case of mistaken identity, that the killer had believed Mandy to be the countess. Yes, of course everyone was always saying they were alike. How small they both were, how Mandy could fit into her cast-offs. But Katharine's hair was browner – it wasn't red like Mandy's. Same fringe, though, I suppose. Same length. In darkness the shape of their heads would have looked the same. Katharine had brown eyes where Mandy's were blue and the countess's were bigger, too, Bambi eyes. (But he had hit her first from behind, in a basement without a light: he wouldn't have seen her eyes.)

Lady Jane watched me as I read. I think she wanted to stop me but I needed to see it written down. Maybe then I would believe it.

The pub landlord said that at 10.30 p.m. the countess 'came staggering in. She was suffering from various head wounds. They were quite severe. She was covered in blood. She was just in a delirious state and kept saying: "I'm dying and my nanny has been killed." She kept on about her children and saying, "My children, my children." '

This is how it was. I've heard it, I've read it, over and over, but I'm only going to tell it once.

Mandy went down to the basement to make Katharine and herself a cup of tea. He must have already let himself in: he still had a key and there were no signs – the police say – of any kind of break-in. He must have been waiting. At the bottom of the stairs. In the dark. Heart beating, forehead sweating. You can only imagine what was going through his mind as he weighed that weapon, bound in Elastoplast, in his hand and listened: heard the door opening on the landing above. He had a mailbag ready. Not Royal Mail, no, I saw it clearly, the photographs the police insisted I looked at. It was an American mail sack.

We know that Mandy came to the basement stairs, carrying empty cups to wash, on a tray. Cups with a bamboo pattern. I think of that, suddenly: her hand with the tender bit between thumb and forefinger, how she showed me it – a blister had formed from that kayaking in Scotland. That detail – the memory of Mandy rubbing at the spot and wincing – makes me the saddest. Because I'd said something like 'Oh, that will soon heal,' and it would have done, it would. But what was the point of her body putting in that effort when someone was about to smash it to a pulp?

At the top of the stairs, before stepping down, she would have tried to switch on the light, but nothing happened. He had taken out the bulb. But she didn't know that. Afterwards it was there, on a chair, with its tendrils snapped. It frightened me, that light bulb, when they showed me it.

So, Mandy, she never lacked courage, did she? She would have just carried on, I know she would. She was proud of her bravery and I agreed. We'd talked about it in The Poplars, why it was, how it was that she bounced back, that she wanted to carry on. She thought she was like a shoot, a strong shoot that kept on growing, no matter what. Beattie, Mr Barr, Thomas, whatever: they could bend her, yeah, she would bend, but she wouldn't break. That was what she used to say. So now she would have drawn on that boldness again, dear brave Mandy, stepping on each stair in darkness, carrying a tray of chattering cups on saucers, her other hand feeling the wall, feeling for the banister rail . . .

It was about nine o'clock and she was wearing the navy court shoes that made a little tap on every step. At nine o'clock most nights Katharine made herself a cup of tea; after eleven years, Dickie would have known that routine as well as we did. Thursday: Mandy's night off. He'd thought his wife would be on her own with the children. He was in some sort of mess – I can't quite picture that. Waiting, waiting at the bottom of the basement stairs.

That moment when I saw her shoes, in the dark pane of the window. Heard her scream, that voice, like a dream where you can't get the words out. How lonely she must have been in that basement.

When I talked to the nice Inspector Raymond, the fatherly one, he patted my hand, shaking his head while I tried to give my statement. My tears were splatting onto the paperwork. 'She would have been very quickly unconscious, wouldn't have felt too much pain, you know,' he said, wanting to be kind.

They'd telephoned me and said I had to come in and give a statement. Inspector Raymond and another, fresh-faced policeman. They questioned me. Those two crucial phone calls. Over and over they asked me, What did the first person say? What time did he call? Was it Dickie? And the second call, from his mother, Lady Morven, asking you to pick up the children, what time was that? What had she said?

This was my answer. I got the first call at about ten o'clock and answered it on the way to the lavatory. The voice was a man's. It was muddled. Maybe he was drunk. I couldn't really make out what he said, or who it was. I think I heard: 'Rosemary? I know you . . .'

Then after that, a second call, this one at about ten thirty, and it was answered by Lady Jane; she came back and said the caller had asked for me. This one was Dickie's mother, Lady Morven, in her croaky old tones asking me to go to the house and pick up the children, and bring them to hers straight away, which I did.

Why show me the photographs? I've seen the pictures anyway. Don't they know I trust my own eyes best? Her little shoes – navy courts, modest heels, square toes. I think she was only about a size four: I could never borrow them. I'd already seen them. I know them well enough. I don't look at the blood – it is just black, anyway, a huge mess of it in a black-and-white photograph. I look at her little shoes, all skew-whiff, empty. I remember them as patent, shiny. She used to clean them with Vaseline and a hankie. And those cherry-red boots she bought the day of her interview. How she loved her clothes, and why not? Clothes loved her back.

In the photographs there's a piano, which I'd forgotten about. Katharine once said she could hear it playing the Death March, on its own. There are framed photographs on the walls: school ones, rugby teams. Portraits, paintings, the Scottish estate. The smashed cups. What a noise they must have made – dropping a cup is dramatic. There's carpet on the stairs. Funny how I never noticed that. I do remember the parquet floor and one shaft of light falling cleanly, and a radiator – a normal kind of radiator, which I can imagine running my hand along, feeling its warmth. Nothing violent or murderous about it. Mandy's hair. In the photograph you can't see the colour. That shiny conker-red, and her scooping it up with one hand, twisting a band around it with the other, before stepping into the sea. Black blood clotting it now.

The other photo is of a mail sack. Oh, I wish they wouldn't make me look at that, but I was in the police station, they were asking me; they'd asked Neville too and we had to. 'She so small she can fit in a pocket,' Neville had said playfully, that night I met him at Annabel's, gesturing to Mandy to come and sit on his knee.

Neville. The newspapers mentioned him, of course. 'The police have questioned the Caribbean boyfriend of the murdered nanny.' I did not want to think about Neville.

Five foot two. In this photo, the second one, she is bundled into a hessian sack.

'Sit down,' the young policeman said. 'Take your time, Miss. We only need you to tell us anything you might notice here, anything different. Was this the basement as you knew it? Can you think of anything that would help us, anything we haven't noticed?'

Tears streamed down my face. My whole face was wet. I couldn't really see anything, or think straight, or be any use to them. They handed me tissues and looked embarrassed. My tea went cold on the table in front of me.

I couldn't think of anything to say. What had Neville said? I wondered. What must it have been like for him? At least he had a cast-iron alibi – so many people in the pub saw him that night. And he was there when Katharine flew in, screaming, 'My children! My children! My nanny's been killed,' so that was how he found out. That was how it happened, for Neville.

The sack was very bloody at one end. Black with it. That's all I could see. I shook my head and they sighed and I longed to go home.

Why did no one else seem surprised that it was an American mail sack, not Royal Mail? And in the photograph her legs were sticking out, and that looked silly, undignified, and Mandy wouldn't have liked that. We had a joke. I used to sit on her bed in the house at Knightsbridge, with my knees up, like a big locust or something, a book resting across them, sometimes not bothering to tug down the brown skirt of my Norland uniform, deliberately flashing my knickers. Mandy would say, 'Now that's not very Lucie Clayton, is it?' You know, the modelling agency. Said in a school-marmy sort of voice.

That was the wrong thing to sneak into my head then, but it did. Rosemary. Look at me. I'm not very Lucie Clayton, now, am I?

I wanted to giggle then, the tears drying on my face. Sitting in that metallic airless room with the sweaty policeman breathing like a horse right next to me, showing me the photographs of the crime scene. I could hear Mandy's laugh, too. Her voice came clearly: 'I've seen it all now. Men. Shown yourselves in all your glory, haven't you? Don't you know *we're on to you*?'

I went to see Katharine at the hospital. After I'd handed in my notice to Lady Jane, and she was cross with me – I could see that she was biting her tongue but wanted to say, How am I supposed to find another nanny at such short notice? – I was in a daze of— Well, all I could think of was Mandy, and I couldn't do my job. I could hardly turn my head when someone called my name. I couldn't pay the children any mind. All I could hear, or see, was Mandy. I wanted to go home. I bought my ticket and telephoned my brother Danny. 'Have you gone and got the sack?' he said. But he'd heard about Mandy, of course. Everyone had. And, like everyone, all he wanted to ask was about the earl. Had one of his posh friends spirited him out of London? Someone with a private plane perhaps. They all had enough money and that was the kind of world they lived in.

'Oh, shut up,' I said.

I thought, Before I leave London, I'll go to see Katharine.

At St George's Hospital there were reporters and a few onlookers hanging around outside, smoking and standing in huddles, muttering. They swelled towards me as I appeared in my uniform but the inspector, the nice one, the fatherly one, put his arm out and told them to 'Back off, boys, let the lady through.' I was carrying grapes in a brown-paper bag and a copy of *Honey* magazine. I thought the uniform would help me, be a disguise, but too late I realised that it made the newspaper men go crazy. The case was about a nanny, a *lovely young nanny*, and here I was providing them with the perfect photograph.

But when I saw her I burst into tears. So tiny she looked. She was sitting up in a pale blue nightie, and she had this big bandage all around her head, like something from a nightmare, and beneath it were her little face and deep brown eyes, and I just thought: Mandy. You're here and she isn't.

She looked frightened when she saw me too. There was a young constable near her bed and the inspector told him to 'pop outside', then nodded to me to go in. He could see I was nervous. He left us both together in the blue space with the humming monitors and the sound of something breathing around us.

'I'll leave you to it, m'lady,' he said. And then just in my ear, away from her: 'You're her only visitor. Doesn't she have any friends?'

I shook my head, feeling in my handbag for a handkerchief to blot my eyes.

'The children – they're all right?' Katharine croaked out.

I thought, No one has talked to her. Perhaps she doesn't even know they're at her sister's.

'Yes, yes, they're fine,' I said quickly. 'I took them to Lady Morven's that same night. But today they've gone on a train to the country, to your sister's.'

She nodded, flashed her eyes. It was hard to make out her expression under all the bandages. Her eyes were swollen, with yellow moons beneath them, and her whole skin had a horrible yellow look to it. I plonked the grapes and magazine on top of a cabinet, took off my hat and gloves and put them there too, then sat down in the chair next to the bed and pulled it close.

'Poor Mandy . . . They must have told her parents by now,' she said, and her voice was scratchy, not quite right. In the papers it said that Dickie had shoved several gloved fingers down her throat and tried to strangle her. I didn't know what to say. That 'poor Mandy' started me off crying again.

'Yes. Beattie. Her mum,' I said. Such a vivid picture then, the small grim figure of Beattie. Yes, I suppose they had told her, but I hadn't dared to ask. Oh, Beattie and Brian and . . . Peter. A little flash then, the three of them, the caravan: how had they been told? I was in such a state, I couldn't think straight. I was having to work hard to stop the chatter in my head and the smell of the house that night from filling it, like smoke.

'She was a difficult mother, I think?' Katharine croaked.

'Yes, but Mandy *loved* her. She had some sort of problem – moods, terrible, spiteful moods. I don't know – was it manic depression, I think you might call it, but Mandy was very understanding of Beattie in the end. It was something – Beattie couldn't help it. It was just how she was. And did you know, did Mandy ever tell you, that Mandy had her own children too?'

'A son, around the same age as James. Yes. Actually one guessed as much.'

'She had *two*. Two boys. One her parents looked after, one she gave away . . . That's how we met. She had a kind of breakdown and, well, we met in a psychiatric place.'

There was no point in hiding it now. The Poplars. Katharine, me, Mandy, all of us bonkers, according to other people. And the only one who wasn't? He was out there somewhere. He'd ended Mandy's life so violently, and tried to kill his wife. Yet he was sane and we were women and crazy.

'I wish I had believed her,' I said. I was starting to unfreeze and in place of the shock was a feeling much worse. How on earth could I have been so wrong about Dickie, about everything? I'd better say it. I should say it. I would feel better if I said it. 'I should have believed her when she said that Dickie . . . I don't know . . . was frightening. I don't know why I didn't.'

Now it was Katharine's turn to cry. She just closed her eyes and let tears slide out. The room filled with grief and with the terrible quiet sense of Mandy all around us but not there with us. I couldn't get used to it. She was still so near.

'It's difficult to explain why one can't easily take it in. It just seems – ridiculous that someone one knows should be capable of such a thing.'

We both cried for a bit and then she said, 'And the boyfriend? Someone should tell him,' her voice just a sound like a scrape. I had to move my chair closer to hear her.

'Neville. He was in the pub. The night you came in. I don't suppose you remember, but he heard you, he saw you, he knows what's happened. The police have questioned him too. They always go for the boyfriend or husband first.'

'And yet in my case they doubt it. You didn't believe Mandy. There seem to be plenty who don't believe me.'

'What do you mean?'

'I've told him, that Inspector Raymond, exactly what happened.' Here a bit of volume came back and she sounded more like her old haughty self. Outraged at not being believed. 'I told them it was Dickie in the basement. That I surprised him there minutes after – after Mandy, and it was he who attacked me. About fighting him off and running to the pub. But Dickie wrote some letters and sent them to some of his gambling friends and then he rang his mother and said he saw an intruder attacking me. It's ridiculous. That bloody friend of his, Susan, she was even on the radio, oh, yes, I heard her only yesterday, being interviewed and saying he was a *sweet* man and she's sure he's innocent. And then, of course, the bastard's buggered off. Why wouldn't they believe me? I mean why on earth would I make something like this up?'

She hauled herself up on her elbows and glared at me, daring me to argue.

'Well . . . I don't know, I suppose *they* would say, to get back at Dickie. So that he couldn't get custody of the children,' I stumbled.

My head was aching. Shame sat on my tongue. Mandy had always believed Katharine's version, believed that he was frightening, that he'd done wicked things to her, not just the sexy things but threatening things too. And, after all, the weapon used on Mandy. I knew about that now. That it was a bigger version of the Elastoplast-bound stick Mandy had seen in Katharine's wardrobe.

Why hadn't I listened? What was it that made it so hard to see Dickie the way Mandy did? I suppose it was unimaginable to me that anyone so handsome and charming and aristocratic could do sordid and shocking things, lose his self-control. I knew that some men beat their wives, of course, I wasn't an idiot, but I always imagined them loutish and thuggish and, well, nothing like Dickie. I thought back to Scotland, Mandy so anxious when we were waiting for him to bring back the children on the boat, or the time when we met Louise at the museum and Mandy was cross with me for downplaying Louise's dislike of Dickie. Yes, *I* had liked him. I'd admired him. And I hadn't liked or admired Katharine.

Once, as a very little girl, my brother Dan had pinched me hard on the upper arm, trying to get some toy off me. I'd run to my dad squealing about it and Dad had just said: 'Oh, go and play, Rosy, and don't make a fuss.' And then turned to Dan, who was protesting his innocence and said, with a wink, 'Girls are born liars.'

Born liars? Are we? Is that what I'd thought about Katharine? I stared back at her now then blurted out, 'Oh, God, your head. Is it very bad?' and broke into sobs again.

Katharine's hand drifted up to her bandages but she didn't take in my question. 'He *told* me, you know. He said, afterwards, after we broke off from fighting, he said, "Don't look." Poor Mandy he meant. Why don't they believe me? How could I make up such a story and stick to it in the state I was in? And what about poor James – James saw him afterwards. James corroborates everything I said. And yet they still don't believe me.'

'They do! I'm sure they do,' I said, hopeless, my heart bunching up in my chest, the sobs just pounding at my temples, but I didn't feel I was convincing. I knew she was right – I'd heard Lady Jane's friends gossiping. It was true that I wasn't the only one to think that Dickie couldn't possibly have done this.

'I hardly believe it myself,' she said. She gestured for a glass of water beside her bed, and I poured her some and handed her the tumbler. 'I suppose sometimes I really was scared of him. I told Mandy. I told one of the nannies before her, Louise. I know she believed me. But a man one is in love with, a person one has shared a bed with, laughed with, eaten with . . . one can't imagine it. Rosemary, do you see that?'

I did. Because I hadn't been able to imagine it, either. I'd insisted that Katharine was crazy and Dickie was just an outraged husband, hurt, upset but not – not *murderous* . . . And yet, and yet . . .

'Even though I saw little Mandy, sticking out from that bag . . .' Here she let out a noise so strange I shuddered from head to toe. I was frightened now. I wanted out of there.

'It should have been me, shouldn't it?' she finished simply.

There was nothing to say. That was her curse. If I'd opened my mouth it would only have come out: Yes. And I wish to God it had been you.

'Tell Katharine it's not her fault,' Mandy says. I'm dreaming. I know it's Mandy but in the dream she is a little jay, rosy pink with a stunning turquoise and black striped wing, hopping between grave-stones, picking up acorns.

'It *is* her fault, it is, it is!' I answer.

The jay is shy. It hides behind a tumbled-down stone, then pops out again: 'It's *his* fault, his alone, he did it, he did it!' the jay squawks. Its little eye is blue, just like Mandy's.

Then there is a fox, a red vixen, really slow, trickling past the upturned urns, the broken pieces of vases. This is a tumbledown place, everything broken, 'On the huh,' as Granny would say. We must be in the Fens, with all that sloping and slipping. A right thrash and tackle. Children screech and sit stupefied in their prams.

James is there and bats at me, like a balloon on a string. Now he's turning into a girl, older. Frightened.

'My daddy is innocent. *Innocent*. It's her fault. She should never have loved him. Then I wouldn't be here,' he says, and floats off.

'It's the same the whole world over, it's the poor what gets the blame,' the jay sings.

She's not poor! She's not poor!

Now the jay and the fox melt into Mandy again. Her red hair, her purple dress. How I saw her once in a storm, in a Fen Blow, blooming, like a really fat seed-pod. There's a big heron sweeping past. Pointed, a warning. Now it's a buzzard, circling and rising higher into the white sky.

And now Mandy is pushing a pram over the beet field and saying, 'Imagine not being married and no one minding, no need to hide it, imagine that day, Rosy.' The wind is whipping up her hair, the baby is sitting up (is it Pamela? Is it Peter? Its face is covered by a bonnet, I can't tell . . .) and smiling and all the village women are gathering round, not to judge but to coo at the infant, to offer presents. The baby is George, of course. They're clapping, they're celebrating, it's the ceremony they used to do in the old days: the Churching of Women, such an old custom – we used to do it before baptism and they're doing it now for Mandy, giving thanks to God for a safe delivery, and no one is asking, Well, did she have a ring on her finger?

'Oh, that day will never come,' I answer, in my sleep.

And the baby is suddenly James, big as he is, too big for the pram.

'Where are my babies now?' Mandy wails. '*Where, where?*'

The heron gave one horrible screech, witchy and blood-curdling. The sound came from somewhere inside the bed with me. I'm shouting in my sleep, waking up. But when I open my eyes the buzzard is still there, high in the sky of my room: a tiny, circling dot.

The police told me I'd be needed at the first hearing. So I couldn't go back home to the farm as soon as I'd wanted. The only good thing about this was that it would postpone the time when I would have to bump into Beattie. The inquest was postponed, and postponed. And the dread settled, and I couldn't sleep. Lady Jane was growing impatient with me and I knew that she wanted me to leave – after all I'd handed in my notice – but the day of the inquest didn't come. That was *his* fault. Because he went missing.

Once, I was standing in the newsagent's and I heard a girl, a dim girl with a big nose and small glasses on the end of it, saying, '*Why*, though? Why did he kill the nanny? Were they having an affair?'

I felt breathless with rage, at her stupidity. How dare she *blame* Mandy for her own death?

'I know. I thought the same,' said her friend. 'Surely he could tell this nanny wasn't his wife.'

In darkness, pumped up, weapon weighted, when he *expected* it to be his wife, it being Mandy's night off?

But mainly all anyone is interested in is not Mandy at all, just the missing earl. Where was he? What had he done when he'd fled the scene? Did his posh gambling friends help him to escape? There were even those who disputed that it *was* Dickie – some said it was a hitman he'd hired; some believed his own story in the letters he'd written afterwards and sent to his friends, that he'd interrupted someone attacking his wife. One person – can you believe this? – one bloke even suggested in a newspaper article somewhere that Katharine did it. Murdered Mandy and then attacked herself to make it look convincing. She had big hands, they said, capable of murder. Because any story at all – a goblin flying in and doing it – seems more believable to some folk than the boring truth that is everywhere around us about who does this stuff.

Those who thought him innocent never could say why Dickie went missing. Why his car turned up in Newhaven with a weapon in the boot, which wasn't the one used, a length of piping wrapped in Elastoplast, but was exactly like it. (Why did he have a duplicate? Had he been practising?) There was no sign of a break-in or of any other means of escape (out the back garden, for instance) at the house. He was seen outside it by several witnesses. James describes him as being in the house in a way that fits perfectly with his mother's account. And Katharine never wavered from the one she gave: she went to the basement to see where Mandy was with that cup of tea. He attacked her too. She managed to grab his testicles and fight him off. And then when they went upstairs to the bedroom (and she believed he would make another attempt on her life), she ran outside to the pub, barefoot and raised the alarm.

At last the date for the hearing came. It was a Wednesday. A red-brick building, Horseferry Road. A tiled floor, the sound of my heels as I tapped across it, like typewriter keys, or a slow clock ticking. Two witnesses called. One of them me. One of them her father, Brian. He'd had to identify the body. A rash, a vivid red stain crept up his throat as he spoke; apart from that he did not look altogether there. Stunned into absence. A big man. All I remembered about him was his singing voice, how unembarrassed he was about singing, a bit like Mandy, always bursting into song. Cheery. A counter-balance to Beattie.

Then the Home Office pathologist, with the briefest of details about the cause of death: 'Blows to the head with a blunt instrument.' Then me: my name. My relation to her: 'friend of the deceased'. Confirmation of her employment with Lady Morven, confirmation of how she had got the job, confirmation that she was nanny to the family from late summer until early November and had not known the family before that date. That was it. I stepped down and my stomach felt as if it had plunged down the steps a few yards ahead of me. I didn't know why the saying of things aloud, the naming of Mandy – Amanda River – could make my legs shake and my stomach lurch.

The weirdest thing was that she wasn't there. Wasn't there to laugh at me, at the pomp of it all. Men pointing cameras. Men scribbling in notebooks. And Mandy wasn't there to narrow her eyes, draw on her cigarette and say, 'Yeah. I see you.'

Another date was set: June the following year for the full inquest hearing. Such a long way off, and yet it meant between now and then that would be all I'd have to think about, no let-up. It wasn't a trial: they couldn't have a trial without the missing earl. The newspapers were full of speculation about where he was – Africa, Switzerland, the bottom of the English Channel, his toff friends had helped him to hide out in France – and we expected him to turn up.

I stepped down and my heels clicked a little more, and a pain sprinted from my heel to my calf muscle. New shoes. Blisters. And the thought came again about the blister on her hand and how Mandy would never, ever feel that ordinary pain again.

His list, the pathologist's list.

Mandy's mother Beattie would have to listen to that, if she came to the full inquest. Three blunt injuries to the face, one over the right eye, one and a half inches, the first group to the head above the right ear, on the back of the head the fifth and sixth splits in the scalp. On the back of the right hand there was superficial bruising: these were protective injuries . . .

And then this. Did anyone else even hear it? The bit where he said: 'In addition to a weapon being used, the lead-piping, there were injuries to the face consistent with a punch with the fist.'

He punched her in the face with his fist. Finally, it came through to me. At last I was able to see it, what had felt so impossible to see. Dickie, Lucky Dickie, Lord Morven, his glorious heritage and his red convertible, his gambling and his cigars and him being the seventh earl and all that, and his escape and all those fascinating, glamorous things about him.

This was the man who also smashed her in the face with his own gloved hand.

'Do you think you're a good judge of people, Rosemary?'

This was Dr Ryan. This was what he asked me, once. I think I was talking about leaving home, about being on my own, away from my family in Chelmsford, how stupid and lonely and sort of *skinless* I felt, how glad I was to meet Mandy when I got to The Poplars because, with Mother gone, I was on my own.

That had been one of our stranger sessions. Walking in the grounds at The Poplars. Magpies hopping across the lawn, daisies, clover, buttercups. He thought this was good for me. A little test. He also said that patients sometimes told him important things when he wasn't looking directly at them. If they thought he would only half hear them. He was looking a bit rough by then, Dr Ryan. Mandy and I had started to feel suspicious of him. Not just the mismatched socks. He often smelt of something powerful and smoky that we wondered about. We thought he was smoking pot, which seemed a bit rich since he was always telling us to stop taking the drugs we were prescribed.

'I don't know. What are you saying? Am I naive, is that what you're saying?' I probably sounded defensive. Angry. I don't know.

'I was thinking about your voices here. I wonder . . . Do they ever tell you about other people? Or only about yourself?'

I had to think. 'Well, mostly they tell me things about myself. You know. *You're stupid. You're not normal. You're ugly.* That kind of thing.'

'And did anyone in your life ever actually say that kind of thing to you? Talk to you that way?'

No. No one did. What does he think, that I haven't thought of that?

'So for understanding other people you don't use your voices as a guide? You don't trust them so you use a more everyday, rational self, is that it?'

Was that true? I hadn't thought about it. It *was* pigeons that told me I should leave Chelmsford, that I should go back home to Ely and throw myself under a train. But right now, walking in the grounds of The Poplars, the voices were mute. And the more I spoke to Dr Ryan, the more silent they became. I didn't want them to leave me entirely. I wasn't ready for that.

'So, apart from telling you you're stupid, or to do away with yourself, they don't actually say much else that's useful? Do they ever – oh, I don't know – give you a warning, predict helpful things?'

This was too much. The magpie hopped right in front of us. How close, how close. No, I wasn't going to tell him. Why should I? My granny was a witch. No one believed *her*, either.

'No. No, they don't,' I said, and walked a little faster, walked ahead of him. He had to trot to catch up.

'You see . . .' he sounded slightly breathless here and I suddenly thought, Does he have a heart condition? '. . . I'm interested, Rosemary, really I am. People throughout history have always heard voices. Joan of Arc. There have always been those who . . . Why should we be so dismissive of this, just because it's rare? Perhaps we'll be able to prove one day that some people have an area of the brain better developed for this sort of thing – extreme empathy, you know, extreme sensitivity, but not something supernatural. Might there not be – one in every million – a simple evolutionary explanation for soothsayers, for those who can help a tribe, predict danger, light the way?'

He'd wanted me to read this book he was obsessed with and given me a copy: *Supernature*. I liked it. Some of it was a bit beyond me but, yes, there was loads in it about all sorts of stuff that maybe science would one day prove I wasn't crazy at all.

Finally, I thought, You're rambling. You're losing it, Dr Ryan. The shine was coming off him, to be honest. Those knitted-together caterpillar eyebrows, that expression of concern. I was a bit tired of his waffling. Mandy and I had laughed about him only the day before. He was wearing some kind of crystal, a little flint on a bit of leather round his neck. 'Who does he think he is?' she'd said. I no longer lay down in his room. I didn't pace my own room either. I'd shrugged off all the medication, just as he had told me to. I held it under my tongue, then flushed it down the toilet. Mandy and I had hatched a plan. 'Come and live with me,' I'd said. 'Come and live at our farm in one of the old cottages. My brothers won't care if we live there – it's a hovel, and they have their own places. I'll help you and I'm good at keeping things secret, too. No need to tell your mum and dad or go back to live in the caravan with them. Come and live with me until the baby's born.' It gave us both something to get well for. I was the best secret-keeper in the whole world. I could keep them even from myself. I'd decided I was ready to leave, ready to be sane again.

There was this one day while we were living in the cottage on the farm and a Fen Blow started. I'd seen one loads of times. It's dramatic, yeah. It happens in the spring when it's too windy and the fine topsoil flies up before the seedlings have really caught hold. It's a disaster for farmers, for Dad. He could lose whole crops that way: black dust floating off the peaty earth. So this day we looked out of the window and Mandy shrieked, 'Oh, wow, look at that, Rosy, the land's *moving*!'

I was scared when she said that. The sky was blackening and the light was spooky. For a second I thought, Is God going to punish us because I'm harbouring her, with the born-out-of-wedlock baby? but I'd learned to keep those thoughts to myself. Mandy pulled herself up towards the window. She'd never seen one, she said, in all her years of living in the Fens.

'Well, you didn't grow up on a farm,' I said. 'Dad hated 'em.' I was trying to play down how uneasy the sight of it made me, how I was trembling a little, watching the land. It was as if *someone* (God again) had picked up a rug and was shaking it out, making it ripple and the dust fly up.

We stood watching it for a bit, from what we call the backus (the back kitchen). Then, as it picked up and grew darker and scarier, Mandy wanted to go outside to look at it. She asked me to take a photograph with my posh camera. I was busy, eating a packet of Cheese Footballs. 'Eating for two' was the joke between us, because it wasn't just Mandy who was getting fatter.

'Rosy,' she said, 'stir your stumps!' This was an expression of her dad's. 'Come on, it's sort of special.' It amazed me how Mandy could be excited by such ordinary things but she was.

Once outside she had to duck from the force, cover her eyes with her hands. I ran out after her, my eyes immediately smarting and watering. The smell — bitter and gritty — I could feel in the back of my nose and throat. She was shouting, 'Whooo! The poplars over there! They look as if they're lit up from underneath, like a stage. Oh, I wish Peter could see this. Peter would *love* this!'

That smell, that taste: smoky, peaty, deep and secret. A sort of *old* smell, something from long ago. I knew it had been there all along. Mandy was laughing. It was as if we were standing on a blanket being shaken. All the birds were hiding and I was scared, I couldn't tell why, but sweat was trickling down my spine, pooling in the small of my back.

'Come inside,' I shouted, trying to reach her in the black swirling cloud. 'We might get blown away!'

But Mandy just put her arms out like a fat windmill, twirling and shouting: 'Look, Rosy! It's like the fen is rippling — you know, like sand does at the edge of the sea.'

That was the only bit of excitement. Nothing much happened at all while we lived there. Her mum visited, just the once. We knew what the village would be saying about Mandy. It wouldn't be Thomas getting any blame, let's put it that way. She wasn't the first in Little Thetford to fall, but boy to hear some women speak you'd think so. Always back-biting. That's all they've got to do round here, make themselves look better than somebody else.

Mandy was ready to pop by then. We'd been at the cottage for four months and her belly was huge. Danny had seen her once in this purple pinafore dress she'd made herself on Granny's old sewing-machine and he called out to her, 'Hiya – Purple Plum!' Stupid bugger fancied her, of course. But mostly she'd been hidden away. I was the one bringing food and money into the house, buying little vests and cot-blankets for the baby. She didn't want to see them, she said. Let the new parents, let them dress it and choose its things.

'You only live once,' she said. That had been her catchphrase lately. To an imaginary Beattie or to anyone else who criticised her impulsiveness, the choices she'd made. I couldn't help myself and blurted that this wasn't true: she could be sure of everlasting life with Jesus. She shook her head, then: 'What a silly way to live. As if you'll get a second chance in the afterlife!'

It was true that Mandy had packed more into her twenty-six years than I had. She had fallen in love and had two babies and tried and tried to *feel* and *experience* things. She had flung off her mother, not once but twice. Remembering this, the sadness and weariness started up again, engulfing me in its great black cloud, sweeping into my eyes, my mouth. Choking me with that black fen dust that only Mandy in the whole world ever found beautiful.

After the hearing they released her. Mandy. The body. We could have the funeral at last. It was nearly Christmas by then and I was back at home in the farmhouse when I got the card from Beattie, inviting me. I thought that was big of her. I knew she'd never liked me.

It was going to be in St George's Church in Little Thetford, near where they lived in that caravan site, the tiny Baptist church that Beattie went to and where Peter was in the Boys' Brigade. So there he was, outside the church in his uniform, and that made me sad. Mandy wouldn't have liked that for him, her being so suspicious about religion. Her little lad looking all lost inside his too-big suit.

There were only six of us: Beattie, Brian, Peter, Mandy's auntie Joan from Upwell, the grey-haired police detective and me. And a cat. Oh, and a few watchers. Funerals in the Fens are funny things. Old people come along and linger at the back of the church sometimes, and there were a few of those too. Funerals mean more in a village. They just go and stand. Morbid, maybe a Londoner would say that, but I don't think so. It's not respect either. It's just . . . Oh, I don't know. They just stand there.

Somehow her parents had managed to keep the funeral date private, out of the local papers. There were no reporters. They hadn't followed us up here. No, these were just random people who didn't even know Mandy. Maybe some old folk like looking death in the eye, trying to stare it down. I mean, it's on the near horizon for them, isn't it? They must be wondering.

The place was cold. It smelt of lilies and furniture polish, pine cones and satsumas. I went to sit in the second row, away from Beattie but close enough to see the bit where the – where Mandy was. There was a wreath of pink chrysanthemums resting against the coffin. Beattie had been looking at it and I heard her say, 'She sent flowers then. Hmmph.'

Katharine. It must have been her – they were sort of posh-looking. You know, the way that things wealthy people buy always look. Stylish. Yes, it would be her. They were tasteful among the flimsy Christmas lights hanging from the trees in the churchyard and the paper decorations near the Sunday-school bit. Tinsel and Christmas angels around the windows. I'd thought of seeing if I could get a letter to Neville at the pub to invite him but, as usual, my pathetic cowardice won out. Now I was back from London, among the quiet again, the emptiness, the flat white page of it, busy, colourful, loud London and everything in it no longer existed. I couldn't imagine Neville in Little Thetford. Blimey, people would have stared! What would Beattie have made of him?

He'd have had to get the train up from London and I'd have had to meet him and bring him – I couldn't do it. I chickened out.

'God sees even a sparrow fall . . .' droned the minister.

He was a very old minister. His head was bald and wrinkled, like a shrivelled-up acorn. I was staring at him: he looked familiar, though this wasn't *my* church and I'd only been for the odd harvest festival. I suppose ministers move around, though.

I wasn't crying. I was dry-eyed by now. The songs chosen were so odd I was thinking about that. Was it Beattie who had chosen the first one? It was Mandy's auntie Joan, her dad's sister, who sang it, all alone, walking to the front of the church. Tip, tip, tip, went her shoes. I stared at her. Easy to see where Mandy got her looks from once you'd clapped eyes on Joan. That side of the family. She was forty-something, she had lovely thick auburn hair and a great figure, shown off by a black suede skirt and a blouse. A bit trendy for round here. And then when she opened her mouth I had to take a deep breath. A beautiful singing voice. She sounded like Mandy. Warm. Confident. She just sang it, a folk number, with no accompaniment. I started to feel strange then. Something rising in me. Something I was keeping down was coming up. My neck prickled. A tiny place where my head joined my body. That was where I felt it, as Auntie Joan sang the fen ballad. A weird little song.

Old Thyme

Come all young women and maids
That are all in your prime,
Mind how you plant your gardens gay,
Let no one steal your thyme.

Once I had thyme enough,
To last me night and day.
There came to me a false young man
Stole all my thyme away.

236

And now my thyme is done
I cannot plant no new,
There lays the bed where my old thyme grew,
It's all overrun with rue.
Rue is running root,
Runs all across amain,
If I could pluck that running root,
I'll plant my thyme again.

And then Auntie Joan came back to her seat, took out her hankie and pressed it to her eyes. Brian, her brother, put his head forward on the seat beside her and folded up. His shoulders shook. I could only see the back of Peter's head, his little neck reddening. He was holding Beattie's hand.

Something in me spiralled up, up towards the ceiling, out through the wooden beams and up towards the sky, up with the birds, while Auntie Joan sang that old, old song.

Mandy, where are you?

We all sat down. My spirit re-joined my body and I felt all right again, sort of calm, cold, I don't know what. The minister went on a bit more about the cruel way that Mandy had been 'cut down in her prime' and how as Christians we must find forgiveness, not hatred, in our hearts. (A sudden, blurted sob from Beattie here.) I was thinking now about Dr Ryan and that funny book he gave me that he loved so much, *Supernature*, and how he said the time when most people heard voices was after the death of a loved one. Even Freud had mentioned hearing a voice, he said, in some lonely days when he was living alone in a foreign city. It was natural, he said, that my voices should arrive after a 'trauma' (his word) or around the time of Mum's death, and I could perhaps assume it might happen again, if I suffered any similar traumas in future. That strange moment, the night she died. What would he have said about that? Now there was the haunting voice of Auntie Joan. Her notes were like a clear bell being struck. We were up on our feet again, the order of service fluttering in my hand. Another song.

People get ready, there's a train comin' . . .

We were all supposed to be singing it. I could only see sky, grey sky, with two swans staring hopelessly into a river. I could only hear the lilting loveliness of Auntie Joan's voice, more beautiful than any bird, calling out a message just for me.

Suddenly, through Joan's singing, I could hear the low rumble of the detective, joining in. He didn't seem surprised by Beattie's idea of a funeral. Maybe he just thought we Fens folk did it that way. His voice was like a slice of reality. He seemed to bring all the sordid memories, the London world, the truth of what had happened to Mandy with him. *I'll never see you again, will I?* And that was when it happened. I looked at the minister's face, his shaky hands, his feeble mouth trying to sing along convincingly, and at last I knew what I'd been trying not to know most of my adult life.

Oh, he wasn't a good man, that old minister, even if he was a man of God, oh, no, not at all. That was what I'd been running home that day, six years old, to tell my mum. I'd got waylaid, distracted by that swan stretching up to shout at me, and the ditch, and the strangeness of it all, but I'd been running home to tell my mum my first honest discovery about people. A minister could be good most of the time – people could like him and he could have a proper job, be sweet, be kind, most of the time. Except when his badness took over and he couldn't stop himself doing something so dirty, so wrong and so cruel.

After the service I went outside and was sick among the mistletoe and dying brambles, the old frorn land, and went home alone.

The inquest arrived at last, and here we were, seven months later, in London again. I had put my Norland uniform in a box and shoved it under the bed at the farmhouse but wondered if I should wear it for the inquest. Would it bring more attention to me or less? I always felt safer in it, like I had status or something, but when I dragged it out I discovered that the moths had got to the hat and made holes in it so at last it was time to put it on a bonfire and be rid of it.

I wore jeans – a new pair, because I'd got fatter, there was no getting round it. A brown polo neck. I wanted to be invisible. I was only required to say one thing and that was about the period after Mandy was – after the dowager countess contacted me. About the phone calls.

First I had to sit through hours of Katharine's account. I hadn't seen her for all that time. She had a headscarf, blue with purple swirls on it. I suppose to hide her scars. We didn't look at one another.

'When did you last see your husband?' she was asked by the coroner. She replied, 'The twenty-fourth of October. I looked out of the window and saw him.'

'What was he doing?'

'Sitting in his car. I noticed he was wearing dark glasses.'

I remembered all the times Mandy had complained of men watching the house, or that time he walked past it and me saying, 'Well, it's not crime, is it?' The strange shaking had started up in my body again. The doctor had given me some tablets for it and I fumbled for them now, tried to swallow one without a drink of water. It was such a crowded room, there was no sense that I could breathe in there, but I had to stay. I had to stick it out.

Then he asked her about Mandy's night off and why she was there on that Thursday. The tablet wouldn't go down. I thought I was going to gag, but at least the shaking had settled a little.

'Was she at home that evening?'

'She was.'

'Why was that?'

'Because her current boyfriend had his evening off on Wednesday and asked if she could change hers to Wednesday as well so that she could go out with him.'

And I saw him then. How could I have missed him? Neville at the back of the packed room squeezed between two women. He had sunglasses on to cover his eyes, and a strange stuffed woolly hat to cover his hair. My hand flew up to wave to him but I stopped myself. I didn't know if he would acknowledge me. I felt scared and tried again to swallow the tablet: it had lodged in my throat.

Inspector Raymond had told me that this wasn't a trial. Without Dickie, it couldn't be a trial. It had some strange legal details. Lady Morven would be able to say some things here against her husband that she couldn't reveal in a future murder trial if there were ever to be one. A wife can't be 'compellable nor competent' to give evidence against a husband, the detective said, and then added: 'Bloody convenient. For the husbands, I mean.' I understood then: he thought that Dickie would never be found. There wouldn't be a murder trial. This would have to do. So the coroner went on, with his plain, quiet voice, and questions and replies were batted softly back and forth, like balls across a ping-pong table.

'We have the crockery,' he said. (Katharine was shown the exhibits.) 'Do you recognise these cups?'

'Yes, I do.'

'And you were watching the news at nine, was that it?'

'Yes.'

'And when did you begin to wonder about the tea?'

'At about a quarter past nine.'

'Did you hear anything unusual at this time?'

'Nothing unusual.'

'So, what did you do then?'

'I decided to go downstairs and find out what had happened to the tea.'

'And how far did you descend in the house?'

'To the ground floor.'

'What did you do when you got there?'

'I looked down the stairs leading to the basement.'

'Was there anything unusual?'

'There was no light on at all.'

'Nowhere in the basement?'

'Nowhere.'

'There is a two-way switch that you can switch the light on, from the top of the stairs, and the other way around?'

'I believe you can. It may be possible.'

'Was the light usually left on?'

'No, you can stop at the door of the basement stairs.'

'Did you try this switch?'

'No, I didn't. I just saw it was dark, and so she couldn't have been there.'

'The light is switched on from the top of the stairs?'

'Yes.'

'Did you call out?'

'I called her name.'

'What happened then?'

'I heard a noise.'

'What sort of noise?'

'Just a noise of somebody, or something, in the downstairs cloakroom.'

'This is where there is a washbasin and toilet?'

'Yes.'

'What happened next?'

'I walked towards the sound, at any rate moved towards it.'

'What happened then?'

'Somebody rushed out and hit me on the head.'

'Did this happen in the area at the top of the stairs, approximately?'

'Approximately, yes.'

'Was there more than one blow?'

'About four.'

'Did you hear anybody speak at that time?'

'Not at the time I was being hit on the head. Later.'

'Then what?'

'The person said, "Shut up."'

'Did you recognise the voice? Who was it?'

'My husband.'

'What did he do then? What happened to you?'

'He thrust three gloved fingers down my throat, and we started to fight.'

'What happened during the fight?'

'It's difficult to remember, it was seven months ago. But during the course of it he attempted to strangle me.'

'From behind, or in front?'

'From in front. Gouge out my eyes.'

'And all this was at the top of the stairs, was it?'

'Yes.'

'And you were on the floor by this time?'

'Yes.'

'And do you remember sitting up somehow between his legs with your back to him or sideways?'

'I would say sideways.'

'Then he desisted a little after that, did he?'

'He desisted, yes.'

'Is it right that you grabbed hold of him during the course of the struggle?'

'Yes.'

'By his private parts?'

'Yes.'

'What effect, if any, did that seem to have on him?'

'He went back – he moved back.'

Quieter we grew in the room. My palms were slipping with sweat now and I felt that I must stop holding my breath or I would faint. Some posh lawyer stood up, a lawyer for the dowager countess, who said he wanted to put forward some evidence favourable to Dickie.

My voices started up suddenly, as the lawyer was speaking. Like a rush, a wave, a mumble at first. I had been trying not to hear from them but they were going, 'Oh, yes, he was a sweet man.' That was something Amelia, Katharine's own sister, had said in the paper. *He was a sweet man.* And hadn't Lady Jane said it too? 'I find it so hard to believe he did it. He didn't have it in him. *I can't imagine him doing anything violent.*' That was another friend. 'People say terrible things in anger. All men are angry when there are children involved in a bitter battle like this.' *He was a sweet man.*

And then Louise: 'Screaming, arguments, yelling at each other. *Frightening* he was . . .'

All these voices clamouring, I wanted to cover my ears. Could others tell I was hearing them? I looked around the room. What would Dr Ryan say about the return of my voices? What was I to do? 'What happens if you take them seriously, talk back to them?' he asked, once. The tablet wasn't helping at all.

Under my breath, I tried muttering: 'No one can ever imagine it. They always say that. He kept himself to himself . . . Bollocks! That's the point!'

I glanced around me. My forehead was now doused with sweat and I was shaking my head a little tiny bit and flapping one hand on my knee in agitation.

'Try imagining it!' This time I definitely said it aloud. I clapped a hand over my mouth. The woman beside me looked at me, alarmed. 'How do you know what people have *in them* until it comes out? How can you really see them? In all its horror, the slip and slap in the blood, the gory goriness – maybe it would be more useful if you could.'

'Sssh, sssh,' people said, on the row of seats behind me.

Next came some discussion about Katharine's state of mind. I couldn't concentrate. My blood was surging. I wanted to shout again and leap up. I didn't think the pill I'd taken was working at all. My breath came in bursts and the woman on the bench next to me kept darting me worried glances and trying to edge away from me. I knew my breathing was loud, louder than other people's, but I wasn't sure what I was saying out loud, what was just in my head.

The quiet voice of the coroner said, 'I don't think this should come into it, evidence about a witness's mental state. There is a lot of scientific evidence to put before the jury.'

'No scientific evidence will show she had feelings of hatred for her husband,' murmured Katharine's lawyer, but he sat down. I took breath after breath and thought, I must keep quiet, I must keep quiet. I was quiet, I thought, by then. I kept my hand over my mouth. I didn't care how strange it looked. I could smell sweat and fear on my hand and it made me feel a bit sick but I held it there, tight.

Next came the evidence taken from James, which was read out by a young woman police constable with ginger hair and a voice so feeble that the coroner had to interrupt her and ask her to speak up. James was somewhere at the back of the room. I sought his blond head. I'd seen him earlier. He sat still as a dummy while it was read out.

Just after Mummy left the room, I heard a scream. It sounded as though it came from a long way away. I thought maybe the cat had scratched Mummy, and she had screamed. I wasn't frightened by the scream, and I just stayed in the room watching television. I went to the door of the room and called Mummy, but there was no answer so I just left it.

At about 9.05 p.m., when the news was on the television, Daddy and Mummy both walked into the room. Mummy had blood on her face and was crying. Mummy told me to go upstairs. Daddy didn't say anything to me and I didn't say anything to either of them. I don't know how much blood was on Mummy's face, I only caught a glimpse of her.

The policewoman came to the end and somewhere in the wood-panelled room I felt I heard breathing again, strange breathing that might have been mine, but was so loud, I couldn't be sure. Then Neville was called. I hadn't seen him in seven months. He looked thinner, and less – what was it? – less brilliant and glittery. He'd always been a cocky devil, but that had gone now. His skin was tinged with an ashen colour. I didn't even know coloured people could look like that. He walked to the stand. He took the sunglasses off. He answered the questions in his strange accent that Mandy loved. His funny phrases and way of putting things.

'In the time leading up to the murder, what was the atmosphere like at the house?' the coroner asked.

'She was living in the shadows,' Neville said, and had to be asked to explain himself. He told about the private detectives, Dickie watching the house. And then questions about the night of the murder and the moment when Katharine came running into the pub.

'What was her condition?'

'Head to toe in blood.'

I closed my eyes. I clenched my fists but my turn was coming. Neville stepped down and my name was called.

I tried to follow the questions being put to me but the voices were loud. It was all about the phone calls, the night of the murder. Lady Morven had already given her testimony, that she had heard from her son that he had seen a man attacking his wife when he was walking past the house, which he was in the habit of doing, had let himself in with his own key and run down to the basement, where he had slipped in a pool of blood as he got down to the bottom of the stairs. The man he had seen attacking his wife ran off. He went to his wife, who was covered with blood and very hysterical. This was what Lady Morven had told me, too. Dickie had told his mother that this man had killed the nanny.

'What did her ladyship ask of you in that telephone call on the night of the murder?' the coroner said.

'To come and get the children and bring them to hers,' I replied.

'And did you – as you told the police – receive an earlier call at your home in Belgravia?'

'Yes.'

You're stupid.

'Who was the caller?'

You're not normal.

'I couldn't tell. It was a man's voice, very slurred. It might have been him – Dickie. He sounded drunk.'

You never will be . . .

'What did this voice say?

'The voice said, "Rosemary? I know you . . ."'

'Is that all?'

'Yes, I think so.'

There were more questions then, about the mention Dickie made of an intruder. Had Lady Morven mentioned this to me? he asked.

'She said that someone had attacked Mandy. A man. I think she said an "intruder".'

This was the story Dickie had put forward, in two mysterious letters he'd written afterwards to his friends and the story he told on the phone to his mother. I'd read it in the papers. I knew it, of course. But it made no sense. If there was an intruder why didn't James mention hearing or seeing him? Why did Katharine insist throughout, even in her shock and hysteria, that it was her husband? How had this 'intruder' escaped? Why were there no signs of forced entry? No evidence of other footprints? No other witnesses who saw him? Why did the car Dickie had used appear with an exact replica of the murder weapon in it? And what a ridiculous coincidence that Dickie was there too, 'passing the house' at just the right moment, seeing his wife attacked in the basement, he said, and running to her rescue.

I was allowed to step down. Relief flooded me as I went back to my seat. A saturated feeling, hushing my voices. At last, quiet again.

The jury were told to retire. This took only a short time and we fidgeted and waited.

They came back with the verdict: *Murder by a named person. Lord Morven. Dickie.*

We were reminded that this was not a trial and only a very rare procedure in a coroner's court. If the earl turned up he would be charged and face a trial, but by then no one believed this would happen.

I plucked my handbag from under my seat. My blood was roaring in my ears but at least there were no voices. People were now standing up, chattering, making for the exits. Had we done Mandy justice? I hoped so.

I tried again and again to tune in, to think about the voice crackling at the end of the telephone line. The one they asked me about. Each time I remembered, it sounded more sinister, more unclear, less human. I had wanted to tell the truth up there. I'd wanted confidence, to look death in the eye, like those uninvited funeral guests. I felt dredged from a nightmare, one of those where you're scared to fall asleep again in case it drags you back under.

Yes, I knew. That voice at ten o'clock on the phone line, saying, 'Rosemary? I know you . . .' It was the voice of that old serpent, the devil himself. He was phoning me from Hell.

THREE

I've plenty to reproach myself with. If it wasn't for me, Mandy would never have come to London in the first place. If it wasn't for me, she wouldn't have gone for that job, ended up in that household. Could I have warned her? Well, I could if I'd understood, if I'd had any sense.

Instead I kept saying – you know – overexcited things. I was a bit taken in. Nobs. Dukes, earls. I used to mock them and sneer – that was my way – but I don't think now that was really how it was. I also used to say how pretty Katharine was. I was all excited by her lovely home and her lovely things, but mostly by the money, really. All those super-trendy Biba and Ossie Clark clothes. Over-impressed. I know I was. I'm ashamed remembering it.

But the real shame was about Dickie. My mistakenness. Knowing that I'd got it so wrong. Who knew what might happen next, what other thing I could appallingly, *fatally* misjudge? The speed of that car as I stepped out on the crossing? The way that person was looking at me? I couldn't trust anything at all. The whole world was fragile and might explode at any moment.

The only person I might have talked to about this was gone. Mandy's judgement had been sound. She perhaps didn't realise *how* bad he was – well, who could? – but she wasn't taken in, that's the thing. I wish I'd— What do I wish? There was no point to anything. It was all curdled, sour and disgusting.

'The lovely young nanny,' the papers called her. *And good nannies are so hard to find.*

Was it just that she was in the wrong place at the wrong time – like Inspector Raymond said? I think Mandy might have said that, too. She often told me, when I said something too 'religious' for her, not to be daft. She didn't believe in a God of any kind, or destiny or Fate, or any of that. She decided this at about the same age as I was the first time I heard the swan speak. She told me that, from her talks with Dr Ryan, she thought she was probably an existentialist. There are some *givens* in life, some facts you know. That we'll all drop dead one day, that there is no meaning, that we have complete freedom to behave well or behave badly, and all we can do is pay attention to our own choices and behaviours.

It was Dr Ryan who talked to her about this stuff. To me he talked about other things but to her it was phenomenology and existentialism and free will and all that. She said we had to look to ourselves, and make sure we weren't *complicit*. (That was a Dr Ryan word.) Like she was talking of her own past here, the children, some *unconscious* forces, that was it. Maybe some deep part of her, secret even to herself, had wanted certain dramatic things to happen, had wanted to flout Beattie or mock the choices Beattie had made. 'But Mr Barr!' I protested at once. 'That wasn't your fault – you're not to blame for his . . .'

'No,' she said calmly, 'but I could have had an abortion. That bit was my choice and I didn't, and I'm glad about that because I love Peter and I'm glad he's here.'

'And George?' I asked, a bit boldly. Why did she give George away?

Mandy bit her lip then, made that little dismissive movement with her head. She glanced down. 'I feel worse about George,' she said. And then she looked at me. 'I think I did it to spite Beattie. Because Beattie would have let me have him. She would have tried to raise another child. She wasn't happy about it but she didn't reject him. She liked being a mother to sons. It was daughters she hated.'

That was our big discussion about Fate and destiny, after we'd left The Poplars, and I felt bad for starting it, for making her cry. But if she were here now, we surely would have the ultimate proof. Because nothing on earth that she did could have predicted her end, could have landed her in this.

Oh, maybe she had some small responsibility for those other things, yes, I can see that's an interesting idea if you don't believe in God – to take personal responsibility for things – but bloody hell, eh, Mandy? How could anyone have guessed – how could anyone – that you would come to *this*?

It was the finish of me. The mistake I'd made about Dickie; the loss of Mandy. I went back to the Fens; my brother Danny said it was just like taking care of a wounded cow. All I did was sleep and he gave up trying to budge me.

In 1985 something horrible happened. I'd thought that Mandy's death was the worst thing I'd ever live through, and it was, but then in 1985 I read about Louise's death, too. It was in the paper. I recognised her, though, of course, she looked older than when we knew her. 'Former Nanny to Missing Earl', she was called. And the horrible thing? She'd been murdered too. Head-butted and strangled by her husband, while their children were sleeping in the house. He'd cut her body up and distributed it in skips and dustbins. He couldn't get rid of her head, so he had to throw it over Hungerford Bridge.

But that detail, imagining all of that, reading that about Louise and then having a sudden flash of her, standing outside the Natural History Museum, stuffing her gloves into her pocket to accept the cigarette Mandy offered her, that wasn't even the worst of it. The worst was the story that journalists and her husband's defence lawyer made of it. Because she'd also worked for Dickie there was already a special interest, this horrible *tragic coincidence*. Her husband's defence was: she drove him to it. Extreme provocation. 'A non-stop form of humiliation and degradation, which drained every bit of respect from a grown man.'

And I thought of Dickie then, and those friends who said (that Susan for one, and other of his gambling friends, interviewed in the papers), 'Oh, Katharine. What a nightmare. Flaky, depressed. She drove him to it . . .'

As if this adult man, the husband of Louise, couldn't walk away or leave, or get a job in another town, if his life with her was so bad. No, head-butting and cutting up her body were the only possible solutions. I read an article in a paper mentioning this new murder, and its relevance to Mandy's case was as follows: how could Louise have been telling the truth about Dickie and Katharine's relationship, about what went on in that house? She must have been unreliable, a bitch and a harridan and a vicious liar. Why? *Because in the end she was murdered.*

Louise's husband got a 'provocation manslaughter verdict'. Six years. The judge said to him, 'Before these dreadful events, you were hard-working, of good character, devoted to your children and a good father . . .'

I read all this at home in the farmhouse, which I had inherited by then, along with my brothers. They worked the land. They'd given up on the Church since Dad died but I belonged to a new one, a spiritualist church, where I was always trying and failing to cross over and get a spirit message from Mandy. Those words: 'good character'. I thought of the minister again then and shuddered. I wondered why the story always seemed to take this shape.

Over the years, all the press talked about was Dickie. Where he was, how he might have escaped, what had happened to him. Rumours and sightings of him were always in the news. All about *him, him, him.* Everyone expecting this story of class and glamour and men and gambling and toffs or the end of the aristocracy or whatever they decided it signified – about *their* world, their story. I'd tried not to read any of the articles and I'd switch it off if it came on the telly, but my brothers were fascinated, like everybody else, and it was hard to avoid. One time I saw a newspaper interview with James. A young man now, studying law at Edinburgh. He actually said, 'My father is innocent until proven guilty . . .'

Poor James. If that was true, he can't have believed a word his mother said. He never went back to live with her. I don't know how that happened. Probably Katharine's depression took hold and in the period of slippage – the period of her life where her story was doubted over and over again, her sanity questioned by the media, by her own family and Dickie's mother too – she lost custody. James and Pamela went to live with Katharine's sister. I never spoke to them again.

How sad for James. That night he lost his father, he lost his beloved nanny and his mother too. I remember him wide awake, with his book, in his pyjamas, when I came to take him to his grandmother's, and I regret the half-baked answers I gave to his questions. I doubt that Dickie's mother answered any better. Hadn't I felt angry with my mother, too, for dying and abandoning me? We don't want people who are supposed to be taking care of us to be vulnerable. We wish they could withstand things, even death. Even murder.

Mandy might have said: 'People show you what they're capable of and you have to see it and not turn away.' That would have been the only way to keep Mandy and Louise and others like them safe. But over and over I find that people make the same mistakes I did. They prefer another story. The story where the woman is too sexy, too crazy or having an affair. They even like stories where the woman is the murderer, and they don't seem to notice how rare that really is. They love the one where she's a liar, a bad mother, selfish, flaky, plain mad. Whatever – it's *her* fault, over and over. If only she had been more honest, sweeter, kinder, faithful, stronger, saner or whatever, she would have been able to stop his terrible violence. In the end this is a comforting thought, I suppose. The world would be so much more manageable if only it were true, if only women *were* in control of men's violence.

Well, one night, I think not long after that shocking bit of news about Louise, I was at church. We had a raffle and we had a couple of new ministers from Streatham and I was all unsettled by that bit of dreadful, *dreadful* news, churning it up again, so I was hoping for some kind of comfort and I found instead, blazing out of nowhere, a question flying at me like a stick of burning corn: *what happened to Dickie?*

Here's how it came: *auditory and visual hallucinations.* That's what the doctors called my visions and my voices. It was just as Dr Ryan had said. I'd had only the two occasions, the one with the swan and the one when my mother died, but the 'significant trauma' of that year, 1974, started them up again. I had medication to take but at the church they didn't mind me so I didn't always take it. And so I think I might have been mumbling to myself, something about Dickie. I was thinking about the mail sack Mandy was shoved into and thinking about it being American and why that had always stayed with me. Thinking again about that friend of Dickie's he sometimes spoke of, the American who was some kind of dodgy fixer for him, something to do with his gambling or his debts. He lived in Newhaven. He'd said he could get Dickie anything. The Yank. I thought, He must have arranged it. The mail sack was organised in advance and I was sure that meant Dickie had had an accomplice. That was how he'd planned to get rid of Katharine's body.

So I kept thinking about this. Newhaven. That was where they'd found Dickie's car. They always said he'd have been too noticeable to escape on a ferry – a tall, distinguished man wearing no overcoat, with his photograph in all the papers. (But a friend could have supplied him with a coat. That Susan, for instance. I know she fancied him – I could tell when we were in Scotland. The papers said he'd visited her after he left his wife's home. The police interviewed her and she was the last person to have seen him before he disappeared.) Newspapers always claimed he couldn't have taken his own life by jumping off the ferry, as Katharine had suggested, because there would have been witnesses.

I remembered how certain Dickie's mother had been that night that she would never see her son again. Was it possible he told her, that when he phoned he told the truth about what he'd done and what he intended to do? And then gave her the story about the 'intruder' to tell the police? Family honour would come first for Lady Morven. She was far too grand to tell a simple copper anything Dickie didn't want her to tell. No, she would have taken that story to her grave.

I was idling, writing their names in the healing book. *Mandy River. Louise Martin.* They needed God's love still, wherever they were. But another part of my brain was ticking over and my heart was ticking too, very fast.

We were in a community hall. Yoga and creative-writing classes. A sign promised healing in the healing room first, then a 'divine service', and then messages. Five minutes earlier I had pushed the wrong door and there were all these boys in green uniforms. I stood there uncertainly and a fat woman in an A-line skirt with slightly goggly eyes came up to me and said, 'Is it the Scouts or the minister you want?' It was a woman called Stella: I hadn't recognised her at first. Our service that week was in a different room. This unsettled me. I felt a bit distracted, not quite with it. I went to the room with the row of bright yellow chairs, and a jam-jar with daisies in it on a table beside our leaflets. A candle gave off a clotted vanilla smell.

I fiddled with a leaflet while Stella said, 'Hello, Rosy, how you doing? It's fifty p. We've got four mediums on tonight. And there's a raffle. Roll-over from last week so there are lots of prizes left.'

I had to give her a fiver – she had no change: fifty p donation and then £4.50 for the raffle. She shoved a great wad of the blue tickets into my hand. I knew she wasn't asking me anything, or accusing me, but I discovered I had butterflies in my stomach and I know I looked shifty.

'Who needs Spirit's grace?' Stella asked. She meant: what had I written in the healing book? I didn't want to say Mandy's name aloud. They'd all remember it. Or Louise's. I'd never get them off the subject.

'Oh, just me tonight. Got a bad back,' I replied.

'Come next door if you want the healing part first,' said goggle-eyed Stella.

The healing was nice, though. She put a hand on my head and one on my back. She stood so close I could hear her stomach gurgling. An even heat radiated from her hands. I suddenly had a memory of my mother, washing my hair as a child, buttoning up my pyjamas, pushing me away with a pat on the tummy as she finished, saying, 'Get on with you now.' Mandy would have laughed so much if she'd been here listening to Stella's rumbling stomach. But, then, would she ever have come with me? Probably not.

At the end Stella showed me her palms.

'Little halos appear – can you see them?' she said. There was a loud snorting sound. I didn't know where it came from but Stella widened her eyes at me, affronted, and moved away.

Where was Mandy? Where was my mother, come to that, or my long ago small pyjama-parcelled self? I'd tried so hard not to think or remember. After the inquest and the funeral, I'd closed up. My voices kept me company, now and then, and I just retreated to the farm and took up the life that seemed always to have been on offer to me: that of the mad girl, the recluse. There was no Dr Ryan to talk to, and no Mandy to laugh with. No point in being a Norland nanny, no London life. At any moment things might suddenly blow and turn bloody, somehow different. There was the church and money that came from Dad's will. That was enough and that was my life now. I didn't want to live as other people did.

Now suddenly it was as if I'd taken a plug out and the memories started streaming again. What about Neville? What happened to Neville? The last time I'd seen him was at the inquest and he was so reduced, suddenly, so flat and so hidden with his dark sunglasses. All his glitter and his vividness, *gone*, like hers. What could I possibly have said to him? Sorry for being jealous of you, of how much Mandy loved you?

I was almost in tears, my eyes filling up, my temples aching. That was caused by the service, the songs. And by the disturbance that news of Louise had churned up. We had to stand up. There were about two dozen people there, mostly people I knew. We were all a bit overweight, quite a few in pinnies and perms, and only two men. There were two young women – I'd say they were about nineteen – all hair-sprayed hair and showing off their boobs in tight jumpers, and they had a lot of dogs with them. Puppy dogs. During the service one of the girls fed the dogs biscuits from a Tupperware box to keep them quiet. 'One bark for yes, two for no,' someone quipped.

I sang along. I even did a bit of harmonising. I felt Stella behind me, approving. I was feeling a bit jollier by then. Spirit's grace, perhaps. I pressed at my eyes with a hankie and sniffed. I felt a bit more pulled together.

Then the mediums stood up. First a woman – a minister – who began by introducing herself and telling us how her mother had 'passed' twenty years ago, and that was when she got her calling. That was when she realised that no one really died: death did not exist. That she herself was a channel for spirit to pass through. Like a drainpipe. (I thought of Stella and her gurgling stomach.)

This woman stood at the front of the room. Her skirt was grey, a strange, slightly fluffy fabric. She was one of the new mediums from Streatham. She was wearing lipstick and a necklace, making an effort. She closed her eyes and opened them with a blink. 'I'm getting a man, yes, he's about forty. He's got a moustache . . .'

A few people shifted in their yellow plastic seats. One of the dogs slurped and crunched on his biscuit.

'He has a smell of cigars, of some kind of *expensive* cologne . . .'

'I can take him,' came a man's voice behind me. I didn't dare look around. I think perhaps I'd been grinding my teeth. My jaw

259

hurt. Yes, you take him, I thought. It's not Dickie. I don't want him.

'I think that's my friend's brother. Gordon. Yeah, he was a cigar-smoker. Well, pipe mainly,' the man said.

'Does this message mean anything to you? He's laughing. He's saying you already know what he's about to tell you. That you saw it yourself before it happened.'

Here he is, that night in the bathroom in Scotland. I couldn't see it properly then but I can now. A cluster of mussel shells at the sea's edge, in darkness. I close my eyes. I see it more clearly: a black sea, crested with white. And a boat, a small one, bobbing on squally dark waves. Two men on it. And one is standing up and the other is hanging something around his own neck: weights, chains. He is swaggering. He must be crazy, or drunk. I see him stepping towards the edge of the boat. And now he's got one leg over and the other man is dark, turned away, and perhaps doesn't look as the one in chains bundles himself over the edge. Tipping, a light spot in that flapping coat, and gone. Not even a splash as the black sea closes around him, like a dark flower pulling in its petals.

Ah, Dickie comes silently, stealthily. He doesn't speak but I see him. It's him all right.

And then here's Mandy, too, with the kids. Standing at the shore, her ribbed polo-neck top, sunglasses, her glorious hair, her loveliness, the glint of an earring at her neck, the baby in her arms. James beside her, gazing up at her. How easily people loved her. The sea a yellow colour, deeper than we ever knew. How long the days seemed, then. Days I have loved. Come back.

And I remembered that argument on the jetty. When we ran there to see where Dickie was on the motor-boat. And how she was frightened, she'd thought he might do something dreadful to himself or the children, and I'd denied it, I'd scoffed, smoothed it over, but she'd persisted. 'I don't know *what* he might do,' she'd said, and her voice had something startling in it. I hadn't wanted to hear it. Mandy was always more willing to *feel* things. To dare to know her feelings. That was why – I suddenly realised – she seemed more *alive* to me than other people.

We stood up to sing. I could barely see to read the song sheet but I knew the words.

> 'The water is wide I cannot get over
> And neither have I wings to fly.
> Give me a boat,
> That can carry two of us
> And both shall row, my love and I.'

There was yearning, there were ghosts in the room. Then came the raffle. I'd won a prize. 'I've got a blue ticket here . . .' Stella said. 'Number twenty-four. Number twenty-four?'

And it was me, and I'd won a tin of beans. I had to go up to the front and get it. And then: 'Right, blue ticket again, thirty-five this time. Who's got thirty-five?'

Laughter, ticket thirty-five, as it was me again. I got off the chair and walked to the prize table, and this time accepted a set of biros. I'd barely sat down before she was calling out another ticket, number forty-six. A 'drawing of a cat' done by Bert. Framed. 'No one claimed it last week so they've put it on the prize table again,' she said. Sniggers came from somewhere; perhaps it was one of the girls with the puppy dogs.

'OK, nobody claiming number forty-six? Well, we'll roll that prize over until next week, shall we?' Stella said, big eyes scouring the room like a torch beam. 'Let's have another song. "Thank You For The Music". Page twenty. I think it's time for more singing, eh?'

And giggling came from somewhere again, as we all stood up, and blue ticket number forty-six fell out of my hand and fluttered to the floor.

Afterword

Sandra Eleanor Hensby (later Rivett) was born in 1945 in Basingstoke, one of four girls. When she was two years old the family emigrated to Australia but returned to England seven years later. Sandra was a redhead, petite and vivacious. Her mother, Eunice, said of her: 'She could make other people happy when they were in her company. She could make a joke out of anything, and I don't think she could make an enemy out of anyone.'

Sandra was twenty-nine when she came to London to take up a position as nanny to the family of Lord Lucan in 1974. Following a failed romance she had been a voluntary patient at a mental hospital in Surrey. In 1967 she married a seaman, Roger Rivett, but was separated from him by May 1974.

In 1964, when she was nineteen, Sandra had a son, who was adopted by her parents. Three years afterwards – after a brief relationship with a married man – she had a second son, who was adopted six months later by another family.

Sandra's time working for the Lucan family was brief: ten weeks. Sandra had told friends that she enjoyed it, that Lady Lucan, Veronica, treated her 'as an equal' and they were on first-name terms. However, the household was pestered by nuisance calls at all hours of the day or night. Sometimes the phone might ring as often as a dozen times in an hour, and if she or Lady Lucan answered they would be met with heavy breathing or silence. The house was being watched, too, by private detectives or sometimes by Lord Lucan himself. Veronica and her husband were estranged and the earl had previously arranged for the children to be snatched by detectives but had had to return them after the court ruled in Veronica's favour. Veronica's account tells how Lucan had been violent to her on previous occasions and had used the stick covered with Elastoplast to beat her before sex.

Sandra's murder happened on the night of 7 November 1974, when she was attacked on the basement stairs by a man, using a piece of lead-piping wrapped in Elastoplast. Lady Lucan's subsequent attack minutes afterwards, and the answers she gave to the coroner about her husband, are included here word for word at the inquest scene that Rosemary attends.

Lady Lucan never wavered from her account and maintained it was the truth until her death in September 2017. Sandra Rivett's inquest in 1975 came to the conclusion that the murderer *was* Lord Lucan, despite his non-show and that there could therefore not be a trial. Sandra's aunt Vera said to newspapers: 'The entire inquest has been devoted to the life of Lord Lucan, and the life of poor Sandra has been almost ignored.'

In the years since Sandra's death this imbalance has only intensified. There have been many books published about 'Lucky' Lord Lucan and his various escapes, his aristocratic world and his gambling associates. The mystery of what happened to him is part of a British collective memory and theories abound. I read many in researching this novel. There have been films and documentaries, too. But, as Sandra's aunt suggested, there is not much at all about the nannies at the centre of this story. The life of a victim is a hard story to tell when there are living descendants (of the Lucan family, too) and others who might still be hurt. My solution was to invent new characters, whose story you have just read.

This novel is dedicated to the memory of Sandra Rivett, née Hensby.